The Power
of a
Woman

The Power
of a
Woman

Suzanne
HIGGINS

POOLBEG

This novel is entirely a work of fiction. The names,
characters and incidents portrayed in it are the work of the
author's imagination. Any resemblance to actual persons,
living or dead, events or localities is entirely coincidental.

Published 2002
Poolbeg Press Ltd.
123 Grange Hill, Baldoyle,
Dublin 13, Ireland
Email: poolbeg@poolbeg.com

© Suzanne Higgins

The moral right of the author has been asserted.

Copyright for typesetting, layout, design
© Poolbeg Group Services Ltd.

1 3 5 7 9 10 8 6 4 2

A catalogue record for this book is available from the British Library.

ISBN 1 84223 093 X

Cover designed by Slatter-Anderson
Typeset by Patricia Hope in Palatino 10/14
Printed by Cox & Wyman

www.poolbeg.com

About the Author

Suzanne Higgins was a radio and television presenter in Ireland for over a decade but she stopped to spend more time with her family. She lives with her husband, three daughters and two dogs in south County Dublin.

The Power of a Woman is her first novel. She has begun work on her second.

Acknowledgements

This is the part where I get to tell everyone who helped me with writing *The Power of a Woman* how wonderful they are!

First and foremost – to my boyfriend, sponsor and husband (who fortunately are all one and the same!) Michael, thank you for everything. Thanks to my girls for your unending patience, including my newest little lady, who helped by not kicking me too much!

I must thank my family (Duffys and Higginses) for their constant encouragement and patience, especially my mum Helen and sister Sinead. You're both brill. I couldn't have done it without you. Thanks also to my mother-in-law, who is nothing like the mother-in-law in this book! Carmel, you're a great friend.

Other friends who were a great help are Berna Williams for the name Innishambles, Helen O'Rian for the legal advice, Paula Boggin for the medical advice and Ingrid Reddyhough for the help on Americans! Thank you to Stephen and Gail Collins for their equestrian expertise. To Jenny, thanks for always being there and never giving up on me (even when I did!). Very special thanks must go to my dear friend Judi Hanna. Judi, you're terrific!

Ireland is currently enjoying a wave of new writers and as such one doesn't necessarily expect help and encouragement from the more established. That is why I owe such a debt of gratitude to Patricia Scanlan and my old broadcasting friend Gareth O'Callaghan.

Thanks also to Helen Litton for being my first line of defence and Deirdre McGee for being so helpful and encouraging. At home, let me thank Juliana and Pat, for keeping the house and home together.

Lastly huge thanks to my brilliant agent Jonathan Lloyd and Tara at Curtis Brown. Thank you, Gaye Shortland, the most patient editor in the world, and thanks also to the terrific team at Poolbeg for having faith in me!

Leaving the best till last, thanks to you – the reader – for parting with your hard-earned cash. I really appreciate your putting your trust in me. I truly hope you enjoy the book and I welcome your comments at my website – suzannehiggins.com

I hope you enjoy reading *The Power of a Woman* as much as I enjoyed writing it! And very finally, if you are a woman reading this, if you get anything out of this book let it be to believe in yourself. You can do anything you want to. You have The Power of a Woman.

Note from the Author

Please let me stress that all the characters in this book have been plucked from my imagination with two exceptions. Woody and Wilma are alive and well. They have been living with me for eight years. Wilma was in no way hurt during the making of this book . . . While both dogs are *utterly nutty*, EVERYBODY else in *The Power of a Woman* is completely fictitious . . . I promise.

For Michael

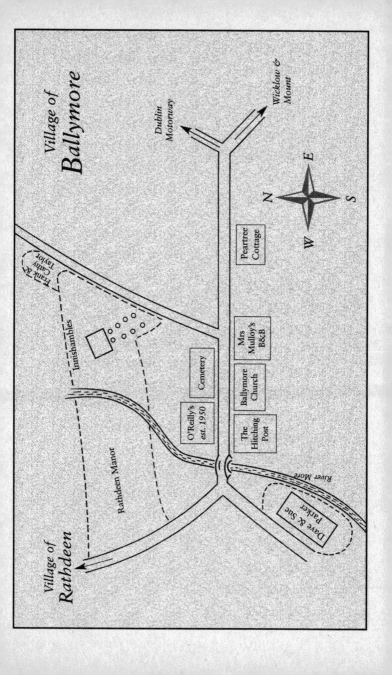

CHAPTER 1

Late in the afternoon, Saskia Dalton was pottering around in the walled garden of her beautiful old house, Innishambles. She was enjoying the last of the summer sun and the last of her freedom. It was even warmer and milder in behind the shelter of the walls. Woody and Wilma, her two Yorkies, were busy helping her. Woody chased away curious birds and Wilma spent all her time licking the gravel. Aware that she would be somewhat busy in a few more weeks, Saskia was turning her thoughts to autumn gardening. She talked to the dogs.

"Do you think I'm crazy pruning so soon, Wilma? If I don't clip the evergreens now they just won't get done this autumn." Another thought occurred to her. "Richard so loved the Christmas hyacinths last year. I'll have to pot up a few sets today or tomorrow."

Wilma ignored her. Saskia continued: "What about

the spring bedding? The time will fly when Junior arrives," she patted her large round tummy. "If we're to have any colour next spring, the bulbs will have to go down next month and that means I'll have to lift the gladioli soon."

Wilma still ignored her. Saskia looked at the fading bed of gladioli.

"Gosh, it seems so premature."

No sooner had she said the word "premature" than a screaming sheet of pain tore across her stomach. Having gone through childbirth three times already, Saskia was in no doubt. Instead of screaming however, she clenched her teeth and staggered to the nearby lavender bench. The chair was up against a sunny wall and nestled in a bed of long lavender. Even in this pain, the soft aroma gave Saskia pleasure and eased her discomfort. As if by some form of female telepathy, Wilma was instantly aware that something was happening. She left her stone-licking and jumped up on the bench beside Saskia, willing her to be OK. The pain subsided as Wilma began to lick Saskia's hand.

"Probably just a Braxton Hicks contraction," Saskia explained to her little dog. "Just a reminder of what's to come – not the real McCoy."

Saskia was half trying to convince herself as well as her little anxious pooch. She had heard of Braxton Hicks or false labour pains but she had never had them. She just kept repeating to herself 'Every pregnancy is different'.

2

"Why don't we have a little lie-down?" she suggested to the dogs.

Wilma hopped down, delighted to see the colour returning to her mistress's face, and led the way into the kitchen.

Edurne was drinking tea and watching MTV. The only help she had been so far this afternoon was collecting the girls from school. Saskia was not altogether happy with her au pair of late. When she had first come to take care of Saskia's daughters, Kelly was fourteen, Lauren was nine and Tiffany eleven. She played with them constantly and was a great help around the house. She was particularly necessary because of the school runs. The younger two were still in junior school in the neighbouring village of Rathdeen, which was south of Ballymore, while Kelly was in Mount Eden, out the Wicklow road in the exact opposite direction. Edu, with a full driving licence, could take Lauren and Tiffany to Rathdeen in the old Micra while Saskia drove Kelly to Mount Eden. Now, however, all the girls were in Secondary, so it was the same school run. Saskia was sure she should have finished with au pairs by now but Richard had insisted Edu stay once he got over the shock of another baby being on the way.

"Edu, I'm going for a lie-down. I'm a little tired. Will you please feed the girls in about an hour?"

"Are you OK. Saskia?" Edu looked concerned.

"I'll be fine after a little rest, thanks. There are chicken breasts in the fridge – if you just toss four of them in

3

butter with a little fresh garlic and onions. There's some fresh cream in the fridge; stick that in too."

"Ees OK. I can cook for ze girls, Sas," Edu interrupted with an understanding grin.

"Oh and boil up some potatoes and veg too," Saskia was fussing, "I'll eat with Richard later, thanks."

"No problem," Edu replied and went back to MTV.

Within an hour Saskia could smell the delicious aroma of garlic and onions wafting up through the house. Richard was right – it was so helpful to have a spare pair of hands at this time. She heard the back door bang and the loud voices of her three girls descending upon the house.

"They always come back to feed," she explained to Wilma, who hadn't left her side. Another lightning bolt of pain shot through her. Again she clenched her teeth and grabbed the bed-sheets. Wilma was concerned.

"Perhaps a visit to the loo will help." Saskia waddled into their en suite. The pain was subsiding but she was now decidedly uncomfortable. She thought she was going for a pee but instead she produced a big globule of gunk.

"Every pregnancy is different," she repeated with a smile. "Wilma, I believe I'm going to have a baby." All thoughts of discomfort and pain left her, replaced by excited anticipation.

She waddled over to the phone at her bedside table and put her first call through to St Helen's. All her children had been born there and Saskia claimed it was

4

the best part of having the baby, with the exception perhaps of actually "making" the baby. She affectionately referred to St Helen's as a Gin Palace or, more accurately, a Champagne Palace. Of course it was extremely professional but more than this, the maternity nurses were absolutely adorable. They really believed in the comfort and wellbeing of the mother. If that meant a glass of Dom Perignon 1961, fine!

The phone rang twice. "Hello, St Helen's."

"Maternity ward, please." Saskia was smiling. The phone clicked.

"Maternity ward, Nurse Ann speaking."

"Hello, this is Saskia Dalton. I'm due to have a baby in two more weeks but I've had some pretty appalling contractions already today and I've just had a show."

"Where are you calling from, Mrs Dalton?" The voice was extremely professional but so warm and welcoming.

"I'm out in Ballymore in Co Wicklow, but I'm sure there's no urgen – ahh . . ."

Another contraction came tearing through her body and Saskia dropped the phone.

"Hello, Mrs Dalton, Mrs Dalton," Nurse Ann's voice had an edge of concern to it. "Can you hear me? Mrs Dalton, pick up the receiver!"

Saskia was holding her stomach and was stooped over the side of the bed. She stretched out her clammy hand to grasp the receiver.

"It's OK. I'm here. I'm so sorry. I didn't mean to give you a fright; it's passing now."

"Did you say you were in Ballymore Eustace?"

"No, no. I'm in Ballymore. It's much smaller than Ballymore Eustace, but people are always mixing us up! Ballymore is in Wicklow, about five miles south-east of Wicklow town."

"Well, it sounds like you're in labour, Mrs Dalton. I think you'd better come straight in to us."

Saskia was regaining composure.

"But that was just my third contraction and I haven't even called my husband yet. I'll have to wait for him to get home." She tried to convince Nurse Ann. "He won't be too long now."

"Neither will you by the sound of things. You've got quite a drive ahead of you. I think you should come straight in, Mrs Dalton," came the sharp reply.

Reluctantly Saskia agreed and hung up. She phoned Richard's mobile straight away.

"The cellphone customer you are trying to contact is unavailable. Please try later."

"That might be a little difficult," Saskia snapped into the phone and hung up.

Wilma was getting quite agitated too. She began yapping. Kelly heard the noise and came up to check on her mother.

"You OK, Mum?" she asked.

"Not really, honey. I think the baby is coming and I can't get your dad on the phone."

"Omigod. It's all right; I'll drive you. Where's your bag?"

Saskia smiled at her beautiful eldest daughter. Kelly's deep chocolate eyes were huge with concern.

"Have I told you lately how wonderful you are, sweetheart?" Saskia asked, bursting with pride.

"Mum, not now!" Kelly grabbed the packed case by the bedroom door and bellowed down the stairs, "Edu!"

Edurne came running.

"I'm taking Mum to the hospital. The baby is coming! Try and track Dad down and get him to meet us there. Where the hell is he without his mobile on?"

"Try the office first, Edu. I've just tried his mobile," said Saskia.

"Do you want me to drive you?" the au pair offered.

Kelly swung around proprietorially. "I'll do it. She's my mum!"

"It's OK, Edu. Thanks for the offer. I think it would be better if you kept an eye on the other two. Kelly can drive me," Saskia smiled.

All three were down at the front door when Tiffany and Lauren appeared, mouths full of garlic chicken, to investigate what all the noise was about. In a flurry of mayhem and confusion, Kelly got the Landrover around to the front door of the house so her mum wouldn't have to walk. Everybody was busy kissing Saskia, suggesting they go with her but secretly hoping she would say no because it was all still a little scary.

Within another minute Saskia and Kelly were gone and the girls returned to their food.

Kelly had received her provisional licence for her eighteenth birthday during the summer, but most of her practice to date had been around the house and Ballymore. The furthest she had got so far was Wicklow. Dublin, however, was another matter. Leaving the village of Ballymore behind them, they approached the motorway.

"Oh bloody hell, Kelly. You have to have a full licence to drive on a motorway. Look!" Saskia pointed to the huge sign that said strictly no hitchhikers, no bicycles and no provisional licence drivers.

"They'll have to catch us first," came Kelly's reply as she speeded up.

Saskia had to admit there wasn't a lot she could do and so she sat back and tried to get comfortable.

"Where the hell is Dad anyway?" demanded a very uptight Kelly.

"Take it easy," replied Saskia, more concerned about the erratic driving than the absence of her husband. "He wasn't expecting any panic calls from me for at least another ten days. You know this may well be a false alarm."

"Not from where I'm sitting," Kelly swung her head around to have an anxious look at her mother, dark mane of curls flying. The car swerved into the neighbouring lane, which fortunately was clear.

"Kelly, please! The best way you can help me is to keep your eyes on the road."

"Shit, shit," Kelly fumed. Even now Saskia marvelled

8

how like her father Kelly was. "Oh double shit, shit shit."

"That's treble shit. What's wrong now, pet?" Saskia asked. Usually she would admonish her daughters for their appalling language but today was probably an exception.

"Oh, Mummy, I'm so sorry. We've got company," she trailed off as the sound of a police siren approaching from behind began to fill the car.

"What a busy day!" Saskia commented philosophically with a little laugh. She looked at her daughter. "Leave this to me, honey. Damn it, we couldn't have a better excuse."

Kelly managed with shaking hands to get the car into the slow lane, onto the hard shoulder and eventually to a halt. The blue and white police car did likewise. Saskia with her huge belly managed to get down from the height of the Landrover and over towards the police car before the garda got out.

"What seems to be the problem, officer?" she asked in her most jovial voice.

"That was some interesting driving, madam. I wonder if I could have a word with the driver." As the garda got out of his own car, he towered over Saskia.

Saskia examined his face and soft eyes. "Sergeant, if I can just explain. Can I ask you your name?"

The sergeant wasn't really listening, however, because Kelly had climbed down from the Land Rover, hands and hair waving in a state of obvious high agitation.

"Bloody hell, garda. Do what you want with me,

throw me in jail for ever, but first let me get my mum to hospital or else get ready to deliver a baby!"

He looked at Saskia suspiciously. "Do you know how many times I hear that story a week? Any woman over three months pregnant tries to use it. Although . . ." he added, looking at her stomach, "that is a pretty big bump."

As if on cue, Saskia had another contraction.

"My name is Donal, madam. Donal Walsh."

Saskia took his hand as if to shake it. She nearly cut off his circulation, however, as she held on until the pain began to subside. Kelly was frantic. Helping horses foal was one thing but your own mother! On the side of a motorway!

Under the circumstances Donal didn't even ask to look at Kelly's licence. Instead, as soon as Saskia could be moved, he gently bundled both women into their car and gave them a police escort to the door of St Helen's.

Kelly was weak with relief at handing her mother over to the professionals who whisked her away and told Kelly to stay in the reception area. This was her first chance to phone home. Tiffany answered.

"Tiff, we're here. Where's Daddy?"

"Oh, Kelly, you're brill. Is Mummy OK? About half an hour after you left Dad got home. When we filled him in, he got straight back into the car. He's right behind you. I'm sure he'll be there very soon."

Then, as an afterthought, she added, "Hey, you made

pretty good time; obviously no problems in the traffic."

Kelly laughed for the first time in ages. "I'll tell you about it later. I'm at the hospital if you need me and I have Mum's mobile."

As she hung up, she realised she was very hungry, having missed out on dinner. She pulled out a box of Marlboro.

"I wouldn't do that if I were you." It was Donal. "This is a hospital, remember."

Kelly was a little shy. "Oh shi . . . I mean yeah, thanks. Thanks for everything."

"Is your mother OK? Hey, are you OK?" His eyes seemed full of genuine concern.

"I don't know what to do now." Kelly's eyes glassed up.

Donal stepped back into policeman mode. He marched up to the reception desk and put his hat back on. He enquired as to the welfare of Mrs Dalton. The little receptionist, always anxious to assist the law, especially the cute ones, phoned the labour ward instantly, to be informed that there would be nothing happening for quite some time because Kelly's mother had stabilised. Mrs Dalton had sent word for Kelly to go home or at the very least get something to eat. This was the news that Donal needed. He returned to Kelly. She looked so small and vulnerable, back to the wall, eyes as wide as an owl's, waiting for news of her mother. Donal couldn't help himself. He put his hand on her shoulder. In uniform it was complete abuse of power. Through the fine-brushed cotton shirt she wore, he felt a very thin bony shoulder. It felt like it might snap if he were to squeeze her. The urge to protect her almost overwhelmed him.

"Your mum is going to be just fine. In fact, now that we have her here, things have slowed down again." He paused, hoping this sounded professional. "Would you like to be driven home? An escort," he qualified it.

Kelly looked at him suspiciously, her guard back up. "I'm staying here, thanks."

Donal knew he wasn't in with a chance. "Fine, but your mother said you should eat something if you're going to stay." He turned to leave.

"Wait, Donal," Kelly faltered. "Thanks for everything."

"Just doing my job." He hoped it didn't sound like some sad movie line.

The smile barely touched her lips but it torched his soul. He smiled back and left.

It was only when he had gone that Kelly realised how much she would have loved some company. She stomped off into the car park to smoke the evening away.

CHAPTER 2

Earlier that evening, Richard Dalton had been content as he gently nudged his car into fifth gear. The three-litre engine purred in response. It really was as if the car knew the way home. They had left the congestion of the city and now they were on the motorway – fast and free-flowing. As the city fell away behind him and fields began to open out the landscape, Richard started to relax. It was late evening and the sky was a clear Mediterranean blue. Not a cloud in sight – a little unusual for Ireland in September. Then the sun began its slow and languid descent; shades of pink and even red began to develop. It was glorious. "Red sky at night, shepherds' delight," he thought wryly. If Saskia was here now, without doubt that's what she would say. Did that mean she was chronically predictable or just dependable, he wondered.

He thought about his wife. Usually so athletic and

full of life, now she was, in a word, huge. He didn't remember her being this big the last time.

Saskia was 39 years old but even Richard knew she looked a lot younger. He supposed some women aged well and some didn't. She always said it was the girls who kept her young. She was kept informed about what was fashionable on a daily basis but she also spent most of her life tearing around either collecting or dropping them off or doing some little errand for them. That's what kept her fit. Richard had to admit she was a fantastic mother. It was difficult not to take her for granted because she never complained. No matter what you wanted done, Saskia would get to it. He really should cut her more slack.

It was just such a pain in the ass to be having another baby at their stage in life. What was she thinking? Of course he wanted a son and heir but he had long ago accepted that it wasn't going to happen. The girls were a hell of a handful and by the time this boy was old enough to golf, he himself would be too old to swing with any style.

A son. He let his mind wander. If Richard's latest business venture was a goer, there would soon be a Dalton Industries to pass on to his son. Rock FM, Richard's main business to date, was proving to be a huge success, a licence to print money in fact. That is what gave Richard the nerve to move up and on to bigger plans. He still remembered the day he read about The Tower in *The Irish Times* property supplement. It was going to be Ireland's tallest building. The article read that it would have some of Dublin's plushest apartments. The penthouse would have the most spectacular views of Dublin city and there was also planning permission for thousands of feet of retail and office space. Finishing the article on a light note, the journalist commented that all it needed was a radio station and it could be a little community unto itself. It was then that Richard realised he had to raise the cash and personally buy the entire Tower. Rock FM could pay an exorbitant ground rent. He could rent out all the apartments to corporate accounts at top prices and letting out the retail space shouldn't be too much of a problem. With a few tax-shelter investments elsewhere in Ireland, he wouldn't have to pay any tax and the whole thing would pay for itself.

Twelve months had passed since that article and so far everything had gone his way. He managed to raise the finance and he reckoned he had already made a few million on the appreciation of Rock Tower, as it was now known. The Irish Property market was going through the roof and so was the value of his property portfolio.

"High risk, high return," he smiled as he envisaged handing the reins of Dalton Industries over to Richard Dalton Jnr.

Of course Saskia would look after the domestic nightmare that the baby would create but inevitably it would also affect him. Skiing in the New Year was up in the air for starters. Sas said she would go skiing on condition that she could bring the child, but it was quite possible she would get too maternal after the birth. Taking a baby on a skiing holiday was a nightmare anyway. This he knew from experience. They had tried it in Europe when Lauren was a baby and it was a fiasco. He remembered they went to the French Alps that year and their au pair at the time was French. Surrounded by her own nationality, she went through a complete personality change and screwed all the locals she could, leaving Saskia to mind Lauren twenty-four hours a day. Well, that would hardly happen this time, he reflected somewhat smugly.

Richard Dalton the second was due in about another two weeks. Richard still couldn't believe they were going to have another baby. Jesus, their kids were reared. He should have smelt a rat. Over Christmas and the New Year last year Saskia was mad for it – morning, noon and night. Throughout their marriage she didn't really initiate sex although she rarely turned him down when he wanted her, but over Christmas he thought she was going through some second adolescence.

Even now it brought a smile to his face.

The Christmas festivities had begun in early December, so it had been a relief to stay in on Christmas Eve and have a quiet if rather indulgent roast wild pheasant. Now of course it was obvious what she was up to but back then he just accepted it. She said the pheasant had been a Christmas present from Barney, the local vet, who was rather well off thanks to Kelly and Tiffany beating a path to his door every other day with some lame horse or half-dead mongrel. Saskia said this would be their only meal together over the Christmas period, what with Grandma Dalton arriving the next day, and it would be nice to have a special family supper. Even Edu was away in Dublin. She wanted to do all her Christmas shopping in one go and so she was spending the night in Edwina's house to get two days in Grafton Street. It was just the family.

The meal was sumptuous: smoked wild Irish salmon followed by roast wild pheasant followed by blackberry tart. Lauren asked if the blackberries were wild too. The drink flowed. Even the girls, usually nowhere to be seen, had scrubbed up and looked quite presentable. In a mood of Christmas benevolence Richard had let them all drink. They were on their Christmas holidays and with any luck they would sleep late with a few glasses of Chateau du Paradis. Naturally enough, unaccustomed to the full-bodied St-Émilion Grand Cru, the girls had got quite skittish and all things considered it had been a lot of fun. They drank into the night and the girls faded one by one until only Richard and Saskia were left. Feeling a little sentimental, Richard told Saskia the girls were turning out fine.

"You really have done a good job on those little women, Sas," he smiled across the dining-room table at her.

Saskia grinned back, "I couldn't have done it without your input."

He was flattered. "We've done all right."

"You've done all right, Mr Dalton."

Saskia got up from her seat and came over to sit on Richard's lap, facing him with a leg on either side of his.

"We're very lucky to have you. You're very clever, very sexy and you make beautiful babies!"

As he thought back on the conversation now, Richard winced. How could he not have seen though this bullshit? At the time it all seemed perfectly reasonable.

"Happy Christmas, darling." Saskia kissed him softly at first then flirted gently with her tongue, enough to give him an idea.

"Sas."

"Yes."

"Have we ever done it on this table?"

Her response was with actions not words. To his delight and utter surprise she wasn't wearing any underwear.

She smiled. "An early Christmas present," was all she said by way of explanation as she got up and bent over the table so he could take her from behind.

"Baby," he exclaimed, "it *must* be Christmas!"

Richard thoroughly enjoyed this brief encounter. Saskia *sounded* like she did too, if perhaps a little unconvincingly.

He gazed around the dining-room as he screwed her. The dusty pink walls were a particularly effective backdrop for the huge gilt mirror, which hung above an exquisitely restored white marble fireplace. It was the fireplaces in Innishambles that had eventually stolen

Saskia's heart when he first brought her here. They had obviously been made for the house as a set.

The dining-room table, which could seat twenty, along with the Chippendale chairs, had been outrageously expensive when he bought them but now it was without doubt a very valuable dining suite. He may have paid more than he really could afford at the time but they were worth ten times that now and he himself was worth a hundred times what he was back then. Now *that* was a real turn-on.

"Damn the begrudgers!" he laughed and came.

Sitting in his large Mercedes right now he laughed again.

"Yeah, damn them," he agreed with himself. His daydreams had nearly brought him the whole way home. He turned off the motorway and was approaching the village of Ballymore.

Ballymore was one of Ireland's best-kept secrets, only an hour outside the city of Dublin on the new European-grant-aided motorway. It was appallingly signposted. This was because the residents of Ballymore made a habit of removing any new signposts that the county council erected! The simple truth was they had a horror of being "discovered" by the ever-growing city of sprawling Dublin. The village had records dating back to 1650 and the church and cemetery (which made up the centre of the village) were picture-postcard beautiful. The only other facilities Ballymore had to offer were a small shop called O'Reilly's – run by Mrs O'Reilly (best not crossed), a pub called The Hitching Post, owned and run by Mick Molloy and a B&B run by Mrs Molloy, Mick's wife. The only thing that put it on the map at all was its hunt, which was really the Rathdeen Hunt – it just sounded posher to call it the Ballymore Hunt, Richard reckoned. Kelly had even joined up with the hunt for a season but she had found the old codgers too lecherous and, Richard suspected, although she would never admit it, Kelly had slight animal-rights tendencies, a trait she had definitely picked up from her mum.

Wicklow town was their nearest big town. The key to Ballymore's anonymity, however, was that it was so complicated to get to. There were about twenty ways to get to Ballymore, all equally difficult. An aerial view would resemble that of a spider's web of roads and lanes, with Ballymore the fly at the centre.

Innishambles was the Dalton residence. A huge house built about a hundred and fifty years ago, it had been almost derelict when Richard had bought it. He spotted it in the newspaper just after he and Saskia got married. He went to view it that afternoon and agreed to buy it on the spot. The fifteen thousand pounds was really for the fifty acres that surrounded it. In the nineteen seventies and early eighties, old derelict houses were being pulled down countrywide to make way for "new developments". Who would have thought they would have become so coveted and valuable? Originally Saskia was horrified when Richard first drove her over the long and windy roads. She had always assumed that they would live in the city but as usual she went along with his plans. Over a few years she grew to love the place and certainly didn't want to leave it now. Dublin city had become so congested.

Innishambles was huge and luxurious. The pace was usually mellow but most importantly there was loads of space. Most of the land was let out to local farmers. The Daltons retained three large paddocks for Kelly's horses and ten acres had been kept as woodland at Saskia's insistence. There was also an assortment of gardens gracing the large house. Saskia's favourite was the walled garden. It had been her pet project over the last fifteen years and it was now returned to its full original splendour.

A large conservatory had been one of the most attractive features of the house when Saskia had first seen it. Although the house itself needed everything from a new roof to damp-proofing to new windows, somehow, miraculously, all the glass in the 30-foot-long, two-storey conservatory had survived. It was absolutely gorgeous. The terracotta tiles spanned the entire length of the room. The *pièce de resistance* was the double doors that led to the garden. These doors were inlaid with the most ornate stained glass. Each door was adorned with a peacock, tail down, looking back disdainfully over his shoulder at the viewer. Saskia had screamed at Lauren over those peacocks more than anything else in the house. Lauren was always in a rush to get out and regularly used the conservatory as a short cut. This wasn't the problem; banging the doors was.

"Mind my peacocks!" was regularly heard reverberating through the house.

One of the nicest features about Innishambles today was its approach. Twenty years ago it had been nothing spectacular; the lane was about half a mile long, but it was dull and dreary. Saskia had planted up conkers in pots (cheap gardening!) when they were new to the house. Much to her amazement, these had all germinated and thrived in the conservatory. When they got through three winters there, she took the plunge and brought them outside to plant along the lane. Again much to her surprise and utter delight they thrived. Now almost two decades later they were all over twenty feet tall, and her favourite had already reached thirty feet. They were like children to her and it was a great cause of concern that over the next couple of years a few were going to have to come out due to overcrowding.

Richard drove past the sleepy village of Ballymore and home without incident. As he turned into his drive, Kelly's horses pricked up their ears. They were in the front paddock that swept up the right-hand side of the driveway. They galloped towards the car. All that kept them at bay was the white picket-fence now covered in Saskia's late flowering clematis. They raced the car towards the house as if it were some form of enemy they were seeing off. Richard was equally competitive and regularly put the foot down just to give Polly and Mooner a run for their money. "Horses against this kind of horsepower," he mused. "No chance."

Saskia had constantly chided Richard for driving a two-door Merc but he claimed that it was his toy, and he loved it; for family journeys they had the Landrover and of course the old Micra.

This evening, however, he took his time. It was so sunny. The house looked magnificent. They had painted it a clotted cream colour once and never had the chance again because Saskia planted Virginia creeper all around the base. Now the vegetation had reached maturity, the house was covered. It was still totally green but this evening for the first time he saw some specks of red. "Autumn must be coming," he thought.

Polly and Mooner gave up the race as the car reached the front of the house, returning to their grass. Dudley and Dexter took up the chase. These were Richard's two black Labradors. They were devoted to him and began to hover around the front door every evening after tea, if Richard was out of the house. They would wait for as long as it took for their master to return, listening out for the sound of his car crunching the gravel outside. If he was away overnight, the dogs could hover at the front door until dawn before giving up. Loud yapping quickly joined their deep barks. Woody and Wilma, Saskia's two utterly nutty Yorkies, were running around in ever-diminishing circles as Richard got out of the car. They seemed very excited but then they always acted like that.

"Daddy, Daddy!" Lauren and Tiffany came hurtling out the front door.

"What a welcome!" He smiled at his two younger daughters.

"Where have you been? Mum's gone in. She's having the baby," they choroused.

"What the . . .?" Richard tried to grasp what they were saying as Edu came out of the house looking flustered.

"I have been thrying to contact you on ze mobile all evening," she explained in her still thick Spanish accent. "You were unavailable."

"Jesus, you know the mobile network is still shit around here. What's going on, Edu?" he asked the au pair impatiently.

"Ees true – Saskia went for siesta earlier because she didn't feel well and zen she came down saying she had to go *now*, she couldn't wait. Kelly took her to St Helen's and I was to thry and thry tho contact you. Zey left about half an hour ago. When I phoned your office your secretary said you were on your way home. I cannot contact you on ze mobile."

For a moment Richard couldn't focus. The baby must be coming early. Kelly, his eldest daughter who

24

didn't even have her full licence, had driven his wife in labour to hospital.

"Shit shit shit," was all he could muster. Then he pulled himself together. "Phone the hospital, Edu. Try Saskia's mobile too, although she's probably out of service now. Tell them I'm right behind them." He turned on his heel and got straight back into the car.

The dogs were going ballistic with excitement. Even the horses had come back to investigate the rumpus. Richard opened his car door, then, practicality prevailing, he decided a quick visit to the loo would be prudent before he hit the road back to Dublin. This was just the chance Wilma needed. As Richard darted into the house, the little Yorkie hopped into the car and hid around the back of the driver's seat. Wilma knew from experience that this was the best hiding place in a car if you wanted to tag along for a drive. She regularly did it with Saskia.

Within a minute Richard was in the car and tearing back down the driveway. The ponies were delighted to have another race. Edu, Tiffany and Lauren stood watching in a cloud of gravelly smoke. Dudley and Dexter began to whine – their master hadn't even acknowledged them; and poor Woody began to run around in even tighter circles looking for his sister Wilma.

CHAPTER 3

Saskia had been delighted to discover that Nurse Ann was still on duty when she arrived. It was nice to have at least one familiar voice in Richard's absence.

"Ah, welcome, Mrs Dalton."

"Please call me Saskia."

"You're very welcome, Saskia. I've got your file here. I see you've three children already. Most of them half reared! Well, sure this will spice up your life again, won't it?" She talked as she took Saskia's blood pressure and temperature with something that resembled a gun. "This goes in your ear now. No more thermometers under the tongue! According to your file, Dr Maguinness is your obstetrician, isn't he? We'll call him when we think you're ready. Will you have an epidural Mrs . . . Saskia?"

It was a little like she was offering Sas a cup of coffee.

"Well, I had thought of going without one, but then

again I had forgotten the pain of childbirth. It's amazing how nature plays tricks on you, isn't it?"

Nurse Ann agreed as she filled in more details on the file and generally fussed over Sas.

"Well, it's your decision now, Saskia, but I'm a great believer in making the whole experience as comfortable as possible. Why put yourself through unnecessary pain?"

"You're absolutely right. What was I thinking?" Saskia was convinced. "I'll have an epidural, please."

Within five minutes a very smooth suntanned man walked into the pre-labour ward. Saskia was lying on her bed in her nightie, watching television. "Good evening, Mrs Dalton. My name is Dr John Moore. I'll be administering the epidural. We'll try and make you as comfortable as possible."

Saskia took an instant dislike to him. He hadn't a sincere bone in his body. He was just spinning out the same line he had said probably six or seven times already that day.

"Do you have anyone with you this evening, for moral support?"

"My husband is en route." For the first time Saskia was really fed up that Richard wasn't around.

"OK, well, let's get you started. According to your file, you've had epidurals before, so you're aware of the risks. There's a one in two hundred chance that we'll have a spinal leak . . ."

He droned on as if he was telling her that there were

27

four emergency exits, two at the front and two at the back . . . Saskia chuckled. He stopped mid-sentence and looked at her quizzically.

"Oh, Dr Moore, let's just get on with it."

"If you'll just sign these, please." He gave her reams of printed paper.

Saskia signed her life away, agreeing not to sue him, the hospital, the state, Santa Claus. God knows what she had signed. She just wanted her baby in her hands.

She lay down on the bed, her back to Dr Moore, lifting her nightie to facilitate him.

"No no, Mrs Dalton. Things have changed." There was a definite tone of condescension in his voice. "We like you to sit up now. Sit on the side of the bed, your back to me, and curl your back forward over a pillow to make it as long and stretched as possible."

Saskia got the gist. Nurse Ann came to stand beside her for moral support as she curled her back forward like a shrimp, giving Dr Moore plenty of long extended back to work on. First came the local anaesthetic so she wouldn't feel the large thick epidural needle pierce her skin. This was her fourth epidural and no matter how many doctors said that you couldn't feel it, Saskia knew she could. The local anaesthetic took away the pain of the thick needle pricking her skin but what Sas felt ran a lot deeper. She could feel the needle scraping its way in between the two vertebrae like chalk between teeth. Then she felt the metal springing off nerves inside her spine. It was like the Starship Enterprise flying blind in a meteor storm. She wasn't in pain because there were no nerve-endings there, but she was just excruciatingly uncomfortable. The nerves that ran down her spinal cord were being pricked like guitar strings. They were sending crazy messages shooting down her body. She felt a tingle in her thigh, next it was her elbow. Then the palm of her left hand pinged.

Never again, she thought. This is barbaric.

Then Saskia felt something she had never felt before. There was a thick warm fluid dripping down the outside of her back. Was it just her imagination or did she hear the smooth and suave Dr Moore curse under his breath? Saskia froze. "Is everything OK?" she enquired, trying to sound as upbeat as was physically possible while bending over a pillow and in labour.

His voice remained smooth but it had a definite edge to it.

"Mrs Dalton, I'm sorry to have to inform you that we may have a spinal leak."

"What the hell does that mean?" Saskia had lost her composure. "Talk to me in English."

"We'd like you to lie down so we can observe you. Try and remain as still as possible."

"I'm in labour," she barked.

Poor Nurse Ann seemed to have vanished into thin air, so Dr Moore did the explaining. He tried to "put it in English" for her.

"The spinal fluid is the liquid that cushions your brain from your skull. It also runs down the length of your central nervous system inside your spine. Occasionally, about one in two hundred times, an epidural needle will pierce the spine so the liquid *might* escape out of your back through the hole the epidural needle made."

"What's this *might* shit? Do I or don't I have a leak?" As she spoke she felt a wave of pain, not a contraction but a headache, like none she had ever had before.

"We'll know we have a problem if you experience any dizziness or headaches perhaps."

"Well, Doc, I can answer that one for you right now. You've got a leak on your hands. Could I please have a plumber to plug up the leak in my back and some very strong headache tablets?" she snapped bitterly.

Dr Moore's tan began to fade. "Ann, we definitely have a spinal leak here. Can you please make Mrs Dalton as comfortable as possible and keep me informed?" Dr Moore turned back to Saskia.

"Nurse Ann will look after you. She's the best." He tried to smile but failed. "I know you're in labour but try and keep as still as possible."

Saskia lay on her hospital bed, staying as still as she could and feeling very tired, sore and alone. She had surprised herself at her outburst but her anger was probably a mixture of shock and fear.

OK it's official, she thought. Now I really am losing my mind, through a little hole in my back!

She was brought into the labour ward a little while later, Dr Maguinness close on her heels.

"I heard about your spinal leak. How are you, Saskia?"

Saskia loved her obstetrician. "Dr Maguinness, help me out of this mess, please. And get this baby out of me."

He looked at Saskia with genuine affection in his eyes. He had brought all the Dalton girls into the world without any problems.

"Why don't we give you some drugs to expedite the labour and get this over with?"

Saskia was so grateful her eyes watered up.

Through screaming headaches and agonising contraction pains, Dr Maguinness and Saskia worked together. Within an hour of the doctor's arrival, the fourth Dalton came into the world. Saskia was too weak to enjoy her new baby. She was asleep ten minutes later.

Five miles away from St Helen's, in the suburb of Foxrock, Wilma decided that it was safe to come out of hiding. She jumped up onto the back seat of the car and then onto Richard's shoulder. Richard didn't know what had hit him. He swerved to shake what he thought was a rat off him and his car ploughed into the other side of the road. Now well off the motorway and in the city, there were no traffic islands separating him from oncoming traffic so the grey Mini approaching him didn't have a chance. Richard's car was like a tank by comparison.

Everything seemed to happen in slow motion for Richard. He saw the girl's face as they sped towards each other. It was a mix of confusion and utter horror. The next thing he remembered was the noise of metal crushing. He heard "his attacker" squeal. He felt a sharp pain across his shoulder and stomach, a bang on his head. Then his body was thrown back with a push.

In the dusk, the glass debris fell to earth. It tinkled like a wind-chime as it hit the road. Then there was silence.

Richard couldn't move. Something was pinning his chest down. He could taste blood and he could hear voices but he was too dazed to make sense of anything. The pressure he felt across his chest suddenly eased and then, concentrating very hard, he realised it was his protective air bag from the steering wheel.

I'll be damned. They work, he thought, through the haze of post-crash trauma.

Within minutes, two fire-brigade men were helping him out of his car. They put him on a stretcher. There was an ambulance beside his car. He tried to look at the Mini. It was crumpled like a piece of spent silver foil after Sunday dinner.

"The girl, the other car?" He was fighting to regain his mind.

"You don't have to worry about her just now. There's another medical team looking after her. We've got to get you to hospital," a kindly voice said. It was a fire-brigade man.

"Hospital – shit. What time is it? You have to get me to St Helen's. My wife is having a baby."

The ambulance men and the firemen, who saw and

heard some pretty wild things in the course of a day's work, looked surprised.

"What's your name?" The ambulance driver took control.

"Dalton, Richard Dalton. Her name is Saskia; she's in St Helen's. Look, we're not far from there now. Please – I have to be with her." He looked at his watch. It was broken. "How long ago did I crash? This is really important." Richard was desperate.

"Dalton," the fireman grinned. "Are you the Richard Dalton that owns Rock FM? Hey, I listen to your radio station all the time! Do I get a prize?"

Richard looked at him in utter disbelief from the stretcher. Sometimes, being publicly successful had its disadvantages.

The ambulance driver returned.

"Well, he's telling the truth," he told his partner and the fire-brigade men who were still clearing up. Then he addressed Richard. "Look, buddy, you've been in a pretty bad accident. We'll have to have you checked over before you go anywhere. There will also be a police report to file. You can do that in a few days. Step into the ambulance and we'll give you the once-over now. If everything is all right, we'll get you over to your wife."

Within twenty minutes, having crashed every red light, Richard and his ambulance-driver friends were pulling up outside St Helen's, the siren still going and lights flashing.

He had more or less recovered from his accident,

although he was still a little shell-shocked; nothing was broken but he was going to have quite a few black and blue bits to show for his troubles. He had a cut above his right eye, which had been sutured in the ambulance before they left the scene of the accident. He still didn't know what had attacked him but the police who subsequently arrived on the scene were satisfied that he hadn't been drinking. Deep down he knew he might have some very serious charges to face – along the lines of dangerous or reckless driving – but he had a good excuse and a damn good lawyer.

"Daddy!" Richard swung around to see his daughter running across the car park towards him.

Kelly had been sitting in the Landrover, having smoked almost a full packet of Marlboro. The noise of the ambulance attracted her attention and an inevitable ghoulish impulse made her look to see what poor unfortunate was going to get out. She was stunned to see her father climb out the back unaided and indeed pumping the hand of the ambulance staff, thanking them for the lift.

Richard threw his arms around her, genuinely glad to see her.

"What are you doing out here? Where's your mother? How is she?"

"What about you? Where have you been? Omigod, were you in a crash? Daddy, what happened?"

"Easy, love, easy. In all honesty I have no idea what

happened. I don't remember. The ambulance guys said that it's shock and I might remember in a few days." Richard could see that Kelly was very upset and confused. She looked like a little girl again. "Have you been out here waiting all evening? Why didn't you stay inside? At least you could have gone up to the canteen, got a bite to eat or watched some TV somewhere."

"I . . ." She faltered. Her father would kill her if she admitted to smoking. In truth Kelly had checked at the reception just twenty minutes earlier and her mother was still in the labour ward. "I was waiting for you."

He chose to ignore the strong smell of cigarettes and they went in together. This time reception told them to go directly up to the third floor.

"She's still in the labour ward, Mr Dalton. I'm afraid there were some complications. Could I have a word with you alone?" Nurse Ann did not want to upset the beautiful girl who was with Richard.

"Daddy." Kelly was scared again.

"Everything will be absolutely fine, love." Nurse Ann put an arm around Kelly's anxious shoulder. "Are you the daughter who drove your mum here? She told me all about you and your adventures. My, you are wonderful. Look, honey, everything really is fine. I just need a brief word with your dad. Why don't you go and have a coffee? I'll come and get you soon."

Happy to be appeased and terrified of seeing her mother in anything resembling discomfort, Kelly headed for the canteen.

35

"What is going on?" Richard asked. Nurse Ann filled him in and explained the necessity for a second epidural to undo the damage of the first.

"It's called a spinal leak. Basically the hole in the bone will not heal itself. It's not like skin. It's bone," she said, stating the obvious.

"How did it happen and how do we fix it?" he asked rather shirtily.

"Well, the best thing is a blood patch. We'll give her another epidural –"

"Stop right there," Richard interrupted. "You want to do it again? No way. How else can it be fixed?"

"I know this is really difficult, Mr Dalton. I also know you yourself were in a crash tonight, so you must be exhausted. Can I get you a cup of tea?"

Richard began to mellow to the soft touch. "How did you know about my car crash?"

She smiled sympathetically, taking in the plaster over his eye. "The ambulance driver rang here. I think that's a first for us, both parties arriving separately, one in an ambulance and one with a police escort."

"What are you talking about, lady?" Richard was beginning to feel his age.

"You didn't know? Saskia . . . Mrs Dalton and your daughter had a police escort. It's been a traumatic day for your wife." She persevered. "But we must settle this matter, Mr Dalton. I understand you don't want another epidural but a blood patch is the only real fast cure for a spinal leak."

"Explain it to me again." He sat down wearily.

"As you know, bone doesn't heal itself very quickly. If we don't treat your wife, she will have particularly bad headaches for months as the fluid surrounding her brain leaks out through this hole. It's a nasty business, Mr Dalton."

Richard winced.

Nurse Ann cheered up a little. "If, however, we get your approval, and Saskia's of course, we will take out some of her own blood and insert it into the spine. This will clog up the hole with a scab. It will act like a plug fixing the leak."

"What if it goes wrong again?"

"We do have to be positive and hope for the best, Mr Dalton."

"What did Saskia say?"

"I think she was a little fed up, to be honest."

Richard smiled for the first time all evening. It took a lot to get Saskia mad but once she was, it took even more to cool her down again. That's my girl, he thought.

"So" he continued, "it is medical belief that a second epidural is the best solution. Am I correct?"

"Absolutely." Nurse Ann felt that she was getting somewhere.

"Fine, I'll talk Saskia around. Now where is she?"

The memories came flooding back to Richard as he entered a very quiet room and saw his wife lying exhausted in a deep sleep. It didn't feel like thirteen years since he had last been down this road.

"She's been through a lot," he smiled at Nurse Ann, who was standing just behind. "Would it be OK to wake her?"

As soon as she heard his voice, however, Saskia opened one heavily sedated eye.

"Richard, you're here. I'm so sorry . . . all the fuss."

Richard shushed her. "Everything is fine, Sas. You're wonderful. Everything will be just fine. You rest. We'll talk in the morning."

He didn't need to tell her twice. She was already asleep.

"Is she under some sort of sedation?"

"She was very uncomfortable so we gave her a little something to help her rest."

Suddenly a flash of excitement came into Richard's face. "Can I see the baby?"

"Of course. Such a cute little thing and the picture of you, I think."

Richard followed her to the nursery to meet his son. It was surprisingly quiet. All these little babies seemed to do was sleep. She led him over to one of the tiny beds on wheels and pointed to a lovely little sleeping baby.

Richard paused to stare at the tiny little fella. Then he stopped.

"Why is his blanket pink?" he asked in horror.

"Why, Mr Dalton, didn't you know? You have a beautiful baby girl!"

CHAPTER 4

Richard and Kelly drove home in the Landrover. It was
after midnight by the time they turned into Innishambles.
Kelly slept for the whole journey. The trauma of her
driving adventure and the excitement of meeting her
new little sister had been enough to knock her out.
Richard had phoned the house to let them know the
good news and fill them in on his own adventures
while Kelly was being introduced to her baby sister for
the first time, so it was hardly surprising that the house
was in darkness when they got there.

"Wake up, love." Richard, who hadn't been in the
mood for talking anyway, was delighted that Kelly had
slept. He spent the journey casting his mind back over
the last few months. Saskia had convinced him beyond
doubt that the baby was a bloody boy. Even the scan
had confirmed it. He was going to sue the scanning
department of St Helen's for a start.

He helped Kelly out of the car and into the house. Without really waking fully, she kissed him on the cheek and shuffled up the stairs.

Richard walked into his study and flicked the light switch. The lighting had an instant calming effect. There was no centre lighting and so the switch worked various wall lights and even some free-standing floor lamps. These were beautiful antique lamps that Saskia had purchased almost twenty years ago.

He poured himself a large whiskey. No ice, no water.

The room soothed him somewhat. It was painted dark green and two walls were covered with antique mahogany bookshelves. For a couple of years, when Innishambles was new to them, Richard's hobby had been antique books. He now had an amazing collection of first editions. He hadn't read any of them but they looked magnificent. The other two walls were covered in pictures, mostly framed photographs. Richard had his "presidential section": three photographs of himself with three different Irish presidents. He also had a framed letter from Bill Clinton. Among the others, there was a photograph of international soccer player Roy Keane and Richard playing football. Another one was of Pamela Anderson kissing him. That was his personal favourite. Owning and running Rock FM had its advantages, especially when Pamela's husband was a rocker! The other prints and photographs couldn't distract him in the slightest tonight, however.

He collapsed into his favourite chair, a large

Victorian armchair with the original faded dark brown leather. It reclined as he did. The reading lamp over his right shoulder cast a soft pyramid of light over his head and body. Dudley and Dexter came trotting in, slightly annoyed with Richard for ignoring them earlier. They had been snoozing on Edu's bed, waiting for his return. He put his glass down on the small table beside him and gave them each a good scratch. He was forgiven instantly as the Labradors rolled onto their backs and thrashed their large tails on the floor, grateful for his attention.

"How are you?" It was Edu standing at the study door.

"A hell of a lot better than my car." He was dour.

"What happened, Richard?"

"Damned if I know. Like I said on the phone, I thought something was attacking me but that is ridiculous. I just can't figure it out. Plus, I nearly killed the young girl in the other car. Poor kid. I phoned Vincent's hospital. That's where they took her and they told me that she's in intensive care. It could go either way. What a fuckin' day!"

"You must be positive, hope for ze best. Where ees Kelly?"

"Gone to bed." Richard rubbed his eyes. He looked tired.

"So eet was a baby girl."

Edu crossed the floor. Even in his exhaustion, Richard couldn't help appreciating the short silk nightdress and the flimsy piece of fabric that was an excuse for a dressing-gown. Edu went behind the armchair and began to rub his stiff shoulders.

Richard heaved a sigh.

"You've no idea, Edu. Saskia told me she had 'fixed it'." He put his fingers up as if he were making speech marks. "She said that she had read books on when to do it, how to do it, even what she had to eat. Then of course the scan. The nurse tonight said it must have been the umbilical cord. Saskia thought it was his dick but so did the doctor doing the scan. Gobshite."

Edu continued to rub his shoulders and gently massaged his chest. She could feel the tension gradually slip as he talked and she worked on him.

As he drained his glass, she took it from him and left the room to refill it. Richard sat where he was. The dogs had settled at his feet. Dexter merely looked up to check that Edu was OK and then dropped his head back to the floor as if it weighed a ton.

She returned and handed the glass to Richard. She had been furious with Richard when he told her that Saskia was pregnant. It had taken all his powers of persuasion and some serious gifts to soften her demeanour. Now, however, she really felt sorry for him.

She returned to her task of massaging his shoulders from behind the armchair.

"Eet's not the end of the world, Ricardo," she purred into his ear.

Hearing her pet name for him and smelling her so

close was serious temptation. His dick hardened instantly. He pulled the arm she was massaging his chest with and brought it down onto his crotch. She gently slid her hand down inside his trousers and began to rub.

"Things are looking up!" he conceded as he leaned back to kiss her on the mouth. "Where are Lauren and Tiff?"

"Fast asleep."

He paused for a moment and then gave in to his urges, "Can you lock the door, sweetheart?"

Edu gently removed her hand and tiptoed over to the door.

Every time Richard promised himself it would be the last. Edu was a little treasure but too high a risk.

When she returned, she shooed the dogs away and knelt at his feet like a little girl. She was adorable – the most amazing mix of little Latin peasant girl and red-blooded woman. Edu knew what pleased Richard at this stage. She gently pulled down his trousers and separated his knees. She began to work on his penis and testicles with her tongue and lips. Over the last three years Richard had taught her exactly what he liked and she had paid attention. It was as if his pleasure was her pleasure and this suited Richard perfectly.

He had never intended having an affair with her. It just sort of happened. After their first encounter, he was furious with himself, certain that Sas or one of the girls would sense something. As the months went by and there were no repercussions, however, he decided to risk it again and again. Edu was so fresh and so willing to please him and there was no passion left between Saskia and him. It had fizzled out years ago.

He pulled Edu up by the hair. "Sit on it, love."

Nimbly she separated her legs and brought herself down on his cock. Her waist was tiny. He held her and guided her pace up and down. A single ribbon tied the light dressing-gown closed. He pulled the bow and the silk fell open. She shook it off her shoulders and in one fluid movement pulled the little nightdress up and over her head. Her breasts were beautiful perfectly rounded toys. They always cheered up Richard. He was a real tit man and Saskia's tits had drooped years ago. Edu's were pert and firm. He held one in each hand and licked around the areolas. Edu drew in a sharp breath. She was always wet and ready for him, another problem with Saskia of late.

She began to purr and spin out some rumblings in Spanish. Christ knew what she was talking about but it really turned him on.

"Come with me now," he whispered. Again on command Edurne acquiesced. She wrapped her arms around his neck and whimpered like a puppy as Richard groaned. Dexter, half-asleep on the floor, looked up and gave a deep sigh, rolling over onto his side. It was nothing he hadn't seen before.

Edurne continued to croon in Spanish for a few minutes before gently slipping off to sleep on Richard's lap. He was still inside her, his trousers around his ankles as he fell asleep too.

It was an hour later before Edurne got a stiff neck and realised what a compromising position they were in.

"Ricardo." It was her name for him only when they were alone. "Ricardo, wake up. We must go to bed." The day's events had taken their toll on him.

With her help, he collapsed into his and Saskia's bed at around four am. Edu tucked him in and tiptoed back to her own room, happy.

It was a little ridiculous that Edu was still with the Dalton family. She had come to au pair in Ireland for one year, four years before, but the time went by so fast and then she became Richard's lover. Everything changed after that. She didn't want to leave him; she was so desperately in love with him. One year had turned into two and then into three. Then Saskia announced that she was expecting another baby.

At first Edu was heartbroken, then she became furious. Richard had insisted that his sex life with Saskia was well and truly dead. It certainly seemed to be, from Edu's perspective. Richard and Saskia appeared to live alongside each other in pleasant companionship, as opposed to passionate love. Edu found it perfectly plausible that Richard and Saskia had given up sex long ago. She still shivered with annoyance when she thought about it. Obviously he had been lying.

At her most furious, Edu threatened to tell Saskia all

about the affair, how Richard had taken her, moulded her, how he had taught her the most frightening and exciting things. He had taught her to be absolutely submissive. He even introduced bondage to her. It was so exhilarating. She had learnt more about life and love with Richard than she had expected to learn in a lifetime. But she was also hopelessly and totally in love with the man. To date their affair had been kept secret only because they had been so careful but tonight for the first time Richard had actually fallen asleep with her. Edu was sure that this was a sign. It would only be a matter of time before they were discovered and then, forced to make a choice, she knew that Richard would choose her over his fuddy-duddy wife.

Edu came from a small village in the north of Spain. Her family were very conservative and strict Catholics. The only reason her dictatorial mother let her au pair in Ireland was because it was another strict Catholic country. Within the safe confines of a wealthy Irish family in the country she could come to no harm.

Edu thought about her family. Her father was considerably older than her mother was, now in his seventies. She was sure that he had only bonked her mother three times to conceive her two older brothers and herself. Pablo just sat around the house these days. He had retired years ago and now it seemed that his only function was to annoy his wife as she pottered around, cleaning an already spotless house. Edu's two older brothers had left the family homestead over a decade earlier. They were both in their mid-thirties, considerably older than Edu. She felt a stab of guilt when she thought about visiting them. She barely rang them any more, perhaps once a month, but she just got grief about when she was coming home. Edu had not been back to Spain in the four years she had resided in Ireland. It had been so long now, it was difficult to envisage going back without being bawled out of it. She busied herself by tiptoeing over to the bathroom to brush her teeth as if to shake away the thought. Her mind wandered back to dear adorable Richard.

There was no doubt in her mind that Richard was her mate for life. Edu loved everything about him and had done so for the last four years. She was convinced that Saskia didn't love him. Sas may have liked him but she didn't love him the way a man of his calibre should be idolised. Richard was so strong, so domineering and he was so handsome. Edu thought back to the first time she had seen him. It was love at first sight.

Saskia had come to Dublin airport to collect her. They drove home together and, at Innishambles, the girls came out to greet them.

It was a glorious summer evening. All the girls were starting to empty the car of Edu's various bags when Kelly's horses pricked up their ears. The dogs began to get fidgety and then she saw the most beautiful jet-black Mercedes cruising up the house's driveway. The horses tried to race it and the dogs went into a frenzy of barking and yapping. So did the girls on this occasion. Perhaps it was the good weather.

"Daddy, Daddy, welcome home!"

A tall dark man got out of this James Bond car. He looked Spanish. Richard was about six foot tall. His hair was very dark brown and his suntan highlighted the most captivating eyes she had ever seen. They sparkled with mischief. The whites were very white, but the deep chocolate brown of his eyes made Edu shiver. His build was stocky, reflecting a youth spent on rugby pitches. He was bursting with energy. What made this man attractive, however, was not his physical appearance, but his aura. He carried himself with such enthusiasm and vitality. He smiled as he got out of the car and Edu's legs went weak.

"Well, that is a nice way to be welcomed home, by the most beautiful women in the country! And," he continued as he walked towards Edu, "I see we've acquired another beautiful woman." Richard took Edu's hand and kissed it as Saskia introduced her.

"Richard, this is our new au pair. Her name is Edurne, but she likes to be called Edu."

He smiled another one of those knicker-melting smiles. "*Buen aquerdo*, Edu," he said in a flawless Spanish accent. "You're welcome."

"Daaaad," the girls chorused, mortified at their father's pathetic efforts to be cool.

Then he swept his daughters into a communal embrace, ignoring their criticisms.

"Well, how are my angels?" He moved into the house surrounded by his girls and dogs, leaving Edu and Saskia to empty the car. Edu didn't mind. She was in love. Saskia didn't even seem to notice that her helpers had deserted her. She was used to doing all the work.

From the first day Edu saw Richard, she wanted to be held by him. She wanted to be loved by him. She just wanted him.

Her opportunity came during her first Christmas at Innishambles. Saskia had taken Kelly, Tiff and Lauren to London for a shopping weekend. It was mid-December. The weather was dreadful and by five o'clock it was raining hard and already dark outside.

Edurne barely heard the knocking on the back door, the weather was so bad. It was Frank Taylor, one of the farmers who rented some of the Dalton estate to graze his cattle. Slowly Edurne had come to know the various characters of Ballymore. Frank was one of the nicest. He was quite old and he always wore a flat cap. When speaking to a woman, however, he took it off and held it respectfully.

"Hello, Eeddie. Are you alone? How are you, *a grà*?" He could never get his mouth around Edurne. "I am sorry to bother you on such a wet evening but I found this down the back field and I thought maybe it was one of little Tiffany's family of foundlings."

Edurne really couldn't understand Frank's thick Wicklow accent but she got the general idea as he took a skinny little dog from under his overcoat. The animal looked terrified and freezing. Edurne didn't know what to do.

"It's OK," Frank encouraged her to take the dog from him. "Sure Tiffany is takin' them in all the time. Just mind it till she gets home."

Edurne took the little animal and thanked Frank.

"*Oiche mhaith*," he mumbled as he turned up his collar and put his cap back on.

"*Oiche mhaith*," she smiled. Saskia had told her *oiche mhaith* was the Irish for good night and *grà*, the Irish for love. Frank was startled.

"Is it Irish you're learning now?" he laughed. "You're a great girl, a great girl. *Oiche mhaith!*" he repeated and he was off.

Alone in the house with the little dog, Edurne thought perhaps a warm bath and some food would cheer him up. First she gave him Woody and Wilma's leftovers. The Yorkies were very fussy eaters and never finished their food but this little one did. He seemed to cheer up very quickly. She took him to the bathroom and ran a big bubble bath for him. She was so preoccupied in talking with her new little friend that she did not hear Richard come home.

"What *are* you doing?" Richard could only see her neat little backside bending over the bath crooning in Spanish to something out of vision.

Richard was a little pissed after yet another Christmas lunch, which had only finished an hour before.

Edurne jumped, surprised to hear another voice, and swung around,

"*Yeazus*, I did not hear you come in."

"It's OK, relax. It's only me. What are you doing?"

"Oh Richard. I'm so sorry. I hope ees OK. Frank Taylor come to ze house with this little, how you say, *perdito* . . . hee has no home. . ." she trailed off as Richard looked into the bath.

Under the influence of the drink and Edu's ass, Richard softened his normal hard line on the adoption of strays.

"What did you say he was – *perdito*? You mean lost. In English it's lost."

"Lost," Edu repeated.

"You're a good student, Edu," he grinned.

"You're a very good teacher, Ricardo. In Spanish your name is Ricardo." She took the little dog out of the bath. Richard laughed.

"There is so much I could teach you, little girl." At this stage he was sitting on the toilet and Edu was sitting on the floor wrapping the little dog in a big warm towel.

"I would like you to teach me everything." She looked straight into his eyes to leave him in no doubt. "Zat is what I am in your house for."

And so their affair began. He took her there and then on the bath-room floor, as the little dog looked on.

Now, three and a half years later, she knew they were

mates for life. The one issue she could not accept was how much of his time was spent working in Dublin. Edu already had plans of moving to Dublin to be with him when their affair eventually became public.

"I leev in Rock Tower," she told her reflection as if she was talking to a stranger at a cocktail party. Her toothbrush was a cigarette in her fantasy. Even though she didn't smoke she thought it looked cool.

"Ah yes, you know it," she continued politely. "Ricardo and I are partners – married actually," what the heck she thought, it was her daydream. "We live in ze penthouse."

Her teeth well and truly brushed, she popped her toothbrush in the toothbrush glass and headed back to her bedroom. As she got into bed, she thought for a second about the poor little dog. They called him Perdito and Richard had said that Edu could keep it as her dog. The little fella disappeared within a week. Richard explained that some dogs were like that. They just had to keep moving on to new pastures.

Not my Ricardo, she thought as she fell asleep. It was almost 5am.

CHAPTER 5

When Richard woke and found himself in bed alone, he remembered the latter part of his evening with horror. Oh shit, he thought, I've done it again. The fatigue mixed with the whiskey and Edu's heady scent had been too much for him to resist.

"Right, that's definitely the last time," he promised himself as he climbed into the shower. Her body was delicious, he got turned on just thinking about her but he knew that she was in love with him and he had to end it.

"The only solution is to find a replacement," he reasoned to himself as he lathered up.

He thought about how he could break it to her,

"Edu, you've been great but –" he tried another tack.

"Edu, I'm worried about Sas –"

Richard realised that Edu would go absolutely nuts if he tried to end his affair with her. I'll have to let her down gently, phase her out, he decided.

53

"No harm done," he announced to his reflection as he got out of the shower. "What you need, boy, is a distraction *outside* of the house. That way everybody is kept happy. Let your new friend know from the start that it's just for fun with no strings attached." He thought about this more as he got dressed. If it was well away from the house, maybe he could find someone who was a little wilder, a little more willing to experiment with him. He dressed feeling a lot better. Ironically his affair with Edu had caused him great guilt but the decision to end it and possibly start another away from the family homestead made him feel positively good about himself.

Tiffany was first to the kitchen as usual. She set the table and fed the dogs. She always thought it grossly unfair that the Labradors had to eat outside the back door and the Yorkies were fed in front of the Aga. Those Yorkies were far too spoilt. Tiffany believed in a fair and just world for all animals. She was a full member of the ISPCA and she had nearly come to blows with her older sister when Kelly once took up foxhunting.

Tiffany had got a little bird-feeding centre for her last birthday and it had to be checked daily to see if it needed refilling. The feeding centre looked more like a birdcage but the theory was that the little birds could flit in through the bars to get to the food inside and the big ugly crows and magpies couldn't. When Saskia pointed out that she was penalising the larger birds just for being large, which was hardly their fault, Tiffany started to throw bird food on the ground around the bird-feeding centre too, so everybody could have a good breakfast.

By the time Tiffany had returned to the kitchen, her father had appeared.

"Who's driving us up to see Mum today?"

Richard had a thumping headache despite his power shower. He was also edgy about meeting Edu. He was always nervous talking to her in front of the family just after he had had sex with her. She on the other hand never looked remotely uncomfortable.

"Nobody. Your mum can't have visitors yet," came his curt reply.

"Daddy," she wailed, "you must be kidding. I have a new baby sister. She doesn't even have a name yet. I *have* to see her!"

"Of course you do. What's going on?" Lauren came into the kitchen at the end of the conversation.

"Daddy says Mummy can't have visitors yet. But we're family. Families are always allowed in." Tiffany continued to fight her corner.

Richard fell into a kitchen chair and Tiffany handed him his usual mug of black coffee. He tried to be patient.

"Look, girls, you know it's not serious, but as I explained on the phone last night there was a complication in your mother's labour. Something went awry with the epidural and it has to be rectified today. You must remember that she has to remain perfectly still in bed. She can't even sit up!" He had their attention. "Now, you know how much she loves you.

If you go up there, your mother is going to want to sit up and talk to you. She'll want to be the one to introduce you to the new baby and so on and so forth, so the best thing you can do is to give her a day or two to get over her medical problems and then go in, when all is well. Now, I know you love her. So wouldn't you rather do what's best for her?" He paused.

Game, set and match. It took a lot more control to keep the head and rationalise with the girls. But it always worked better than blowing his top. He took their silence as a sign that he had won this round.

"I'll tell you what. I'll drive you to school this morning. Where are the other two?"

"Kelly and Edu are both still asleep," Tiffany answered. "I'll get them."

Richard stopped her, "You may as well let Edu sleep in. There's no point in her getting up if I'm driving you to Mount Eden. Then I'll be going straight up to St Helen's. As soon as the doctors give me the all clear, probably tomorrow, I'll take you guys up. What do you think?"

"We don't have much choice, do we?" Lauren studied the floor.

"That's my girl," Richard patted her on the head. "Hey, you're not the baby any more. How does that feel?"

"Daaad!" She pulled away from him, still fed up at the idea of going to school. Lauren had assumed that she would miss school that day and so she had skipped all her homework. After her mother and Kelly had taken off to St Helen's the evening before, she had high-tailed it off into the woods to wander and mess around. Tiffany's situation was somewhat similar.

She went to pull her narky older sister out of bed. Kelly was a nightmare in the mornings. She hated school anyway, especially this year because it was her Leaving Cert. Kelly constantly threatened that she wasn't going to sit the Leaving. She was going to run away or something. Even Tiffany knew that Kelly wasn't the brightest one in the family but what did it matter? She was so beautiful she would just marry money. That's what Grandma Dalton said.

"Kelly, it's time to get up. We've got to go to school." Tiffany tried the direct approach.

"Fuck off," came a muffled reply from deep under the downy quilt.

Kelly's bedroom was next to her parents at the front of the house. The sun streamed in both windows. It was very bright from early in the morning, a constant source of annoyance for Kelly. The view, however, was spectacular. First you could see the front lawn, then beyond that were Polly and Mooner grazing for their breakfast, and the chestnut trees were magnificent, sweeping up the driveway.

"Kelly, will you bloody well get up?"

"I'm not going to school today. I had a very traumatic day yesterday between babies and motorways and cops. I'm not going." A pillow came hurtling through the air at Tiffany and caught her off guard as she was gazing out the window.

"Bitch," was all Tiffany said and she flounced down to her father and little sister.

"Kelly won't budge," she told Richard, expecting him to go crazy.

"It was a very late night for her. We'll leave her where she is."

Tiffany and Lauren objected in unison.

"That's not fair," came the familiar reply from Tiffany, believer in all things being *fair*.

"She is so spoilt. Kelly gets everything her own way. That cow is your favourite." Lauren was seething.

Even Richard had to admit that it looked like that from the outside. But Grandma Dalton was right. Kelly wasn't the most academic of his girls although she was a bright girl in her own way.

"She was up very late last night. I'll tell you what, girls. Why don't I take you out for dinner tonight as a celebration meal for the arrival of the newest Dalton? Whatever her name is!"

This cheered them up. "What about Diana? That's a nice name!" suggested Lauren, who still hadn't got over the death of the Princess of Wales.

"Gross," argued Tiffany. "How about Joan? As in Joan of Arc!"

"Joan Dalton," Richard winced. "You must be joking. How about Robin?" He could not think of a name without a person connected to it. Robin Maher worked for a PR Company called Corporate Affairs and Richard had just contracted them to do the massive relaunch of his radio station Rock FM. The radio station was already the most successful in the capital. He just wanted to do a big publicity boost because Rock FM was, at last, moving into Rock Tower. In all likelihood, the entire area around the tower would experience a lift in property value as it became a hub of activity. Richard liked Robin.

Robin was a real PR bird. He laughed at his own little pun. Robin – bird.

Robin Maher had an hour-glass figure and the obligatory blonde shoulder-length hair which needed constant flicking. It was more than that however; she had the look – the one that said, "Go ahead, play with fire if you think you can handle the heat". That was her biggest attraction to Richard. Robin gave him all her attention at their meetings and laughed perhaps a little too indulgently at his jokes. He knew she fancied him and he definitely fancied her. She was about thirty and she was ambitious. Having only become an account manager at Corporate Affairs a few months ago, Robin was already working with the big accounts. Richard fantasised about getting her into bed.

"God, I love women," he said aloud.

"Good," giggled Tiffany, "because you're surrounded by them. Now come on or we're going to be late."

Tiffany was the worrier in the family. She had them all early for planes and on time for family or social outings. She was the one to remind her father that Saskia's birthday was coming up or perhaps their wedding anniversary. She reminded everyone about everyone else's birthday, which is why they nearly always forgot hers, unless Saskia remembered at the last moment. In Saskia's absence Tiffany always took on the mother role, even though she wasn't the eldest. She handed her father his mobile phone and car keys and gave Lauren a quickly prepared packed lunch. Next Tiff shot upstairs to inform Edu that they were letting her sleep in and to tell Kelly that Richard had said she could have a sleep in too.

Somehow she managed to get Richard and Lauren out to the Land rover on time and they were off.

When Tiffany had first heard that Saskia was going to have another baby, she was horrified. Women of her mother's age shouldn't be shagging and her father was definitely past it. The private embarrassment was one thing but having to break the news in school was utter mortification. Practically all the girls at Mount Eden came from privileged backgrounds and most of them from small families. As it was, the Daltons were one of the few families to have three girls at the school at one time and now there was another Dalton girl. Originally Tiffany had thought about keeping the whole thing quiet. Saskia had told them of the new addition to the family in early April. Tiffany thought if she could keep it hushed up in school for a mere three months, that would take her to the summer holidays and her secret might be safe. Perhaps the baby would be born during the school holidays and forgotten about by the time school started again in September. No such luck, however. Kelly, who thought the whole thing utterly ridiculous, told her classmates the next day. It was the talk of the school within hours and Tiffany's fate was sealed. By their final year the girls were not so bitchy but at fifteen, Tiffany's classmates were pretty merciless about Saskia.

"Can you believe she still does it?" was one catty comment. Another was, "Isn't it illegal for fogies to do it?" Tiffany took all the slagging in silence and buried it deep inside her.

Lauren didn't have this problem because she had started in the school only that term and if anything she had a higher standing in the class than most because she was well used to the school, having been there many times visiting her older sisters on family days.

The only backbiting she had to contend with was over the few days when the news broke in her class. One aspiring bitch simpered: "Imagine your dad and your mum still do it!"

Lauren replied as quick as a flash, "Well, we know your mum did it but are you sure about your dad?"

The circle of girls listening burst out laughing, backing Lauren, and nobody took her on again.

The morning passed more pleasantly for Tiffany and Lauren than it did for Saskia Dalton. A morning in school facing the trials and tribulations of not having your homework done was easier than facing another epidural.

By lunchtime, however, it was all over. The

procedure had taken longer than she had expected but it had been a success. Dr Moore was definitely more subdued – perhaps even a little more attentive – or was that just her imagination? Whatever the reason, things were getting better. He took about a pint of blood from her arm and gave her another epidural, effectively dumping the blood into her spine so it would scab over the hole from the previous day's muck-up. Then all she had to do was lie very still for as long as possible.

Richard was her first visitor.

Saskia was kept in the labour ward overnight and in the morning she had been moved to a beautiful room. It was a private room on the corner of the building, so she had two large windows and a balcony overlooking the immaculately kept lawns of St Helen's. Her en suite was nearly the same size as the bedroom. It housed a huge bath and a terrific power shower. She longed to soak in a deep bath but she was under strict instructions not to move yet, not without the aid of a nurse.

Richard arrived with a huge bouquet of lilies and a bottle of champagne.

"Darling, how are you feeling?" He beamed love and affection.

"Oh Richard." Her eyes glassed up, the trauma of the last twenty-four hours spilling over when she saw her husband.

"I'm so sorry. I had no idea the baby was coming early and a baby girl . . ." she looked up into his eyes anxiously.

"Hush," he crooned, gently caressing her forehead. "She's beautiful. I love her already," he lied.

"Oh, Richard, she is beautiful, isn't she? I love her too. Everything is so tiny and those Dalton eyes. She has your eyes."

Richard hadn't even seen her eyes. He hadn't really noticed anything once he had seen that the blanket was pink.

"What's her name?"

"Well, I know I've always picked the girls' names but we were so sure that she was going to be a boy and I know you wanted a boy."

Richard shook his head in denial. "As long as she's healthy. That's all that really matters, darling."

"Well, why don't you pick her name?"

Just then the door burst open. Nurse Ann was back on duty, arms full with another two bouquets.

"More flowers, Mrs Dalton." She stopped when she saw the very attractive man sitting beside Saskia.

"Ann, this is my husband Richard. Richard, this is my new friend Ann."

They smiled at each other.

"We met late last night," Ann explained. "Your husband was a little the worse for wear after his ambulance trip. You look a lot better today if you don't mind me saying so, Mr Dalton."

"I feel a lot better too, Ann." He stood up to help her with the flowers and gave her one of his grins. Nurse Ann was smitten.

Flowers had arrived from Richard's mum, Grandma Dalton, who had been phoned first thing that morning by Richard. Saskia had also received flowers from Rock FM, and numerous business associates of Richard's, some of whom she didn't even know. Elizabeth, Richard's frighteningly efficient secretary had obviously been busy on the phone.

Saskia and Richard spent lunchtime talking, filling each other in on their adventures of yesterday and convincing each other that no permanent harm had been done. Richard's Merc would survive, although he would probably sell it as soon as it was fixed. He loved that car. Long, sleek and black, the two-door sports car attracted a lot of attention, but he was superstitious about crashing it. He would never trust it again. He knew nothing of the other driver, except that she had been taken to hospital. With any luck, she would be OK and the insurance companies would look after everything. He still had no clue what had caused him to lose control of his car.

"Not to worry," he smiled. "I've had it for just over a year now; it was time for a change."

"What about my old workhorse?" Saskia teased.

"Who, Edu?"

"No," Saskia laughed, "that poor old Landrover. You have no idea how banjaxed it is and I caught Lauren driving it up and down the lane again last week. She's so hard on the clutch."

Richard was not surprised. "Lauren will probably get her driving test before the other two."

"Before the other three," Saskia corrected him gently. "Would you like to see her again?"

Richard smiled. "I'd love to but don't you have to lie very still?"

"You could go down to the nursery and get her if you like."

"Fantastic," he beamed a perfect lie.

Richard left Saskia's large room and walked out into a long corridor. He always felt uncomfortable in hospitals, particularly maternity wards. They were excessively hot and surprisingly quiet. There were always at least two or three women walking up and down the corridor with 'ready to pop' bumps. This day was no exception. He tried to smile an encouraging/apologetic sort of smile and hurried past.

Richard had to walk the full length of the corridor to get to the nursery. He was even more uncomfortable there than in the rest of the hospital. There was a young girl being taught how to wash a small baby and another was being shown how to change a nappy on a tiny infant. The infant was screaming in protest, which in turn started the hormonal mother off into floods of tears.

I'm too old for this shit, he thought to himself as one of the nurses looked up.

"Can I help you?" she asked proprietorially.

"Hi." He smiled his 'friendly dad' smile. "I'm Richard Dalton. I was hoping to bring my daughter up to my wife's room for a while."

The nurse's face softened instantly.

"Ah, Mr Dalton, your little lady is right here." The nurse walked away, leaving the new mum bathing her baby to her own devices. She brought Richard over to a sleeping baby.

"She's just been fed. You do know your wife has agreed to bottle feeds in view of her condition?"

"I didn't actually but I'm delighted. She needs all the rest she can get."

"A few bottle feeds won't make much difference."

"Thank you," Richard replied with a broad smile. Perhaps there was going to be a benefit to this epidural fracas. If this kid wasn't breastfed, he could get away skiing after all.

He took the little bundle in her baby bed, which was on wheels, and headed back up the corridor, pushing it in front of him. He remembered that you weren't permitted to carry the babies for insurance reasons. As he walked up the corridor, he had his first really good look at his newest daughter. He couldn't understand how people saw one side of the family or the other in a newborn. To him they were all just small little pink shit-machines and, of course, bill-builders. Christ, the bills! Keeping the Dalton girls in the style to which they had become accustomed was costing him as much as it would cost to run a small country. Naturally, under the umbrella of "the Dalton girls" fell Saskia, Kelly, Tiffany, Lauren, Edu and his mother – hardly a Dalton girl, nonetheless a large expense.

"Mother." Richard looked up as if his thoughts had

come to life. There stood Grandma Dalton, large as life. "We weren't expecting you for another few days," he smiled weakly.

"Nonsense! I wanted to see my newest granddaughter." Edwina Dalton had been heading for Saskia's room but, seeing Richard, came straight over and picked up the baby.

"Mum, you're not meant to carry the babies in the corridor. Let me at least get her into Sas's room."

"Honestly, I carried you on shinier floors than these," Edwina snorted, looking down her nose at the immaculately polished floor. Then she turned on her heal and headed for Saskia's room, child in arms, leaving Richard standing there with the empty little cot.

"Saskia, how are you?" Edwina boomed into the room, ignoring the "No visitors" sign.

Saskia jumped bolt upright in the bed. She always jumped when she met Edwina Dalton.

Edwina sat down and began to study the little girl.

"Oh, I think she's another Dalton. Well done, Saskia. But really I can't understand how you didn't have a boy, honestly."

"Well, Edwina, as you know we take what we're given," Saskia sniped back. Richard was an only child and Saskia knew that Edwina would have loved a few more.

"How are you?" Edwina changed the subject. "Richard said you had a few problems. I did warn you about those epidurals, very dangerous things don't you know. I told you. You remember, Richard? I said Saskia don't have an epidural, but did you listen? Do either of you ever listen to your poor old mother? Not that I know why you're having another baby at this late stage anyway. When I told the bridge girls that you were having a baby they thought I meant Kelly was pregnant. Of course, her not being married, well to be honest I don't know which is worse."

"Mother," Richard glared at Mrs Dalton senior, "that's enough."

Edwina stopped dead in her tracks. "Well, I only meant to say," she paused, not knowing what she meant to say. "Well. For God's sake, what name are you going to give the child?"

With that another bunch of flowers arrived, this time a beautiful bunch of red roses. Saskia took the card from the nurse.

"Richard, aren't they beautiful? They're from Corporate Affairs, the marketing agency you've just teamed up with."

Richard smiled, "I haven't *teamed up* with them, Saskia – I've just contracted them. They work for me. There is a difference!"

He looked at the flowers. Richard had sent a very similar bunch to Robin Maher last week after a particularly flirtatious lunch.

"What do you think of the name Robin?" he asked the two Mrs Daltons.

CHAPTER 6

Everybody in Ballymore loved Barney Armstrong. Barney always had a smile on his face, the kind of smile that made you think he had just been given some really good news of a personal nature. He walked with a happy spring in his step and never seemed to be in a bad mood. At five foot six inches he was smaller than many of the women in Ballymore. It may have been his stature that made him uninhibiting to people, but whether it was his height, his smile or general demeanour, everybody loved Barney.

He could not be described as good-looking, being quite stocky. Perhaps he was when he was in his twenties and he had all his own hair. Now, having just reached the ripe old age of thirty-three, what was left of his hair was swept right back, unashamedly showing off his ever-growing forehead. Nor was he the slimmest man in Ballymore. That said, people loved him and he was very huggable.

Barney came from Carlow town, where his father and all his uncles had been vets, so it was only natural that he went into the business. Just as he did with people, he seemed to have a way with animals. It was generally agreed that he could talk to animals and they understood. He could soothe the wildest pony and have it eating out of his hand in minutes. Like Tiffany Dalton, however, he had more strays in Peartree Cottage than was probably legal.

Peartree Cottage got its name from the little pear-tree orchard out the back. Barney would laugh and concede that there was barely a pear left these days since Owl had discovered he could jump the little hedgerow between his paddock and the orchard. Barney said the old horse was as wise as any owl and so the name stuck. Owl was more of a pet than a working animal. If anyone gave out to Barney for the crazy expense of keeping the animal for no valid reason, Barney would saddle up the old beast and do his rounds on him for a few days, thereby giving his old banger of a Nissan Patrol a rest. Usually, however, Owl's days were spent relaxing in the orchard of Peartree Cottage.

It was barely half a mile from the Cottage to the village, so Barney usually walked it for the exercise. That evening as he strolled along, the Daltons' Landrover drove past. Richard Dalton was driving and he had his three daughters packed in. The car stopped and reversed.

"Barney, Barney, we have a new baby sister!" Tiffany was beaming.

"Well, that's terrific. How's your mum?"

"She had all sorts of problems, but it's OK now. We're going to call her Robin. What do you think of Robin Dalton?" Lauren asked.

"Well, that sounds lovely." Barney looked at Richard. "Is Sas OK?" he asked with concern.

"Yeah. Problems with the bloody epidural."

Barney frowned. "Messy business those things. Give her my very best. I'll see her when she gets home – and give the little one a special kiss. Robin Dalton. That's lovely. Did you give yourself a bit of a bump as well, Richard?" Barney asked, taking in the plaster over Richard's eye.

"Dad was in a crash last night!" Lauren gushed.

"It's fine. It's fine really, Barney. I'll pass your kind wishes on to Sas," Richard insisted, eager to terminate that particular line of chat.

"We're going out for a bite to eat now, to celebrate the arrival of little Robin."

"Do you want to come? Even up the numbers a bit?" Tiffany asked.

"Tiff!" Kelly and Lauren whined at her in unison. The whole Dalton family knew that Tiffany fancied Barney like crazy but he was far too old for her. Tiff cowered back into the car seat.

"It was only a suggestion," she whimpered.

Barney smiled a big-brother smile.

"Thank you very much, Tiffany, but this is a special family time."

71

The Landrover took off again towards Dublin and Barney continued on to O'Reilly's shop in the village.

It was an old-world shop that hadn't changed much since it opened. Mrs Maureen O'Reilly took great pride in the fact that she was the third generation of O'Reillys to manage the shop. Her mother-in-law ran it before her and that woman's father-in-law had started it back in the 1950s, so it had always been called O'Reilly's. The little bell rang over the front door as it was pushed open or closed and Mrs O'Reilly would scuttle in through the multicoloured plastic ribbons that acted as a separation in the doorway at the back of the shop.

"Barney, it's yourself. How are you this evening?"

"Very well thanks. How are things with you? How's Hudson?"

"Oh, he's fine." Maureen seemed distracted. Hudson was her old tomcat, called after Rock Hudson, Maureen's idol; she had nearly died when she found out that the film star was gay. Barney had his suspicions about the cat being that way too but had thought better than to tell Maureen.

"Well," she grinned furtively, "I have the most interesting news." Maureen O'Reilly couldn't keep news to herself if her life depended on it.

She was one of the few women in Ballymore who looked up to Barney, physically. Maureen was only five feet tall and almost as wide. She had a strange habit of whooshing up her ample bosom with her folded arms as if they were constantly slipping, but, as Richard had once commented to Barney when they were discussing it over too many whiskeys, Maureen O'Reilly's boobs couldn't slip any more if they wanted to.

She always wore what she called her housecoat. Barney would have called it an apron. It fitted over whatever she was wearing underneath, but the result was that she really always looked the same. Her hair was a most unnatural blonde, slightly curly, with a side split. It was combed over to one side. She nearly always wore slippers.

Barney had noticed years ago that when Maureen had news she wanted to impart, she had a habit of darting her eyes from left to right as if checking that nobody was eavesdropping. This was a little ironic because if the shop were full, she would still have passed on the scrap of scandal and thoroughly enjoyed the fact that she had a larger audience than usual.

"What do you have for me?" he asked conspiratorially, the grin never leaving his face.

"Well," she began, "it all started a few weeks ago. I knew something was going on but I wasn't sure exactly. There were three very strange men in the village. They were American!"

Barney's grin broke into a broad smile – American would definitely qualify for "strange". Ballymore had never promoted itself as an attraction for tourists and it was so difficult to get to, very few passed through and even fewer actually stopped.

"What were they doing in Ballymore, Maureen?"

He called her Maureen to unsettle her. Everybody called her Mrs O'Reilly because she was married, not living in sin. She raised a disapproving eyebrow but ignored his impertinence this time, not wanting to get distracted from her story.

"Well, I saw them myself that time. They came down from Dublin in a stretch limousine no less and drove around the village a few times. Very suspicious activity altogether. They had lunch in The Hitching Post that day – three club sandwiches," she qualified.

Barney had to stop himself from laughing. So he pasted a fascinated expression his face. Maureen loved telling Barney news – he was such a gratifying listener. She went on. "Now, I don't know what they had to drink but I could find out."

"What were they doing here?" he repeated, trying to get her back on track. These little stories could take up to half an hour if you didn't keep her to the point.

"Well, the first time they were just driving around, you know looking, but they were back yesterday, Barney, two of them and they stayed in Mrs Molloy's last night and they were still here today!"

Barney tried to look suitably shocked. The fact that they would stay overnight and still be here the following morning was not worth rationalising with Mrs O'Reilly.

"Well, Mrs Molloy got talking with them over their full fry this morning. You know her, can't keep her nose out of anybody's business." She raised her eyes to heaven in disgust and went on. "They were asking her lots of questions about the village and you'll never guess . . ." She was fit to burst with excitement at this stage.

"Tell me."

"They wanted to know about Rathdeen Manor!"

"Wow," Barney tried to sound as excited as she wanted him to be. "Why do you think that is?"

"Ah, Barney Armstrong, would you wake up, boy. They're obviously thinking of doing a movie up in the old ruin or something like that. They were American. What else could it be indeed?" She had it all thought out.

"Might they have been tourists?"

"Well, why were they here two weeks ago, in that car and in suits I might add, and back now. If they were tourists, they wouldn't come and go like that and, anyway, who would visit an old wreck like Rathdeen Manor?"

Barney thought about it. She had a point.

Rathdeen Manor was a beautiful old building but of no great historical interest. If anything it was ready to be demolished. It had become dangerous since the roof fell in a few winters before. It got its name from the neighbouring village but in fact the Manor was much closer to Ballymore. In truth Ballymore village had probably been built to house the working staff for the old mansion, but if that was the case it was long forgotten in history. Rathdeen Manor had been boarded up decades earlier and "trespassers will be prosecuted" signs were posted everywhere.

Just then the shop doorbell chimed again. Barney and Maureen swung around like two guilty children caught with their hands in the cookie jar. Edu looked at them suspiciously.

"Congratulations," Barney smiled. "I hear you have a new baby in the house. Robin Dalton; that's lovely."

Edu smiled. "Yes, ze girls have gone out with Richard to celebrate. I prefer to stay at home. Eet is so quiet up in the house now. I love it."

Barney laughed.

"Well, I never!" Maureen knew nothing of the new arrival and was very put out. "You should have told me, Barney. Was it bread you wanted?" She was now anxious to get him out of the shop so she could get all the news from Edurne.

"It was, and a pint of low-fat milk, please." He smiled. "I'm watching the waistline!" He knew she was dismissing him and it suited him fine.

Barney left the shop with his bread and milk, leaving poor Edurne to handle the inquisition.

The sun was setting by the time he had strolled back up the road to Peartree Cottage. He pondered on Mrs O'Reilly's news. A film being made in Ballymore would certainly spice things up. Would it be over Christmas or next spring? Probably the next summer, he reflected. That didn't make sense, however. Rathdeen Manor was too dangerous to film around. It had to be that somebody was buying the property. It piqued his interest. He wondered would the new owners keep horses.

He admired his little cottage as he pushed the gate open. The garden was delicious. He would rarely notice how beautiful it was, but this evening, with the sun setting behind him and the garden drenched in golden streams of light, it was impossible to miss. On either side of the path were fragrant bushes of lavender. These he recognised, but he had no idea what most of the others were called. He also knew the gladioli because Cathy Taylor was particularly proud of them and the Canna lilies. She took those bulbs out every autumn and replanted them in the spring, which struck Barney as an inordinate amount of work, but looking at the results it seemed worth it now. On the left of the cottage were the most wonderfully fragrant rose bushes, scramblers and standards. Cathy had all kinds and all colours, from blood-red to sunshine-yellow to baby-pink. Barney loved the result.

Frank Taylor's wife, Cathy, maintained Barney's garden meticulously. A few years before, just after Barney had bought Peartree Cottage, Cathy Taylor's Jack Russell had run into serious difficulties delivering a large litter. Cathy was beside herself with worry and Frank was out with the cattle, uncontactable. Frank would have seen to her if he was there but he wasn't and Cathy genuinely feared for the poor bitch's life. As luck would have it, Barney had been out on a job and just popped in to see how the Taylors were. The fact that he knew Mindy was due to deliver around that time was incidental! Mindy survived her ordeal and

Cathy and Frank were forever grateful and thought him the best vet they had ever known.

Cathy tried to pay Barney for his services but he would have none of it. That the little dog was happy and well was payment enough. Then they got on to talking about his recent purchase, Peartree Cottage. Barney had been renting the house for years before he bought it but now it was his and he was delighted. At that time the garden was in a dreadful state and that was when Cathy took it upon herself to fix it up for him. He was delighted for the help because, whatever talent he had for healing animals, he had no understanding of things horticultural. Cathy, on the other hand, could make anything grow anywhere. She had a key to his house and came and went when she had time. The relationship developed and Cathy became a sort of surrogate mother to Barney; his own mother had died when he was very young. Before long Cathy was cleaning the house and ironing his shirts. She loved mothering him since her own two boys had moved to the States.

That evening with the garden glowing a welcome home to him, he thanked her silently again. The only sound was the bees working over the lavender and some birds chirping to each other. Barney loved Ballymore and prayed that the Americans were not thinking of harming their little village. Suddenly the yapping started. Thanks to Barney's DIY efforts, Peartree Cottage had the unusual feature of a doggy-flap in its front door. Nina came bailing out when she heard the gate of the cottage creak in protest as it was opened.

"Hello, girl." He bent down to pick her up and opened his front door. Nina was one of Mindy Taylor's pups from that difficult labour. She was definitely a mongrel. Barney figured Woody Dalton was the father because Nina had shaggy long hair just like him. He only had one other lodger at the moment, a great big Afghan hound that just wandered into his garden over the summer. Usually strays came and went from his house. Some stayed for a week, some for years, but at the moment it was Nina, his own dog, and just one other. Barney called him Orinoco, nothing to do with the river of the same name. Orinoco was one of the Wombles, the fattest and the laziest as it happens. The dog certainly looked like a Womble with all his hair and he was lazy as sin, only getting up to eat and pee. Barney used to love the Wombles and so the name fitted perfectly. As with all the strays that crossed his threshold, he was trying to track down the owner. This guy looked like a pedigree so he would have cost a couple of hundred pounds but, judging by the condition Barney had found him in when he wandered into the front garden, he had obviously travelled quite a distance. Anyway thus far he hadn't had any luck finding the owners so, for the time being, Orinoco lived happily with Nina, Owl and Barney.

Barney put his shopping and his little dog down on the floor. He looked around his lovely homely sitting-room, drenched in evening sunshine, and then flopped into his big Laura Ashley second-hand armchair. He had bought it in an old bric-à-brac shop years before because the pattern on it was lots of different breeds of dogs! Nina was instantly up on his lap again.

"Well, sweetheart, there's something happening in paradise," he confided to the dog. Like most of the locals Barney liked Ballymore the way it was and didn't fancy any changes. Nina turned her head sideways, as if this would help her understand her master better.

"Nina, Nina, Nina" he repeated, laughing at his adorable little dog. She rewarded him with a big wet lick.

"I saw Edu this evening," he changed the subject with his little friend. Nina's ears pricked up at the familiar name.

When Barney was first given Nina as a pup, he called into Innishambles to introduce his new little friend to the Daltons. Edu had only been in the country a few months at that stage and her English wasn't too hot. Barney fell in love with her instantly. She asked in her broken English was the pup a *perro* or a *perra*; a boy dog or a girl dog. "Eef it was a baby we would ask *nino* or *nina* – to know if it is a baby boy or a baby girl. *Perro* ees the Spanish for dog." Edu explained. Barney found this utterly disarming and instantly christened his little dog Nina because she was as smart as any human he knew. He also made Edu her godmother, a role Edu enjoyed, and she regularly called in to Peartree Cottage to see how her little god-dog was doing!

Barney still reddened when he thought of his one

and only effort to date her. It was an unmitigated disaster. He was so desperately shy for so long that he did nothing the first year she was in Ireland. During that year Edu's English became more or less fluent. In Barney's eyes she seemed to get more beautiful by the day and he loved the fact that she would often call in unannounced just for a chat or a coffee. In fact, truth be told, Barney secretly hoped that she might have a crush on him too.

One evening it was particularly sunny and so, instead of their usual coffee, Barney retrieved a bottle of white wine he had in the fridge for just such an occasion. They sat outside on the front lawn of Peartree Cottage. Back then the garden was just beginning to take shape under Cathy Taylor's expert hands. After their first bottle, a second seemed like a great idea and then a third. Neither was a big drinker and so they were well oiled when Barney mentioned his secret love.

"Barney. You are een love?" Edu asked in delight. "So am I!"

"You arrrre?" Barney couldn't believe his ears. "Shince when?" he tried to speak coherently.

"Oh Barney, ziz is so hard to talk about for me. I 'ave been in love from ze very beginning. I sink eet was love at first sight."

"Zat's amazing you too, I mean me too!" He tried to sit upright beside her on the lawn. "Edu, you are so beautiful, any man would be mad not to want you."

Edu looked like she might burst out crying but instead she threw her arms around Barney's neck.

"You are ze best, Barney!" She tried to kiss him on the cheek.

He made his move and kissed her on the mouth with all the passion he had been storing up inside for the last year. Under the influence of three bottles of Chablis, it took Edu a moment to figure out what was happening. There was a muffled squeal from under Barney's embrace and she pushed him away.'

"What are you doeeen, Barney?" she yelled. "Bastard. You get me drunk to do zis? You make up stories . . ."

She trailed off as she realised through a white-wine haze that Barney had been trying to confess his love for her when she had jumped in with her own story, and in the alcoholic confusion, he understood that she was in love with him. She did a complete U-turn, which was probably even more humiliating for Barney.

"*Yeazus*, Barney, *chico*. Eet is me you love?" she put her hand to his cheek affectionately. Barney couldn't meet her gaze. He just looked at the grass. "I am so sorry. I do love you, Barney, but not like zat. Perhaps I should go." She stood to leave as he mumbled an apology for the confusion.

The next time they met, they both pretended it hadn't happened and slowly their relationship grew back to being 'just good friends'. Any time he thought about it, Barney cringed and so he pushed it to the back of his mind. There was however one lingering confusion for Barney. Who was it that Edu really did love?

CHAPTER 7

When Dave and Sue Parker had moved to Ballymore three years ago there was quite a ripple of excitement. He was the nearest thing Ballymore had to a celebrity. Richard Dalton might own a big radio station in Dublin, but Parker's – the chain store was famous all over Ireland. Everybody knew Parker's. There was one in practically every town in Ireland now. Parkes specialised in clothing for the whole family, not exactly high street fashion but none the less very affordable and certainly very well known.

Maureen O'Reilly was in a tizzy for a whole week, fearful that they would open a Parker's in Ballymore. This was a little ironic as she didn't even sell clothing but she did feel threatened. As time passed, however, she realised that her fears were unfounded. The Parkers had moved to Ballymore for the peace and tranquillity, not to develop their chain store even further.

Sue Parker got to know the entire village quite quickly because she was out most evenings after they moved in, walking her new baby to sleep in her designer pram (definitely not bought in Parker's). The baby's name was India, and Guy, born just last year, arrived next.

Dave Parker had stopped for his customary pint in The Hitching Post on his way home. He had become quite good friends with Michael Molloy who owned and ran the pub. Michael had bought the pub thirty years earlier and when the house down the street came up for sale a few years later he had sufficient funds set aside to buy it and convert it into a B&B. Bridget, his wife, who ran the bed and breakfast, had insisted that they move into it, primarily because she didn't like living above the pub but she also reasoned that it was easier for guests coming and going and for breakfasts if she was in the house.

As with most things in their married life, Mick went along with her. In truth it actually worked out much better because the old men visiting the pub were a lot more relaxed in the absence of a woman.

Mick was a gentle creature who didn't impose. This is what Dave Parker liked most. He did not come for the chat or the gossip, quite the opposite. Mick and he might give a cursory nod to the weather or the traffic but it was usually quiet and calm in the old pub. Dave could rest after a hectic day in the office and then he could recharge his batteries for the pandemonium he knew he would face when he got home.

This evening was a little different, however. Frank Taylor had already arrived. He usually popped in just for the one pint, like Dave. Harold O'Reilly (Maureen's husband) would have three or four most evenings. "Just to keep Mick company," he would say.

Mick Molloy, Harold O'Reilly and Frank Taylor had their heads together, deep in hushed conversation, as Dave walked in. They swung around when they heard his cheery "Hello", but they relaxed when they saw it was only himself.

"Jesus, Dave, ye gave us a fright," Harold smiled at his neighbour.

"You lot look like you're up to no good," he replied, looking at them quizzically.

The three whisperers looked at each other and Mick from behind the bar sighed. "Sure you might as well tell him. He'll hear soon enough."

Dave Parker became concerned. "What's wrong?" he asked.

Harold looked like he had some very grave news.

"An American has bought Rathdeen Manor."

Mick, Harold and Frank stared at him waiting to see his response. Dave froze for a moment and then he burst out laughing.

"So?" he asked. "Isn't it a good thing surely that somebody has bought it and now maybe it'll be developed into something instead of being the old dangerous ruin it currently is?"

Frank spoke first. "Ah, David, if he's American, he'll

hardly bring something *positive* to Ballymore. You know they're all so loud."

Dave Parker, having come to the neighbourhood relatively recently himself, knew how xenophobic his friends were. How could they dismiss one of the most dynamic and progressive nations in the world just like that? It appalled him, but he understood that it was pointless trying to convert them and so he adopted a softer approach.

"Lads, lads, lads, three years ago you all hated me and look at us now? Won't this be the same?"

Michael disagreed from behind the counter. "Ah, but we knew about you before you came here."

Dave smiled in acknowledgement. He had been treated like royalty for the first few months, being Dave Parker of Parker's clothing.

"Well, what do we know about this American?"

Harold was the one with all the news. Working in an accountancy firm in Wicklow he often got news from the town before it reached Ballymore village.

"I was working this morning and bumped into the wee one working in the estate agent's next door. She's only a slip of a girl," he looked for a reaction. "Barely out of school," he added.

"'Hi, Mr O'Reilly,' she says to me." Harold took the top off his pint. He licked his lips. "'I suppose you heard we sold Rathdeen Manor to an American client last week,' and then she looks at me. Naturally I had to say that I knew all about it."

Harold took another sip.

"Ah Harry," Dave tried to control his temper. "Could you not have got a little more out of her than that?"

Harold looked dejected.

Mick spoke up. "Well, there were those fellas here a few weeks ago. They stayed with us, and Maureen did say they were interested in the Manor," he offered.

"Look, don't lose any sleep over it yet," Dave offered. "I'll make a few calls tomorrow and see what I can find out. It could be one of those Hollywood babes – did you think of that? Lads, we'd all be made!"

The other three cheered up at the prospect and went back to their drinks. The conversation moved on to Hollywood women and the mood was decidedly lighter as Dave downed his pint and left for home.

"Daddy, Daddy," the children squealed as they came hurtling out of their playroom to see their hero.

"I've painted a picture of you," India offered up a still wet cacophony of colour to her father.

"It's a picture of me and you and Mummy, but not Guy," she added. Dave glanced up at Sue who had just joined them in the hall. They were having terrible problems with India. She was so jealous of Guy's arrival on the scene even now, a full year on.

Dave spent the next two hours playing and talking with his two children. They chased and tickled. He bathed them while Sue watched television. And then he read them the story of *Beauty and the Beast* for what felt like the hundredth time that month. India liked it because she could be the Beauty and Guy the Beast. Guy didn't care what was read to him. He just loved the attention of his father.

Dave Parker doted on his children. India was very feisty but a real little princess. She was adored by both her parents and spoiled rotten. It already looked like she was going to be a beauty. Guy on the other hand was a complete animal. He was only just over the year old but he had been walking since he was ten months. Guy's main objective in life was to destroy. He had done more damage in the last few months than India had done in her entire feminine life.

Even before he could walk Guy had discovered the pleasure of breaking dishes. If a cup or a plate were inadvertently left at the edge of a kitchen counter or on the table where he could reach it, he would pull it down and smash it with great glee. India was horrified by this behaviour. David Parker looked at the bigger picture. Guy was obviously one hundred per cent testosterone. Surely this was a good thing in a boy and he would be well able for the challenge of taking Parker's retail chain to the next level, perhaps going international or maybe even floating the company.

By nine o'clock he had them both in bed. They were happy and exhausted and so was he. Then he came down into his drawing- room and remembered the other reason he was so happy. Sue Parker was his reason for living, his sole motivation. She was the most beautiful woman he had ever seen and she was all his. This evening she was sitting on one of their large luxurious sofas with her feet up. She was as always impeccably dressed. Sue's clothing and dry cleaning bills were fantastically high but Dave didn't mind when this was what he came home to.

Tonight she wore a simple but classically elegant summer dress. It was tailored, of course; even Sue's summer wardrobe was well cut and quite probably handmade for her. This evening she wore a sandy-coloured, "Jackie O" dress – round neck and sleeveless. It fitted down her long thin body and was cut to about four inches above the knee. To this she had added large gold earrings, a long gold necklace and a matching bracelet. He looked at her in wonder. She could have been on the cover of *Vogue*.

The sandy-colour dress highlighted her deep tan and as she sat the short skirt rose up her thigh, reminding Dave what ravishingly long legs she had.

Sue turned and smiled at him. "Welcome home, darling."

"God, you're gorgeous," he replied as he crossed the room to hug her.

"Dinner is ready. Would you like to change first or do you want to eat straight away?" She ignored his amorous greeting, but brushed his cheek with hers as if to air-kiss him.

"Dinner can wait if you fancy helping me get out

of these clothes," he grinned at her, one eyebrow raised.

"David, you're incorrigible," she gently pushed him away from her and went to busy herself in the kitchen.

David stiffened with tension as he followed her.

"Honey, is there something you want to tell me? What's wrong?"

Sue had her back to David, so he couldn't see the panic on her face.

"What are you talking about?" she asked with a flippant chuckle.

Dave went to the fridge and pulled out a bottle of chilled white wine. He opened it as Sue served up two plates of salmon steak with new potatoes and baby carrots tossed in lemon.

"Looks great, honey."

"Thank you." Sue's voice was artificially good-humoured in an attempt to keep him away from his old topic.

Dave sighed. "If I knew what was wrong maybe I could help," he tried. "You don't want me near you at all now," he persevered.

"Don't," she pleaded. "Don't start this again. It's nothing. Look, I'm tired, I'm hungry. It's been a long day with the kids. Just because I don't want a quick shag as soon as you get in the door doesn't mean I'm frigid, Dave." She was beginning to get aggressive. It was the same routine every time. Dave didn't know what was going on in his wife's head but he did know he didn't want a fight.

"OK, OK," he smiled, backing down yet again. "I'm just a randy old sod!" Dave saw Sue's hand gently release the kitchen chair she was clutching for support. Her knuckles were white. After years of negotiation and confrontation in the business world, having bought out many retailers throughout the country and indeed aggressively taken over others, Dave Parker knew a lot about human nature and he knew his wife was keeping something from him. He just didn't know what.

"This smells terrific," he reverted back to the safe topic of food as they sat down. "You've been working hard."

"Not at all." She was calmer. "How was your day?"

"Same old, same old. I had a bit of fun in The Hitching Post, however." He filled her in on the evening's events as he refilled his own glass and gave Sue her first drink. "The lads are in a state of high agitation because some American has bought Rathdeen Manor."

"I can go one better," she laughed as she took a drink. "I can tell you who has bought it!"

"Bloody hell, Sue, even the estate agent wouldn't know that! Where do you get your information?" Dave asked incredulously, laughing at the same time.

"Who needs Sky News when you have Rathdeen Golf Club?" she asked with a white-wine giggle. "It's Nicolas Flattery!"

"*The* Nicolas Flattery?" Dave asked incredulously. "As in the movie *Freedom* – that we saw only last month!"

"The very same. Nicolas Flattery fell in love with Ireland when he was making the movie and now he wants to live here."

Dave took a gulp of wine to get over the shock. "Jesus, Nicolas Flattery will be living up the road from us! I assume he's bringing his drop-dead gorgeous wife. What's her name again?"

The two laughed and talked about when they would have their new neighbours over to dinner and, most importantly, who with. Anybody in Ireland would be impressed to dine with the Flatterys. Sue explained that the husband of one of her golf ladies' was the solicitor liaising with Nicolas Flattery's lawyer in LA. Work on the house was to start instantly and the hope was that Nicolas would be in residence by Christmas.

"Perfect," he exclaimed. "We can have a huge Christmas drinks party and we'll invite them so they can meet all their neighbours!"

Sue was the first to even consider the other possibilities. "You know they probably chose Ballymore because it was so quiet and unobtrusive. Maybe they want to be left alone."

Dave pondered on this for a while. "Sod that. If we're going to have internationally acclaimed neighbours we may as well enjoy it!"

Sue laughed in agreement. "I'm sure the price of houses will go up too." With that, there was an almighty crash from upstairs. "If the house lasts that long – I know that sound, Dave." She jumped up. "Guy has managed to turn his cot over again. God, he's such a nightmare, that child."

"I'll go." Dave got to his feet, draining his glass as he did so.

"Thank you, darling. He'll listen to you. He never does what I ask anyway."

"He's got the Parker punch," Dave explained, inflating his chest with pride. "When I was a kid I was the same." He left the kitchen.

Sue ignored him as she started to clear away the dinner things. She didn't trust herself to look him in the eye.

Dave Parker was her one true love. How could she have let the situation develop to this?

She knew that Dave loved her absolutely and totally. In fact, he had never loved anybody else. Dave and Sue met in first year in college. He was studying business and she was doing languages. The first time he met her he told her that one day she would be his wife and Sue laughed at the little man with the big ideas. At five foot eight, Sue looked like a model and she carried herself like one too. Her own father had been very old-fashioned and always had the view that she was being sent to college to be married off. It was with an open mind then that she began dating the ebullient David Parker. Sue, being quiet by nature, loved Dave's effervescence. Dave, loud and bursting with life all the time, idolised Sue's serenity and classic style. He claimed he had found his queen and he would never let her go.

The relationship was strong enough by the end of their first year at college to survive when Dave announced that he was quitting. He was frustrated by the amount of time it was taking him to learn what *they* claimed he needed to know and so Dave Parker jumped into the rocky world of business without his degree.

Sue had grown accustomed to him by then and she was quite happy to date a man with a salary, even if it was only a shop assistant's wage. When they were both students, they had been permanently broke.

Sue's father was not too convinced until Dave bought the shop that he was working in within the year. He bought his second and third shops while Sue was in third year and then began his meteoric rise.

Dave himself put his success down to bloody hard work and being in the right place at the right time. Most importantly he believed in motivating his staff because they were the ones keeping the whole operation going. Whatever his beliefs, in the space of one decade he had become a household name and now employed many of his old college classmates.

David claimed that he too was five foot eight, but Sue knew that she was a fraction taller than he was, not that it mattered. The day Sue graduated Dave proposed to her with a four-carat solitaire diamond ring. Then, instead of going on the piss with his old classmates and his girlfriend, he whisked her over to Paris in a private Lear jet he had rented, where they had a quiet candlelit dinner and she accepted his offer of marriage. Even her father approved by then!

Sue could not and would not imagine a life without Dave. She had betrayed him, however, and she knew it was the one thing he would not be capable of forgiving her for. Dave was not a malicious man with his friends (work was another matter). With his loved ones, however, he was absolutely loyal and naturally expected that they would be the same. If Dave discovered that Sue had not been a loyal wife, he would quite simply crumple. It might or might not destroy him but it would definitely destroy their marriage.

CHAPTER 8

Saskia was very happy to get home from hospital, even if it was St Helen's. She had originally thought that she would only be in for a couple of days, but with all the problems, she was in fact in there for almost a week. She never would have thought that the house would continue running without her to hold it all together but surprise, surprise, it had.

Of course, a mountain of washing and an empty freezer greeted her but all things considered, the house was relatively intact. Richard had, in fact, yelled at the girls and Edu just before he left Innishambles to go and collect Saskia from hospital. He told them to get the house in shape before Saskia's return and he gave them all individual chores.

Kelly was put in charge of vacuuming the house about which she complained bitterly, claiming that she was never in the dining-room or study and so why should she have to vacuum them? Tiffany didn't mind doing a little housework. She would have ended up doing it all without any help if her father hadn't taken control of the situation. She offered to wash the kitchen floor and clean out the fridge and cooker, which were frightful messes after a week of Edu's cooking and Richard's heating up old dinners. "Men really are such scatterbrains!" she said. Lauren, who was still treated like the baby, was given the job of polishing which everybody knew was a complete doss. All you had to do was walk into each room of the big old house and spray a squirt of polish into the air and hey presto, the room smelt like it had been polished.

Edu stripped all the beds and daydreamed. She fantasised about Innishambles being her home and Richard her husband. If Saskia was out of the picture she could become the woman of the house. The girls would just have to get on with it and it would be she, Edu, who accompanied Richard on all his business trips and who went to the Christmas charity balls with Richard and it would also be she who gave him his much-coveted son. The fact that Saskia did not currently go with Richard on his business trips, Edu took to be a failing on Saskia's part. What Edu did not know was that Richard would not let her go. He claimed her place was with their girls and business trips were just a lot of long frustrating meetings. He could not burden her with such hassles.

Just as Edu fluffed the pillows in the master

bedroom, finishing off the last bed in the house, she heard Dudley and Dexter begin to bark and howl at the front door. Since Wilma's disappearance, a much tighter rein had been kept on all the animals.

Woody had been utterly miserable for the last week in the absence of both his little sister, Wilma, and his mistress, Saskia. He slept with Tiffany every night and she took him everywhere with her to try to console him. Tiffany felt terrible because she had not taken Wilma's disappearance seriously for days. The little dog was often missing in action, especially at mealtimes. Wilma liked to eat alone and would never stoop so low as to run around Tiffany's feet when she was preparing the dogs' meals. Dudley, Dexter and Woody were always on hand at mealtimes, but not Wilma.

On the evening Saskia went to hospital Tiffany had assumed that Wilma was somewhere around the house, probably sleeping on somebody's bed or in their laundry! The following morning, she hadn't even noticed Wilma's absence, she was so preoccupied with being sent to school instead of getting up to St Helen's.

Now as she cleaned the kitchen floor, she worried as she watched Woody lie forlorn on his blanket in front of the Aga. He had given up rushing out to meet Richard. Tiffany looked at the little mutt. He didn't move when Dudley and Dexter began to bark at the approaching car.

"Woody!" His ears pricked up just at the tone in her voice. "I think that's Mummy!" The dog jumped at the sound of the familiar name and hurtled across the wet kitchen floor, slipping and sliding in his excitement to get to the front door.

"Slow down," Tiff chortled, mopping up his paw-prints quickly and running after him.

Lauren came running out of the study where she had been playing on the computer. Edu and Kelly came thundering down the stairs. Lauren got to the front door first and threw it open as Tiffany and Woody arrived from the kitchen in time to see Richard's brand-new black Mercedes glide up their gravelled laneway with their mum, dad and their new little sister. Polly and Mooner gave chase to their new adversary which looked exactly like their old one.

As with all her new babies, Saskia was most anxious that the elder ones did not feel jealous. Even with the large age gap, she did as she had always done on returning home. Robin Dalton was asleep in her baby seat in the back of the car and Saskia got out of the Merc without the baby to greet her older girls. Kelly, Tiffany and Lauren had each held their baby sister in hospital and so their curiosity was slightly sated. They were just happy to have their mum home.

"Hi, welcome home. We missed you!" Lauren threw her arms around her mother, holding on very tight. Slightly winded, Saskia returned the bear hug, if perhaps a little more gently.

"The house is spotless. You just put your feet up," Tiffany volunteered, joining in on the hug.

"Well, at least we'll get some ordinary food now you're home." Kelly looked at Edu as she kissed her mother's cheek. "Welcome home, Mum. We really missed you."

Edu was the only one who hadn't seen the baby. She stared in the car window at the tiny little person, so incomprehensibly small. She could not believe that it was real. "*Yeazus*, Saskia. She is so small. She is so beautiful!" Edu was mesmerised.

Richard took the baby out of the car, leaving Saskia completely free to hug and hold her other girls. Still in her baby seat and sound asleep, Robin Dalton looked like a doll. They all gathered around Richard, to stare at the little bundle of pink. Saskia had been so certain that her new baby was a boy, most of her new Babygros were blue. Thankfully Kelly had visited her mother in hospital via Grafton Street and blown a small fortune on pink outfits. She arrived in St Helen's with enough clothing for three children!

Annoyed with the lack of attention, the dogs began to bark. They were all quickly hushed by the entire Dalton clan in unison as Robin stirred a little as if to wake. Then she fell back into a baby-sleep again. The family breathed a collective sigh of relief. It was then that Saskia spotted Woody by himself.

"Where's Wilma?" she asked as she picked up Woody. Richard caught Tiffany's eye, while Lauren and Kelly looked at the ground. Edu was still transfixed by the baby. Saskia felt the change in mood.

"Tiff, what's going on?" she asked with a slight smirk, expecting to hear about some devilment that they were up to.

"Oh Mum, I wanted to tell you, but Daddy said you had enough on your plate," wailed Tiffany.

Saskia looked at her husband. "Richard?" Everybody looked at Richard, even Edu.

"Saskia." He paused, wondering for a fleeting second if he could fob this conversation off till later – not a chance. "Look, we don't know exactly. It appears Wilma has wandered off."

"What?" Saskia's face told him all he needed to know. This was not going to be easy. Saskia had got Woody and Wilma over ten years ago and they went everywhere with her. She was extremely attached to both of them. Saskia clutched Woody for support.

"You bloody well should have told me, Tiffany. Your father was wrong." Sas was very upset and this upset her girls.

Kelly, who also loved Wilma, tried to explain. "We've done everything that we could think of, Mum. We've been on to the police, the dog pound. We've even had an ad in the *Wicklow Tribune* and *The Irish Times* for the last week."

Sas was not appeased. "What do you mean she wandered off? Wilma is far too intelligent for that." She directed her venom at Richard. Her eyes were ablaze with anger. "For Christ's sake, when was she last seen? Who saw her last?"

Richard tried to take control. "Saskia, hush," he tried to embrace her but she shook him off.

"Hush nothing!" she stammered, close to tears. "Every day that passes, the likelihood of finding her alive slips." Her voice began to choke. "Not my little Wilma."

The girls gathered around their mum, each feeling guilty for not trying harder to find her dog.

"Lauren and I could ride out this afternoon and search every inch of the woods," Kelly volunteered.

"I can take Dudley and Dexter around the village to try and pick up her trail if you like," Tiffany chipped in.

"We really are trying to do everything we can," Richard smoothed Saskia's hair in an effort to calm her a little.

Robin Dalton was the one who managed to distract her mother however.

She shifted in her baby-seat and all eyes descended upon her again. Even Woody, safe in his mistress's arms, was curious about the little bundle.

Robin opened her eyes and looked at her family en masse for the first time. At the tender age of one week she gave a broad gummy grin to everybody and they all, even Richard, said "Ahhhhh," together.

Edu and Tiffany, anxious to keep Saskia's mind off Wilma, quickly threw lunch together. A huge Caesar salad was set in the middle of the table. Kelly had been dispatched to O'Reilly's to get a few baguettes. She went on Polly who, Richard said, was looking too fat lately. Richard retrieved a few bottles of Dom Perignon from the fridge "to wet the baby's head," and Saskia had settled down to feed Robin her bottle.

"I thought you were going to breastfeed the baby," Lauren commented as she set out cutlery and glasses on the big old pine table.

Saskia looked up and smiled with a look of resignation. "Alas, Lauren, with all the problems I had over the birth, I think Robin had settled with the bottle by the time I was fit enough to feed her," she explained. "Would you like to hold her?" she asked her daughter. "The advantage of me not feeding is that you can all get a chance to feed this little dote."

Lauren was a little nervous but very curious. She walked over to her mother and baby sister and had her first good look at her replacement as "baby of the family". When Lauren had heard the baby was a girl, a wave of relief washed over her. Here was another person to share or even take over the burden of guilt for not being a boy. Now, as she looked at the little baby, all she felt was compassion.

"She's so small," was all that she could say at first. The sofa that Saskia sat on was very old and worn. It had been there, in the kitchen, by the wall opposite the Aga since they bought the house. Dogs slept on it, children lounged on it. Richard and Saskia had got pissed on it and now Lauren held her tiny baby sister on it.

Robin stared intently at Lauren, which made the teenager laugh.

"She's just like a tiny person!" she giggled, gently taking the tiny hand. "Omigod, her fingers are like skinny matchsticks!" Lauren was fascinated.

"Where the hell is Kelly?" Richard, who had skipped breakfast to collect Saskia on time, was starving. The dogs started up again, bounding off towards the front door.

"That's strange. They don't usually get excited by the sound of Polly's hooves," said Tiff as she put the final touches on the table.

The dogs changed direction and milled from the front door, through the house and the kitchen into the conservatory, barking all the way.

"That can't be Kelly." Richard headed after the dogs.

"Yoo-hoo, anybody home, other than these filthy animals?" Edwina Dalton walked in.

"Dudley, Dexter, Woody. Heel!" Richard took out his aggression on the poor dogs. "Into the scullery." He locked them in and went to embrace his mother. "We weren't expecting you."

"I thought it would be a nice surprise, pet. I know you have no *professional* help and everybody says it's at times like this that you need the mothers!"

Saskia was speechless as she took in the suitcase in Edwina's hand. This was the last thing she needed.

"Where's my grandchild?" Ignoring Tiffany and Lauren, she scooped Robin out of Lauren's arms and sat herself down on the sofa. "Now, Saskia, you don't worry about a thing. I'm here to keep everything under control but I am starving. There's a good pet, fetch me a cup of tea while I feed this little thing and there's some fresh bread in the plastic bag beside my case. I know you don't have such luxuries living in the country. It's *Cuisine de France* you know. It's only a few hours old."

"*I* suddenly feel a lot older," Saskia mumbled under her breath as she stood up to make the tea.

"At least we don't have to wait for Kelly to get back with the bloody bread now," Richard offered. Tiffany, Saskia and even Edu glared at him.

After a rather fractious lunch during which Edwina Dalton managed to irk everybody at least once, Saskia hauled Richard into the study.

"What are you going to do about her?"

"Sas, that's my mother you're talking about."

"God knows I wish I wasn't talking about *Edwina*, Richard. I think I'd rather have anybody in the house than her for the next few days. She's not staying."

"For Christ's sake, what do you want me to do about it? She only came down to help you!"

"Did you hear what she said to Edu?" Saskia was not going to back down. She mimicked her mother-in-law, "Are you *still* here?"

"That was a bit harsh," Richard conceded, "but Edu is able for it. Look, Saskia, I actually think it's a good idea. Perhaps she should stay for a few weeks just until you get settled into a routine again. Remember you're going to be up in the middle of the night for feeds. You need all the help you can get."

Saskia stared at him, mouth wide open in shock, and so he persevered. "Mum can be a little indelicate at times –"

"*Indelicate?* No, Richard, a bull in a china shop is indelicate compared to your mother. Edwina Dalton is a loud, opinionated, ignorant old bat!"

"OK OK, you win, honey. God, but you're a hard woman."

The tension and anger began to leave Saskia's face as she listened to him.

"I'll talk to her. I understand that this is your house and you need your space. She can only stay for a week – at the outside." He was out the door of the study before she could respond.

Saskia returned to the kitchen just as Tiffany was storming out with a thunderous expression on her face.

"Everything OK?" she asked as cheerfully as she could.

Edwina started up again, "Saskia, why are you letting Tiffany do that transition year in school? It's common knowledge that the girls just while the time away and, Lord knows, the Devil finds work for idle hands."

Sas now knew why Tiffany had stormed out of the room. She tried to control her own temper. "Well, Edwina, we would disagree. The theory of a transition year is that the girls take some time out to look at the bigger picture. They do projects and work experience, to figure out what they want to do after school."

"I still say it's another example of your generation utterly spoiling the next generation. I don't know where it will finish – total disintegration of the moral infrastructure and backbone of society."

Saskia burst out laughing and so did Edu, who was finishing up the dishes. Edwina, who was born without a sense of humour, couldn't see the joke and so she handed Robin to her daughter-in-law.

"Yes, well, I need to powder my nose now." Edwina headed for the bathroom in a huff of indignation, but she stopped when she got to the kitchen door. It was as if a thought had struck her. "I still think you're mad coming home today no matter what you say. Yesterday or tomorrow would have been OK but not today."

Saskia stopped laughing. "What are you talking about?"

"Why, Saskia, you know," Edwina paused for effect, "Saturday's flitting makes for short sitting."

"What?" Edu was lost, so Saskia explained.

"It's an expression, Edu, an old superstition." She stressed the word old. "If you leave hospital on a Saturday, you'll be back there again, pretty soon. It's rubbish, of course!" But Saskia didn't feel like laughing any more.

Chapter 9

Katie Anderson had been in a coma since the car crash. She was in intensive care and a machine was breathing for her. The doctors had told her father that it was still not certain whether or not she would be able to breathe without the aid of the machines ever again, such were her injuries.

He had not left her bedside in all that time. He could not. Tom Anderson's wife, Jilly, had died in a car accident five years ago. He had never really recovered. Jilly was the lively one in their marriage, so full of energy and spontaneity. Tom had always assumed she would bury him. He was not prepared to bury her and live without her but that is exactly what he had been forced to do. Katie was their only child, for reasons known only to God. The Andersons had always wanted a large family but it just didn't happen. After Jilly's death, Katie moved home to Sligo to be with her father.

She claimed she had had enough of Dublin and it was what she really wanted. Tom had his doubts. He loved her to distraction, however, and didn't want to discourage her from moving home to be with him. He was very lonely without his wife. Katie settled down quickly. She genuinely seemed to be happy to be back in Sligo.

It was where Tom and Jilly had lived all their lives and so Katie was born and reared there. She quickly joined back up with her old friends. In fact she insisted that life in Sligo was considerably better than it had been Dublin.

Katie returned from Dublin with a terrific track record of experience. She had references from the Burlington Hotel and so she quickly got a job in the Yeats Country Hotel in Rosses Point, just outside Sligo. She claimed that she was just very lucky and that her timing had been good. Tom, on the other hand, was convinced that she was an absolute stunner with a mind as sharp as her mother's had been.

What really stuck in Tom Anderson's gut today however was that Katie wasn't even meant to be in Dublin at the time of the crash. She had spent the weekend in Sligo as she usually did. It had a great social life and Katie had no problem finding fun. One of her Dublin friends rang her complaining that they never saw her any more and so Katie decided to visit her city set.

She spent the day with her friend. That night they

were having a dinner party for some others and so she popped out to get some more wine. Returning back to the house with her goodies, some madman driving a tank of a car came head-on into her little Mini. She didn't stand a chance.

Tom Anderson had been awoken by the doorbell at two fifteen in the morning. When he heard the ding-dong, the first thing he did was look at his bedside clock. He trundled down the stairs hoping it was some neighbourhood kids playing a prank, but when he opened the door, he was in no doubt. A policeman and woman stood side by side with a soft expression on their faces. Before they even spoke he fell back, pleading with them.

"No, no, go away, not my baby, not her as well." They broke it to him as easily as they could and urged him to delay travelling up until the next day. Tom was as polite as he could be under the circumstances, but as soon as he got them out of his house, he threw a few belongings into a bag and drove like a demon from Sligo to Dublin. Tom was sitting at Katie's bedside by sun-up the morning after the accident. He hadn't moved since.

"Da," the girl's throat was choking before she could get a full word out.

He thought he was dreaming when he heard the familiar voice.

"Da?" Katie's voice was barely a whisper.

"Hush, child. Yes it's me. I'm here," he took her

hand and squeezed it. Looking over his shoulder he called for the nurse who sat only ten feet away. She was over in a flash.

"Welcome back, Katie. Can you see me?" The nurse was all business even if it was in a soft and gentle tone. Katie was more interested in her father. Her eyes were focused on him, a combination of fear and incomprehension.

"Rest, pet. The reason you can't talk properly is because you've got a tube down your throat. Don't fight it. God, it's so good to have you back. We have really missed you. I love you, Katie."

She closed her eyes again.

Tom looked at the nurse for reassurance. "This is good, Mr. Anderson, very good. Now, however, she must rest." The feeling of relief that flooded over him was like a tidal wave. He moved out of the intensive care ward for a minute and collapsed into a chair. There, he wept and wept for joy.

The nurses that worked the intensive care unit were special. They regularly had a patient's life in their hands. They were also the most compassionate and loving people, helping ordinary mortals through these most traumatic of times. Victoria, the nurse Tom had come to know and like best, followed him out of the ward and sat next to him.

"How are you bearing up?"

"Much better now," he wiped away the tears.

"This is terrific news, there's no doubt about that,

but Tom, you know we're not out of the woods yet?"

"She's out of a coma, Victoria. Isn't that a start?"

"Yes, and a very good one. The fact that she came out of the coma relatively quickly bodes well but you do know, with the other complications, even if she does stay conscious there are still a lot of bridges to cross. She may not be able to breathe unaided, for example."

"Fine, well, we'll just have to live with that bloody big machine until the medical world comes up with a pocket version!"

"That's the spirit," Victoria encouraged him. "You need to be strong for your daughter. I know it's not easy alone but she loves you very much."

"You think?" he asked. Even though he knew the answer, he liked being told.

"My God, you saw her just now. I couldn't get her attention for a minute. She only had eyes for you, Tom!"

"Please make her better, Victoria. Please." Victoria knew that Tom could not accept that Katie would never be as she had been, but she had pushed him enough for one day. She hugged him like a little boy and rocked gently.

"Do you know what you should do? Do you know what Katie would really appreciate?" She had Tom's attention. "You should go back to your hotel and have a rest. Then get up, have a shower, a shave and a hearty meal. After that, come back here this evening fresh and dapper!"

Tom faltered.

"Look, she's out of the coma. She does need to rest however and I'm not sure that she'll rest if you're here. When she wakes next, I'll tell her that I sent you home for a few hours and that you'll be back this evening."

The idea that he might be a source of exhaustion to his daughter was the deciding factor so he complied with Victoria's wishes. He returned to Katie's bedside for one more look at his beautiful daughter.

She lay so still; she could have been dead. The machines that were so inhibiting last week were now his old friends. The constant beep, beep of her heart monitor informed him that she had a steady pulse. The only time that that sound had changed was when she woke. The beeping had sped up alarmingly but now they were stable again.

Her skin was a clammy grey. Her eyes were lightly closed, so still that he could see the tiny blue veins dotted across each eyelid. Her long eyelashes rested gently on her cheekbones. Her mouth however was snarled and ugly because it was forced open so this huge tube could fit down her throat to fill her lungs. Then it was taped in place so it was airtight. The other end of the tube was connected to the respirator and as the bag inside the glass jar rose and dropped it took a breath for his darling daughter. He knew that this was the machine actually keeping Katie alive but he still wanted to take it out of her mouth so she could be comfortable. Both her hands had tubes inserted into her skin bringing much-needed fluids, nutrients and painkillers.

"I don't want to tire you out, Katie, so I'm going to leave you to rest for a little while. I'll be back soon, pet." He kissed her forehead as best he could around the tubes. "Don't go anywhere!" he teased and left the ward.

It was lunchtime Saturday and Tom was starving.

Kelly trotted Polly up the main street of Ballymore past Bridget Molloy's B&B. The pony suddenly stopped outside Ballymore Church because she wanted to do a pee.

"That's a charming view to have as I eat my Saturday brunch, Kelly Dalton!" a voice yelled at her from outside The Hitching Post. It was Barney Armstrong.

"It's not my bloody fault. You, of all people, should know that!"

"Yes, but outside the *House of God*? Could you not push her on a bit?" Barney teased.

Polly had finished anyway and so she was happy to move on at Kelly's request, especially when she saw her old friend Barney dining outside the pub next door. He was having lunch with a friend.

"I hope Father Conway didn't see you," he teased.

"So what if he did?" Kelly turned to the girl having lunch with Barney. "Hi. I'm Kelly."

"Jenny, Jenny Quinn. I think I've seen you around. I'm the Parkers' new nanny."

"I thought I'd introduce Jenny to the wild social life of Ballymore," Barney laughed.

"Well, this here is about as wild as it gets, I'm afraid.

114

Nothing much ever happens in Ballymore. Does it, Barney?"

"Actually it has been fairly busy this morning, hasn't it?" Barney looked to his lunch-mate for support and then he turned to Kelly again. "Did you hear about Rathdeen Manor? Jenny has been telling me that the word is – on the complete QT of course – that Nicolas Flattery has bought the Manor and he's moving over here."

"Who is Nicolas Flattery?"

Jenny and Barney both looked shocked. "You can't be serious! Everybody knows Nicolas Flattery! Jesus, Kelly where have you been?" Barney explained when he saw her blank face. "Nicolas Flattery is the guy from *Freedom*, probably the biggest actor in LA right now."

"Oh, the *Freedom* fella, why didn't you say? Wow, he's moving over here? Why?"

This silenced Barney. He turned to Jenny who had told him the story in the first place "Why, Jenny?"

She shrugged.

"Are you working today, Jenny?" Kelly asked. "Are the Parker kids still little twerps? I used to baby-sit for Sue and Dave a bit."

"No, it's only a part-time job. I only mind them a few days a week when Sue has stuff to do," Jenny explained.

Kelly caught Barney's eye and winked. So this was a date then. Barney looked suitably guilty. He coughed to clear his throat.

"Anyway, as I was saying, it's been mad busy all morning. The noise outside Peartree Cottage this morning of trucks passing by eventually got my curiosity going. So I had a little look."

"Mrs O'Reilly, eat your heart out!" Kelly teased him.

"Feck off, Kelly Dalton, or I'll tell Fr Conway that Polly was piddling on the pulpit! Do you want to hear this or not?"

"Hardly the pulpit," she mumbled. "I'm sorry, Barney. I'm all ears."

"They were all delivery trucks, dropping tons and tons of building equipment up to Rathdeen Manor. We went up there. It's actually like the scene from a movie."

"We can go home that way and have a look," Kelly said, giving Polly a pat on the side of the neck. "It's unusual that those guys deliver on a Saturday, isn't it?"

"Especially so early. God, it must have been around seven o'clock when they started," Jenny groaned.

Barney glanced at Kelly nervously but he knew that the damage was done by the broad, knowing grin on her face. She understood perfectly. Barney was not on a lunch date with Jenny Quinn. It was in fact a Friday night date that was still running!

"Well," she said expansively, "we don't want to overstay our welcome, do we, Polly? Hate to pee and run but I'm actually on a shopping expedition. I have to get some bread for our lunch. Mum's back from hospital with my new little sister! Lovely to meet you, Jenny. Oh, and welcome to the charms of Ballymore!" She winked at Barney again.

"Mmm," Jenny swallowed the end of her club sandwich, "nice to meet you. I'm sure we'll meet again."

"Bye, Kelly. Send my regards to your mother." Barney called after her, as she trotted Polly across the wide main street of Ballymore, to O'Reilly's shop.

Just as she was about to dismount, a car came tearing down the road and beeped loudly at her. It was one of those old horns that played the first five notes of some nondescript song. The car was travelling very quickly and it gave Polly a ferocious shock. She reared up on her hindquarters and Kelly held on to her neck for dear life. The horse kept rearing and whinnying, eyes rolling. Polly, in her confusion, was trying to throw Kelly. All Kelly could do was hang on. Barney was over in a flash. He stopped at a distance of about twenty feet and began to softly whisper to Polly.

"OK girl. OK. Down now." His voice was barely audible. He stood like a scarecrow, arms outstretched, very slowly moving them up and down.

After what felt like an eternity to Kelly, Polly fell under Barney's spell and allowed herself to be soothed. The huge animal began to snort indignantly and slowly calmed.

"Shit, shit, shit and shit those bastards!" was all she could muster. Kelly was as shaken as Polly but not at all hurt.

"You're a bloody good horsewoman, Kelly." Barney took her arm to steady her as she slithered off Polly.

"Thanks for being here, Barney. That could have been a lot sorer."

Barney was stroking Polly, calming her a little more. "Go and get your messages and I'll hold this animal until you get back," he suggested, and then he looked over to see if Jenny was watching the action, from the safety of the pub bench. "You see," he laughed, "never a dull moment!"

Kelly bought her bread, bade goodbye to Barney and Jenny for a second time and, on Barney's advice, decided to walk Polly home.

"I'm taking you home the scenic route, Polly. If we go along the river and up the back way to Innishambles we'll see all the action Barney was talking about. Plus we avoid the risk of meeting those lunatics again!" Kelly took Polly on a loose rein to let the horse's head hang comfortably as she walked along beside her mistress.

O'Reilly's shop and The Hitching Post were opposite each other on the main street of Ballymore. Next to them, at the end of the village was a little bridge that could grace the front of any chocolate box.

Being September, the grasses and brambles were at their full height. Wild lilies, glowing bright orange, grew along the water's edge. The River More was not particularly dangerous. Its pace was languid and it was not very deep, thus it made the most wonderful bubbling and gurgling sounds as the water splashed and spluttered merrily over large rocks and boulders.

Kelly and Polly made their way down to the river's edge and they walked along the bank breathing in the atmosphere and enjoying what was definitely the last of the summer sun. Kelly fumbled around in her various jacket pockets until she found her cigarettes and her lighter. She lit up and took a deep drag.

"You know, Polly, that was the first time you ever tried to throw me. I didn't think you had it in you." The animal nuzzled into her side as if to apologise.

"Don't worry, girl, I would have probably done the same thing in your shoes! What utter horrors though. If I ever see them again, I'll give them a piece of my mind."

Polly snorted in agreement.

Rathdeen Manor, like Innishambles, was a big estate. It started with a large road frontage and swept down the side of the valley spreading over acres of good grazing land. The estate ended at the River More. Both estates had fishing rights. The only difference was that Rathdeen Manor was on the north-facing side of the valley while Innishambles had the south-facing side, and so the land enjoyed more warmth and sun.

As they approached Innishambles, they also approached Rathdeen Manor land because the two estates started at the same point along the river.

As Kelly reached the boundaries, she craned her neck to see any sign of life on the Manor's land but down by the river there was none. Feeling slightly guilty she slipped back up onto Polly's back and bribed her with some fresh baguette.

"I'm sorry to mount you after your big shock, pet, but just a quick look, Polly. Obviously all the action is up in the old Manor itself and at the roadside. I can't see anything from here." Polly acquiesced and broke into a soft canter.

As they rose to the top of the valley, Kelly whispered urgently to her big four-legged friend.

"Woah girl, I've seen enough." It was pandemonium. They got a full view of all the new building materials that Barney had been talking about. Kelly also spotted the bashed-up little blue Cortina that had made such a rumpus and nearly killed her half an hour earlier.

"They're bloody builders!"

She turned Polly around and galloped for home.

CHAPTER 10

Lauren was thoroughly fed up. Robin was a little dote – of that there could be no doubt – but so much fuss. To top it all now Grandma Dalton had descended upon the house. Terror and frustration would reign until she saw fit to leave or until she was kicked out.

Lauren thought about last Christmas with a cringe. The best night was probably the night they all got pissed on Richard's delicious red wine and they ate Barney's wild pheasant. Nobody expected Edwina to arrive at eight-thirty the next morning. God knows what time she left Dublin! Edwina's habitual bitching and nitpicking ruined the entire Christmas. Comments like "Oh, Saskia, had I known you weren't going to make the cranberry sauce yourself, I could have done it," were not appreciated.

Her presents were even worse. Kelly got a book on *How to improve your IQ*. Tiffany received an acrylic blouse with huge frills. Lauren was sure it was one of Edwina's own blouses that she was recycling because it was a size sixteen and it must have been at least 30 years old! Lauren drew the shortest straw on the Christmas presents however. Grandma Dalton gave her a Bible!

"I know you're starting secondary school next year, pet, and your mind will be opened to many new ideas, so the timing of this gift is perfect. Keep it near you always and you won't go far wrong."

Tiffany hid her chuckles under her new blouse and Kelly shook with laughter behind the pages of *How to improve your IQ*. Saskia tried to sound polite and positive about Edwina's choice of presents until she discovered that her present was a year's subscription to *Unislim*.

"The only way you'll shift that spare tyre is with the help of professionals, Saskia, and let's face it, I think you could do with all the help you can get!"

Richard did best of all, of course – a Tricot Marine jumper. The girls cheered up a little when they saw it because Edwina still thought Richard was as trim as he had been the day he got married. She invariably bought a few sizes too small for him and so the girls would get most use out of it.

"How is the studying going, Lauren?" Edwina interrupted her daydream.

"Fine."

"You know now is the time to lay down the foundations if you want good grades in your final year."

"I know, so you keep reminding me."

"Lauren!" Tiffany cut her sister a warning look, "Be nice," she whispered.

"Why?" Lauren mouthed back.

"Well, pay heed that you work hard now, girl. I gave Kelly the same advice and did she take it? Not a bit of it. That girl spends all her days dreaming and where does it get her? Mark my words she'll end up on the shelf with no means of supporting herself."

"Maybe she'll have a rich son to support her," Lauren teased her grandmother, with a veiled reference to her and Richard's relationship. It went straight over Edwina's head, however.

"Sure who'll marry her if she's not a nice, well-educated girl?"

"Maybe she'll just get pregnant, Grandma, you know without the benefit of matrimony. Then we can have a shotgun marriage!"

Edwina went puce and so did Tiffany, who was mortified at Lauren's flippant comments. She glared at her little sister and tore out of the kitchen before she got pulled into the conversation.

"Good God, girl," Edwina spluttered. "Where do you get your ideas? Kelly may not have worked very hard at school but she's a good girl. She'd never –" she was lost for words.

"She'd never have sex outside wedlock. Is that what you're trying to say, Grandma?"

"Sorry I'm late," Kelly arrived into the kitchen, as if on cue.

"Are you *late*, Kelly? That's funny because Grandma and I were just discussing how sexually promiscuous you were. Care to join in on the conversation?"

Kelly stopped in her tracks and stared agog at Lauren. She broke into fits of laughter when she saw how excruciatingly uncomfortable her grandmother was.

"Whatever turns you on!" she said. "Hi, Grandma, are you down for the day or what?" Kelly gave her grandmother a gentle kiss on a particularly puce cheek.

"Kelly, we weren't. I wasn't –"

"Relax, Edwina. I know how Lauren operates." She was actually beginning to feel sorry for the old lady. "Where is everybody? I've got the baguette – well, half of it. We had a little accident with the other half."

"What was the accident?" Lauren asked.

"Polly got hungry."

"Well, you're off the hook anyway. Edwina brought bread with her. It was *Cuisine de France*, you know." She slightly mimicked her grandmother.

"Why the bloody hell did I go to the village in the first place then?"

Saskia arrived back without Robin.

"Where's the baby?" her mother-in-law asked.

"I think the exhaustion of having her nappy changed was enough to knock her out. She's asleep again, so I put her in her crib."

Edwina looked dejected. "Well, I expect I'll go and unpack then. Am I in my usual room, Saskia?"

"Yes."

Kelly looked at her mother in horror as Edwina left the room. "Unpack? Please don't say she's here to visit."

"I'm afraid so, pet." Saskia checked at the door to ensure that Edwina was well and truly out of earshot. "You must remember that she's your father's mother and we're the only family she has. It must be very exciting for her to have another granddaughter."

"Then why don't we send Robin up to stay with her?" Lauren interjected bitterly.

"Lauren, you don't really feel that way about your new baby sister, do you?" Saskia hugged her daughter. "I know things are a little topsy-turvy at the moment but it will settle down soon. Who knows, Edwina may even be of some help."

The girls looked at their mother incredulously and burst out laughing.

"Well, maybe I'm being a little optimistic there!" Sas agreed with their laughter.

"Mum, I'm really sorry about Wilma. She just vanished," Lauren said.

She and Sas sat down at the kitchen table. Saskia took the girl's hand and stroked it maternally. "I know, pet. It was nobody's fault. Sometimes these things just happen. I shouldn't have lost my temper. I'm sorry."

Kelly who was fixing herself a sandwich with what was left of the baguette turned to her mother. "How do you end up apologising? We're the ones who lost her. I'm really sorry too, Mum."

"Really girls, it's OK. All I ask is that you help me out over the next few weeks and cut your grandmother a little slack." She looked directly at Lauren who was toughest on her grandmother and raised her right eyebrow questioningly.

"Ah, Mum, you spoil all our games!" Lauren teased. "I'll go easier on her – a little easier," she qualified.

Saskia looked at Kelly for a promise.

"Don't look at me. I didn't do anything. I just got here." The conversation moved on and Kelly told them all about Barney's news and the famous Nicolas Flattery moving next door. Sas and Lauren were very excited.

"He has a gorgeous son who's fifteen years old!" Lauren enthused.

"You are not allowed within a mile of that young man, Lauren Dalton," her mother interceded.

"Why the hell not?"

"For once I sound like my mother-in-law, but I know about those LA kids. I read *Hello!* too, you know. I'm serious, Lauren. You can be polite and neighbourly but no friendlier than that. Do I make myself clear?"

"Mum, I can't believe you're being this irrational. He doesn't even live here yet and wait till you get a look at the dad. Now, he's really gorgeous."

"Hands off. He's mine," giggled Kelly.

"That would make you my mother-in-law," gushed Lauren.

Saskia threw her hands to heaven as Richard and Edu walked in.

126

"What's this?" he asked. They duly filled the others in on the morning's gossip. Kelly also told them about the mad builders with the wonky horn in the old bashed-up Cortina.

"That's bloody ridiculous," Richard thundered. He was really furious. "They could have killed you. Thank God for Barney. I think I'll go over there right now and give them a piece of my mind."

"Daaad," Kelly pleaded, "let it pass; no damage was done."

"Perhaps not this time, Kelly, but if these builders are going to be around for the next few months, they're going to have to learn how to behave in the country. You certainly don't go around scaring the shit out of horses."

"Richard!" Saskia reprimanded him on his language out of habit.

"No, that's it. I'm going over there." And he was gone.

"On a slightly lighter note. It looks like Barney has a new girlfriend!" Kelly said.

"Oh God, don't tell Tiffany!" Lauren suggested.

"Don't tell Tiffany what?" She walked into the kitchen.

"I'm afraid it looks like Barney has a new girlfriend, Tiff," Kelly continued. "Jenny Quinn is the Parkers' new nanny. All I know is that they were sharing a lovey-dovey Saturday brunch outside The Hitching Post today and she woke up in Barney's house this morning. Must have been a good night!"

Tiffany looked crestfallen. She sat down beside her mother. "He was mine! Has she no honour?"

Saskia stroked her daughter's hair. "Don't worry, darling. There's plenty of fish in the sea."

"I don't want any other fish. I want Barney."

Edu who had been sitting quietly, listening to the chat, was surprised to realise that she felt a stab of jealousy when she heard about Jenny Quinn. Obviously she didn't fancy Barney. That was Tiffany's little fantasy. Barney was her dear friend, however, the one she ran to when she wanted some time out or if she wanted to talk and relax. How could she do this if he was going to fall in love with Jenny Quinn?

"What is she like?" Edu asked Kelly.

Kelly paused and thought about this for a while.

"She's a tall girl, I think. She was sitting down."

"Kellyyyy," Tiffany whined, "tell us what you do know, not what you don't know!"

"OK, OK. Jeez, she's blonde. She has a nice smile. She looks a little like Sophie Rhys Jones!"

"Forget it so!" offered Lauren. "He'll probably marry her."

"Thanks for your support, sis!" Tiff snapped at Lauren. "Hey, maybe they're still outside The Hitching Post. Who wants to come for a walk?"

"Where were you thinking of walking to?" Saskia asked, already knowing the answer.

"Well, I said I was going to take Dudley and Dexter out this afternoon to look for Wilma. But we could start our search outside the Hitching Post!"

"Looking for love, more than looking for poor Wilma!" chided Kelly.

"I'll come with you if you like," Edu offered, her curiosity piqued.

"Don't look at me," laughed Lauren. "I'm not interested in spying on poor old Barney Armstrong, now that he's found love. Anyway I want to look up the Net and see what I can find on Nicolas Flattery and his totally dishy son."

"OK, let's go, Edu." Tiffany called the two black Labradors and she was gone with Edurne within minutes of discovering that Barney had a new woman in his life.

"I don't know who I feel sorrier for, Tiffany for losing her first love or Barney who's about to learn what it's like to be stalked," Saskia sighed.

"Spare a thought for poor Jenny Quinn," Lauren exclaimed as she rose to leave the kitchen. "She'll feel the heat of Tiffany's hatred burn her from a hundred yards! I'm off to surf the Net." She left.

"What about poor Dudley and Dexter? They think they're going out for a good walk. All they're really going to do is hang around a pub door!" Kelly was, as usual, thinking about the animals first and people second. "I've got to brush Polly down."

This left Saskia alone in her kitchen. The room suddenly seemed deafeningly quiet. She rose to switch on the radio. It was always tuned to Rock FM. In hospital she had heard a wonderful new station playing classical music only, but it was more than her life was worth to change stations. Richard would hit the roof. Saskia thought Rock FM was fairly OK. It was an AOR station – adult orientated rock – so they did play a lot of stuff that she recognised but it was always so energetic and feisty. Sometimes she just longed for the peace and tranquillity that the classical music brought. She was about to fix herself a cup of afternoon tea when she heard the tiny but insistent sound of a newborn baby's cry on the baby monitor.

No rest for the wicked, she thought, and left the room.

Lauren did not feel she should be obliged to listen to her father's radio station all the time. During the week, it was actually quite good and she was fairly happy to listen to it, but at the weekends Rock FM played what they called *classic rock* – absolute crap. She had never heard of most of the bands. Who the hell were Deep Purple, T Rex and Supertramp? The worst one of all was Survivor with a song called "Eye of the Tiger"! Richard had tried to get the girls to watch "a classic film called *Rocky*," to appreciate how good this song was. They thought he had really lost it and told him so.

When Lauren entered the study, the first thing she did was switch Richard's sound system over to Club Fm. It was an illegal radio station; Lauren had heard a rumour in school that the radio station was broadcasting from a private house somewhere in Wicklow. Whatever, she thought – it sounds great.

Pirate radio stations tended to come and go, as the police found them and shut them down. Richard gave out about them all the time. He said they were costing him a fortune because Rock FM was a legitimate business. It paid all its taxes, royalties to musicians, licence fees etc. Pirate radio stations rarely even paid their DJs!

Club Fm only played club music. As Lauren sat down at the computer she used the remote control of her father's fantastically expensive sound system to crank the volume up. The high-energy pulsing music reverberated through the room. And upstairs she heard Robin start to cry.

"Oh, shit," she whispered under her breath. She hit the mute button in time to hear Saskia pass the study door and head up the stairs. As the minutes passed she realised she was going to get away with waking her baby sister, and so she gradually turned the sound up to what her mother would describe as a moderate noise level.

Lauren hit the space bar and the computer cranked into life. The fan in beside the hard drive began to purr and the menu popped up. Most of the stuff was her father's files, none of which interested her. One of the options however was Internet explorer. She clicked the mouse on that.

The little egg-timer appeared, telling her to wait for a moment. Then within minutes she was on line. Fortunately Richard had had the foresight to install a few phone lines a couple of years ago when faxes became a necessity for him. Now there was a line dedicated to e-mail and the Net, another one for faxes and two phone lines. Even then, sharing the house with so many women, he often complained that this wasn't enough.

The screen was full of suggestions on where she could go and what she could do, but she knew what she wanted. There was an empty box beside the Search command and she typed in the name, "Nicolas Flattery".

Another egg-timer appeared and she waited.

"Sorry, there are no matches. Please try another word or phrase," came back the reply.

"Damn," she muttered as she clicked back to the front-page menu. "Where are you, Nicolas Flattery, and more importantly where is your son?" Then to her delight, on the front page she found the title *Hollywood Hits*. She clicked once and got a list of the top ten movies in the UK that week. *Freedom* wasn't one of them. The screen provided another option, top One Hundred Movies.

"That's it," she squealed. Number twenty-five was the film *Freedom*. She clicked on the name and up popped a picture of Nicolas and his co-star Julia Roberts. "God, he really is a ride!" She read on. It was mostly bumf about the movie, on how successful it had been, on how its timing had been really good coinciding with the peace process in Ireland and what a success it had been for *Mr Flattery*. The script Lauren was reading was printed on the computer screen in black, but *Mr Flattery* was printed in blue indicating that there was a web-site dedicated to him. She clicked on his name and up popped his page.

"Thank you, God," she muttered as she began to read about the man and his life.

The piece started with a picture of Mr Flattery and his wife and their totally gorgeous son.

"Nicolas Flattery has been acting for fifteen years, but really came to prominence in the last year. He is forty-three years old and lives in LA with his wife, Jessica Bell, and their son Nick Jnr." The blurb went on but Lauren had all she needed to know. The name of her new neighbour was Nick Junior! "How American," she squealed in delight. Lauren tried to double-click on his name but nothing came up. She read what there was about Nicolas. He was a method actor blah, blah, blah. That was why he came to Ireland in the first place to *get into the character*. On reflection, Lauren thought he sounded like a bit of a bore. Then she clicked on the name Jessica Bell to find out more about his wife. Jessica Bell had been famous in Hollywood for the last ten years, much longer than her husband had. As Lauren read down the list of her films, it struck her that this woman had passed her sell-by date. Perhaps that was why she had gone a little wild. Rumour had it that she had been in and out of rehab but she was OK now.

"They'll love you down at The Hitching Post!" she told Jessica's picture.

CHAPTER 11

Furious though he was, even Richard was distracted when he saw the astonishing transformation in Rathdeen Manor. He pulled his car in at the entrance to have a good look. There were JCBs lined up, a fleet of cement mixers. Three huge moxy trucks had just arrived with tons of sand and cement. It looked like a quarry, or, as Kelly had said, the scene of some movie. Richard got honked at from behind. He looked in his rear-view mirror. A brand-new Ford van was flashing at him to get out of the way. He moved his Merc forward to let the van into the building site. The driver waved thanks to him but Richard couldn't see his face because furry dice were hanging from the van driver's mirror. The Ford's stereo was up full blast. Richard watched the mayhem.

The beautiful Manor was a hive of activity. A massive sign, *Cantwell Construction*, had been erected on the front wall of the building, and then Richard noticed a sign just beside him at the front gate. *This is a hard-hat area*, it read.

"Bugger to that," he exclaimed. Just as he got out of his car he heard the car horn that Kelly had been talking about.

Got you! he thought. A man stood beside the light blue Cortina. He had beeped the horn to attract the van driver who duly beeped back and went to park alongside.

Richard marched over to them.

"Oy," he started, "are you the owner of this car?"

"Who wants to know?" The builder's face lost its broad smile the moment he heard Richard's tone.

"I want to fucking know. Are you the one who drove this car through Ballymore village an hour ago?"

"Why?"

"Look, some little shit nearly killed my daughter at lunchtime today. They were driving this car and they blasted her out of it on the main street of Ballymore. She was on horseback and the animal got scared to death. It tried to throw her and damn lucky for you it didn't or you could be in a lot more trouble!"

"Connor!" the builder yelled. "Get your arse around here now!"

A boy in his teens came around the corner of the Manor.

The builder glared at him. "When I lent you the car at lunchtime, where did you go and what did you get up to? I want the truth."

Connor looked at Richard. "Ah Paddy, you know what I did. I went into Wicklow to get a load of McDonald's for the lads."

"Did you blast some girl out of it in Ballymore village?"

"Me?" he asked incredulously.

"You nearly fucking killed her," Richard butted in.

"I what? I was only messing."

"I'll show you messing." Richard looked like he was going to take a dig, or at the very least a swipe at the youngster but Paddy was too quick for him.

"I'm very sorry, mister. The boy is under my charge. He's learning the trade and I let him off to get the lunch. This is his first job in the country. Maybe he's a bit over-excited. I'll take it from here."

The look of horror and fear in Connor's face was enough to appease Richard. "Well, see that you do. If you're going to work here, you have to learn to respect that this is the country. You can't go around scaring animals."

"I'm really sorry, sir. Please convey my humblest apologies to your daughter. If there's any way I can –"

"Leave it out, Connor," Paddy butted in.

Richard stared at the boy. He was dressed in jeans and a top. They were both caked in dry cement. He looked like the consummate builder or labourer but he spoke very eloquently. His eyes were bright and intelligent and he was a good-looking lad. Sallow skin, dark eyes and sandy-coloured hair peeping out from under his yellow hard hat.

"Is there a problem?" Richard had not noticed the brand-new Jeep pull up beside them. He swung around. The driver got out and shut the door behind him. On the door was the name, Cantwell Construction.

"No, Kevin, just a little misunderstanding." Paddy tried to brush aside the problem.

"Paddy. You're a great foreman but a lousy liar!" The man turned to Richard. "Hi, I'm Kevin Cantwell. Can I help you with anything?"

"Richard Dalton, I live just across the river." He shook hands with Kevin as he continued. "One of your trainees was just getting a bit of a driving lesson this morning. I'm trying to ensure it doesn't happen again. At least not around my daughters when they're on horseback!"

"Hi, Dad," Connor said rather demurely.

"Connor, are you getting us a bad name already?" Kevin Cantwell asked his son, then he turned back to Richard. "I'm really sorry. I'll see to it that it doesn't happen again."

Richard let the matter drop. Young Connor was the developer's son and he got the feeling that Kevin Cantwell was a man of his word.

"Now that you're here," Kevin interrupted his thoughts, "why don't I show you around? After all, this is your neighbour."

"I'd love that! You're doing a massive job. Will it take you long?" The two men walked towards the manor entrance. Kevin grabbed a hardhat from a windowsill and gave it to Richard. "First put this on. If you don't, you're not insured on the premises."

"Ah right, sorry. It is true your client is Nicolas Flattery, isn't it?"

"Yes. I think that's in the public domain at this stage. Yes, Nicolas Flattery has commissioned this job and I don't mind telling you, Richard, he's paying through the nose, top dollar."

"How long will the whole job take?"

"Well, we're on penalty clauses after December fifteenth. He wants to be living here by then. That shouldn't be a problem, to be honest. I have an army of lads on this job because the money is so big."

"Money talks!" Richard agreed.

They had reached the front door of the building. The first thing that struck Richard was the amount of men that were working. He could count at least nine or ten in this area alone. Kevin Cantwell continued: "Did you know he wants to build a stable yard?"

"No, I didn't, but I don't think he'll have any problems with that. This is a very horsy area and he certainly has the space."

"Well, I just thought I'd tell you because the planning application will be posted up today, so doubtless the entire village will know by tonight. That part we won't have finished by mid-December, I've explained to Nicolas, because we'll have the Ballymore planning authority to contend with."

Richard guffawed. "That bunch. They are real

sticklers. I've had to deal with them myself. Shower of lefty, environmentalist feminists!"

"I take it you don't like feminists, Richard."

Richard thought he might have gone too far. "Well, let's just say that I didn't get what I wanted and that really pissed me off!"

"What did you want?"

"A helipad. No big deal."

"Ah, noise pollution problems?"

Richard stared at Kevin. "How did you know?"

"I had the same problem with a client I was building for in Killiney in Dublin. His planning permission was turned down on the grounds of noise pollution."

"So what did you do?"

"We built a tennis court with the best foundations in Dublin!"

"Foundations strong enough to take the weight of a helicopter?"

Kevin grinned and gave a very faint nod. Richard got the feeling that he had made a new friend. "Talk me through the house. What there is of it."

"Well, this is the reception hall." They were standing at the front door looking into a room that measured about twenty by twenty feet.

"Jesus, this is huge. He's going to have massive heating bills."

"Well, he wants underfloor heating throughout and treble glazing. The entire building will be insulated thoroughly so it may not be that big a problem. One of our biggest issues has been the fireplaces – as you can see, they were all pulled out years ago and they're huge. God knows where the originals are now." They walked over to the gaping hole in the reception hall.

"It must have been about six foot high," Richard suggested.

"Try ten foot. That's the hole, the mantelpiece went much higher. Anyway, they all have to be tailor-made for the house so Nicolas has commissioned some guy himself. An Italian guy. I've spoken to him on the phone and he sounds like a right queen. He's also overseeing the staircase.It's being hand-carved somewhere in Germany. I just hope he can deliver on time. That's the sort of thing that could hold us up from completion."

All around them men worked. There were two men taking measurements of the door frame and window sizes. Another three had been taking out rubble in wheelbarrows. One guy was unravelling miles of wires, obviously bringing an electricity supply to the various rooms, and two others were working with Kango hammers.

"What are they doing with those?" Richard asked, pointing to the hammers.

"They'll shave about three inches off all the walls, to remove all the dead and chipping plaster. It's a bitch of a job in a building this old because they used anything and everything to construct the walls, one hundred and fifty plus years ago. The lads might hit a large granite rock that will take hours to break down. It's a tough job." As they left the reception hall behind them the Kangos started up again. The noise was deafening. Richard glanced back. All the men were wearing protective earmuffs; everything was definitely being done by the book.

Kevin took Richard around the rest of the ground floor of Rathdeen Manor. What struck him most was the sheer size of the building. It seemed much bigger on the inside than from outside. He had lost count of how many reception rooms he had been in. Having come through what would be an amazing reception hall he had entered a long passageway, which went right and left. Off this were many even larger reception rooms.

"I'm afraid I can't take you upstairs yet. It's not safe."

"Actually I didn't even see the stairs."

"No, as I said they're still in Germany. We go upstairs the old-fashioned way!" Kevin pointed to a ladder resting harmlessly against a wall. He caught sight of Paddy in an upper room.

"Everything OK, Paddy?"

"Peachy!" came the reply.

"There's a basement as well but I don't think you'll want to go down there until we've had Rentokil in."

Richard winced. "No rush. It is going to be huge, isn't it?"

"About ten thousand square feet, including the basement. When you consider your average family home is sixteen hundred, yep, it's going to be massive."

Richard felt a sharp stab of jealousy. This house was going to be a mansion. Innishambles was six thousand square feet. He suppressed the feeling. He had other fish to fry right now, like Rock Tower, and on reflection Kevin Cantwell would be a good man to know.

"Look, can I buy a drink? This has been terrific, seeing around this old place."

Kevin looked at his watch. It was almost five o'clock. "I'd love you to tell me where the local is because today is *day one* of a new job and I have a sort of tradition of buying the men their first drink. That's all the more important today, it being a Saturday. That said, we'd love you to join us."

"The local is The Hitching Post, in Ballymore main street. Christ, I'd better warn Mick Molloy. His usual Saturday night would be three or four locals."

Kevin Cantwell laughed. "Please do warn him – I have thirty men here and they'll all be hungry and thirsty. Tell him we're right on your heels."

Richard drove back to Innishambles in considerably better form than when he had left it. He made a quick stop at The Hitching Post to warn Michael Molloy that it was going to be a very busy evening.

"You better prepare a few tons of scampi and chips and put on another keg, Mick," Richard teased.

"I will, and you better not darken this door later without Lauren and Tiffany with you. Tell them I'll pay them twice the norm if they work on such short notice."

"I'll tell them," Richard laughed. "It's a Saturday night so I doubt their mother will complain."

Richard had forgotten about his own mother, however.

"You're not leaving me here with her to entertain by myself, Richard!" Saskia snapped, when he filled her in on the afternoon's events.

"Honey, this is business. What can I do? Look, this guy is an expert on helipads and you know the trouble we had. Now I really need a helipad on the top of Rock Tower and this is the man to organise it for me. I won't stay long."

Saskia could tell by his tone that he had already made up his mind. Nothing she could say would change it. "Well, you can be the one to tell your mother."

Within an hour Lauren, Tiffany and Richard were heading back to The Hitching Post. It was already heaving.

"Where the hell have you been?" Mick Molloy looked at his two helpers.

They knew him well and ignored his harmless grumbles. Quickly and efficiently, the two girls moved around the pub, picking up pint glasses that had already been emptied and fetching new orders.

"Richard, over here," Kevin Cantwell yelled from the back corner. He was sitting with Connor and Paddy and a few other men. Connor Cantwell was preoccupied, however. He had clapped eyes on Lauren.

"Who is she?" he asked Richard.

Richard turned around to follow his gaze. "Connor, that's my daughter. Don't lay a hand on her or I'll kill

143

you. That I won't leave in Paddy's capable hands." The older men laughed at Connor's lovestruck face, but not Connor. He took the matter perfectly seriously. All night he watched her; as the other men drank, he sipped a pint of Guinness. The first time she came to serve their table, Richard introduced them.

"Lauren, this is Connor Cantwell. He's working on Rathdeen Manor." Connor smiled shyly at her.

"Daw – well, I guessed that, Dad. Every man in here is working on Rathdeen Manor, except you, and he doesn't exactly look like a brain surgeon!" She looked at his clothes. He quickly looked down at his own clothes, covered in dry cement and muck. He suddenly felt awkward and stupid. Richard and Kevin burst out laughing. "Jesus, give a guy a chance, Lauren," Richard said.

"What do you mean?"

"Well, you could at least be civil to the young man, honey."

She looked at Connor. "Welcome to Ballymore and have a nice day." She turned to her father "Happy?" and she flounced off. Connor was crushed and retreated into his pint.

Lauren was secretly flattered but mortified that her father was so open about Connor's crush on her. He did look cute but she was saving herself for Nicolas Flattery Jnr.

"Barney!" Tiffany squealed with obvious delight. "You're back. I mean, welcome to bedlam!"

"Hi, Tiff," he gave her a peck on the cheek. "Mrs O' Reilly told me there was a bit of a shindig going on over here so I thought I'd pop in."

"Where's your new girlfriend?" she teased.

Barney blushed. "What girlfriend?"

"Barney, over here," Richard shouted across the little pub when he saw his neighbour. "Let me buy you a drink. I hear you saved my daughter's life earlier today!"

For the rest of the night Tiffany served her father, Barney and the Cantwells, eager to be near her true love, so Connor didn't get another chance to talk to Lauren. He watched her from a distance. She was dressed in grey wool trousers and a tight black wool top. She looked very elegant in them, even in this pub environment. She was tall and dark, like her father, quite unlike her sister who was shorter than her and fair-skinned. Her hair was so dark it looked almost black. It was cut short, almost tomboyish but her cute cherub face softened the look. He kept catching her eye by mistake and then he would look away for another five minutes but as soon as he looked back she caught him staring again.

As the Saturday night progressed it got rowdier and rowdier. Builders who were meant to be driving back to Dublin were making arrangements to stay in Mick's B&B down the road. Everybody was pissed by midnight and the mood was very festive. Richard had invited the Cantwells to stay at Innishambles.

"You'll shtay, shure you will!"

"Dad, I can drive," Connor assured his father. "I've only had one pint."

Kevin Cantwell tried to focus on his son but this was difficult as he was seeing double. "You're a good lad. No, Rishard, We'll goo, Mrs C – that's the missies – doesn't like it whin we don't come home, does shee, Connor."

Tiffany couldn't control her laughter. He was hilariously drunk. Connor helped his father to stand and somehow managed to get him out of the pub and into the jeep.

"I think we're going," was all Kevin Cantwell could muster before he fell asleep in the passenger seat of the Cantwell Construction jeep. Connor returned to his table to say his goodbyes and this time he walked straight up to Lauren.

"Nice to meet you, Lauren Dalton. I hope you meet your brain surgeon soon."

She was taken aback by his curtness and instantly felt guilty for being so rude herself.

"Bye, Connor," she said with a smile, but he had turned away and her voice was drowned out by the strains of "Danny Boy" now starting up in another corner.

As Richard began to feel the room rotating he called for Tiffany. "Honey, I think it's time you took me home. I'm a little tired." Tiffany was far more concerned about how Barney was going to get home, considering he was now having a conversation with thin air since Kevin had left. What was even more worrying was that Barney didn't seem to have noticed!

"Daddy, don't forget that you've got the car. If we were really clever, we would get Lauren to drive you home. She's a much better driver than me."

Richard was so pissed, it didn't even occur to him that both Tiff and Lauren were way under legal driving age, but he did like the idea of getting the car home, instead of having to walk down for it in the morning. He tried to stand but swayed dangerously. "You're a good girl, Tiffany, good thinking! Where's Lauren?" He called for his younger daughter.

Those two safely dispatched, Tiffany cleared the pub of all the stragglers and thanked Mr Molloy for the hefty pay packet.

"I'm going to walk home now but I'll set Barney on the right road too," she offered.

Michael Molloy thanked her and waved Barney and Tiffany off as he closed and locked the front door of The Hitching Post. It was almost two o'clock. If this was what life was going to be like in the Ballymore of the future, he was happy. He cast his mind back to the day he, Harold O Reilly and Frank Taylor had worried about their little village, and laughed.

"Rock on," he said, mimicking Lauren Dalton. "Rock on."

CHAPTER 12

Tiffany had to use all her strength to keep Barney vertical. He kept zigzagging and falling into the hedge. As they neared Peartree Cottage, he turned to her.

"You know, you're a great girl, Tiff. Any man would be lucky to get you!"

"I'm glad to hear it, Barney. Now let's just get you home."

"They're a lovely bunch, those builders. What did you think, Tiff?"

"I think it's great news about the stables, Barney. Nicolas Flattery will make you a rich man."

"Yea, and then I'll be a good catch, won't I?" He laughed.

"You're already a good catch, Barney Armstrong."

He looked at Tiffany. Although his eyesight wasn't the best thanks to umpteen pints, she was still lovely. He already knew she had a huge heart. Tiffany was worse than he was when it came to taking in stray dogs, birds and mice.

"Do you remember the time you brought the rat with the broken leg to me?" he smiled.

"Of course." She was trying to open his front door with his key.

"Do you know I had to put it down?"

"You told me you fixed it and then set it free."

"Tiffany, I'm sorry. It was a rat. They're vermin."

"Try telling that to his wife and kids! You're a shit." She opened the door and marched in, letting him stagger in the rest of the way himself. Nina was delighted to see them even at this late hour. Orinoco ignored them.

"You've a heart of gold, Tiffany."

"Well, you've a heart of ice." She had stormed into his little kitchen to put on the kettle. Barney needed strong black coffee. He followed her in.

She continued. "If I'm such a darling and such a pet, why don't you ask me out?"

Even through his alcoholic haze, he was stunned. "What?"

"You heard me. You think I'm so bloody wonderful, what are you doing with Jenny Quinn?"

"Tiff, you're a dote and God knows you're cute, but–"

Tiffany stopped him mid-sentence. She walked across the kitchen and kissed him. For a moment his arms flapped in protest and then they melted around

149

her, holding her tightly, and he began to kiss her back.

Tiffany's head spun. She was only fifteen and he thirty-something. But that didn't matter to her. For so many years she had dreamt of this moment. She could feel his breath quicken and his penis harden against her. It excited her. She wanted him to want her the way she wanted him.

Barney stopped for a second and looked into her eyes. She couldn't help noticing that he was still very drunk but if that was what was necessary to break the ice, so be it. He also stank of booze but she let it pass. He brushed back her hair with his hands and kissed her again, this time more urgently. His hands began to explore her body, quickly finding their way under her cotton blouse. He undid her bra strap and began to massage one of her breasts. She gently pushed him away.

"Not here," she whispered. Tiffany knew Barney's house well from regular visits over the years and guided him to his bedroom.

Barney was too drunk to undress himself so she had to do that bit too. This certainly wasn't the way she had fantasised this particular scene but she persevered. The Y-fronts were another shock.

"Wow, even my father doesn't wear those!" she teased. Then Barney began to get sick. Tiffany rushed to the kitchen to get some sort of bowl and by the time she returned he had stopped and fallen asleep.

Utterly fed up, Tiffany cleaned up the mess around

him. He didn't budge. She covered him in his quilt and left Peartree Cottage.

"Where the hell have you been? It's after three."

Tiffany jumped, expecting everybody to be in bed by the time she got home.

"Hi, Lauren. I was trying to seduce Barney."

"How did it go?"

"An utter failure."

The girls looked at each other for a few moments and then burst into laughter.

"Here, Tiff, have the rest of my sandwich and tell me all about it."

"God yes, I'm starving. We didn't get anything to eat tonight, did we? What are you making there?"

Lauren and Tiffany sat down and had a midnight snack as Tiffany told Lauren about the strong smell of whiskey, the puke and the Y-fronts. The Y-fronts caused the biggest laughs. Lauren told Tiffany about Connor Cantwell who was quite cute and obviously had a crush on her but then she ruined it all by being so rude. Then Lauren took Tiffany in to the computer to introduce her to the real love of her life.

"This Tiff, is my next boyfriend, Nicolas Flattery Jnr."

Tiffany watched as the computer flashed into life and his picture formed. "God. He's gorgeous!"

Lauren had managed to enlarge the family photo of the Flatterys. Then she cut out the picture of Nicolas

Jnr. This she saved as her new screensaver, so as soon as the computer was switched on the first thing anybody would see was a photo of her intended!

"I'll bet he doesn't wear Y-fronts either!" giggled Lauren. "Oh cheer up, Tiff. There'll be other opportunities."

"Do you want to know the funny thing, Lauren, I don't think I fancy him any more."

"I don't believe that. You've fancied him for years."

"Yea, but tonight for the first time, I met the real Barney Armstrong, not my perceived lover."

"Didn't match up, heh?"

"No way. I'd say sex is a very messy business. The first bit was a bit of fun but as for real sex!"

"Jesus, what are you saying? You *are* sure you didn't have actual intercourse with him, aren't you?"

"Lauren! What do you take me for? Of course I'm sure – I didn't. Besides it would have been illegal. I'm under-age."

"He could go to prison, Tiff. Do you think he knows you are fifteen?"

"No, I think he thinks I'm a little older!"

"Why?"

"I told him I was!"

"Bitch."

"Shh, what was that?" Tiffany looked at the kitchen door anxiously.

"What was what?"

"I thought I heard somebody on the stairs or in the hall."

"It's just your guilty conscience!" Lauren teased.

"Come on, I've had enough excitement for one day," Tiffany suggested, relaxing a little.

"Goodnight, Nicolas, parting is such sweet sorrow." Lauren kissed the computer screen and switched it off.

The alarm on the life-support machine shrilled out in the small hours of the morning. The nurse rushed over to Katie Anderson's bedside. She pressed the emergency pager button and a full medical team joined her within one minute.

"She's flat-lined."

"Clear," the doctor sent a huge surge of electricity through her. No heartbeat.

"Clear," he did it again. Nothing. Then as if by magic, the soft but insistent beep beep beep of the equipment assured staff that Katie Anderson wasn't going to give up just yet.

The doctor looked at the Intensive Care clock. It was three thirty am

"That was a close one!" he smiled and went back to his half-eaten supper in the night canteen.

When Victoria clocked on at seven am on Sunday morning she was given both the good news and the bad news. Katie Anderson had escaped death but she was back in a coma. Not a good sign.

She didn't know how Tom would take it, but at least Katie hadn't died. She was pretty sure that would be too much for the man to take.

Tom arrived just after eight with all the Sunday papers, a box of chocolates and two bunches of flowers.

"One for you and one for my daughter, the two most wonderful women I know," he told Victoria. "Is she sleeping again? That's good."

"Tom, good morning," Victoria started with a broad smile. "Flowers? How lovely but I'm afraid, we'll have to take them straight out of here. No flowers allowed in Intensive Care."

"Oh, I'm sorry. How's my little girl?" Tom asked expecting a healthy progress report. Victoria took him by the arm and guided him to a quiet pair of seats by the window just outside the care unit.

"Tom, I'm afraid we've had a little setback."

"What are you talking about?" Concern flooded his face. "Victoria, we've come too far. She's out of danger. You said as much yourself."

"Easy now, Tom. The truth is we just don't know. She had a little turn last night –"

"What's a little turn, in God's name? What happened?" He was beginning to panic and stood to go back in to his daughter.

"Please, Tom," Victoria drew on all her resources. No matter how long she worked in Intensive Care, she knew the one thing she would never get used to was handling the pain of those watching a loved one fight for their lives.

"Tom, Katie nearly slipped away last night, but she

didn't. That's what you must focus on. She didn't. I think she's a fighter but she has been in a terrible accident and all we can do is stand by and hope and pray. She didn't die. She's still with us, Tom, but I'm afraid she did slip back into a coma."

Tom collapsed back into the chair and let his flowers and papers slide to the floor.

"Jesus, please no. Sweet Jesus – don't take my baby too. I couldn't live without her." He covered his face with his hands and began to weep. Victoria thought her heart would break for him. She wrapped her arms around Tom and hugged him as he cried over his only living relative. Unable to give him anything positive to hang on to was so difficult. The uncertainty was the worst part.

Damn the man who crashed into this poor unsuspecting girl. Damn him to hell, she thought silently.

CHAPTER 13

Edwina Dalton was the first up on Sunday morning. She was horrified that everybody else slept so late.

"The best part of the day is gone," she grumbled.

Kelly was the next to appear. "Where's Mum?" she asked.

"God only knows. Today is Sunday. Doesn't anybody in this house go to Mass any more?"

"No, Gran. We're a shower of heathens! Well, the girls were working so my guess is we won't see them until some time mid-afternoon and likewise Dad. I heard him singing "Danny Boy" – a very bad sign."

"Unless I'm mistaken, young lady, he was only looking out for your welfare," she chided, always ready to defend her son.

Kelly started to fix herself some breakfast. "Well, I heard him talking to Mum when he came home around teatime and I think he was more concerned about helipads and new business contacts than he was about me and Polly."

"Ungrateful child."

The doorbell startled both of them. Kelly reached the front door at the same time as Dudley, Dexter and Woody. The dogs were barking furiously, annoyed that they had been taken by surprise. Usually Sunday mornings were a totally laid-back time in the Dalton household. The girls rarely surfaced before eleven in the morning, with the exception of Kelly who was up and out early to give both her horses a good ride.

Saskia had been up four times during the night with a hungry little Robin and so she slept right through the commotion.

Two policemen in full uniform stood at the door, looking very serious.

"Is your father in, please? We're looking for Mr Richard Dalton." There was no warmth in his voice. He looked very austere which made Kelly nervous.

"Why do you want him?"

"That's something we need to discuss with him," the younger of the two explained, admiring Kelly's fine physique in a pair of jodhpurs.

"Dad, you're wanted," she yelled up the stairs.

There was no response.

"Dad!"

Edwina came out to see who was at the door on a Sunday morning.

"Oh my, gardai! What seems to be the trouble, officers?" she asked in her most polite accent.

"Madam, we would like to talk to Mr Richard Dalton right away, if you could get him, please."

Edwina left them at the front door and scooted up the stairs as fast as her legs could take her. She rapped on Richard's door.

"Richard, Richard, get up! It's the police! They look very serious. They want to talk to you. Get up!"

Reluctantly, Richard dragged himself out of his deep sleep. The first thing he was aware of was his mother banging his bedroom door down. This was quickly followed by a thunderous headache. His joints ached, as did his throat. His stomach was in a real mess.

"Hang on," he mumbled into the pillow. "Sas, whas going on? Sas?" He reached over to her side of the bed but she wasn't there. Then he had a vague memory of accidentally waking little Robin with his singing when he came in the night before. He had met a furious Saskia on the upstairs landing just as he was getting going. She told him to belt up and she took off to Robin's bedroom for the night to soothe her.

"Richard, hurry for God's sake! It's the police," Edwina repeated.

He managed to get himself over to his bedroom door and opened it ajar.

"What do they want, mother?"

She backed off at the smell of booze, "You."

"Tell them to wait a minute and fix them a cup of tea, please?" he managed a weak smile.

Edwina scuttled down the stairs, somewhat relieved to see that her son was not in the least bit nervous. She decided that he must have been expecting them. She headed back to the front door.

"He'll be down in just a jiffy. Will you come in and have a pot of tea and something to eat?"

"We'll wait here, thank you, madam." Nervous again at their overt hostility, Edwina left them and headed back to the refuge of the kitchen where Kelly was also waiting. Within minutes Richard was meandering down the stairs. He hadn't even considered why the cops might be at his door at this time of the morning. Without Saskia's help, all he had managed to find to wear were the clothes he was wearing the night before. His chinos were creased and beer-stained and his polo shirt was in dire need of a wash. Richard hadn't bothered with socks; he just pulled on a pair of loafers and headed down to meet his unexpected guests.

"Mr Richard Dalton?" the elder policeman asked.

"Yep, what can I do for you men?"

"Mr Dalton, we'd like to talk to you about the car accident you were involved in last week."

Richard looked at them incredulously. It was the crack of dawn on a Sunday morning.

"Is this some kind of joke?" he asked.

The younger guard looked at him.

"Mr Dalton, do you realise how serious an issue this is? There is a thorough ongoing investigation into the accident. You know dangerous driving is an imprisonable offence?"

"Who said anything about dangerous driving?" Richard tried to control his very short temper. He failed. "For fuck sake, lads. It's Sunday morning. This is a matter you'll have to take up with my lawyers in Dublin. I'm not saying another word to you." He was about to close the door but the police stopped him.

"In that case, Mr Dalton, perhaps you can accompany us down to the station and answer our questions there."

"OK, now I know you're joking," Richard laughed uncertainly.

"Do I look like I'm joking?"

"I can't make a statement without my lawyer and he's in Dublin."

"If you want him present, maybe you should call him."

"OK, OK, I don't know who has it in for me but you win, guys. Is it OK at least if I take a shower and follow you down to the station in half an hour?"

The older of the two cops looked at Richard's clothes and tried to ignore the whiff of booze from his breath. "That's no problem, Mr Dalton. Are you sure however that you'll be OK to drive. Is it possible that you have a large amount of alcohol in your system?"

Richard was about to laugh out loud when he

remembered all the stories he had heard of guys getting done for drunk-driving the morning after the night before.

"You could come with us now and call your lawyer from the station if you like," the garda suggested.

"Richard, what's going on?" Edwina asked from behind him, her voice trembling, on the edge of hysterics. "Richard, are you being arrested?"

That's all I need, he thought to himself. "Mother, nothing's wrong. Nothing at all. I'm just going down to Wicklow garda station with these nice gentlemen to clarify some details about the accident last week."

He turned to the guard. "I think it would be easier if I go with you now."

"You're being arrested?" Edwina shrieked.

"I'm not being arrested."

"Oh my God, What have you done?"

"Mother, I'm not under arrest."

"Daddy," Kelly wailed. "What's happening?"

"Get your mother," he answered. "Get her to call Barry McCourt. Everything is really OK, I promise, honey."

"What has he done?" Edwina begged of the police who were now putting Richard in the back of the police car.

"On the fifth of September last, as you probably know, Mr Dalton drove into an oncoming vehicle, head on. The lady driver is still in a critical condition in hospital."

Kelly was in floods of tears. "Daddy, what have you done?"

Edwina stood rooted to the spot with her hand over her mouth, lost for words. Richard was too hung-over to think straight.

The two policemen got into the car and drove off with Richard in the back.

"Mummy!" Kelly came screaming up the stairs. Everybody woke when they heard the urgency in her voice. First Kelly tore into her parents' room and when she saw Saskia wasn't there she ran into the nursery. Saskia had just woken to her screams. Little Robin was nestling in her arms.

"Dad's been arrested!"

"What?"

"He's just been arrested. Two policemen came up to the house in a cop car and they took him away. He could be charged with dangerous driving. The girl he hit might die."

Saskia was up and out of the bed. She rushed to the window, as if to confirm Kelly's story. Then she rushed to the landing.

"Richard!" she yelled.

Edwina, who had regained the use of her legs, had now reached the upstairs landing.

"He hasn't been arrested, Saskia. Richard insisted that he was just going to help them with their enquiries."

"On a Sunday morning?" Saskia asked in shock.

"You have to call Barry McCourt. Dad said so."

Lauren, Tiffany and Edu had reached the landing by now. The two younger sisters were exhausted and could barely take it in. Edu on the other hand lost the run of herself and began crying and praying in Spanish.

"Cop yourself on, Edu," Saskia snapped. "You're being melodramatic. Here, take Robin and I'll phone Barry McCourt."

Everyone descended into the kitchen and copious pots of tea were made. Edwina had even forgotten about Mass. Saskia disappeared into the study. She switched on the computer because all their contact names and address were stored there. The screensaver was the first thing to pop up. It had been changed. Now it was the face of a young boy, and a good-looking one at that, bouncing up and down in front of her. Saskia tapped into the contacts file and got Barry McCourt's home phone number.

She phoned him immediately.

Donal Walsh was at home making himself some breakfast. He had also had a late night and ended up in some nightclub with his friends. He knew he didn't want to be there even as he was going in, but the crowd were, and so he tagged along. His friends never seemed to tire of doing the same thing every weekend. They went out, got jarred and then pulled women. They were now at the pulling stage of the night. It wasn't that difficult either, as they were a good-looking group of men and inevitably they pulled *en masse*. Donal was the only one in the gang who didn't go along with this plan of action. It just wasn't his thing. Last night, however, had been very awkward. He with his friends were a group of five and as luck would have it they met a group of five girls. The lady he was paired off with was more than keen and she dragged him onto the floor for a slow set. As the music played he could see through his peripheral vision all of his friends getting off with their various partners. Unfortunately, his dancing partner saw this too. She wrapped her arms around him and snuggled in so tightly Donal could hardly breathe. He saw his friends rummaging inside blouses and down the back of skirts. All Donal wanted to do was get out of there and so that is what he suggested.

Looking back on it now he felt a little guilty. He had definitely implied that he wanted to take her home to have his way with her. Since he had met her he had been polite but distant. Then, suddenly, he took her face in his hands and gently kissed her. Nothing too romantic, just a little butterfly kiss.

"Would you like to get out of here?" he had asked.

"Oh yes, that sounds like a good idea."

They returned to their seats only to retrieve their coats but they were spotted as they walked past the dance floor towards the door of the nightclub.

"Go on, ye wild boy!" one friend yelled at him

"Don't do anything I wouldn't do," one of her friends shouted. Then another of Donal's gang barked like a dog at him. Out in the night air, it was a lot less claustrophobic.

"That's much better," he said and then, continuing his little charade, he asked, "Now, where do you live?"

"Rathmines," she giggled.

"Taxi!"

Donal cringed as he thought back to it. He really had been very impolite, not that she gave him any choice. He opened the back door of the cab for her, as she gave him the exact address. Then he repeated the address for the cab driver and gave him a tenner, closing the car door again. He didn't get in. He waved goodnight at her through the car window and turned on his heel. The car began to drive off before she could react although Donal was pretty sure he heard a muffled "Bastard!" from behind him.

The shrill of the phone shook him out of his thoughts.

"Hello."

"Donal, hi, it's Peter Madden. How are you?"

"Fine, all things considered. You missed another session last night."

"Yea, I was on duty. Did you score or did you do one of your wimp-outs again, Walsh?"

"Ah, that would be telling. Tell me, what are you doing up this early on a Sunday morning anyway?"

"I'm still working. I was on a late last night and an early this morning. That's why I'm ringing. Do you remember the car we escorted to St Helen's a few weeks ago?"

"How could I forget? What a babe!"

"Yea, I thought this might interest you. Her dad is

in the Wicklow station, assisting garda with a dangerous driving investigation."

"Jesus, on a Sunday morning! What's going on? How did you find out?"

"They were checking up on his story about his wife being in labour and he told them about the escort. Anyway, our report popped up on their computer as soon as they tapped his name into it."

"But bloody hell, dangerous driving? Was anybody hurt?"

"It was a young girl, single – mid-twenties, I think. She's on life support in Vincent's as we speak. The press is going to love this. It gets better, Donal. Richard Dalton is Rock FM Richard Dalton – the guy who owns the station and he bought The Tower a few months ago. Do you remember the story?"'"

"Jesus."

"Well, I thought you might like to know, in case you wanted an excuse to phone Kelly Dalton!"

"Yea, she'll really love me now that her Dad has been dragged off by some of my workmates. Why have they pulled him in?"

"One of the guys in Wicklow is going out with one of the nurses in the Intensive Care unit. She called him this morning and gave out shit about the bastard that hit this young girl – Katie Anderson, I think her name is. Anyway the nurse asked if maybe they could make this Dalton fella a little uncomfortable, so instead of questioning him next week as planned, two guys took a little saunter out to his mansion this morning. Poor bastard was seriously hung over. He voluntarily went with them but he's suffering all right!"

"Look, Peter, I really appreciate the info. Keep me informed on any developments that you hear about, will you?"

"No prob. Get on to Wicklow yourself, though. They'll tell you exactly what's going on."

"Good idea, thanks again."

"Good luck with that babe, Donal." Peter hung up.

Peter Madden was one of Donal's best friends. They often worked together and they usually socialised on Saturday nights together. Peter was one of the few who accepted that Donal wasn't into shagging complete strangers every weekend, not that he understood it. He just accepted it. Peter was devilishly good-looking. He stood over six foot and had blonde hair and blue eyes. Any Saturday night he wasn't working, he went out and got laid.

He was honourable however. In the code that governed who Peter and his mates chased, the general rule was whoever sees the girl first has rights on her. This meant Kelly belonged to Donal, sadly. Peter thought she was a real cutie!

Donal hung up the phone and rushed to get changed. He knew if he thought about it he would stop and so he got straight into his car and headed for Wicklow.

After a quick stop at the Wicklow station, Donal found himself driving up the beautiful driveway of Innishambles by lunchtime. He thought about turning back as he got to the rather formidable front door but the dogs were barking already and so it was too late.

When he rang the doorbell the dogs went even wilder. An elderly lady answered the door and looked aggressively at him.

"Yes?"

"Hi, my name is Donal Walsh. I'm an, er, acquaintance of Kelly's and Mrs Dalton's. You see, I'm a policeman."

"What do you want? Are you going to arrest them too?"

"Who is it, Edwina?" Saskia approached the front door.

"Hi, Mrs Dalton, it's me – I don't know if you remember, Donal Walsh. I, eh, we gave you an escort to the hospital when you were in labour. I just heard about your, er situation and wondered if I could help."

Saskia had been keeping up a brave face all morning for the sake of the girls but when she heard his kind and understanding voice, she crumpled. He instinctively reached out and put his arms around her.

"There, there, it's OK. It will be OK. I'm sure it will."

"How do you know that, Donal? Do you know something new?"

"No, no." They walked into the kitchen together and Saskia introduced him to everyone.

"Girls, this is Garda Donal Walsh. Kelly, you

remember Donal. He's the nice man who gave us an escort to St Helen's."

"Hi, Kelly," he smiled at her. She was even more beautiful than he remembered.

Edu was holding Robin.

"So this is the new arrival. She's gorgeous. May I?" he gestured to take the baby. Edu looked to Saskia for approval and she nodded.

"You're good with babies," Saskia commented. "Her name is Robin."

"This one's a beaut," he smiled at the baby who smiled back and gurgled. "Hi, Robin."

"Have you heard any news, Donal?"

"Well, I stopped by the station on my way here. Richard is being helpful with their enquiries, which is a good thing. His solicitor – McCourt, is it?" Saskia nodded. "Well, he's on his way down. He'll be home soon enough and everything will be OK, I'm sure of it."

The girls heaved a collective sigh of relief.

"Would you like a coffee, Donal?" Kelly asked.

"Nonsense, he'll have lunch. You'll have lunch with us, won't you, Donal?" Saskia interrupted.

"If I'm not intruding." He looked to Kelly for reassurance and she smiled at him.

"Intruding? You've brought me the only word I've had so far today. You're better than Barry McCourt!" Saskia took the baby from him,

"Kelly, would you take Donal for a walk around the yard just while we're fixing lunch."

"Sure."

"Why does she get to miss the work?" Lauren complained after Donal and Kelly had gone out the back. "I could have taken him around for a walk."

"Mum made Kelly go, because Kelly is the real reason our Sgt Donal Walsh is here. He fancies her like crazy!" Tiffany explained.

"How do you know?"

"It's obvious."

"Mummy?" Lauren looked at Sas.

"I think Tiff is right, honey. Donal is here to help us all but he has a special interest in Kelly."

"Well, really," Edwina snorted, disgusted at the idea and annoyed that she hadn't spotted what the others took as obvious.

Edu watched them from the kitchen window. He was an attractive man with very caring eyes but, most of all, he appeared to love babies. This she found very attractive. After all, perhaps she would be a mother soon herself . . .

Out in the courtyard Kelly and Donal walked up to Polly's stable.

"This place is beautiful," he said.

"Thanks," she replied a little sheepishly.

"Are you OK?"

"Yea, considering my Dad is looking at a possible jail sentence, I guess I'm bearing up all right."

"Now, you know that's not true, Kelly."

"Isn't it? Don't people go to jail for dangerous driving, especially if someone dies?"

"Hey," Donal gasped. "Nobody is dead! Look, your father is a fine upstanding member of society. This is just the investigation. He's not going to jail. I'm sure of that!"

"I'm sorry, Donal. Every time I meet you, you seem to end up minding me."

"Well, that is why I arrived on your doorstep today. I reckoned you might need some support."

"Thanks. It really is kind of you."

"What's this fellow's name?" Donal patted Polly on the nose.

"Her name is Polly. She's a girl."

"Oh, I am sorry, girl, I didn't mean to get personal." Donal addressed the horse.

Kelly laughed. "How would you know?"

"Well, I could have had a look, but surely that's a little rude, considering we hadn't even been introduced."

Kelly laughed again and moved to the next stable.

"This is Mooner. He's a boy!"

"That's a relief, otherwise I would be seriously outnumbered! Hi, Mooner! Where did you get that name?"

"I was there when Mooner was born; it was during the summer holidays four years ago. Barney, he's our local vet, he was delivering the foal. Anyway, Mooner tried to enter the world butt first. Unlike humans, horses can't do that."

"Well, I don't think women like it much either, to be honest, Kelly."

"No, I know but it's possible." She was positively animated as she talked about her horses.

"Go on," he encouraged her.

"Well, Barney had to push Mooner back up inside his mum and whoosh him around so that he would come out the right way."

Donal winced but Kelly continued, "Anyway, the weird thing is Mooner will regularly turn around and moon at people he doesn't like or know very well, right up to this day!"

"Amazing!" Donal replied. "Well, at least he's not mooning at me, so he must like me."

Kelly looked at Mooner. It was true. He was nuzzling up to Donal like an old friend, which was quite unusual.

"Do you ride yourself?" she asked.

"I used to but not in years."

"Perhaps you would like to come out for a ride this afternoon, after lunch?"

"I would love to, on one condition," he said

"What's that?"

"You promise not to laugh at me."

She laughed now. "I promise."

CHAPTER 14

Lunch was a surprisingly merry affair. Everybody made an effort to be positive about Richard's situation. Saskia was the only one who couldn't settle.

"Really, Saskia, you should trust in your husband more," Edwina chastised.

"I know, but no matter whose fault it was or wasn't, that poor girl is hanging on to her life by a thread."

"Mrs Dalton, why don't you phone the hospital if it makes you feel better?" Donal suggested.

"Have some wine, Donal," Lauren offered. She and Tiffany were having great fun with their unexpected visitor at Kelly's expense.

Lauren had already asked him if he planned to marry her eldest sister. Kelly nearly died, especially when he said that it depended on her. Edu, who had complained that she wasn't hungry, was up in the nursery with Robin, singing her to sleep.

In an effort to keep busy, Saskia had thrown together a feast of chicken carnation on a bed of fluffy rice with an avocado salad on the side. There was garlic bread and fresh coleslaw and gallons of wine. Kelly, however, was as quiet as a mouse. She didn't talk at all over lunch. She just gave her sisters the occasional glare when they gave Donal a hard time. The irony was that he could take it happily. It was Kelly who was getting addled. She had already shocked herself by inviting him out for a ride that afternoon. It was just that she remembered how wretched she had felt after he left the hospital and she didn't want to feel that way again. She didn't want him to go, not yet anyway.

The other women were equally glad to have him around. For the most part he had calmed them down regarding Richard's sudden exit. Lauren and Tiffany just loved the distraction.

"Where are you from, Donal?" Tiffany asked.

"I'm from a lovely little town in the midlands called Birr, Tiff."

"Do you have any brothers or sisters?"

"Yes, Lauren, I have three brothers and four sisters. I'm the eldest."

Edwina, Saskia and all three girls gasped in unison.

"Eight children, your poor mother!" Saskia sighed. "I have my hands full with four."

"It's not right, morally," Edwina grumbled as she stood up to clear the table.

"Your father must have been a real goer, Donal!"

"Lauren, stop that!" Saskia interrupted her daughter.

"It's all right, Mrs Dalton, nothing I haven't heard before," he laughed. "I don't know how my poor mother managed but it was and still is a crazy, happy, totally topsy-turvy house."

"I can relate to that myself," Tiffany grumbled.

"So tell me about your brothers. Are they all as cute as you?" Lauren went on, shameless as ever.

"Ah, they're much better looking, Lauren!"

The phone interrupted them. Tiffany and Lauren lunged for it at the same time. It was usually a race to see who could get to it first. In fact, Kelly would usually compete as well but she was obviously on her best behaviour at lunch because of Donal.

Today Tiffany won the race.

"Hello, Dalton residence." She paused and listened. "Mum, it's for you. It's Barry McCourt."

"Put it on hold." Saskia was already halfway out the door. "I'll take it in the study." She was gone.

"Barry, is that you? What is going on?" Saskia let her guard down once she was in the privacy of the study. "What has happened to Richard?" Her voice was drenched with concern.

"Hi, Sas. Stop worrying; everything will be fine. They were questioning him all morning but things have mellowed out a little now. There's no doubt, it has been a terrible turn of events; the young girl has slipped back into a coma – well, it's just a terrible business. Sadly, there are no mandatory drink-driving tests done at the scene of car accidents, but the ambulance driver and his partner will be good witnesses and, of course, he was on his way to meet up with you. A new baby is probably the best excuse in the world for fast or er, dangerous driving. Please don't worry, Saskia."

"Well, can they detain him? When is he getting out? Can we keep it out of the papers? Oh Barry, he'll go crazy if this gets out."

"Saskia, he'll be home in a few hours – he has not been arrested, you do realise that, don't you? I'll bring him home myself. I do have one bit of good news. A police car did arrive at the scene of the crash and they were satisfied that he hadn't been drinking. That is a big plus."

"Oh thank God," Saskia exhaled. "So what now?"

"The next thing is a file has to be sent to the DPP. Please don't worry. He needs you to be strong."

She hadn't thought of that. "Oh yes, of course I will. Can I speak to him?"

Barry paused, "Not just at the minute, Sas. Look, I'll have him home this evening. Please stop worrying."

Reluctantly she hung up and returned to the kitchen where everybody was waiting for news. On seeing their expectant faces, she pasted on her cheery face and smiled.

"Well, the good news is Barry says everything is going to be fine and he'll have Daddy home tonight."

"Just as Donal said," Lauren tittered and looked at her new friend.

Kelly decided that her little sister was getting way too familiar. "Are you ready for that ride?" she asked her guest.

Lauren and Tiffany giggled at the double entendre.

"You bet," he replied, "as long as you don't laugh!"

Kelly and Donal were let off doing the dishes and headed straight out into the yard.

"Which one is mine?" he asked, nervously looking at Polly and Mooner, who in turn were both eyeing him up.

"I think you'd better have Mooner. Polly can be a bit – feisty."

"And Mooner?"

"Oh, he's a pet. I promise."

"Yea, I believe you, but does Mooner know that he's a pet?"

Saskia watched them from the kitchen window. There was no doubt that they made a handsome couple. Doubtless Richard would do his nut if he knew that his princess was with a cop but in truth Donal was a kind and very caring young man. That was what Kelly needed. For some reason, she seemed distant and untrusting of men. Donal could make a nice first boyfriend.

"Where are we going?" Donal asked, once mounted.

"I could take you down through the little woods to the river at the bottom of the valley. From there I can show you where Nicolas Flattery is going to live."

177

"*The* Nicolas Flattery, the guy that was in the movie *Freedom*?"

"The very same."

"I didn't know he lived in Ireland."

"He doesn't. He's moving here soon, when the house is finished."

"Come on. What are we waiting for?" Donal squeezed his long legs around Mooner's sides and the horse responded instantly. They took off towards the woods at breakneck speed. Kelly looked on in amazement. It took her a few moments to realise that he was, in fact, in total control of Mooner and then she galloped after them.

"You shit, you're well able to ride!" she chastised him when he eventually slowed down and she caught up.

"Why am I a shit?" he laughed.

"You said you couldn't ride."

"No, I didn't. I said that I used to ride a long time ago. I just haven't ridden in years but I have to admit now that I'm up again, it is just like riding a bicycle, isn't it? You never really forget."

"Where did you learn?"

"We have a farm in Birr. There are always a few old nags knocking about."

Polly and Mooner walked alongside each other companionably.

"It sounds nice."

"Perhaps you'd like to come and see it sometime," he offered.

She looked at him in shock, "Oh, I didn't mean, I just meant, well," Kelly got all flustered.

Donal thought she looked gorgeous. "What did you mean, Kelly?"

"Oh, I don't know what I meant."

"Kelly, I have to be honest with you. I did come here today to lend my support and to see if I could be of any help, but my main reason was I really wanted to see you again."

Kelly could hear her heartbeat thundering in her ears. She was delighted by what he said but also a little nervous.

"Come on. Here's the River More. Polly and Mooner love walking in the water."

Donal watched the excitement in her eyes. She was the most beautiful girl he had ever known. Her eyes were like giant saucers and her skin had a warm Mediterranean look. She was very sallow. Even now, with a riding hat on, her rich dark curls danced down her back. He had to fight the urge to stroke her or to touch her hair.

Polly gently found her footing into the water and Mooner followed.

"Look at me, Kelly," he insisted. Gradually she drew her gaze up to meet his. "I'm really serious. I can't stop thinking about you. You're the most beautiful girl I've ever seen." He pulled his pony up along-side hers and reached over to stroke Kelly's cheek waiting for some sort of reaction. Brave from the amount of wine she had at lunch, Kelly rose out of her saddle and leant towards him. She kissed him gently on the lips.

"God you're gorgeous," he exclaimed as he kissed her back. Unlike Kelly, Donal hadn't touched a drop of the wine that the girls had poured him. He wasn't a big drinker anyway and certainly never when he was driving. It did rather surprise him that Tiffany and Lauren were drinking – they seemed so young – but he thought better than to say anything.

Mooner was the first to lose interest in the two riders kissing and so he began to walk along in the river pulling the couple apart. They burst out laughing, as Donal was taken further away from Kelly. "Wait for me," he pleaded as if he were the hero of some old war movie.

"Romeo, Romeo, wherefore art thou?" she giggled and walked along behind.

Kelly pulled Polly out of the river on the Rathdeen side.

"Come on, I'll show you Nicolas Flattery's new mansion." She turned and galloped up the hill. Donal galloped after her.

"Would you like something like this after we're married?" he asked.

Kelly swung around in horror but was relieved to see the expression on his face was only jest. "Oh no, darling, I want something much larger."

Now it was Donal's turn to laugh. "Not on a garda's salary, you won't!"

He dismounted and tied Mooner to a nearby cement mixer. Kelly did likewise.

"Tell me about yourself, Kelly. I want to know everything."

"Gosh, what is there to tell?"

"What are your hobbies? What's your favourite pastime?"

"Skiing! I love snow skiing, and pastime? That would have to be shopping. Mum usually takes us to London every December to stock up on clothes and stuff."

Donal looked stunned. "Wow, poor little rich girl! I've actually never gone skiing. Where do you go?"

"Well, for the last ten years we've gone to Europe, so we're really hoping to try out the US this year. Hey, I'm not a poor little rich girl, feck off!"

Donal didn't comment.

"Where did you go to school?"

"Mount Eden," she whispered, aware that he had said *did* and not *do*. Shit, he thinks I'm older than I really am, she thought in panic.

Donal let out a low whistle, "What is that now? Five or six grand a year."

"Seven," she mumbled, now feeling decidedly uncomfortable. "Will we have a look around the house?" she asked, desperately trying to change the subject.

"Is it safe, structurally, I mean?"

"Just a little look," she suggested.

"I know what I'd much rather have a little look

around." Donal had crept around behind Kelly and wrapped his arms around her.

"What *do* you mean?" Kelly asked, pretending to be shocked.

"I mean this beautiful face," he kissed her again. "This beautiful hair." As she shook her mane free from the riding hat, he took a handful and buried his face in it. "And this exquisite body." He dropped both his hands onto her buttocks, gently pulling her towards him. Kelly loved how it made her feel. In truth she had never had a boyfriend before. The plonkers that hung around Mount Eden were sad excuses for men but Donal was different.

"What did you have in mind for this exquisite body?" she asked playfully.

"Well, I'm not sure that I could tell you."

"Well then, why don't you show me?" She took him by the hand and gently led him into the building site that was Rathdeen Manor.

"What room do you reckon this is?" she asked him. Donal was momentarily distracted from Kelly.

"Jesus, this is huge. It's more like a hotel than a house. Is everybody in Ballymore a multi-millionaire?"

"Well, this must be the front door." Kelly had wandered down the corridor and chose to ignore his comment. "We must have come in through the back door. Where are the stairs?"

Donal caught up with her. "You want to go upstairs, mademoiselle?" he teased and kissed her again.

"Not necessarily," she kissed him back.

His hands began to explore her clothes. She shook off her riding jacket. The blouse was a little more difficult. He squeezed his hands down inside her jodhpurs.

"Oh, ow, just wait a minute, Donal." Awkwardly she undid her zip and pulled her jodpurs down. Even on Kelly's thin body, they weren't easy to peel off. Then there was nowhere to lie. Everything was covered in cement powder and it was considerably colder than Kelly had anticipated. "Stop!" she yelled.

Donal jumped back in shock. "What's wrong?" he asked.

"You have to ask? Donal. Look at me." Kelly stood in the middle of the huge reception hall with her jodhpurs around her ankles and her blouse half-open. He had pushed her bra above her breasts but it was still attached at the back so it looked utterly ridiculous. Her riding jacket was covered in grey dust, lying on the ground. To top it all, she was freezing. The old building had yet to have windows and doors installed, let alone heating. This was enough to sober her up fully and quickly.

"Somehow I think this is not the place, whatever about the time," she snapped. Donal was still fully clad. But he was so turned on, this was not what he wanted to hear. "Kelly, where's your sense of fun?" he pleaded.

"I'll tell you where, it's somewhere a lot warmer than here."

"Yea, like Bermuda probably," he grumbled.

"And what is that supposed to mean?"

"Ah come on, Kelly. You and I – who are we kidding? You were born with a silver spoon in your mouth. I'm a regular guy. We're not exactly a match made in heaven!"

She pulled up her trousers and down her bra. She tucked in her blouse and gathered up her jacket and walloped the dust off. She put it back on and glowered at Donal. "Come on, Casanova."

"What the hell did I do? This was your idea."

"Oh yea, who came around to whose house?"

"What's suddenly got into you? Jeez."

"Well, that's just typical. There's something *wrong* with me because I don't want to have sex with you. You men, you're all alike."

"Why? Does this sort of thing happen to you often?"

"What?" Her bottom lip began to quiver. "I've never done this kind of thing before, never."

Donal knew that in anger he had gone too far.

"I'm sorry, Kelly." He went to hug her. "Really I'm sorry." He paused, as if something had just registered with him. "What do you mean you've *never* done anything like this before?"

"Who the hell are you two?" a loud voice interrupted their little chat.

Kelly and Donal jumped, startled at the intrusion. Standing in what would eventually be the front door of

Rathdeen Manor was a young, very broad, very tanned young American.

"Didn't you see the signs, dude? This is private property." He addressed his aggression at Donal.

"Omigod, you're Nicolas Flattery!" Kelly exclaimed, fantastically relieved that she had stopped Donal when she did, otherwise they would have been caught mid-bonk.

"Tell me something I don't know, lady," he snapped with a surprisingly strong American twang.

Unfazed, she walked straight up to him and stuck out her hand. "I'm Kelly Dalton. We're neighbours. Oh, and this is Donal Walsh, a friend."

"Nice to meet you Kelly, Don," he nodded in Donal's direction but he kept Kelly's hand. "Well, neighbour, what are you doing here? Do you know this is a strictly hardhat area? It's still very dangerous."

"Oh, we didn't know. We came in through the back door. We must have missed the signs."

Donal kicked himself for being so careless. It wasn't like him.

"We should be getting back, Kelly, It's getting late."

"Yes, the horses will be getting cold. Nicholas, it was lovely to meet you. Sorry about the intrusion. Please come and visit us – at least we have windows!" She laughed but neither of the men did.

"We will soon," Nicolas snapped, slightly stung.

"Oh, I didn't mean . . . " Kelly stuttered. "This is going to be a fantastic house!"

"Yea, whatever. Pity it's on this side of the Atlantic," Nicolas replied.

"Kelly, we really should go," Donal tried again.

"Well, it was nice to meet you. Please call around to our house just to say hi. It's Innishambles, just across the valley." She smiled weakly at her new neighbour, who seemed very foul-tempered. Then she followed Donal back out to the horses.

"Well, he's a bunch of laughs." Donal mounted Mooner.

"We *were* in his house," Kelly tried to excuse him.

"You think that justifies his attitude? You tried to explain that we didn't know." Donal looked around. "There are no signs around here."

"No, maybe they're all along the road. They probably didn't expect to get invaded by their next-door neighbours – from behind!"

"You're cutting him a lot of slack," Donal observed jealously.

"I'm just being neighbourly. I don't want to start off on the wrong foot."

"You richies have to look after each other."

"That's just not fair," Kelly objected.

"Actually, it's not, but you have to admit, Kelly, this is a pretty exclusive place. I mean millionaires and movie stars. I'm not sure that your dad would be too impressed if he knew what I did for a living."

"Well, we were just going out for a ride together," she looked at him and smiled shyly.

"Yea, a horse ride. That's the only riding that we should be doing together, for both our sakes." He hesitated. "There is something else you have to be honest with me about, Kelly. How old are you?"

She bit her lip and looked at the ground.

"Kelly?"

"Eighteen, last month."

"Oh Jesus."

"What's wrong with eighteen?" she asked indignantly.

"Oh, Kelly. My youngest sister, my baby sister, is twenty, for God's sake. It just never occurred to me, when I met you on the motorway. You look about twenty-four. Christ, I'm thirty-four!"

"Thanks," but she knew her romance was over.

"You're still the most beautiful woman I've ever seen – but the age gap. It's just too large."

Donal couldn't believe he was saying these words, but he knew it could never work – she was too young and too rich.

"Let's just stay friends, for the next few years at least," he suggested.

"Ha, the 'just good friends' line. OK, if that's what *you* want."

Lunch had been a long affair and the time had flown by in each other's company, so they were surprised to realise that it was almost five o'clock by the time they got back to Innishambles. They reached the house as it was getting a good deal colder. They unbridled the horses and went inside.

187

Saskia was preparing the Sunday dinner.

"How was your ride?" she asked merrily, folding the soufflé.

"Lovely. You have lovely lands here, Mrs Dalton."

"Please call me Saskia." She gave him the benefit of a motherly smile. "Will you stay for dinner, Donal?"

"No, thank you very much, Saskia. I'd best be on my way. Thank you for a lovely lunch. And Kelly," he turned to face her, "thanks for the lovely afternoon."

"Sure," was all she said.

Edu came into the kitchen with Robin. "Teatime for ze leetle one."

"Can I hold her one more time?" Donal asked.

This time Edu handed Robin over straight away, not waiting for Saskia's approval.

"You like ze babies," she smiled at Donal.

"Yes," he conceded, as he cuddled and crooned to Robin who was delighted with the attention. "Now I really must go. Thanks again for everything. I hope things work out OK for Mr Dalton. I'll leave my phone number if you like. If I can be of any more help just call."

"That's very kind, Donal. Just stick it up there on the noticeboard. Please do feel free to pop in any time you're in the neighbourhood," Saskia suggested, but she knew her eldest daughter well and, from the veiled expression and hooded eyes, Donal Walsh would not be rushing back.

CHAPTER 15

Barney Armstrong saw Donal Walsh tear down the Innishambles driveway. The driver barely looked as he pulled out of the gate.

Lucky bugger, Barney thought, I'd love to be leaving Innishambles instead of just arriving. Barney didn't know Donal but it was pretty obvious that the guy was in a hurry to get away from the house.

"I know how he feels," Barney told Owl. He had taken the old horse out for the exercise. He also thought he needed a little moral support for the trip. He wasn't sure that his legs would be able for the short walk from Peartree Cottage to Innishambles. Barney was still pickled with alcohol, utterly hung-over. He hadn't drunk that much in years, if ever, he thought. It had been a great night and he remembered laughing a lot, but it was the latter part of the evening that had him making this reluctant journey now.

"How could I have done it, Owl? Tiffany is a honey but not in *that* way." The horse snorted in agreement and continued his stroll up the driveway.

Out of habit, Barney went to the back door of the house and there he met Kelly brushing down Mooner and Polly.

"Hi there, fancy doing another one?" Barney asked playfully.

"Oh God," Kelly jumped. "Barney, it's only you."

"Hey, are you OK?"

"Oh yeah, it's just I thought you were someone else."

"A guy with sandy brown hair, by any chance?"

"Yes, how did you know?"

"I think you can relax, Kelly. He could qualify for Formula One at the rate he just tore down your driveway. I'd say he's in Dublin by now."

"Whoopee."

"Didn't quite go to plan then?"

"Oh Barney. I just don't understand men. They can't all be plonkers, can they?"

"Well, actually, I'm not really the one to ask."

"Well, you're not a plonker, are you?"

"Oh, Kelly, don't go there. I'm a prize plonker. Believe me."

Kelly burst out laughing. "You can't be a plonker if you say you're one!"

"Yeah? That really makes me feel better." He winced. "Tell me, is Tiff around?"

Kelly paused. "To be honest, today isn't a very good day, Barney. Could you come back tomorrow?"

"What's wrong? Can I help?"

Saskia walked out into the yard to look for Kelly and overheard Barney.

"Kelly," she snapped. "Can't you keep anything a secret?"

"Mom, I didn't say anything," Kelly scowled, flashing her big brown eyes at her mother. She turned and put Mooner into his stable for the night.

"She didn't, Saskia, honest," Barney added, trying to help. He had dismounted and saw the worry in Saskia's eyes. "Looking at you, however, it's obvious that something is wrong. Please let me help."

Saskia looked at Barney and saw the concern in his eyes.

"Oh Barney, come on in. You may as well hear it now." Then she turned to Kelly, "Finish up here, will you, honey? Dinner will be ready soon. Barney, would you like to stay for dinner?"

They walked into the house together, leaving Kelly where she was happiest, surrounded by horses with Polly, Mooner and Owl.

Barney was shocked to hear about Richard and it lessened his own trauma but there was no sign of Tiffany in the Dalton house. He eventually mustered up the courage.

"Eh, Saskia. Is Tiffany around? I wanted to talk to her about minding Orinoco and Nina for a few days."

This was a complete fabrication, but he suddenly felt that he needed an excuse to talk to her.

"I think she's doing her homework in the study, Barney."

"Homework? Oh, of course." He broke into a sweat. He knew that Tiffany was only in her transition year but he had forgotten. God, what age was she anyway? He knocked gently on the study door.

"Tiff?"

"Come in."

Barney stuck his head around the door. "Hi, girls." Tiffany and Lauren were studying together.

"Hi, Barney," Lauren teased in a singsong tone. It was obvious that she knew. "Perhaps I should go and leave you two lovebirds some room," she added. Oh shit, Barney thought. Lauren danced out the door singing an old Boyzone song.

"Hi," Barney began.

Tiffany continued to study, looking down at her books.

"How are you?" he persevered.

"Fine," was the muffled reply.

"Tiff, please look at me. We have to talk, about last night."

Tiffany looked at Barney. "What's there to say?"

"Well, lots."

"Barney, it's over. It was just one of those things. Let's just forget it."

"What?" he couldn't believe his ears.

"Let's just let it go."

"Ah no, Jesus. Tiffany. What about you. Are you OK?"

"Yes, I'm fine. Everything is fine. Just forget it."

Barney had not anticipated how the conversation might go but this was definitely not what he had expected.

"If you're sure," he faltered.

"It was nothing, Barney. Jeez, just let it go, will you? Look, what I'd really like, if it was all right with you, is if we could just get back to being friends. Forget all about it, OK?"

"If that's what you want. Sure." Barney heaved a sigh of relief.

"God, I can't believe you're taking the whole thing so seriously. Chill out, boy." Tiffany stood up, took him by the hand like an old friend and brought him out to the kitchen. "Dinner smells great, Mum!" she chirped.

Everybody descended upon the kitchen when the familiar sounds of the carving knife started up. Kelly and Barney brought the dogs out to the scullery because they were getting so giddy. Usually they were let sit by the Aga while the family ate but Edwina gave out so much about them being unhygienic, it just wasn't worth it.

"You look a little weird, Barney. Dad is OK, you know – he'll be home tonight," Kelly smiled.

"No, it's not that," he looked at her. "Well, if you don't understand men, don't worry, because I'm damned if I understand women!"

They laughed together. "Come in and have dinner. You'll feel a lot better after it," she said.

If lunch was a sumptuous affair, dinner was even better. Saskia had been hoping that Richard would be home by then and so she had pulled out all the stops. The homemade potato and leek soup didn't last a minute. She had even made fresh bread to go along with it. The main event however was a roast rack of lamb with roast potatoes, minted peas and mashed carrot and parsnip. Everybody ate with great relish.

"Hey, we met Nicolas Flattery today," Kelly remembered.

Lauren nearly choked on her peas, "Which one, junior or senior?"

"Oh, junior! Actually he's kinda cute!"

Lauren could hardly contain herself. "Why do you always get all the excitement? What did he say? What does he look like in real life, Kelly? What is he doing here now? The house isn't nearly ready."

Saskia interrupted, "Will you relax, Lauren? You'll give yourself indigestion."

Kelly continued, "Anyway, I don't know. He wasn't very nice. He didn't say much. He just told us to get off his land."

"You were trespassing?" Edwina was horrified.

"We were only having a bloody look."

"Well, what does he look like at least? Surely you can give me that much."

"Good-looking. He looks very American!"

"What does that mean, for God's sake?"

"Do you want to know or not?" Kelly was enjoying her limelight. "He looks like the boy in *Dawson's Creek*. What's his name again?"

"Do you mean Dawson by any chance?" Lauren suggested barely able to hide her impatience.

Kelly continued, "In fact, Lauren, I'd say he's about eighteen years old, more suited to me than to you."

"Don't you dare, Kelly. He's mine. I saw him first."

"He's fifteen actually, but I agree with you, Kelly. He does look older." Barney spoke. Everybody looked at him.

"That means he's perfect for me," Tiffany added gleefully.

"How the hell do you know?" Lauren asked Barney, ignoring Tiff.

"I met him yesterday. He was staying in Molloy's B&B for the weekend, just to get his first look at his new home, I guess."

"What the hell? Who was he with?"

"His mother."

The table broke into chaos as everybody chastised Barney for keeping this to himself.

"I kinda got the feeling that they wanted to be left alone," he tried to explain.

"Still, I would have loved to get a look at Jessica Bell," Saskia added.

"I invited him to come and visit us sometime," Kelly remembered.

Everyone began talking together again. Saskia was worried that they might arrive tonight and the house was in total disarray after the day she had. Edwina disapproved of Jessica Bell and she was sure the son would be damaged goods as a result. Edu was the only one not caught up in the excitement. Her mind was elsewhere.

After the main course, Saskia's soufflé was duly devoured and Barney eventually made his farewells.

"It's Robin's bath time," Saskia yawned. "Can I trust you girls to do the dishes without fighting? Edu has been a great help to me today, and I actually think she's quite upset about Richard in her own way, so I've told her to relax."

"It's been traumatic for us too, yeh know, Mum," Lauren whined, still recovering from the shock that she had missed Nicolas Jnr. Before he left, Barney explained that he was sure Nicolas and his mother were only in Ballymore for the one night and so it was not worth her while heading down to Molloy's B&B at this late hour.

Left alone, Tiffany and Lauren began to interrogate Kelly.

"Well, what happened?"

"Nothing." Kelly began washing the larger saucepans in hot, sudsy water.

Tiffany didn't believe her; "You were gone too long for nothing to happen. Something must have happened, Kelly?"

"OK, well something nearly happened but I stopped it. It would have been a mistake."

"Do you not like him after all?" Lauren asked.

"I thought I did, but it's difficult to explain. He was so nice the night Mum had Robin, really masterful!" The other two giggled, but Kelly continued. "Well, he certainly wasn't masterful today. To be honest, he freaked when he heard that I was just eighteen – I mean eighteen. I could get married if I wanted to! I'm glad nothing happened. It would have been a mistake. He also had a real problem with the fact that we're really rich."

"We're not really rich," Lauren scoffed.

"He seems to think we are. Anyway that particular romance is over so I'm young, free and single again."

"You and Tiff!" Lauren added.

"What are you talking about?" Kelly didn't understand, but Lauren had turned to Tiffany already.

"What was he doing here today? Is he in love?"

"I think he might be," Tiff conceded. "He was so serious. He wanted to discuss it and talk."

"Oh barf," Lauren giggled.

"What are you talking about?" Kelly asked again and so Lauren explained. "Tiffany and Barney had the much anticipated romp last night and it was a fiasco. But the biggest bit of news out of their escapades is that Tiff is over Barney. Now it seems Barney is in love with Tiff!"

"You what?" Kelly looked at her sister. "Tiffany, you didn't do anything *too* wild, did you?"

"I didn't bonk him if that's what you mean," she

replied a little indignantly. "Anyway, I'm nearly sixteen." Then she told Kelly all about her adventures the night before.

"Actually now that you mention it, he did keep staring at you during dinner. I wondered what was going on," Kelly said. "Well, what did you say to him?"

"I asked him if we could just be friends." The three girls exploded into laughter. "Just good friends," they chorused.

As the last pot was dried and put away, they heard the front door open. The dogs, who had escaped from the scullery as soon as Edwina retired from the kitchen after dessert, tore out to meet their master.

"Anyone home?" a familiar voice yelled.

"Daddy!" The girls descended upon their father, as did Edwina. Saskia soon joined them from upstairs, little Robin safely bedded for the night.

He was warmly welcomed and brought into the kitchen where his girls waited on him and served him his dinner.

"What a day," he sighed.

"Was it awful, Daddy?" Tiffany asked, eyes wide with worry.

"It was fairly arduous, honey, but it's over now."

"What happens next?" Saskia asked nervously.

He looked at his wife, "Well, a file is sent to the DPP."

"And then?"

"Who knows? With any luck there'll be no charges!"

The girls heaved a collective sigh.

"Well, I know it was a dreadful accident, but something did attack you, Dad. It wasn't your fault," Tiffany tried to make him feel better.

"I know, pet. Now there is something I must discuss with all of you. We must keep this inside the family. I don't want any outsiders to know about our little family drama." He saw the guilty look on their faces.

"Who knows already?" he asked.

Saskia was the one who had told Barney, so she replied. "I did tell one person today but he's absolutely confidential, Richard. Damn it, he's a close family friend."

"Not any more," Kelly muttered.

"Barney?" Saskia asked her eldest daughter in surprise.

"Oh, I thought you meant Donal Walsh."

"Who the hell is Donal Walsh?" Richard asked incredulously. "And why does Barney know?"

The conversation went downhill from there. Richard was furious that already two people knew about the trauma, and damn the police for contacting this Walsh fella. He was equally furious that Saskia had let Kelly fraternise with him. Richard maintained that he could have been a plant or spy or God knew what!

Eventually everybody sloped off to bed. The day had ended fairly badly. The only two remaining were Richard and Saskia.

"So what's the worst case scenario?" she finally asked.

"Oh, for Christ's sake, Saskia, why do you always have to be so negative?" he snapped.

"Damn you, Richard. You have spent the day in the Wicklow police station and you have the audacity to give out to me. I have held this house together while you were away and I have to be prepared for any outcome. Now don't try to placate me and don't beat about the bush. I need to know the whole picture. Obviously we hope it doesn't come to this, but what's the worst thing that could happen?"

Richard looked deflated. He paused as if thinking about what she had just said and finally he replied. "Prison."

"Oh, my God," Saskia was horrified, her hand over her mouth in disbelief. "But they can't put you in prison for something that wasn't your fault. This is all a dreadful mistake. For how long?"

"Years – four, maybe five."

"This can't be. This is a nightmare. A bad joke. Richard, say you're not serious."

"You wanted to know, now you do," he added bitterly.

Tears began to roll down Saskia's tired face. He looked at her without any compassion or love.

"Shit, Saskia, you said you wanted to know. You wanted to get prepared, so stop your bloody crying. I've had a lousy day. The last thing I need is to have to try to console you!"

He grabbed his whiskey and stomped off up to bed, leaving her alone.

"I guess I didn't want that much honesty," she whimpered.

CHAPTER 16

Robin Maher had been looking forward to this meeting all weekend.

Friday night she spent with her boyfriend, Joey, but she sent him home after a romantic supper and a shag. Joey wasn't too impressed at being kicked out of bed in the middle of the night, but Robin didn't care. She knew that she would be kicking him out of her life soon enough. For the present, he was a pleasant diversion who kept her satisfied.

For the remainder of the weekend, however, Robin needed to be alone, to think. She wanted to play this meeting just right because she had two very important objectives. Firstly, she had to get Richard Dalton to agree to the Corporate Affairs' publicity campaign and get his signature on the dotted line. Her second objective, however, was much more personal. She was determined to become Richard Dalton's mistress. Not just any old mistress, but his official, long-term, not-to-be-messed-with mistress. Robin Maher was no easy pushover. She knew he had been eager to get her into bed ever since he met her, but she held out. "Treat 'em mean and keep 'em keen," she always said.

Robin knew that she didn't want children. She didn't know why she lacked what her mother called the maternal instinct but she did. What's more, it didn't bother her. For this reason, Robin had no great need for marriage, but she did have a serious need for money. She loved it and what it brought.

Dressed this Monday morning in a black Escada suit with large gold buttons, she knew that she looked a million dollars. She had planned what to wear as soon as she heard about the meeting over a week ago. The jacket was short and figure-hugging. With the top two buttons open, Richard would get a very clear view of her exquisite cleavage. Under the suit, she wore a black silk camisole and stockings. The skirt had been adjusted too. She had had it shortened marginally, just enough to show off her finely shaped legs without looking at all tarty. Escada suits were so well cut anyway; it would be practically impossible to look cheap. The suit had cost her over fifteen hundred pounds; more *mistressy* than *tarty*, she smiled to herself. This was her first meeting with Richard alone. She wanted to blow his mind. Even her boss at Corporate Affairs couldn't ignore the sexual tension between Mr Dalton and Robin and so, ironically, it was he who had suggested that Robin carry the Rock account herself. She was thrilled, and promised to give it her *everything*.

Robin's figure was excellent. She worked out three times a week, which was probably more than necessary, but she enjoyed it. Thanks to the gym and an industrious weekend, she was in glorious condition. She spent Saturday with her hairdresser, Brid. Now Robin's hair was blonder than ever and cut straight just below the shoulder. For the first time, Brid had convinced her to have a fringe cut into the style and eventually, Robin gave in to her old friend's advice. The result was spectacular. She didn't have to flick her hair any more, which felt a little strange at first, but she was able to look out from under her new fringe in a most flirtatious way!

It didn't stop there. Robin booked herself into Dublin's most exclusive beauty clinic for all of Sunday. She had her legs, underarms and bikini line waxed. Then she had a total body exfoliation and moisturising treatment. Her skin felt like silk. She had followed this with a facial. She also had her eyebrows shaped, her eyelashes tinted and by Sunday evening, she just had enough time for a manicure and a pedicure.

By the time Robin fell into bed, alone on Sunday night, she knew her body was absolutely perfect!

Richard Dalton's profile was steadily climbing, since he had bought Rock Tower. He was beginning to get a name as one of the City's players and movers. He was now the sole proprietor of the station.

Damn it, Richard *was* Rock FM. This was already known in business circles, but *everybody* would know Richard Dalton's name by the time Robin had finished her PR drive and as for owning the Tower, Donald Trump, eat your heart out!

A shiver of exhilaration went up her spine as she arrived at Rock Tower. It was much taller than she expected it to be. Naturally she had driven past it quite a few times over the last few weeks, but this would be her first time inside the building.

She drove her black Audi TT down the slipway into the underground car park where an iron gate greeted her. A security guard approached her and she zapped down her automatic window.

"Can I help you, ma'am?"

"I have an appointment with Richard Dalton."

He turned to the security intercom beside him and pressed the call button.

"Rock Tower," a polite voice responded.

"I have a Miss –" he paused, waiting for Robin to tell him.

"Maher, Robin Maher," she didn't like his condescending tone.

"I have a Miss Robin Maher, here. Says she has an appointment with Mr Dalton."

"Please park your car and take the lift to reception, Ms Maher. Thank you." With that, the gates began to open and Robin was able to get away from the nasty little man.

She parked her car and headed for the lift. As she approached the doors, they automatically opened and an automated female voice spoke.

"Welcome to Rock Tower. Please enter your access code now, or alternatively press the button marked reception."

Slightly inhibited by the talking lift, Robin pressed the reception button.

"Thank you for your co-operation," the lift responded. It glided so smoothly that Robin wasn't sure whether or not she was moving until, seconds later, the doors slid open again and the lift told her that she had reached reception and to have a nice day. She moved out of the lift fairly smartly and found herself in a large reception area.

The floor was black marble. About ten feet in front of her was a water feature incorporating a huge rock with water pouring over it. The reception desk was also made of black marble. In fact now that she looked around, she realised that everything was black marble. The effect was bright, clean and airy, however, thanks to very strong spotlights in the ceiling.

Then, to her amazement, she saw that behind the reception area, through a large soundproof window, Rock FM's Studio One was in operation. Gerry Dempsey, probably one of Ireland's most popular DJs, was sitting there, pressing buttons and looking at CDs.

Rock FM had begun broadcasting from Rock Tower.

"Hi, you must be Robin." The chirpy young receptionist interrupted her thoughts.

"Yes, I have an appointment with Mr Dalton."

"God, no one calls him that!" the young girl laughed. "He'd kill you if he heard you call him *Mr Dalton*. I've told Elizabeth you're here. That's his PA. She says to go on up. They're on the top floor."

"Do I need some sort of access code?" Robin asked, a little uncertainly. "The lift said something about –"

"Oh, ignore Bessy. That's what we've christened her. There are going to be access codes for the different apartments when they're let out, but they're all still empty. No, just press one and three for Richard as in thirteen – he's on the thirteenth floor."

Unlucky for some, Robin thought, as she punched in the numbers.

"*Penthouse*," the lift commented succinctly as it glided effortlessly to the thirteenth floor. "*Have a nice day.*"

"You too," Robin found herself talking to the lift.

As she stepped out, Elizabeth Wright greeted her.

"Miss Maher, welcome to Rock Tower. This is your first visit, is it not?"

"Yes, it is actually. To date, we've, I've met Richard at our offices down town or in the Burlington."

"Well, we're still only getting settled here ourselves. As you probably know, we only moved in last week so things are still a little chaotic."

"I didn't realise Rock FM had begun broadcasting from here."

"No. We were hoping to keep that quiet for a few

weeks until any teething problems were ironed out – you know, equipment failure and so on. Then it will be announced as a *fait accompli*."

Robin was a little annoyed that Richard hadn't seen fit to inform Corporate Affairs that the move had already taken place. They were, after all, meant to be managing all publicity.

"Would you please come this way?" Elizabeth broke into her thoughts and began to walk towards another room.

Robin glanced up and realised that the huge reception hall was two storeys tall, topped off with a glass pyramid. There was an internal balcony on the upper level and she could see doors leading off to various rooms. The walls were made of what looked like sandstone, light brown in colour. The floor was tiled with a similar shade. The effect would have been quite cold had it not been for the magnificent tapestries that adorned most of the walls.

"Of course," she said, annoyed with herself that only now was she copping on. "The marble in reception, the large stone, the tiles here. They're rock – Rock Tower."

Elizabeth ignored her, or pretended not to hear. "This way, Miss Maher," she beckoned.

She followed Richard's PA into what looked like a large drawing-room. It was beautifully furnished with three large white sofas. The coffee table in the middle was glass. Robin realised that there were fish in it. She couldn't contain her surprise.

"My God, it's a fish tank."

"Yes," Elizabeth smiled. "It's a coffee-table-fish-tank. But it's strong enough to carry a large pot of coffee! Mind you, I wouldn't try sitting on it."

"How unusual."

"The interior designer wanted to use the theme of water and stone for the entire building. Fortunately I think he only got his way in the penthouse and in the reception area. The other floors are fairly regular."

"No, I like it," Robin thought that she might have offended.

"It's not a question of taste," Elizabeth continued. "It was the cost. Outrageous!"

Robin moved to the window. It was in effect a wall of glass because it covered the entire side of the room.

"Oh my God. This is spectacular."

Robin could see across the whole of Dublin city. There were no other buildings obstructing her view. The cars down below looked like toys and the people like ants.

"Is this the tallest building in Dublin?"

"Liberty Hall is thirteen floors tall and you're on the thirteenth floor now. But Richard's office is upstairs on the fourteenth floor. He's as high as you can get."

You got that right, sister, Robin thought smugly.

"Can I get you a tea or coffee, Miss Maher?"

"I would love a black coffee, please." Robin returned to enjoying the view while Elizabeth left her.

One day, she thought, all this could be mine. It would

be inevitable that Richard Dalton would take a mistress when he hit the headlines. His profile was going to be huge. Now that Robin had seen all of this, she realised that he was going to be even more eligible. The sooner she installed herself here the better. She began to look around the room. Again, nothing had been left to chance. Tapestries were used to great effect on the stone walls. The sideboards were made of a dark wood, distressed to look aged. She sat down and contemplated the fish, swimming merrily on the thirteenth floor of this spectacular building.

Elizabeth returned without the coffee.

"Richard will see you straight away." She escorted Robin back out into the reception hall and up the sweeping stairs to his study. Robin could hear the man before she could see him. He was on the phone. What she didn't know was that he was on to his private investigator. Richard had already told him to find out all he could about one Donal Walsh. The other chore was to find out everything he could about Kevin Cantwell. It was at this point that Robin moved into earshot.

"Who did he pay off and how much? I want dates, times and figures."

Elizabeth coughed as if to clear her throat as she entered the room with Robin. It was obvious that she was alerting Richard to their presence. He looked up and beamed as he caught sight of Robin. He gestured to her to come over and sit at his desk. Richard's study was even bigger than the room Robin had been in downstairs. Such space, she thought. This room is bigger than my entire apartment.

"OK, as soon as you can. You know what I want. Bye." Richard hung up without waiting for a reply. He turned to Robin.

"Robin, honey. How can you look so good on a Monday morning? Can I get you a drink? Tea, coffee, something stronger?" He raised an eyebrow playfully.

"Black and strong," she paused. "Please."

Richard's eyes didn't leave Robin's. In fact he stared at her even more intently. "Elizabeth?"

Elizabeth was beginning to feel uncomfortable just standing there.

"Two coffees coming up," she gushed and left quickly.

Robin knew that Richard was already playing with her but she had to get the business part signed up before anything else and so she changed the tone.

"Richard. You've begun broadcasting from here already. Is that prudent?"

He pulled himself back into business mode.

"It was necessary. Radio stations are like living animals. We had to get it used to its new cage before we put it on display."

"What happens if word is leaked?"

"We play it down until it suits our purpose. Simple."

"Can I discuss the final points of the campaign with you now?"

"Sure."

Elizabeth interrupted them on the intercom.

"Richard, your estate agent is returning your call on line four."

Richard picked up the phone.

"Ollie, having a late start again? You call this first thing in the morning? It's almost lunchtime, for Christ's sake." He listened for a while and watched Robin as she took out her plans and artist sketches.

Richard sighed as if to indicate that he was getting bored with the conversation.

"Ollie, I have the sixteen best apartments in Dublin to let and you have had them on your books for the last four weeks. If I was to say if you don't have them let by next Friday you're fired, would you think I was being unreasonable?" He stopped to listen for a second and then continued. "Fine, let's say Friday week." And he hung up before Ollie could reply. He smiled at Robin who looked up shocked, unable to ignore the severity of the conversation.

"Where were we?" he asked.

"The plans."

"Ah yes."

"Can we confirm January third as the relaunch date?"

"Yes."

"Can we confirm two hundred buses with this logo?" She handed him the artist's sketch of the slightly modernised Rock FM logo and the slogan, *"Rock FM – Shattering The Competition"*.

"Yes."

"We'll also book five hundred bus shelters with that same logo and the slogan – *The Best Just Got Better*".

"Yep. That's assuming the new figures put us further ahead in the listener figures."

"All indications are that Rock FM continues to increase its market share."

"Good."

"You are also happy with the radio and television airtime that we've bought on RTE in January?"

"Yes. Their rates are cheaper than ours are, actually. Do they not mind advertising the competition?"

"They have no choice legally, under the Monopolies Act. That said, we have taken the liberty of implying that Rock Ltd. is the company name for a well-known brand of cement!"

Richard laughed. "Smart girl. Yes, that all sounds fine by me. In the publicity celebrating the new listenership figures, we'll launch Rock Tower, the home of Rock FM."

Robin continued, "That brings us to your profile. As the sole owner of Ireland's most successful radio station, we feel confident that we can generate a lot of publicity for you. As you know, *Hello!* magazine is looking to Ireland a lot more for personality profiles. We want to sell you in the Richard Branson guise."

This had been discussed and approved before with Richard, but following his experiences of the day before, he was no longer sure.

"Can we discuss that at a later stage?"

"Is there a problem, Richard?"

"No, it's just, well, I'm not sure that I want to part with my privacy."

"Think what it will do to the value of Rock FM shares, all of which you own," she watched his eyes brighten. "And what about directorships on other boards? This is only for your benefit, Richard." And for mine, she thought.

"Yea, of course you're right. OK, let's forge ahead with that too. What's next?"

"Just sign here."

Richard took her pen and signed the contract, indicating his agreement with the entire campaign. In the back of his mind, he had a niggling worry about sticking his own head so far above the parapet. Spending the previous day in Wicklow Garda Station had really shaken him and obviously given his self-esteem a real shudder, but Robin Maher had a way of making him feel really good.

"Let me be the first to congratulate you, Richard. This will be a massive campaign. I think we'll enjoy working with each other." She lowered her face, so she could peep up at him demurely through her new fringe. It had the desired effect.

"Let's have lunch together to celebrate," he said.

"I'm starving," she smiled. "All this negotiation has given me an appetite." She was back to flirting outrageously with him, now that her first objective was safely completed.

Elizabeth arrived in with the coffees. Their entire meeting had only taken ten minutes.

Richard stared at her, understanding the change of mood.

"We could of course stay in," he offered. "Thrash out those final points one more time?"

"You know Richard, I think that's a good idea." Robin spoke barely above a whisper.

Richard turned to his PA. "Elizabeth, could you have some lunch sent around from The Galloping Gourmet. Set it up in the dining-room. I'm going to show Robin the rest of the Tower."

Elizabeth had gone scarlet. The fizz between her boss and his PR woman was palpable. She couldn't get out of there fast enough.

CHAPTER 17

"Have you seen the view?" Richard asked as he stood up from his desk and walked over to the window. Just like the room downstairs, this one had a wall-to-wall window. Richard's study was obviously directly above the room that Robin had waited in, because the view was almost exactly the same, only from a slightly higher perspective. He gestured for her to join him.

"Richard, it's breathtaking."

"You approve?"

"Very much."

"Yes, I like it too." They looked across the city together. "Do you recognise that?" he asked.

"What?"

Richard stood close behind her so he could point over her shoulder. "That. It's the Obelisk, in Phoenix Park. We're looking right across the city from here."

"Oh, I think I see," she said uncertainly. She didn't

have a clue what he was pointing to, but she liked feeling him so near.

"God, you smell good," he murmured into her hair, breathing in the heady scent of hairdresser's shampoo.

"Now it's your turn to approve," she whispered.

"You know I've approved of you for a long time now, Robin." Standing behind her, he wrapped his arms around her waist.

"Richard, I had no idea you felt this way!" she teased without turning around. Ever so gently, she rubbed her buttocks into his crotch and he was instantly aroused.

"You little liar. You've known from the start," he argued and began to nuzzle for her neck through her hair.

Robin turned to face him.

"We had business to see to. Now that you've wrapped all that up however," she let the sentence hang on her semi-open mouth.

Richard continued for her. "Now that the business is wrapped up, I can unwrap you. Is that what you're saying?" but he was already opening her jacket and admiring a bust-line even better than Edu's.

"Black silk," he stroked the camisole that outlined her breasts and her flat stomach. "You're a traditional girl."

"Very," she purred. She tilted up her head, as if to kiss him, but he wouldn't.

"No hurry, pet. I always like to thoroughly check

out the product before I commit. You of all people should know that."

"Gosh, you're talking about commitment already, Richard," she teased.

A shadow crossed his face, as he looked at her in shock. Commitment was the last thing on Richard Dalton's mind. Then he realised that she was just teasing, and so he laughed hollowly.

"Oh, yes, dear. Absolutely," he agreed.

Robin couldn't believe how happy this made her feel. She had thought it might take some time to pull Richard into some sort of solid relationship but it appeared that he had already made up his mind. He wanted them to be together. Then to her horror it occurred to Robin that Richard might be thinking of leaving Saskia. She already knew, through gentle questioning, that his wife was not very involved in his city life. Robin wanted Richard, but not as a husband and all the baggage that that would entail.

"We can keep this our little secret, Richard. Can't we?" she purred.

"Whatever you say, honey." Richard knew that he fancied Robin Maher and that she fancied him but he couldn't believe how lucky he was getting this morning. She showed no signs of stopping him. This is perfect, he thought. It's just the sort of distraction I need, well away from home, with no commitments . . .

He removed her jacket and stroked her arms as if inspecting one of his pet dogs.

"Very nice," he said, as he kissed her biceps.

"Firm and silky," he rubbed under her arms. Robin sent up a silent prayer of thanks that she had been waxed so well the day before.

"Take off your skirt," he whispered in a very firm tone. It shocked Robin a little but she didn't think that this was the time to argue. Anyway, she knew she had a good body. She undid the button and zip at the back of her skirt and let it slide over her silk stockings to the floor.

He stared at her as she stood in his study wearing only a black silk camisole with suspenders and black stockings. She was still wearing her black patent high heels.

"You're in very good shape," his voice was deep, as he examined her body from different angles. His eyes were as black as coal. "Clever girl, it's very important that young fillies stay in shape."

Robin was getting aroused from the way he was looking at her. "Especially if we want to play with stallions like you!"

A broad smile spread over Richard's face. "Come here," he commanded. "You are hot to trot, aren't you?" He rewarded her with a kiss, strong and powerful. She drank him up. Robin had been anticipating this moment since she first met him and she wanted him inside her already. Richard was so masterful and dominant, she had never been with a man with such powerful magnetism. He wrapped his arms around her firmly, rubbing her body confidently. It was obvious that he was very familiar with how a woman likes to be stroked and explored, teased and indulged. There was no clumsiness. His movements were fluid and purposeful as he undid the buttons at the bottom of her camy and gently began to explore her. Robin let out a gentle moan of gratification that at last he was beginning to touch her in the right places. Equally competently, he pulled the silk camisole up and over her head. She stood by his large office window naked but for her stockings, suspenders and shoes.

"You have excellent breasts," he told her. Robin could barely speak.

"What about you?" she whispered, "I want to see you too."

"Patience, child – believe me, you'll get all of me in time."

Robin was weak with lust and affection for him. He turned his attention to her beautiful round full breasts. He stroked them so gently that she could barely feel him. "Harder," she yearned, "stroke me harder and take me now."

"No. Silly girl. Good things *come* to she who waits." He was treating her like a young impetuous student and she was amazed how turned on by it she was.

He gently rubbed his index finger around her nipples. Then he introduced his thumb, as he tweaked them to attention. "Hello, boys, I'm your new boss." He brought his mouth down onto her nipples.

"Oh Richard, please take me to your room," she begged.

"Why do we need a room?" He guided her back to his desk. Slowly and deliberately he put his files in various drawers. He even stopped to put his signature on one, before he put it away. Then he patted the desk.

"Get up here, honey pot," he ordered her.

"Oh," she giggled. "I've never had sex on an office desk before."

The desk was huge, about six feet long and four feet wide and so she could lie on it as if it was a bed. The leather that covered the table felt cold on her back.

"Now, pet," he continued, "let Dr Dalton do what he does best."

"What about you?" she pleaded.

"Will you stop talking, girl!"

Robin shut up instantly, terrified of annoying him. If it was his pleasure to pleasure her, why not just go with it?

"Now," he continued, "are you willing to trust me?"

She looked up at him and nodded subserviently.

"Good," he smiled and kissed her conclusively. He began to rummage through the drawers of his desk.

"Here it is," Richard pulled out some thick adhesive tape and cut off a large segment with his teeth.

"This may hurt a little. But you know that with pleasure comes pain." Robin's lust was fading fast but she knew she couldn't stop him now if she wanted a relationship with him. Somewhere in the dark recess of her mind, she was curious. Richard covered up her eyes.

"Without vision," he explained, "the other senses are heightened."

As she lay there motionless, she heard him undress, slowly and deliberately. She even thought she heard him fold his clothes.

"Now, Robin, I want you to trust me, but you do want me to enjoy myself too, don't you?" She nodded in agreement, not sure what she was agreeing to.

Richard removed Robin's stockings and suspender belt, carefully and very slowly.

"OK," he said, "you can have your wish." He climbed on top of her. Without any more attention to her needs, he pushed himself inside her body. Moving up and down, she could hear his heavy breath as he was approaching his climax. Hungrily she explored his body with her hands, rubbing his back and stroking his broad buttocks. His tongue ploughed into her mouth, insistently working its way around her teeth and right down her throat.

"Fuck, this feels good," he mumbled. "I'm going to come inside you, girl. Are you ready?"

She wasn't, but he didn't wait for an answer. He came before she had any chance of catching up with him.

Robin jumped when the intercom button clicked into life beside her right ear sixty seconds later. She couldn't move however because she was pinned down by Richard's body.

"Yeah," he growled at the phone.

"Sorry to interrupt, Richard, but your lunch is served in the dining-room when you're ready."

"Great, I'm starving," he said, as he disengaged himself from Robin, "Thanks, Elizabeth."

In one harsh and sudden movement, Richard removed the tape from Robin's eyes. They stung and watered in protest. She wondered why she had bothered paying a fortune to have her eyebrows professionally shaped the previous day, God knows what they looked like now!

"You did very well, honey pot," he crooned. "Very, very well."

"What were you talking about when you asked me to trust you? Was it the blindfold?" she asked nervously.

"That," he answered succinctly and pointed to a camcorder standing on a tripod next to them. It was still in record mode.

"You filmed us?" she asked in horror.

"Just for fun," he took her in his arms. "Robin, you did say that you trusted me just a few minutes ago." He gave her one of those butter-wouldn't-melt-in-his-mouth looks and she gave in.

"Why do you want to film us?"

"We can watch it later and see if it acts as a turn-on!"

Robin laughed nervously.

"Or," he nibbled her ear, "we could study it to see how we can improve our technique."

Robin began to relax as he spoke and felt slightly exhilarated by the idea of being filmed. "Well, as long as we keep the video cassette well hidden under lock and key."

"In the Rock Tower safe," he assured her.

"Now, Mr Dalton," she teased. "Can you tell me where the Rock Tower toilet is? I need to put my clothes back on."

By the time she had returned dressed, with a new layer of Lancôme, he was dressed and looked fresh and revived, every bit the respectable, successful businessman she fancied.

She privately worried about Richard's slightly depraved tendencies. Were the Joeys of this world and all her ex-boyfriends just boring old farts, or was Richard genuinely sick? For the sake of her sanity, she decided that Richard had the right attitude. All the lovers in her past were just old fuddy duddies, who didn't know how to explore the realms of sexual fantasy. That decision made, Robin realised that she was going to learn a lot of new games over the coming months.

"Hungry?" he asked.

"Now I'm really starving!" she said. "And Richard?"

"Yes."

"Do you have many more blank cassettes?"

The smile started in his eyes and spread over his entire face.

"Oh yes, honey pot, crates of them, but let's have lunch first."

Elizabeth had out-done herself. As it was already one thirty, she had gone to the canteen for a bite to eat, but she left a note in the dining-room for Richard.

Dear Richard,

I didn't know what Robin would like so I just got a bit of everything. If you need me for anything, I'm in the canteen. List of phone messages herewith. Back at two.

Liz.

He read the note and checked his messages. Nothing too urgent.

"This is wonderful, Richard," Robin said. But she was looking at the room, not the food.

"Yes, the penthouse is fairly spectacular. I still haven't given you the guided tour!"

"How big is it?" she asked, her eyes drinking up the luxury of the large dining-room. "It's more like a home than an office."

"Well, I do spend a lot of time here."

"Does Saskia ever come up here?"

He looked at her guardedly. "Never."

"She's mad. If I were her, I would live here."

Richard pulled Robin over to him by her hand. "Yes, well thankfully, you're not her." He kissed her again and she responded with the enthusiasm of a new mistress.

They spent lunch talking about the campaign and Richard was delighted to note that Robin seemed quite comfortable with the fact that he had a wife, kids, and even a new baby! *If this is feminism, I like it,* he thought smugly.

Lunch consisted of mussels in garlic and a crab-claw salad. They had a bottle of wine, which didn't last long. As they started their second bottle, Richard sat even closer to Robin, allowing him easy access to her body. After the food, his sexual appetite returned. He began to play with Robin's breasts again. He made her open the buttons at the bottom of her camy, so that he could touch her when he felt like it. He moistened her with wine and was just getting aroused when there was a tentative knock at the door.

"Richard?"

"What is it?" he snapped at Elizabeth.

"Just checking if everything is OK."

"Fine, leave us." She didn't need to be asked twice.

Robin had pulled away however and so he got up and went to the dining-room door.

"Liz," he yelled and she came running back.

"Take the rest of the day off. Switch the phones back to Denise at the main reception and tell her that on no account am I to be disturbed. Miss Maher and I have a lot of business to get through. Is that understood?"

"Yes Richard. Thank you. I'll see to everything." Elizabeth understood perfectly.

When Richard came back into the room, he had that look on his face again.

"Now, honey pot, when you've finished your lunch, I think there are a few more things that I have to *go over* with you."

CHAPTER 18

Barney still couldn't get a handle on it. He spent half his time trying to put the whole sordid affair out of his mind and the other half trying to figure out what the sordid affair actually was. Almost a week had passed since his wild night in The Hitching Post and now, as he sat in his living-room, he still couldn't figure it out.

The weekend had started so well. He had bumped into Jenny Quinn a few times around the village. With her gentle encouragement, he eventually got the nerve to ask her out for a drink, on the Friday night. That had gone so well, she came home with him. One thing led to another and she spent the night. He liked her, but he wasn't sure that he wanted to go out with her. It wasn't in Barney's nature to hurt anybody and so he said that he would call her. To his shame, however, he still hadn't got up the nerve. The one slight consolation was that he hadn't actually had sex with her. She put a stop to it at the last minute, saying it was all happening too fast. Little did she know how much *had* happened since then.

His first inkling that Jenny wasn't the girl for him came when Kelly's horse went wild outside O'Reilly's. Barney nearly lost his life. He was panic-stricken when he thought some harm might befall Kelly. It was Barney who calmed down Polly and defused the situation, but he couldn't believe how much it had unnerved him. Did he care for *Kelly*? This was ridiculous. He was behaving in a most out-of-character way and it was driving him nuts

He was so upset at seeing Kelly *almost* hurt that he drove Jenny home after their lunch together. Jenny was definitely a little put out. She had already said that she had the day free and nothing planned but Barney made up some excuse about needing to make some calls and so he drove her home to Wicklow.

Barney didn't actually do anything for the remainder of Saturday afternoon. He just moped around Peartree Cottage. Later, he took Nina and Orinoco out for a walk down to O'Reilly's to get himself something to eat for supper. Mrs O'Reilly was like a chicken on a hot griddle.

"Barney, I can't keep up with the action here today. You know I'm going to have to start making sandwiches next!"

"Busy day, Mrs O'Reilly?" he tried to sound interested. "Surely it's calmed down now, though. Haven't they all gone home?"

"Home? You must be joking. I've just sold out of cigarettes. They're in and out like yo-yos. They're all over in The Hitching Post. The place is crammed but, with the Dalton girls helping Mick Molloy, sure it's faster to hop across the road than to be waiting for those girls to serve you if it's cigarettes you want."

"The builders from Rathdeen Manor are over in The Hitching Post and the Dalton girls are serving?"

"You have it now, Barney. I don't see any sign of her ladyship Bridget Molloy working, mind you."

"Mrs O'Reilly, I'll just have a pint of milk, please. Thanks."

As he thought back on it now, he couldn't understand why he was so eager to see Kelly again. At the time, he put it down to her near-accident. He just wanted to check that she was OK. Having dropped the dogs home however, when he got to The Hitching Post, it quickly became apparent that it was Tiffany and Lauren who were working. Kelly wasn't even there. Barney was crushed and sat down with Richard Dalton to get pissed.

That said, he had a great night. It had been ages since he got really rollicking drunk. The builders were a dab hand at it and he took their lead. He remembered eating scampi and chips that Tiffany brought him and he remembered talking a lot of shit with the other men. One topic that he remembered very well, however, was when Kevin Cantwell told him about the stables he was building for Nicolas Flattery. Barney couldn't remember the exact details but he did know it would mean more work in the neighbourhood, which was good news. It also meant more work with horses, which was by far his favourite. His next memory was of the pub emptying, which surprised him. It didn't feel that late.

At the time, he was delighted that Tiffany took the initiative of taking him home. He needed a little help. Sitting in The Hitching Post, everything felt fine, but when he hit the fresh air, his head began to spin furiously. Tiffany helped him home and into Peartree Cottage. The next thing he remembered they were kissing passionately in his kitchen. He remembered undoing her bra and caressing her breasts. It was always at this point that he shied away from his memories. Christ, she was only a child – not that she acted like one that night.

Barney's biggest worry, however, was that after the kitchen scene, he really did draw a blank. He remembered going into his bedroom with her and then, nothing, or at least what he remembered made absolutely no sense.

In yet another effort to make sense of that night, Barney forced himself to focus on that part again. It was all so hazy and confusing.

He fixed himself a cup of tea and sat in his favourite chair, the one with the print of all the dogs on it, and tried to figure out the night. Nina jumped up on his lap and Orinoco ignored him.

"OK, Nina, I know I was pissed and I know Tiffany came home with me. What happened next?"

The little dog licked his nose.

"A lot of kissing. Is that what you're saying?"

Nina continued licking.

"I know we went to the bedroom. This is where I really get confused. Did I barf at this point and then crash out?"

Nina was no help, she just looked at Barney, her head slightly at an angle as if she was trying to think too.

"There was sufficient *evidence* around to suggest that I did puke," Barney offered, slightly shyly.

"Why then do I have a vivid memory of shagging Tiffany? I know what I know and I'm sure I got laid last Saturday night. Not just the fact that I woke up naked but I woke up feeling – refreshed, if you know what I mean." Nina didn't.

Barney stroked the top of her little head between her ears and pondered on the evening.

"It just doesn't add up. Tiffany is so relaxed about the fact that we shagged. I *know* we shagged! I was drunk, but I wasn't that drunk and I must have been her first, she's so young." He didn't want to think about that.

Then Barney became quiet as he pondered on the most sinister part of his memory.

"How could I do that to poor Tiffany? She's so nice. How could I fantasise about another woman when I was taking her virginity? I don't even fancy Edu any more. Nina, I'm going mad."

The truth was Barney could only think of Edu when he was thinking of the bonking part of the night. He vaguely remembered his jocks being removed . . .

"Tiff? What are you doing?"

"Shhhh, darling. Teeefany here. You relax and enjoy. Zis will be very good for you."

He felt her lips around his dick and expert hands massage his balls. Just before he came, she moved up and sat down on his cock and moved in unison with him.

"Good boy," she purred. "Now you must sleeep."

It was definitely Edu's voice.

Barney got up to fix himself another cup of tea. No matter how many times he thought about it, the night just didn't make sense. He felt so guilty. He should have rung Jenny. He shouldn't have gone near Tiffany and he shouldn't be fantasising about Edu, the one innocent person in his crazy mixed-up mind.

Up in Innishambles, Edu wasn't feeling quite so innocent. Unlike Barney, her method of dealing with last Saturday night was to put it out of her mind. She had been fortunate enough to overhear Tiffany and Lauren's conversation. That alone was amazing. It was genuinely a coincidence that she woke up at that time, to visit the bathroom. The truth was she was sleeping very badly. When she heard the voices downstairs, she thought it might be Richard. She was desperate to be with him now that she was sure she was ovulating but since Saskia came home that morning, there hadn't been an opportunity. Now, to make matters worse, his mother was in the house and Edu hated Edwina.

Seeing little baby Robin had made Edu even more desperate to have her own child. The truth was Edu had been trying to get pregnant for almost six months and still no joy. Some time after she discovered that Saskia was pregnant again, Edu decided that the only way to deal with fire was with fire. She gave up taking the pill. Somehow she thought if she produced a son for Richard, things would come together for them but so far, she hadn't managed to conceive. Over the last few months, it began to occur to Edu that perhaps there was something wrong with either her or Richard. Was he getting too old? He had managed to get Sas pregnant but was that to be his last child? Worse again, was it possible that she was not able to carry children? That was unthinkable. The more Edu thought about it, the more she worried. She began to monitor her cycles very closely to figure out exactly when she was ovulating. She was certain that Saturday night was the night. Perhaps that was why she was sleeping so badly. It was appalling luck that both Saskia and Edwina had descended upon the house that very day. If they had arrived just one day later, she was sure that she could have seduced Richard. That was not the way it happened however and so she just had to play the hand that fate dealt her.

Naturally she could not discuss this with Richard

because she was fairly sure that he would be furious. She would not tell him until she was a few months pregnant.

When she overheard the girls talking about Barney, she knew it was a sign. It was too good an opportunity to overlook. Quickly and quietly she ran upstairs and threw on an old tracksuit. She ran all the way to Peartree Cottage. Catching her breath before she went in, she crept in the back door. The dogs knew her well and so they didn't even bark. Barney always left his back door unlocked because that's just the kind of guy he was. He always thought the best of people.

Poor dear sweet Barney – the rest was easy for Edu. She quickly undressed and gently peeled off his jocks. He stirred but she soothed him and, to her relief, he still thought Tiffany was there. It was easy to arouse him with a little encouragement. The idea of conceiving was enough to turn her on. As soon as she reckoned that he was ready to come she deftly moved up on top of him and gently guided him into her body. She moved with him steadily until finally he arched his back and groaned a long slow satisfied groan. It was done. He pulled her down on top of him to kiss and embrace her but she slipped away quietly as soon as his snoring became regular again.

Exhilarated at the idea of possibly being pregnant, she dressed quickly, slipped out the way she had come in and skipped the whole way home.

Barney need never know about what had happened

between them and if she were lucky enough to be carrying his child, she would simply tell Richard that it was his. Richard would not doubt it as he never suspected that she would be capable of having sex with another man. Under normal circumstances, of course she wouldn't. Richard was her reason for living. She loved him with all her heart. This little escapade she excused as a necessary exercise to progress her relationship with Richard, her one true love. It was almost six o'clock by the time she slipped into her own bed, giddy and utterly remorseless.

CHAPTER 19

Before Saskia could say Trick or Treat, it was Halloween. She spent weeks worrying about Richard's dangerous-driving problem but it didn't seem to bother him or, if it did, he was capable of hiding it very well. She tried to put it out of her mind, as he obviously did. She just had to assume that Barry McCourt had the matter in hand. All would be well.

She never told Richard but once a week she phoned Vincent's hospital to see if there was any improvement in Katie Anderson's condition. There wasn't. The girl had been in a coma for almost two months now.

As she prepared dinner that evening, it saddened Saskia that she no longer had little girls to dress up and take around the neighbourhood. Frank and Cathy Taylor were always so generous with the girls. The children would go into the little cottage and show off their outfits and in return they would be showered with sweets and biscuits. The same thing happened with their visit to Michael and Bridget Molloy, but the Dalton girls always saved the best till last. When it was darkest, probably around six o'clock, they would descend upon Maureen and Harold O'Reilly. Being the owner of the sweet shop they had a huge supply of chocolate and sweets. Even at their young ages, however, the girls had their system worked out. Lauren, especially, had discovered that she could wangle even more out of Maureen O'Reilly by exaggerating how much she had received from Bridget Molloy. Not to be outdone, Mrs O'Reilly always came up with some extra goodies.

"You look like you were miles away," Kelly interrupted her mother's thoughts as she walked into the kitchen.

"What? Oh, yes. You're right, I was. I was just remembering when you were young and dressing up to go around Ballymore for Halloween."

"Mum! Where do you get these notions? That was ages ago. I'm amazed you even remember."

"Thanks a lot, darling – it wasn't *that* long ago, you know. Anyway, it won't be that many years before you have to baby-sit your little sister around, to do it all over again." Saskia took Robin out of her Moses basket, which was in the kitchen, just as the baby began to mooch.

"Don't remind me," Kelly groaned.

"You don't mean that, surely? She doesn't intrude upon your life too much. Does she?" Saskia was holding Robin protectively.

Kelly realised that she had upset her mother, who seemed quite uptight most of the time recently.

"Oh Mum, no. I didn't mean it at all. I love Robin. She's a dote and she's not an intrusion in the least. In fact, I love her to bits." She reached out to take her little sister from her mother's arms.

Saskia's shoulders dropped with relief as she handed her youngest daughter to her eldest daughter.

"I just want everybody to be happy," she trailed off as Tiffany and Lauren barged in together.

"Is dinner ready? I'm starving," Lauren was fresh-faced and out of breath.

"Where have you been?" Kelly asked.

"We were just checking out Rathdeen Manor to see how it's coming on. It's incredible. They're throwing it up. It looks like something out of *Ideal Homes*. It's amazing!"

"OK,OK, we get the gist," Kelly wasn't as impressed.

"No, for once she's not exaggerating," Tiffany backed up her younger sister. "The change in the last few weeks is literally amazing. I wouldn't believe it if I didn't see it myself."

"Do the builders mind you being over there? I mean you're not in their way, are you?" Saskia asked.

"Mum, are you nuts? They love the distraction. In fact there's one guy who is always hovering around Lauren," Tiffany teased.

"Shut up," came the reply.

"Well, it's true." Tiffany continued.

"Connor Cantwell, Connor Cantwell," the girls began to tease Lauren.

"Slag all you want, but you'll be the jealous ones when I snare Nicolas Flattery."

"Ah Lauren, have you not given that up yet? I'm sure he's tucked away in some snooty little boys' school in L.A. He hasn't been around since that time Kelly bumped into him," Tiffany tried to dissuade her sister.

"He's hardly going to go to school on the West Coast of the States if his parents are moving to Ireland. Sure what's the point in moving over to Wicklow if they're going to leave their young and impressionable son behind them? They're probably moving over here for his sake!" Lauren argued.

"I know I wouldn't trust *you* out of my sight for two minutes, Lauren Dalton," Saskia laughed.

Kelly was happy to hear her mother laugh again. She seemed to be depressed a lot lately. She put it down to the fact that Sas was still up several times a night feeding little Robin.

"Can I help with dinner?" she asked.

"Kelly, you're a pet. If you would mind the baby, that's help enough. It's roast chicken, roast potatoes, lemon carrots and colcannon. The bad news is that I'm out of cream," she looked at her daughters. "Who is going to be the angel that goes down to O'Reilly's?"

They all looked at the floor.

"Lauren?"

"Ah Mum, why does it always have to be me?" she whined.

"I'll go, Mum," Tiffany volunteered.

"No, you're very good for offering, but you always end up going, Tiff. I think it's Lauren's turn," she said firmly.

"Can I drive?"

"You're thirteen!"

"I know but I'm still able to drive."

"Don't go there," Kelly warned, realising that they were ominously close to talk of dangerous driving. "Come on, twerp. I'll drive you."

She handed Robin to Tiffany and took Lauren out to the car.

"Look, will you muck in a bit more, Lauren? Can you not see that Mum is knackered."

Lauren looked crestfallen. "I didn't mean to upset her."

"And like, hello, have you forgotten about Dad's current dangerous driving problems? You might lay off that too, for a few months."

"Oh, shit. I didn't even think."

"Yeah? Well, think a little more, please."

Kelly drove the Landrover out of one of the stables that Saskia used as a garage in the winter months. There was a definite nip in the air. The house had been a glorious shade of burnt orange and fiery red for the last two weeks. Now suddenly, all the Virginia creeper leaves had fallen and Innishambles looked stripped, covered only in a web of brown stems and branches. The clocks had gone back the previous night and so it was darker than the girls were used to, for six o'clock. There was a sinister feel to the evening.

Lauren shivered, "I wouldn't like to be trick or treating tonight."

"Look on the bright side. You wouldn't have to dress up!"

"Feck off," Lauren scoffed. "Speaking of looking lousy, what do you think is bugging Edu? She looks like shit lately."

"I agree and she's no help to Mum either. I think she's just burnt out. She probably needs a man!"

The two girls giggled.

"What about you, Kelly? Do you not want a man?"

"God, I don't know what I want." She fumbled through her jacket for her cigarettes. As they reached the gate of Innishambles, she slowed the Landrover down to light up. She glared at her little sister over the naked flame. "Not a word of this to Mummy. She has enough on her mind."

"I won't say anything if you give me one," Lauren retorted.

"I don't believe you! You're not smoking, are you?"

"What's the big deal? What age were you when you started?"

"Christ, I don't know," Kelly took a long drag and threw the cigarette box at Lauren in disgust. "You shouldn't get hooked, you know. I really regret it."

"Yeah, whatever," Lauren lit up like a pro and blew a few perfect circles at her sister.

"Where the hell did you learn to do that?"

"School."

"Lauren, you're not smoking in school? You know you can be expelled for that!"

Lauren snorted at her sister, "Jeez, Kelly, you're so innocent. All the girls in my class smoke!" She took another drag. "Where's Dad tonight?"

"Where is he *any* night? I think he's moved to Dublin permanently."

Lauren frowned. "Why does he work so hard?"

"Probably so he can afford to keep us in school. Don't forget he has a fourth daughter to pay for now as well."

"Somebody else to fight for the inheritance," Lauren laughed.

"Now, now," Kelly knew that her sister was joking, "age before beauty." She pulled up outside O'Reilly's. "You go on in. I'll wait for you here and finish this." She took another drag of her cigarette.

"Ah Kelly, drive around for a bit, I only just lit this cigarette. Come on, I'll show you Rathdeen Manor. You'll see for yourself how amazing it looks."

Kelly had been wondering what the commotion about a bloody house was and so she agreed without a fight.

They drove out the Rathdeen Road and up to the Manor. Kelly was dumbstruck.

"See. You wouldn't know it was the same house, would you?" Lauren sounded self-satisfied.

"It's a palace," gasped Kelly.

"Dad was saying that the builders have a huge penalty clause if they're not out by mid-December, so I know that my beau will be in situ by then!"

"Lauren. Give it a rest. Remember Tiffany and Barney. She can't stand the guy now. Be careful what you wish for, in case it comes true."

At just that moment a car came tearing out of Rathdeen Manor's driveway and nearly careered straight into them.

"Bloody hell, did you see that?" Lauren asked aghast.

"See it? He almost killed me. This place is bloody dangerous."

"I think it was a Porsche 356!"

"Lauren, who gives a shit what it was? Come on, you're getting the cream and we're going home." Kelly turned the car and headed back to O'Reilly's shop.

"Look, it's here. The Porsche. It must be Nicolas Flattery, or," Lauren got all flustered, "oh God, Kelly, maybe it's Nick Jnr."

"And maybe it's The Grim Reaper. Happy Halloween! Will you get the bloody cream?" She reached across her sister and opened Lauren's car door. "Go!"

Lauren stumbled out, all self-confidence suddenly dissipating in the cold evening air. She walked into the familiar little shop and heard the familiar little bell as the door swung, but she felt like she was in a strange place. Maureen O'Reilly's voice brought her back down to earth.

"Here's one now," she said. "Lauren, this is Jessica Bell, your new neighbour."

"How do you do?" Lauren managed.

"Well, how do *you* do, young lady?" Jessica repeated.

"Welcome to Ballymore. Have you moved in?" Lauren managed.

"Naw, we're just surveying the work," she explained with an incredibly broad American accent. "Say, are you the one that Nick met in the Manor a few weeks ago?"

"No, no, that was my sister, Kelly. She's out in the car. Is that your car outside, the Porsche?"

"Hey girl, you know your cars. Neat, isn't it? Yep it's mine, I brought it over with me. The thing is everybody here drives on the other side of the road." She used her hands a lot as if that made more sense of what she was saying. "Anyway, I keep forgetting which side I should be on. I nearly crashed coming down here just now. It was totally real."

Lauren didn't want to admit that they had been snooping and so she said nothing.

"What was it you wanted, love?" Mrs O'Reilly came to the rescue.

"A pint of cream, please."

Lauren mustered up all her courage, realising that Jessica was about to leave the shop. "Has your son come with you?" she tried to sound as casual as possible.

"Yea, he's up at the Manor. Say, I've just had an idea."

Lauren sent up a quick prayer.

"Why don't you come up and meet him?" Jessica continued, "You're going to be neighbours after all."

"There's an idea. He probably knows nobody." Lauren tried to look surprised.

They exited the shop together. Kelly nearly swallowed her second fag when she saw Lauren walking over to her side of the car with an incredibly glamorous blonde woman.

"Kelly, this is Jessica Ball. Jessica, this is Kelly, my sister. She's the one that Nick, er met."

"How do you do?" Kelly asked through the car window, accidentally blowing cigarette smoke into Jessica's face.

"How quaint, do you all say the same thing? How do *you* do, Kelly?"

Jessica turned back to Lauren. "Do you guys know where you're going? Just follow me," and she was gone.

"What's going on?" Kelly asked, already knowing the answer.

"Kelly," Lauren whined, "this is my big chance. We've been invited up to the manor to meet Nick Jnr. Omigod, Omigod. How do I look? Is my hair OK? Shit, I *would* be wearing these jeans. They make my bum look big. Shit, shit shit."

"Look," Kelly said soothingly, "you wanted to meet the guy. Now you will. You look great. Just be yourself, only calm down a little." They followed the car as it moved up the Rathdeen road.

"Is she drunk?" Kelly asked, "She's all over the road."

They followed Jessica Bell into her driveway.

"Welcome," she said expansively as they alighted from their cars. "Hey, you're our first visitors. Neat."

She pushed open the massive oak door. "Hi, we're home. Nick, Kim?"

Kelly and Lauren looked at each other, mouthing the name Kim at the same time.

"Who is Kim?" Kelly whispered to Lauren as Jessica walked on.

Her sister shrugged. She was looking around the reception hall. It was stunning. The floor tiles were black and white marble, high-lighting the huge black marble fireplace. Lauren walked over to it. It was considerably taller than she was. A fire roared in the massive grate.

"This is lovely," Kelly offered.

"Thanks, we think it's awesome." Jessica returned to the girls, having yelled for Nick and Kim a few more times. "I think I can hear the others coming now. I have to apologise, I can't offer you a soda or anything. The kitchen was only fitted today and we haven't stocked it with food yet," she laughed.

The footprints grew louder on the tiles as Nick and Kim appeared.

"Hey, you guys," Jessica started in true LA style, "I've met some of our neighbours!" Jessica did the introductions as Lauren squirmed. Nicholas Flattery Jnr was considerably better-looking than the photograph she had downloaded from the net to act as her screen saver. Kim, it transpired, was an interior designer, all the way from LA!

"Nick, why don't you show the girls around the house. Kim and I still have some decoration decisions to make."

"Sure," he offered. He didn't seem to be even slightly embarrassed as Jessica and Kim left him with two strangers.

"Say" – He looked at Kelly, and so she saved him the trouble.

"Yes, I'm the one you caught snooping around your house a few months ago. Look, I'm really sorry. We didn't know."

"Ah, forget it. To be honest, I was in a pretty crap mood and it was easy to take it out on you!"

"Why were you in a crap mood?" Lauren asked.

"I had just moved to Ireland, for Christ, sake."

"We're not *that* bad," she offered.

Nick looked at Lauren properly for the first time, "Naw, I guess not," he smiled.

"Can we have a look around your beautiful home?" Kelly asked.

"Sure. That's what you're here for, isn't it?"

He brought them around the massive manor. It was spectacular. The entire building had been restored to its original glory with large chandeliers and rich colours on the walls. The cornices and woodwork had been lovingly restored. The only exception to this faithful restoration work was the basement. Originally the kitchens and sculleries, it had been totally modernised with spotlights in the ceiling and thick shag carpets in what was now obviously a den or TV room.

The kitchen was like something out of a sci-fi movie. It was wall-to-wall chrome. No Belfast sink, no AGA cooker, but the largest three-door fridge that the girls had ever seen.

"My, you have the best of both worlds," Lauren gushed.

"Yeah well, this old style is pretty neat but you need your creature comforts too," Nick explained.

"Tell me about it," Kelly grumbled. "We live in an old house too. In Innishambles, there's always something that needs fixing and no matter how well they're insulated, you still have draughts in old houses!"

"It's a pretty weird name. Innishambles," Nick commented. "I've heard of Yeats's Innishfree and Innishboffin, but never Innishambles. Is it your father's homeland or something?"

The girls burst out laughing. "Dad's from Clontarf in Dublin!" Kelly said.

"No, when Mum and Dad first moved in, almost twenty years ago, the house was in a mess – it was practically derelict," Lauren explained. "Mum once complained to her mother-in-law that it was *in a shambles*, in other words, in a bad state. Edwina, that's our grandmother, misunderstood or misheard and thought that Mum said that the house was Innishambles and so the name stuck."

247

"Has no one told your grandmother in all these years?" Nick asked, amazed.

"Why?" Kelly asked blankly.

"Does your grandmother know the expression in a shambles?"

"Probably not," Lauren reflected. "Or else she just wasn't listening properly which is nothing new."

"She's a bit of a pain," Kelly admitted. The two girls looked at each other and burst out laughing again.

Kelly glanced at her watch. "Omigod, we're going to be killed. We're late, Lauren."

"We'd better go," Lauren agreed unenthusiastically.

Kelly headed back towards the front door. Lauren, however, hovered.

"Are you going to school in Ireland?" she asked Nick.

"Yea, but it's not as bad as I thought it was going to be. It's the American College in Blackrock in Dublin. Most of the kids are American and the syllabus is the same as home."

"Wow. I didn't even know that there was an American school in Dublin. Where are you living while the house is being done up?"

"I'm boarding this term. Next term I'll commute, when we've moved in here."

"Well, if you want any company or any advice on local stuff, just call." Lauren hoped she sounded friendly as opposed to desperate.

"I don't have your number," he said. They had

reached the front reception and there was no sign of Kelly.

"Do you have a pen?" she asked, again trying to keep the enthusiasm out of her voice. He produced one and gave it to her.

Her hand was shaking, she was so nervous. She, Lauren Dalton, was giving her phone number to Nicholas Flattery Jnr.

"Well, bye," she said simply as she ran to join Kelly in the Land- rover.

"See you around," Nick waved from the door of Rathdeen Manor. She's cute, he thought to himself, and she certainly looks game! Perhaps an Irish girlfriend was a good idea. He fingered the piece of paper, now snug in his jeans pocket.

CHAPTER 20

Innishambles was a frenzy of activity over the Halloween mid-term. When the girls were on holidays, there seemed to be twice the washing, twice the cleaning and twice the cooking, not that Saskia minded. She loved having a full house. Robin was a very good baby. Barely two months old, she was beginning to sleep for most of the night. Saskia had even slept in her own bed the previous night. Sadly, however, Richard was based in Dublin for the entire week. He explained that he was working very hard on the relaunch of Rock FM.

"Keep the chin up," he had said to her on the phone. "When this comes off, we'll be very rich! By the way, Sas, I had a meeting in that new hotel, The Belleview, last night. It's magnificent. I'll take you there soon, when the work load eases off, OK?"

Saskia phoned him on Halloween night to say

"Happy Halloween," but he hadn't contacted her since then and that was almost a week ago. Every day she hoped that he would call, but he didn't. Thankfully the girls didn't seem to notice. Kelly was busy getting her horses as fit as possible before they inevitably fattened up over the winter. Tiffany was always doing some project for school or trying to decide what she was going to do after she left school.

Lauren gave Saskia more cause for concern, however. She had fallen hopelessly and totally in love with Nick Flattery Jnr. They had numerous fights over it but Lauren quite simply did what she wanted. The house had been insufferable after Kelly and Lauren visited Rathdeen Manor. Lauren was like an anti-Christ, waiting for the call. Thankfully, however Nick Jnr phoned Lauren two days after her visit to the Manor and they had been more or less inseparable ever since. Saskia was worried about what her thirteen-year-old might be getting up to. Ultimately, however, she knew that she had to trust Lauren.

It was the last day of the Halloween break and Saskia had suggested to her daughters that she take the three of them into Dublin to get their Christmas outfits. Kelly and Tiffany were delighted but Lauren said that she didn't want any new clothes and she didn't want to go into the city.

"That's the last straw, Lauren. You can't spend every bloody day with this boy. You barely know him."

"This is my last day with him before he has to go back to school, Mum," Lauren wailed.

"You'll both be on Christmas holidays in no time. You can see him then, and anyway I really don't think it's healthy spending so much time with this young man."

"I'm not going to town!"

"You will have to discuss this with your father," Saskia threatened.

"Like he cares."

"Lauren Dalton, take that back. If your father isn't here as much as we'd like, it's only because he's working flat out."

"Flat out on top of who?" Lauren quipped.

Saskia smacked her daughter across the face in fury. She had never struck any of her girls in the past but none of them had ever come out with something so terrible before.

Lauren burst out crying. Clutching her red cheek, she ran to her room. Saskia collapsed onto a kitchen chair and also started to weep.

"What in tarnation is going on here?" Tiffany walked into the kitchen some minutes later and found her mother still crying. "I leave you for half an hour and I find you like this? Where's Edu? Where are the others?" She wrapped her arms around Saskia.

"Oh, Tiffany. Am I losing it altogether? I can't seem to control your sister at all. She's just running wild and I'm terrified that she'll get into trouble if she doesn't watch out. I do know about these things, believe me."

"Is it Lauren or Kelly, hardly Robin?"

Saskia looked at her middle daughter and smiled through her tears. "I've just slapped Lauren for the first time in her life."

"Well, she must have deserved it! I'll get the little wagon." Tiffany gave Saskia a reassuring squeeze and headed out into the hall. Sas heard Tiffany yell for her sister and stomp up the stairs.

God, I wish Richard were here, she thought. But he had been little or no support with the girls for as long as she could remember. She missed the Richard of old, the loving, playful man that she married. It seemed as if all the affection and fun was gone. He hadn't tried to have sex with her since she told him that she was pregnant with Robin. It was April when she broke it to him – Christ, that's over six months, she thought in horror. I must do something about that.

"Just what the hell do you think you're playing at?" Tiffany yelled at her sister as she stormed into Lauren's bedroom.

"Oh, Tiff. What have I done? I said the most terrible thing to Mum," Lauren wailed.

"What did you say, in God's name?"

"I suggested that Dad was, was, well that he was messing around."

"Lauren! Where did that come from? Dad? Are you mad? He wouldn't know how!"

"I don't know – it's just that, well, he's around so little these days and Nick asked me were he and Mum still together."

"Dad's around all the time. He's just away this week. God, you have a vivid imagination. Look, you have to apologise to Mum. You've really upset her and if you're that freaked out about Dad being away so much, why don't you give him a phone call? Tell him you miss him."

Lauren still felt awful but she cheered up at her sister's suggestion. "Yea, you're right. Maybe I'll even visit *his tower*!" she managed a chuckle.

Tiffany burst out laughing. They thought the name Rock Tower was "totally pathetic". It was fairly cool having a Dad who owned a radio station. It was just a pity it wasn't one of the *good* ones, but calling the building after the radio station was fairly naff, they thought.

"That's the spirit, Lauren. First, though, go and apologise to Mum."

Edu lay on her bed feeling absolutely appalling. She was now in no doubt that she was pregnant. Three tests had proved positive and from the amount of puking that she was doing, she didn't need to be a rocket scientist to figure it out. Sadly for her, however, the vomiting was not restricted to the mornings. She felt ill practically all of the time and she had no energy.

Edu knew Saskia was beginning to get fed up with her and that was saying something, because Sas was usually so laid back. The au pair was treated like another member of the family. Over the last few weeks, however, she had spent so much of her time in bed that Saskia had to yell up the stairs just to get her down to the kitchen in the mornings. Originally, Edu told Saskia that she had some sort of tummy bug. After a few weeks, however, she had to say she was better because Saskia was beginning to talk about getting a doctor to have a look at her.

It would all be worth it in the end, Edu reflected. She would say nothing until after Christmas and then it could be her New Year surprise for Richard. She was going to have his baby. This morning, lying on her bed she pushed away thoughts of Barney and the fact that he was most likely the real father. Nobody need ever know that.

"Mummy, I'm so very very sorry. I'm a silly eejit and I don't deserve a mum as terrific as you." Lauren came rushing into the kitchen and into Saskia's arms.

"Hush, child. It's OK. I'm not such a wonderful mother. I'm so sorry I hit you."

"I deserved it."

"No. No child of mine ever deserves to be hit," Saskia argued as she hugged Lauren and stroked her hair.

Tiffany walked into the kitchen.

"Peace!" she smiled. "Mum, I've been talking to Kelly. We're all happy to delay going to Dublin for a shopping spree until the Christmas holidays. That's if it's OK with you."

"Yes, I think that's a good idea," Saskia conceded. "Let's all just take it easy today and do absolutely nothing."

"Is it OK if I do nothing with Nick?" Lauren asked sheepishly from under her mother's embrace.

"Will you never learn?" Saskia sighed. "Yes, it's OK."

Lauren didn't need to be told twice. She kissed her mother on the cheek. "Oh, thank you, thank you. You're the best mum in the world," and she was off to grab her coat.

"Mind my peacocks!" Saskia yelled as Lauren tore out through the conservatory and the doors carrying the precious glass designs slammed shut behind her.

"No, Mum, she'll never learn," Tiffany laughed. "What are you going to do this afternoon, now that we're not going to town? I hope you're not going to do housework. You look a little tired."

"No, pet. I think I'll go for a nice walk while Edu takes Robin. Where is that girl? She really is getting slack."

"I'll bring Robin up to her," Tiffany offered. "You take your walk but don't tire yourself out."

"I'm not tired from lack of sleep. Robin is being an angel and sleeping through the night. It's just –" she paused.

"What's wrong, Mum?"

Saskia shook herself as if she had been woken from a daydream. She regained her composure in front of her daughter and pasted on her *everything is fine* face. She smiled at Tiffany.

"Absolutely nothing, pet. I'm fine. Thank you for taking the baby to Edu. I'm going for a bracing walk."

Out in the fields of Innishambles, Saskia was able to let her mind wander. She had taken Dudley and Dexter for company. Inevitably Woody trundled along too, even though some of the terrain was tough and he couldn't manage the walls without Saskia's help.

All the trees had been stripped bare over the last few weeks and the land had become barren and hard for winter. The day was dark and the clouds looked menacing. I'm glad we didn't go to Dublin, Saskia thought. She hated driving in bad rain and it looked like it might pour any minute. Wrapped up in her thermal-lined puffa jacket, Saskia didn't mind if it rained while she was out with the dogs. She was prepared for bad weather.

What she hadn't been prepared for, however, was Lauren's comment earlier. Lauren had insisted that it meant nothing and that she was just blabbing off, but Saskia couldn't let it go. Forced to face the issue, Saskia knew that there was something not right between herself and Richard. Yes, he was working hard and that explained his need to stay in Rock Tower. He was under enormous pressure having purchased the building personally and now trying to get retail and corporate tenants to fill it, but there was more than work pressure on Richard's shoulders.

As Saskia crossed the fields and wandered aimlessly towards her little forest, she realised that she and Richard hadn't had any time alone together in months. The girls were always around or, worse again, his bloody mother would arrive unannounced. Any moments that they had managed to grab together, they seemed to end up fighting. She pondered on this and on Richard's strange distance for hours before she realised that she was in fact walking around in large circles. Saskia headed down the valley purposefully towards the little river. Her mind dragged her back to her family. Lauren's comment about Richard being with another woman, had struck her like a bolt of lightning. It was as if somebody had suddenly shaken her into reality, she thought in horror.

"My God, is it possible?" she asked herself in disbelief. It would explain why he never pushed her for sex any more. It would also justify why he stayed in Dublin so much recently. Most of all it would explain why they had been growing apart for the last year or more. Richard always had an eye for the ladies but Saskia never thought it went any further than the odd flirt. He and Sue Parker had disappeared for twenty minutes at their Christmas party the year before last, for example, but she never thought any more about it, considering they came straight back. Richard wouldn't do anything crazy with Sas and Dave Parker in the other room. Would he?

"It's just not possible!" she chided herself out loud.

"Anything is possible," a voice answered her.

Saskia jumped at the sound of another person.

"Oh my, I didn't see you there." In truth, Saskia hadn't even realised that she had arrived down to the river. A man stood facing her from the other side of the River More.

He looked amused at her discomfort.

"You must have been deep in thought, because I've been standing here admiring the scenery for the last twenty minutes. I thought you were actually walking over to me!" He smiled at her.

"Oh no, no, I was just out for a walk. I needed some fresh air."

"Well, it doesn't get much fresher than this," he added just as a cold blast of wind whistled down the river between them and caused Saskia to wrap her arms around her body.

She snuggled deeper into the warmth of her puffa. "Yes, it's getting pretty windy all right. I think it's going to get worse."

He smiled. "It's true what they say – come to Ireland and talk about the weather."

"And if you don't like it, just wait a few minutes. It'll change," Saskia added.

He burst out laughing, revealing the most spectacular set of teeth Saskia had ever seen. They were whiter than his shining eyes and more perfect than the ones in toothpaste commercials.

"Well," he continued from the other side of the river, "I'm Nicolas. I'm going to be living here soon." He gestured in the general direction of Rathdeen Manor.

"You're Nicolas Flattery!"

"Eh, yes."

"Oh, I'm Saskia Dalton, your neighbour. I live back that way in Innishambles. I'm your nearest neighbour!"

"Well, it's nice to meet you, neighbour. Sorry I can't shake your hand."

Saskia thought he was a lovely-looking man but not at all like the guy from the film *Freedom*.

"If we walk this way, there are little stepping stones further down the river about a hundred and fifty yards down here," she gestured.

"Sounds good to me."

As they arrived at their stepping stones, Saskia looked over to him and asked, "Do you want to cross over here or will I go over there?"

"You're most familiar with those stepping stones – in fact, are you sure they're safe?" He looked concerned.

"Nothing to it, when you're used to them," she added as she hopped over them like a teenager. The dogs just bounded through the freezing water, even Woody.

He reached out his hand to help her across the last couple. Then he took her hand to his lips.

"What an enchanting way to meet my closest neighbour!" He kissed her hand in an old-fashioned gesture.

Saskia laughed. "Delighted to meet you too," she

curtseyed. "Welcome to Ballymore." They began to walk companionably along the riverside.

"You said your name is Saskia?"

"That's right."

"I've never heard that name before. Is it Gaelic?"

"No, it's Dutch actually. The only other Saskia I know is connected with Rembrandt the artist. You know him?"

"Yes."

"Well, his wife was a Saskia, although she was no oil painting, if you'll pardon the pun!"

Nicolas looked at her and laughed.

"You, on the other hand, are a masterpiece."

Saskia was embarrassed at his compliment and so she changed the subject.

"Have you moved in yet?"

"Gawd no. It's still a hell of a mess up there I'm afraid, but we'll be in by Christmas I hope."

"It must be a huge move. I mean, well, that is to say . . ." she faltered, feeling a little awkward. She glanced up at him. "Well, it's just that I know who you are obviously, and so I know you're moving from LA."

"I get the feeling that in Ballymore everybody would know my life story whether or not I was in the movie business."

Saskia laughed, "Well, that's true. There are no secrets in Ballymore."

"None?" he had stopped and was staring at her profoundly, one eyebrow slightly raised.

261

"What do you mean?" Saskia asked.

"Well, it's just that you looked like you were trying to unravel a few yourself when we bumped into each other."

Saskia was pulled back to reality with a thud. Her face must have shown it because Nicolas Flattery immediately apologised and changed the subject. He began asking her about the locality and Innishambles. That led them on to her children and her new baby. He seemed genuinely interested.

"I can't believe you have a child as old as eighteen," he exclaimed "You look too young."

"I certainly don't feel it," she sighed. "Not young enough to have a new baby anyway."

"I would have loved more kids," he spoke openly. "Jessica, that's my wife, well . . . let's just say that it wasn't possible."

"Oh, I'm sorry."

Nicolas shook himself, before his mood went deeper.

"Say, could I see your baby?"

"Of course," Saskia was thrilled that somebody should show so much interest in her and her baby. "Why don't you come up to the house now? I can introduce you to everybody. Who knows, you might even meet your son up here. He and one of my girls have become inseparable, but that's another story." Saskia was not willing to discuss her misgivings about Nick Flattery Jnr's intentions towards Lauren just yet. "There's just one problem." She hesitated and looked at him.

"What's wrong?"

"Well, you're going to have to risk the little stepping stones. Do you think you're up to it?"

He laughed. "Let's risk it!"

When Tiffany heard the dogs scampering into the scullery she called out to her mother.

"That was one heck of a walk. You've been gone hours." She jumped as she saw a tall dark stranger walk in behind her mother. "Oh."

"Tiffany," Saskia introduced them, "this is our new neighbour, Nicolas Flattery."

"Hi, welcome. Your house is coming on really fast now. I guess you'll be moving in soon."

Nicolas spoke to Tiffany with the same calm attentive manner that he did with Saskia. Half an hour later they were still sitting in the kitchen drinking tea when Kelly arrived in. Saskia had fetched Robin from Edu, who promptly went back to bed, complaining of period pains. She didn't even come downstairs to meet the movie star.

Nicolas spent the entire visit holding Robin and walking the kitchen with her. The baby was as enchanted by his soft voice and eyes as the other girls were.

"Would you like to stay for dinner, Nicolas?" Saskia asked eventually.

"Oh no, I think I should be going."

Kelly and Tiffany tried to convince him to stay but he politely declined.

"Well, at least let me drive you home. It looks like we were right about the weather." Saskia peered out at the dark evening and saw hailstones beginning to tap insistently at the window panes.

"I would appreciate that, if it's not too much trouble. It's just that it seems to have gone very dark and I don't think I could manage those stepping stones without being able to see them!"

"No problem," Saskia said willingly.

"We can take Robin for the spin," Nicolas added enthusiastically.

"Gosh, you really have got it bad, haven't you?" Kelly teased. "Tell you what, we'll stick you on the baby-sitting rota if you like!"

Everybody laughed, especially Nicolas. "I'd love that and I would baby-sit this little lady any time as long as she doesn't – well, use her nappy." He reluctantly handed Robin back to Kelly.

That night, as Saskia was getting ready for yet another night alone in bed, her mind was on Nicolas Flattery, not Richard Dalton. As usual, her husband had not phoned. This evening, however, for the first time Saskia didn't care. Her afternoon and evening had been filled by another man. Nicolas was the most charming neighbour any family could have.

She couldn't believe how they had talked so amiably, considering they had never met before. It was like they were old friends. He seemed genuinely interested in every little thing she had to say and he talked openly and candidly about his own life. The time had flown by. When she drove him home they talked again for a while in the old Landrover before he got out. It was only when she got home that she realised she had been gone for over an hour. The car journey should have taken about five minutes.

Tiffany was the first to comment to her mother.

"Mum, I can't believe you brought Nicolas Flattery home! I mean *the* Nicolas Flattery. He's famous and you didn't even warn us."

"You know that didn't even occur to me. He just seems so, so normal!" Saskia tried to defend her actions.

She didn't see anything sinister about spending the time with Nicolas either. It was only when Lauren arrived home and heard about his stay in the house that she teased her mum.

Lauren had obviously forgotten about her little tiff with Sas that morning and so she continued in her usual carefree manner.

"Be careful, he's a fine thing, Mum, and I don't think there's any love lost between him and Jessica Bell."

"Lauren, how can you say such things?"

"Well, they're going to be sleeping in different rooms. Nick was showing me around the house," she explained, "and they have different bedrooms, that's all."

Saskia was so distracted that she didn't even ask Lauren what she was doing upstairs in Rathdeen Manor.

Nor had she bothered to inform her girls that she was meeting Nicolas Flattery again the following day.

CHAPTER 21

On the first morning back to school after the Halloween break, Saskia woke as giddy as a schoolgirl. She roused her three elder daughters to strains of "Santa Claus is Comin' to Town" and showered to her own special version of "Singing in the Rain".

She was in such surprisingly good form that Kelly commented,

"Well, you obviously got enough sleep last night, Mum."

"Yes, angel, it's a wonderful morning. The sky is clear blue and all is well with the world."

"What drugs are you on?" Lauren snarled over her Special K.

"The drug of life! Come on, girls, put a spring in your step. Mid-term is over. You've got to go back to school so you may as well do it with a smile on your faces. It's time we got going." Saskia left the kitchen to wake Edu.

"What the hell's got into her?" Lauren asked again.

"I don't know, but it's great to see the old mum back," Kelly sighed.

"Yeah, she has been a bit down lately," Tiffany agreed. "Now come on, you lot. Here's your packed lunches. We're going to be late as usual."

With the girls safely deposited at Mount Eden, Saskia whizzed home to Innishambles.

She walked straight into Edu who was shuffling up the stairs in her dressing-gown and big fluffy slippers, holding a cup of tea in one hand and Robin in the other arm.

"Honestly, Edu, I don't know what's got into you lately. You're like an old granny," Saskia complained.

"I am tired."

"You went to bed at eight o'clock last night! Is there something you're not telling me? Are you sick? Do you want me to get the doctor?"

"No, no. Actually I'm fine. I just didn't sleep zat well. Sorry."

"Well, Edu, I know the cure for that. You've been moping around this house for weeks. It's a glorious day, so what you need to do is get the two of you dressed and head out with the pram for a good old countryside walk."

Edu looked decidedly unenthusiastic.

"It's the only way you'll get out of a visit to the doctor," Saskia continued. "If you don't have enough energy to go for a simple walk, you definitely need to see a doctor!"

The choice was simple. Edu was not ready for a medical.

"We would love a walk, wouldn't we, Robin?" she looked at her little charge and then smiled weakly at Saskia.

"I'm delighted to hear it and I think Dudley, Dexter and Woody would like the exercise too. They can chaperone you."

Back in the privacy of her bedroom, Edu cursed Saskia.

"Just you wait, Mrs Dalton. Are you in for ze shock of your life!" She stared at her reflection and patted her still flat stomach. "Just you wait."

Saskia had also returned to her bedroom. It was just over two months since she gave birth to Robin and she had got a clean bill of health at her six-week check-up. Looking at her reflection now, however, she was surprised to see her favourite trousers looking baggy and shapeless on her.

During the mid-term, she had pulled out all her old slim-fit clothes, the ones that she had been forced to put into storage six months earlier, as her pregnant belly grew and grew. It was a great source of delight and surprise to her that they all fitted so well already. She had assumed that it would take three or four months to get back into shape but the weight seemed to have fallen off her.

"All the worrying," she commented to her reflection. Saskia thought about Richard. For the first time, she felt a slight pang of guilt about spending the afternoon with Nicolas Flattery. Am I being unfaithful? she wondered. She picked up the phone on her bedside table and dialled Richard's office.

"Hello, Rock Tower." Denise answered the phone.

Saskia already knew her from previous phone conversations. "Hi, Denise, It's Saskia. Is Richard there?"

"Hi, Sas. I'll put you through to Elizabeth."

"Good morning, Richard Dalton's office," a much less friendly and more serious voice clicked on the line, before it even had a chance to ring.

"Hi, Elizabeth. It's Saskia here. Is Richard there?"

There was a pause, "Eh, hi, Sas. I'll just see."

When he answered the phone, Saskia knew that she was on one of those speakerphones. He knew that she hated them.

"Hello, Saskia, what's up?"

"Nothing, Richard. It's just been over a week since we've spoken. I thought it would be a good idea to touch base and to remind you that you have a wife and kids."

He picked up the handset instantly. She heard him talk to Liz, so she *had* been in the room.

"OK, Liz, you can leave that." Then he turned his attention to Saskia and talked into the phone.

"Jesus, Saskia, don't get all bitchy on me now. You know that I'm working flat out on this relaunch."

Saskia winced when she heard the expression *flat*

out. She remembered Lauren's words, "Flat out on who?" She shook herself out of it. Get interested in his world, she reminded herself.

"How is it going?"

"Well, it's pretty hectic, to be honest. As you know the radio station has moved into Rock Tower, but there was some technical problem and the damn thing went down yesterday."

"As in Off Air?" Saskia asked appalled.

"Yep, the radio consultants reckon it will take up to three weeks to make up for the lost listeners."

"Surely not! How long were you off air?"

"Only twenty minutes, but that's not the point. Ninety-nine per cent of our listeners will have switched stations when we went down and now we have to get them to switch back again. Some will inevitably stay listening to their new choice of radio station."

"Bummer."

"Yeah, it really is. The only consolation is that the research for next month's new listenership figures is already completed. So this won't jeopardise that."

"Poor Richard. You didn't need that."

"I do have some good news though. Levels three and four in the Tower?"

"The retail units?"

"Yeah. You'll never guess who I've got in as a tenant."

"Who?"

"Dave Parker! He's taking all of level three."

"The entire floor? My God, it'll be a huge department store."

"I never thought he'd take the whole storey. There is a slight eggs- in-one-basket feeling to it, but damn it, I need the income."

"What about the apartments? Any takers on any of them yet?"

"Even better news there. You know Megazone, the internet company?"

"Yes, Richard, even I know them. They're one of the bigger internet companies. I think you call them search engines."

"I'm impressed, Sas. Well, they've just moved into their new head office, about five hundred yards down the road from us here and so they have rented all the apartments as a job lot for the senior staff."

"Richard, are you telling me that all the apartments are let?"

"That's exactly what I'm saying."

"That's fantastic."

"All I need to do now is rent out level four and the building is fully occupied and one hundred per cent owned by yours truly."

"Well, you and the banks, but congratulations."

Richard ignored her clarification. "The best part is I have the nicest office in Dublin practically rent-free!"

"I must come up and see it soon."

"Oh, Saskia. That's not such a good idea. We're working all the hours we can here. You'd only be in the way." His words stung her much more than he realised. "How are my girls?" he continued.

"Everybody is fine. Edu is being a bit of a pain in the neck recently. Honestly, she's about as useful as a rubber crutch these days. I don't know what's wrong with her, Richard."

"Look, Saskia, I have to go," Richard didn't want to talk about his au pair.

"Oh, OK. By the way I have one bit of interesting news. I met Nicolas Flattery yesterday. He seems very nice."

"Great. Befriend that guy, Sas. God knows when he could come in useful. Better still. Invite him over to dinner with his drop-dead gorgeous wife. We'll have the Parkers too. Maybe over Christmas. That's only around the corner. Gotta go, honey." He hung up before she could even say that she was meeting him that very day.

"Bye," she said to the dialling tone.

Saskia gazed out her bedroom window and saw Edu pushing Robin's pram down the gravel driveway with the dogs in tow. The little group were about as energetic as a used Duracell. She opened her window in frustration.

"Put some effort into it, Edu!" Saskia yelled.

The au pair looked over her shoulder up at the open window and waved indifferently.

"That's it. We have to do something about that girl," she promised herself out loud for the hundredth time.

Saskia went back to her wardrobe. Feeling the large amount of room between her waist and the waistband of her trousers, she began to toy with the idea of her really old jeans, the ones that hadn't fitted her for years. She began digging through the stuff at the bottom of her wardrobe. This was where she threw clothes that she didn't know what to do with.

Usually Saskia put her summer clothes in a big box for the winter and vice versa, but the bottom of the wardrobe was no man's land. Even the girls had stopped looking for outfits there. First she pulled out some old tops with massive shoulder pads. Then she pulled out a couple of stray ankle warmers. Finally she got to the stuff that she was looking for, clothes that she really loved, but had grown too large around the rear for.

"Hello, stranger," she greeted a pair of faded denim jeans. The cotton was soft from wearing and they were full of creases, having been squashed at the bottom of so much junk for many years. Saskia pulled them free from the rest and had a good look at them.

"I'd never fit into those, would I?" she asked herself.

She pulled off her trousers and slipped into the old favourites. It was like a hand fitting into a glove. They fitted her perfectly.

She stood in front of her mirror in wonder. She looked positively skinny.

"Thank you, God," she laughed as she pulled them down again to have a look at the size on the label. It was at the back. Sitting on her bed with her old jeans around her ankles, she attempted to read the label upside down and back to front.

"It's an eight. I can't believe it but they really say eight. OK, so it's an American eight which means ten here but I, Saskia Dalton, have returned to my old size eight jeans." She was thrilled.

The phone rang beside her.

"Hello," she answered it cheerfully, trousers still around her ankles.

"Saskia?"

"Yes, hi, Nicolas," she recognised his soft mid-Atlantic tone instantly.

"Hi, I can't believe it's you. You sound so young on the phone. I thought you were one of your daughters."

"Thanks. No, they're all at school this morning. How are you? You're still on for your tour of Ballymore today, aren't you?" A note of concern entered her voice.

"Oh, yes, absolutely. I've been looking forward to it. It's just, well, I was wondering if you would like to take Robin with us, or are you tired of having her around you all the time?"

"Oh, Nicolas, that's so sweet. No, I'd be happy to take her with us only she's just gone out for a walk with Edu."

"Oh well, some other time. Hey, are you nearly ready?" He changed the subject. "I'm in the car. Sorry, I think I'm a little early," he added sheepishly.

"*A little*? I wasn't expecting you for at least another hour!"

"Oops! Look, don't worry. I can go over to the house and check in with Kevin to see how they're getting on today. I'll collect you at one o'clock as planned."

"No, Nicolas. I'm ready. I mean," she didn't want to sound too enthusiastic, "I'm just wearing an old pair of jeans and a jumper. That's OK, isn't it?"

"You're asking me?" he laughed and so did she.

"OK, I'll be there in about fifteen minutes. See you then."

"Bye," she hung up and panicked.

Saskia pulled up her size eights and began to tear through her jumpers.

"Typical," she fumed. "A chest full of jumpers and nothing to wear."

She began to rifle through Richard's clothes and found the navy Tricot Marine that he had got from Edwina the previous Christmas. She pulled it over her tussled hair as she rushed back to the mirror. It actually looked great. As usual, however, her hair was a fiasco. Saskia had got up especially early that morning to wash it and have enough time to blow dry it properly, but all the rushing and changing had made it look like an unmade bed again.

She ran into her en suite and attacked the hair with a comb. "It's no good," she wailed. Nothing was going to persuade it to stay in place. The truth was that her hair needed a good cut. It hadn't been seen to in months and it was only now that she realised it had grown a good three inches. Saskia flew out of her room into

Kelly's. She had the longest hair in Innishambles and so she had any number of baubles, go-gos and squidgeys for her hair.

Saskia threw open Kelly's top drawer but stopped dead in her tracks when she saw the box of cigarettes.

"Kelly," she shouted at the empty room, "we need to have a serious chat!" Then she continued her rummage for a suitable tieback.

"A navy go-go, that's what I need," she told herself but then to her horror the doorbell rang. Without Dudley and Dexter in the house, she didn't get her usual thirty-second warning that somebody was on their way up the drive.

"Yikes," she squealed as she threw all her hair in the first go-go she touched. She ran down the stairs like a teenager and threw the door open.

"Wow," Nicolas Flattery smiled.

"What?" she asked sheepishly.

"You look amazing, Saskia."

"Me? I'm an absolute mess!" but she smiled at him. "I still have to find a pair of socks and I have no make-up on yet. Come in, sit down. I won't be a minute."

She turned to fly back up the stairs again, but he was faster than her and he caught hold of her hand, pulling her back.

"Saskia," he said softly, "don't put on any make-up. You're beautiful." His eyes were so intense, she felt a shiver tingle through her. Was he looking at her face or into her very soul?

"OK," she whispered and she slowly walked back upstairs to get a pair of socks.

The panic she felt prior to his arrival had dissolved into thin air. Now she felt calm and utterly comfortable.

"I am sorry that I'm so early," he shouted up the stairs at her.

"No problem," she yelled back as she stole a pair of Kelly's Lacoste navy socks.

"Where are we going?" he asked.

She stopped. "Gosh, I don't know. What would you like to see first?"

"Well, we could wander around the land. You know I've just bought over fifty acres and I haven't even seen it yet?"

"That's dreadful," she called. "We have about the same and I must admit, there's a lot that I haven't been around for a long time. Let's start with a long walk. Then I can take you for lunch in The Hitching Post and we can take it from there."

"That sounds perfect."

She came back downstairs and found him in the study.

"I'm sorry. I didn't even offer you a cup of coffee or anything. Have you just driven down from Dublin?"

"Yes, but I had one of those traditional Irish breakfasts – awesome! I don't think I'll have to eat for another week."

Saskia laughed at him. He stared at her as if transfixed by her face. She got uncomfortable and shifted from foot to foot. Nicolas snapped out of his daze and looked around the study.

"This is a beautiful room. Did you use interior designers?"

"God no," she guffawed, "the paint was probably going cheap! Everything that happened in Innishambles more or less happened by accident, Nicolas." With that, the computer monitor blinked into life. Richard had adjusted it so that it switched on automatically if there was any motion anywhere near it. Up sprang the screen saver of Nick Jnr's face. They both saw it at the same instant. Saskia was so embarrassed she rushed over to switch the thing off but it was too late.

"What is that doing there?" he asked.

"Oh God, Nicolas. I'm afraid my daughter Lauren is in love with your Nick."

"Lucky Nick."

They looked at each other for a brief moment and then Saskia turned.

"If we're going to walk out in the wilds, I think I'm going to wear wellies! What are you wearing on your feet?"

"Wellies? What are you talking about? I'm wearing a pair of trainers."

"That's the first time I've really heard you speak with an American twang! I call them wellies, you probably call them galoshes."

Saskia took Nicolas out to their scullery where they had a massive selection of wellingtons and Barbour

278

jackets. They each found suitable footwear and rainwear.

"The weather is so mild. Are you sure we really need these?" Nicolas asked as he examined his jacket.

"Do you remember our conversation about the Irish weather yesterday?"

"Yea, I guess. It's very changeable. OK, we're ready. Let's go!"

Saskia took Nicolas out to her walled garden and on to the stables.

"Who are these guys?" he asked.

"This is Polly and this is Mooner. They belong to Kelly."

"Did you hear what I want to do with Rathdeen Manor yet?"

"Gosh, I just thought you were going to live there."

"Well yes, there is that. I also want to make it an animal refuge." He hesitated.

"Nicolas, that's wonderful. What an amazing thing to do!"

"You approve?"

"Absolutely. Why wouldn't I?"

"Well, I was a little worried that our neighbours might not like the idea of a home for homeless animals right beside them."

"Nonsense. It's the nicest thing I've ever heard of. The girls will be beside themselves, that is if I'm allowed to tell them yet. Am I or is it still confidential?"

"No, no. Tell who you want. We're having the stables built as soon as the Manor is finished. We'll also get proper kennels and the land will need to be fenced off professionally. Did you know that deer can jump a twelve-foot fence?"

"Deer?"

"Eh, yes. They're culling them in England so I want to save them too."

"Nicolas, you're a big softie."

"I'm just relieved that you don't mind."

"No, I don't mind. In fact I think it's a very noble thing to do. You're an amazing man, Nicolas Flattery."

"You're the one who's amazing, Saskia."

She blushed when she heard what he said and so she moved away, changing the subject.

"You know my daughters think I'm very casual about the fact that you're a world-famous movie star."

Nicolas burst out laughing, "I wouldn't go that far!"

"Well, you are. We all knew exactly who you were before you even moved to Ireland."

"Really?"

"Yep, What's it like being world famous?"

He laughed again. "Well, firstly I'm not *world famous*. I'm sure that they've never heard of me anywhere in Asia or Oz or anywhere else in Europe for that matter. Like, I'm not Stallone famous! *Freedom* has done fairly well here and in England but that's mainly because the movie is about the north of Ireland. It did pretty well in the States too because there are so many Irish-Americans, but I wouldn't be famous by LA standards."

"Oh, sorry!"

"Don't be. To be honest, the taste I've had of fame, which I must stress has only been a small taste, nonetheless was enough to put me off it for ever."

"Why?" Saskia asked genuinely amazed.

He tried to explain. "If you're famous, people are happy to walk up to you like they know you and comment on your life. It's very intrusive. Don't get me wrong. I like the money, but the fame thing? It's definitely overrated."

"Gosh, I never would have thought."

"Well, actually, that's one of the reasons we have moved to Ireland. The Irish are so good at ignoring famous people."

Saskia was embarrassed. "I'm sorry. I shouldn't have mentioned it."

"Not you, Saskia. I'm happy to discuss it with you."

He gave her one of those deep penetrative looks again, the ones that made her very uncomfortable.

"Come on," she said, changing the subject again. "We have a lot of land to cover before lunch."

CHAPTER 22

It was Lauren who said that she was dreading going back to school after the Halloween break and that she would love a little more time off. Nick didn't need much encouragement, however. He suggested wagging instantly.

"What's wagging?" she had asked.

"Not going to school," he explained

"Oh, you mean mitching!" Then they hatched their plan.

It was surprisingly easy. Saskia dropped the three girls at the gate of Mount Eden as usual. They each went their separate ways, only Lauren went to the bicycle shed where she swapped her school uniform for a pair of jeans and her sexiest top. Over her trousers, she pulled her Mount Eden tracksuit and her long coat. Lauren looked innocent enough walking out of the school gates. Girls often ran back to their Mummy's

Mercs or Daddy's BMWs to retrieve forgotten lunches or gym bags.

Then, she walked further and further away from the school gates until she was clear of all the parents' cars. When she felt there was a sufficient distance between her and the school she reached down and pulled her tracksuit bottoms up above her knees. When Lauren stood up straight again, she just looked like a girl in jeans and a long coat.

Exhilarated at the idea of getting away with it and terrified by the possibility of still getting caught, she half-skipped, half-ran to the bus stop for the Dublin bus. Luckily, she didn't have to wait long for the next one to arrive. The bus driver didn't bat an eyelid. Safe, down the back of the bus, where nobody could see her, she peeled off her tracksuit bottoms and shoved them into her schoolbag.

She was on her way to Dublin to meet her boyfriend as her classmates were on their way into double biology.

It was considerably easier for Nick to mitch. The American College was right beside the suburb of Blackrock in Dublin and the students didn't have school uniforms. They usually wore jeans and sweatshirts.

Half of the students were boarders and half day-students, sons and daughters of diplomats and American businessmen living in Dublin. The boarders were given plenty of freedom. They often went into Blackrock for breakfast if they didn't like what was on offer in their own canteen. The American College was run more like a university than a secondary-level school. As long as the fees were paid, the principal didn't really mind what went on.

As arranged, Nick was in Café Java at eleven o'clock. He had just sat down to have a cup of coffee and a bagel when Lauren arrived, wide-eyed and breathless.

"Hi," she smiled conspiratorially.

"Good morning," Nick mumbled. "Sorry, I'm not really awake yet."

"My God, are you only just up? I've been on the go for ages!"

"You sound out of breath. Why?"

"Nick. I've just run down the full length of Mount Merrion Avenue. I was so terrified of being seen by one of Dad's or Mum's friends."

"Why?"

"Why? Because the bloody bus doesn't come through Blackrock. It goes into Dublin on the dual carriageway."

"Oh."

"What about you?" She changed the subject. "Did you have any difficulty leaving school?"

He looked at her in slight bewilderment. "No. We come and go as we please."

"Won't your teacher be cross?" she asked amazed.

"Naw, I'll just tell him that I had a doctor's appointment."

"Will he not need a certificate?"

"Gee, Lauren, I'll just tell him that I forgot to ask for one. Easy."

"Our teachers wouldn't accept that."

"Yea, well, your school sounds more like a prison than a school."

"Compared to yours, I suppose it is!"

"You wanna coffee?"

Lauren looked around the busy coffee shop nervously. It suddenly occurred to her that she was still in public and could easily be seen by any of her mother's friends. So many of them shopped in Blackrock.

"Let's get out of here, Nick," she suggested.

"Sure, where do you wanna to go?"

"I don't know. Town maybe."

"OK," he paid for his late breakfast and they left. On Lauren's suggestion, they caught the train. Away from the main roads into town, she was less likely to meet anyone who knew her.

As they walked onto O'Connell Street, she had the brainwave.

"How about a movie?" she asked.

"Fine by me," he agreed, "as long as it's not *Freedom*!"

"Saskia, I had no idea it was going to be this beautiful." Nicolas Flattery was awestruck by the view from the highest point on Innishambles land.

They had reached the northernmost tip, next to Frank and Cathy Taylor's house.

"From here, you can see across our little forest, over the top of our house and down into the valley," Saskia explained.

Nicolas craned his neck to see more. He even climbed up onto the wall that separated the Daltons' land from that of the Taylors'.

"I've seen the name Bally in a number of towns in Ireland," he continued. "Do you have any idea where it comes from?"

"Well, some people say Bally is a derivation of the Irish word *baile*, which means town and the more part would be the Irish *mòr*, meaning big," Saskia explained. "That would make this Bigtown!"

Nicolas looked unconvinced. "That can't be right. It is gorgeous but big it ain't."

"OK then," Saskia laughed. "How about if Bally was a derivation of the word valley? That would make sense – big valley."

"That sounds more credible," he agreed, and continued, "What if Bally was a derivation of valley and more was always meant to mean more?"

"What are you getting at?" Saskia asked.

"Well that could make it the valley of more, as in the plentiful valley, the bountiful valley."

Saskia laughed, "Well, if that was right, Ballymore is the valley of more what?"

"More – beauty? Look around you," he enthused. "Or more laughter, or more happiness –"

"Eh, I think you're getting carried away by our clean

air, Nicolas," she laughed. "Too much pure oxygen for you, not like LA."

Nicolas turned his attention back to the panoramic view, "I think I can see the river at the bottom of the valley."

"Well done, I've never seen it!" she said. "In all these years."

"Come up here," he offered her a hand to pull her up.

Standing beside Nicolas on the wall, however, while the view was better, Saskia had to concede that she still couldn't see down to the river.

"I'm too short," she giggled.

"Let me lift you." He didn't give her the opportunity to say no. He turned and lifted her, like lifting a little child up over a crowd to see a parade.

"Nicolas, put me down," she pleaded. "You'll do yourself an injury."

"Saskia, you're as light as a feather. Now tell me first, can you see the River More?"

"My God, actually I can. Now please put me down."

This time he did. He put her down on the wall beside him again.

"You really are very light, Saskia," he smiled at her.

"Well, I'm not used to being carried. I'm usually the one doing the carrying!" She jumped down from the wall and Nicolas followed her.

"How long have you lived here?" he asked.

"It seems like for ever. We've been here for close on

twenty years now. What about you? What will you do? I mean, your business is the movies. So will you come and go as work dictates?"

"The truth is I don't know. I told you about the Refuge yesterday. That has been my life ambition. To see it becoming a reality is awesome."

Saskia was captivated by the animation in his eyes.

"Now that I'm building my dream, I don't really want to leave."

She began to protest, "But you're a movie star –" she cut herself off mid-sentence, remembering what he had said the day before.

He looked at her and laughed. "No, I'm not a movie star! I've done one successful movie. It has made me enough money to build this dream home and enough to live on for a few years. To be honest, I would be very happy if I never had to do another film. What I'd really love to do now is to write!"

"My God, that's a heck of a change. Most of the world wants to get into the film business and you want out."

"Not really. Look at how many broken marriages there are in the business. I don't think many people in LA are truly happy."

"Do you think you could be happy here?"

"Yeah, I'm sure of it."

"What about your son and Jessica?" Saskia knew that she was no longer imagining it. There was a definite change in his mood when she mentioned Jessica.

"Well, we'll see. This is a much healthier environment for Nick to grow up in. He can come and live at home as soon as the house is completed or he can continue to board if he likes. Jessica? Well that's another story," he trailed off.

"Oh, I'm sorry. I didn't mean to pry." She continued, trying to lighten the mood, "Would you like to meet your other neighbours?"

"Who?"

"Come on. Frank and Cathy Taylor are lovely people. This is their house just here!" She clambered back over the wall, into their garden. Nicolas watched her.

"Come on," she urged and so he did.

"What will we do now?" Lauren asked, slightly demoralised. The new James Bond movie had been fun but she could have seen it any Friday or Saturday night without risking mitching off school to do it.

"Jeez, Lauren, I don't know. I mean this is your city. You should have a better idea than me," Nick snapped back. He obviously felt the same way she did.

This was not exactly Thelma and Louise stuff as they strolled down O'Connell Street aimlessly together.

"Are you ready for lunch yet?" she asked, clasping at straws.

"Hey, good job," Nick perked up. "Let's go to a pub and get a big burger and fries."

"OK," Lauren smiled, glad that he was cheering up.

"How about here?" he asked as they passed the Gresham Hotel.

"It's not really a pub," she laughed, "but it will have nice food I'm sure. Come on." She affectionately pulled him by the sleeve and they strolled in together.

Nicolas carried himself with such ease and sophistication that he inspired Lauren to do the same. She strolled straight up to the restaurant door and threw it open. Nick followed her. The maitre d' looked down his nose at her.

"Yes?" he enquired in a condescending voice when he saw the two teenagers clad in jeans walk into his restaurant.

"Table for two, buddy," she requested in a mock American accent. "And step on it, we're pushed for time."

"Does madam have a reservation?" he asked, peering down at his time sheet for the day on the rostrum next to him.

"I think you'll find she does, dude," Nick interrupted, putting a twenty-pound note on his precious time sheet.

"Ah, yes here it is," he smiled at his two young VIPs. Lauren didn't even see where he put the money, it disappeared so fast.

They were ushered to a little snug at the back of the restaurant instantly.

"What can I say? Money talks in every country in the world," Nick commented dryly.

"Yeah, isn't it great!" Lauren laughed.

He studied her face for a second and then laughed too. "Yeah, what the heck! OK, what do you want to drink?"

Drink hadn't even occurred to Lauren, but spurred on by Nick's free spirit she thought about it.

"How about a vodka and tonic? You can't smell that from your breath," she suggested.

"Good thinking, Batgirl," Nick answered. He had been thinking about having a beer, but he was not going to be outdone by his guest and so when the girl came to take their order, he requested two double vodka and tonics with their burgers and chips. The waitress, barely older than them, was foreign and didn't bat an eyelid at the request for alcohol from her young clients. She simply walked away and returned presently with their orders.

"Cheers," Nick raised his glass. "To happy days."

"To happy days," Lauren agreed, raising her glass to meet his.

After the popcorn in the cinema, the two were thirsty and they were quickly on their second vodkas. Thankfully Lauren put in the order and so she made them regular as opposed to doubles. She was nonetheless feeling light-headed and decidedly giddy.

They wolfed down their food as only teenagers can and then paused for a rest.

"Do you think you're getting settled in Ireland now?" she asked.

"Well, it is getting better as time goes by. But my Gawd, the weather! Does the sun ever shine?"

"Oh Nick, this is the winter. It will get better in June and July."

"June and July? Jeez, that's nothing. In LA we have sun over eleven months of the year."

"Yea, well in Ireland we have rain over eleven months of the year!" She tried to make a joke but it sounded funnier in her mind than out loud.

"How about another drink?" he smiled.

"OK," she giggled, definitely feeling a little light-headed.

"What about you? Do you think you'll live in Ireland all your life, like after college?" he asked having put in another order for drink.

"Well, to be honest I hadn't really thought about it. I don't know what I want to do with my life yet," she answered truthfully.

"I'm gonna direct movies," Nick said proudly. "It's the directors that have all the real power in Hollywood, not the actors." Lauren looked at him, fascinated, and so he continued. "The actors have all the headaches, finding the right roles, getting the right pay deals. It's so bogus! They also have all the bullshit that goes along with stardom. Directors enjoy a practically anonymous life."

"I thought fame was one of the most attractive parts of the Hollywood thing."

"Only to the uninitiated," Nick explained. "Do you have any idea how many nutters are out there? Even Dad has had problems. Some fruitcake decided that she was in love with Dad. She even went through our garbage! It was totally gross, man." Nick's accent became stronger the more he drank. He obviously got upset talking about the stalker.

"We don't have to talk about this if you don't want to," she tried to calm him.

"Naw, it's OK. It might help you understand our totally weird family a little more."

"I don't think you're weird," she tried.

"If you don't, that's only because you don't know us well enough yet."

"Nick, you're very hard on yourself."

"Do you have any cigarettes?"

Relaxed from the amount of vodka in her system, Lauren didn't even flinch as she extracted a box of Camel from her schoolbag. She didn't usually smoke Camel but she thought they looked cool and so she had bought them from the little sweetshop beside Mount Eden that was infamous for selling cigarettes to the girls.

Nick lit up and took a deep drag of the nicotine. He looked really cool when he smoked, Lauren thought. She lit up too. There were no filters on the cigarettes and so she got a heck of a shock at the amount of smoke that rushed down her windpipe. She began to cough and splutter.

Nick burst out laughing; he moved over to her side of the booth and began to slap her on the back. "Hey, are you OK? Take a drink of this and you'll feel better."

He handed her the vodka and she gulped it down like it was water,

"Not my usual brand," she explained as he wiped the tears away from her eyes. She began to laugh at her own misfortune and so he joined in. Then she realised that she couldn't stop laughing.

"Shit, I have a fit of the giggles," she spluttered.

So did Nick.

Even in the privacy of their own booth, they were beginning to attract curious glances from other people in the restaurant.

"I think it's time we left," Nick said.

"Ah Nick, let them look. That's the price of fame," she exploded, laughing again at what she thought was a hilarious joke.

"OK, but I'm going to get you a milder cigarette. Stay here. There was a shop in the lobby. I'll be back in a second."

As soon as Nick left, the waitress arrived at the table. She had been sent over by the maitre d' to see if there was anything else that they wanted or perhaps the bill.

"My God, we don't want the bill yet," Lauren responded, horrified at the idea of leaving. She was very comfortable and didn't fancy the idea of standing. "I know, we'll have Irish coffees!" she exclaimed. "I'll show Nick the charm of the Irish," she explained to the waitress, who looked at her blankly.

"I-r-i-shhhhh co-fff-eee," Lauren said again. The waitress nodded and left.

"Here, these are what you should be smoking," Nick announced on his return. He threw a box of extra mild cigarettes on the table as he sat back down on his side of the snug.

"Ugh, these are like smoking thin air," she complained, picking up and opening the packet.

"Suit yourself," he mumbled. "Will we go?"

"We can't. I've just ordered you a surprise," Lauren was now giggling incessantly and Nick was getting a little tired of it.

The Irish coffees duly arrived. He looked at his, shrugged and settled back down into the chair.

"I must say, you're pretty cool about the time," he commented.

"What are you talking about?" she asked, trying to focus on lighting another cigarette.

"Well, it's three o'clock now. What time did you say you finish school at? Four thirty? Is there an express train that you're catching back to Wicklow?"

"Nick, what are you talking about?" Lauren didn't understand.

"Your mom," he explained. "Won't she be expecting you at the school gates at four thirty?"

"Oh, no. Four o'clock," Lauren replied. Then, what he was saying hit her.

"Omigod. What time did you say it was? I have to go. Shit, shit shit. I'm dead. I'm so dead."

Nick was startled by her sudden change of mood.

"OK, chill. Four o'clock. This is going to be tight! I

think we'd better get the bill and get the hell outta here."

They had been getting so rowdy, the maitre d' was happy to swipe Nick's gold American Express through quickly and bid good day to the young couple.

Lauren's problems only began when she hit the air, however. She reached for Nick's arm to steady her.

"Nick, I really don't feel too good," she said uncertainly. He took one look at her.

"Aw Jeez, Lauren. We need to get you back into the rest rooms – and fast." He turned her on her heel, back into the hotel but unfortunately it wasn't fast enough. Lauren sprayed everything that she had eaten and drunk over the last three hours on the beautifully shiny floors of the Gresham Hotel lobby. Some businessmen were leaving the restaurant and nearly walked into the puddle of puke. A French woman, obviously a resident of the hotel, started to shriek and pontificate in loud French.

Nick turned to the tourist and unashamedly yelled, "Put a sock in it, lady."

The businessmen looked at him stunned, as he walked Lauren around the large puddle and towards the toilets. He smiled at them a little more sheepishly. "I hope you didn't eat the shellfish!"

Nicolas and Saskia had ended up having lunch in the Taylors' house. They spent a wonderful afternoon, easy in each other's company. Having walked through the little forest in Innishambles and through the fields down to the river, Saskia suddenly realised that she would have to go.

"Goodness, Nicolas, it's three thirty. I have to collect the girls."

"But you haven't taken me around the Manor land yet," he put on a dejected face. "And I thought I could show you around the Manor itself, not to mention a drink in The Hitching Post."

"Oh, Nicolas, there's nothing I would like more, but the girls will be wondering where I've got to. I'm always there on the dot of four o'clock."

"Well, when will you finish showing me the delights of Ballymore?"

"Gosh, I can do this any time," she smiled.

"Same time tomorrow?"

"Oh, OK," she agreed shyly.

He took her hand as if to shake it but he kissed it instead. "Thank you for such a charming day, Saskia."

"Thank you, Nicolas. Now I really must go." She turned on her heel and scampered up towards Innishambles.

"Saskia!" he yelled after her and she swung around again. He marvelled at how young she looked. Far too young for him. "I've just remembered, my car is at your house."

"Oh, yes. What were we thinking? OK, come on then," she called to him. He tried to run up the hill to catch up with her but he was out of breath.

"God you must be fit," he exclaimed.

"I spend my life running after three, now four girls!"

He took her hand as he reached her, for support, but neither let go as they walked the rest of the way home. It felt too good.

At four o'clock on the button, Saskia pulled up outside Mount Eden.

Kelly arrived first. She was in a thunderous mood.

"I hate school," she snarled as she threw her schoolbag on the floor of the car and sat in the passenger seat. Tiffany arrived next.

"Hi Mum, how was your day?" she asked cheerfully.

"I had a wonderful day, thank you, darling. What about you?" Saskia asked, eager to get off the subject of how she had spent her time that day.

"Oh, you know. Same old, same old," she replied light-heartedly.

"What's taking Lauren so long?" Kelly snapped.

"Temper, temper," Tiffany reprimanded her sister. "Just because you were first for a change. We all usually have to wait ages for you, Kelly."

As she spoke, the back door of the Landrover swung open.

"Hi Mum, sorry I'm late." Lauren looked flushed and pale at the same time. Her mother looked at her as she got into the back seat.

"Are you OK, Lauren?" she asked with concern.

"Eh, no. I think I've got a bug or something. I don't feel too good."

"Maybe it's the same thing Edu has," Tiffany offered.

"Yeah, maybe," Lauren answered, unconvinced. She glanced behind her. About a hundred yards behind the Land Rover, the Dublin taxi had not yet moved. Nick and the cab driver were obviously waiting to see if she was going to be all right or if perhaps she was going to be turfed back out onto the road.

Nick saw Lauren look out the back window of the Landrover but he didn't risk waving, fearful that he might attract Saskia's attention.

"I hope she's worth it, son," the taxi driver grinned. "This is going to be one hell of a cab fare."

Nick wasn't so sure.

"What the hell is wrong with you?" Tiffany whispered. "Mrs Dunphy asked me why you weren't in double biology this morning. I had her this afternoon. Where were you?"

"Just cover for me," Lauren mumbled back, turning green as she did.

Tiffany turned back to Kelly and Saskia in the front of the Land-rover. "You know there's a vicious bug going around the school. One of the girls in my class had to go home early, she was puking so badly," she announced happily.

Kelly winced. "Spare us the details."

"I hope you don't have that, pet," Sas cooed from

the driver's seat as she tried to get a look at Lauren in the rear-view mirror.

"If you'd all just leave me alone, I'll be OK," Lauren groaned. Then she promptly fell asleep.

CHAPTER 23

Lauren couldn't believe that she got away with the day in Dublin. Her mother had taken her at her word and assumed that she had a tummy bug. For some reason, Saskia seemed very distracted. Tiffany had been a bit of a pain and wanted to know all about it. In return, however, she nursed her little sister and brought her tea in bed. Lauren had brought up most of her lunch and vodka in the foyer of the Gresham and so there wasn't much more to show for her day with Nick Flattery Jnr. It was late in the evening when he phoned. Tiffany was first to get to it.

"Hello, Innishambles."

"Hi, is Lauren in?"

She knew his accent instantly. "Nick, is that you?"

"Eh, yeah, who's that?"

"Hi, it's me, Tiffany. I met you a few weeks ago when you were collecting Lauren, remember?"

"Ah, right, hi. Is she around?" He didn't sound like he wanted a conversation.

"Just about, you got her into a rotten state, Nick. She's still sick as a parrot."

"Sick as a what?"

"Oh, it's just an expression. What were you thinking? You know she's under-age, *way* under-age!"

"Hey, anything we did, we did at her suggestion. Anyway I don't feel too good either and neither does my American Express."

"Did you really catch a taxi from the Gresham Hotel to Mount Eden? How much did that cost?"

"He charged me eighty pounds, the shit. I had to catch the bus home. Why don't you girls go to school in Dublin?"

Tiffany laughed. She knew that she liked Nick a lot, but she would never do anything to hurt her sister.

"Do you want to talk to Lauren?"

"Well, I just wanted to know if she was OK really. Is she gonna be alright?"

"Let's just say she'll be better before your American Express is!"

He laughed, "Tell me about it. I've blown my month's allowance in the first week of November. I don't know what I'm going to do for Thanksgiving now."

"When is that?"

"The end of the month, but being in the American College, we obviously make a really big deal of it. Probably even bigger than Christmas."

"Oh gosh, I'm sorry, Nick. I don't know what to suggest."

"Hey, don't sweat it. It's not your problem. I guess it was my fault that I went so wild. The problem seems to be that Lauren and I bring out the wild side in each other."

"Well, to be honest Nick, even my Grandma Dalton brings out the wild side in Lauren. I'm not sure that she has a demure side."

"Yeah? Well, tell her I rang and I hope she's OK. She can call me at college when she feels better."

"I will. I hope everything works out for you too. You didn't get into trouble for mitching today, did you?"

"Naw, it's cool here. What about your mom. Did she smell a rat?"

"No, amazingly. She seems very distracted these days."

"Hey, don't knock it." She could hear the smile in his voice. "Well, I guess I'd better go, Tiffany." Was it her imagination, or was he also lingering on the phone?

"OK, well, we'll see you when you move in next month. Give us a call if you want any help."

"Yeah, of course. I forgot about that. See you then, Tiffany."

"Tiff!"

"What?"

"Everybody calls me Tiff, as in fight!"

"What are you talking about?" he asked confused.

"Tiff. That's what most people call me. It's less of a mouthful than Tiffany. I don't know about in the States, but over here a tiff is a sort of a little fight."

"I don't think I would fight with you, Tiffany!"

She blushed – he was definitely flirting with her. "OK, bye." She wanted to get off the phone.

"Bye, Tiffany." He hung up.

She waited for her colour to return to normal before she bounded up the stairs, two at a time.

"Lauren, that was Nick. He was just phoning to see if you were OK."

"Oh, please say he's gone. I can't talk to him. Not tonight, not ever."

"What's wrong? He's lovely. He is gone. Relax."

"Oh, Tiff. He is gorgeous to look at but he's wild. I don't know if I can keep up with him."

"I can't believe that I'm hearing this from you! Kelly maybe, but not you."

"Oh, Tiff. Today was a fiasco. I still feel sick as a dog. I have Mrs Dunphy to contend with tomorrow and it wasn't actually that much fun at all."

"Well, you got to spend the day with Nick, instead of going to school. Surely that was worth something?"

"I guess," Lauren, responded, unconvinced.

"Look, why don't you just calm down in each other's company? Who knows, you might even find that he likes a softer, calmer you."

"Hey, I try," Lauren snapped from her sick bed. "He just . . . I don't know. He just brings out the rebel in me."

"Well, I think what your rebel needs right now is a good night's sleep."

"Where's Mum?"

"With Robin, why?"

"You're sure that you can't smell booze or fags from me?"

"Lauren," Tiff answered impatiently, "how long were you in the bath for? An hour. You smell of lavender and primrose! Now get some sleep!" With that she got up off her sister's bed and went to the bedroom door, switching off the light as she passed it.

"Tiff, thanks for everything."

"Don't mention it. I'll tell Mum that you're asleep. Goodnight."

"Goodnight."

By mid-December, Edu had begun to feel positively healthy again. In fact, she couldn't believe how well she felt. Her skin was glowing, her hair was shining and she was constantly in a ridiculously good mood. Bloody hormones, she thought as she laughed her way through the morning with little Robin gurgling by her side.

When the dogs started to bark, she assumed that it was the postman. Richard regularly had business post directed to the house and there was often a mountain of it. If that was the case, the postman couldn't get it through the letter box and so he would have to ring the doorbell. It ding-donged right on cue.

The dogs bounded forward, with more gusto than usual, but Edu fought her way through. When she opened the door, she was not greeted by good old reliable Declan the postman, but by a young man, maybe twenty-five or thereabout. He was at least six foot six. Edu had never seen such a big guy. He was wearing a white t-shirt and black jeans – no jacket in December! He was built like a body-builder, his biceps as wide as Edu's neck.

"Hi, babe!" He liked the look of her too. "Is this Rathdeen Manor?"

Edu couldn't look over his shoulder, even though she was on a step above him and so she looked around him. There on the gravel was a massive removal truck, with *Transal* written on the side, in six foot lettering.

"Ziz is not ze manor. Ave you come from America?" she asked, wide-eyed with wonder.

"Yes, ma'am, we're a long way from home. We've been travelling for eight days now. This here is the Flattery cargo for their new home. It's come all the way from the west coast of the US of A," he announced proudly. "Transal stands for Trans Atlantic!"

"*Yeazus!* Well, you are nearly zere." Edu gave them the directions to the manor.

"Say, you're not Irish, are you?" the talking t-shirt asked.

Edu blushed, "No, I am Spanish!"

"Cool, *grass-ias!*" he said in a broader than broad west-coast accent. "I'm Brad, but people call me Butch

306

because I look like this." He flexed a bicep at her. Edu giggled.

"Elo, Bush."

"Well, we better get truckin'. Nice to meet ya, *sinorita!*"

"Goodbye, Bush!" she laughed again. She had never seen such a large man, and so toned! "Are zey all like you in LA?" she wondered aloud.

It was pandemonium in the manor.

As the Transal truck pulled up, Kevin Cantwell was getting the last of his builders out of the house. He had complained bitterly that it wasn't his fault that Guiseppi Marloni had given the wrong measurements for the Gothic stairs. Typically, they arrived a week after Guiseppe had promised and then they didn't fit. Kevin had a team of carpenters and plasterers working around the clock to alter the stairwell space to facilitate the new measurements. The temporary stairs, a simple wooden structure, had been removed on the day Guiseppe promised his would arrive. For a week, the builders and the Flatterys were forced to revert to the ladder while they waited. It had been only twenty-four hours earlier that the Gothic stairs had arrived. The woodcarving was exquisite and they were absolutely beautiful but, to Kevin's horror, they didn't fit. He went over his figures again and again, until he realised that it was in fact Guiseppe who had given him the wrong measurements in the first place. The last twenty-four hours had been hectic and Jessica Bell was fit to explode. That said, everything was now complete.

The builders still had another month's work on the stables and various outhouses, but the manor was finished just before Christmas and, most importantly for Kevin, before the penalty clause came into effect.

Butch rang the front door bell, even though the door was open with builders walking in and out, moving all their materials over to the stables. Jessica arrived presently.

"Hello again, Jessica. Here we are!" he announced proudly.

"You're welcome. I'm afraid the place is still a little upside-down but at least we're in and the developers are out."

"OK, let's get this show on the road," he smiled at Jessica. "Do you want to direct?"

"Nicolas," she yelled down the corridor for her husband. "Transal have arrived."

Nicolas had been dreading this day. Even though he was very glad to be moving in finally, he hated the hassle of settling. He came to the front door to lend his support and generally endorse the decisions that his wife was making. She and Kim had everything organised, down to the last detail. Kim, the interior designer, was making a bigger production of this move than any movie Nicolas had been part of. The cargo began to pour in. Beds were moved upstairs, books down to Nicolas's den. Tables and chairs were sent to their various destinations and then paintings and sculptures began to appear. By lunchtime, Nicolas was tired of acting interested. In truth he had nothing to offer because the move had been Jessica's little project. It had taken him all his powers of persuasion to get her to leave LA in the first place. He had glamorised Ireland to her, convinced her that it was the totally trendy place to live. Nicolas had omitted details like the weather. Finally Jessica had agreed to make the move on the two conditions that she could take her friend Kim and that Nicolas never complained at how much she chose to commute between the US and Ireland. He agreed.

Unsure of what to do while his home was so full of strangers, Nicolas retreated to the den. He had already fallen in love with Ballymore. It felt like he was coming home. There was no bullshit here like back in LA. There were no pseudo-personalities as Jessica called them. The neighbours were all real and genuine. Even the weather was real. Much to Nicolas's surprise he found he preferred the Irish climate to the constant blue skies that he had left behind. The fact that it was constantly changing was a source of comfort to him. And Saskia? She was more than he could ever have imagined. He pushed her out of his mind yet again. She was married and so was he. There the story must end for his own sanity. There were promises that had been made that could not be broken. Saskia could be a friend – no more.

"Nicolas, Barney is here. He said you asked him to

come over." Jessica stood at the den door. Nicolas snapped out of his daydream about Saskia.

"Oh, yes that's right," he went out to greet Barney.

"Hi, Nicolas. How are you?" The vet was his usual pleasant self.

"Barney, it's good to see you. Come on in. I'm afraid it's a little mad around here today. We're finally moving in and that means chaos."

Barney glanced around. "I see what you mean."

"Don't worry. The den isn't too bad. Come on down." They wandered down companionably through the hall, past upturned tables and beds propped up on their sides and finally they reached the refuge of Nicolas's den.

"This house is terrific. You're going to have a fine home here," Barney enthused.

"I sure hope so. Naturally it has cost considerably more than we anticipated. I guess, on reflection, I really should have known that. Have you ever heard of anyone coming in under budget on a house?" Nicolas laughed.

"True. In fact I'm amazed that you got in before Christmas. That's very unusual. Builders are notoriously slow. Something always comes up, doesn't it?"

"Well, we were lucky there. Kevin Cantwell is a real pro and there is the small matter of the penalty clause that was due to come into effect as of tomorrow!"

"Ouch," agreed Barney. "Not the kind of *Claus* you want to be greeted with in December!"

"Ho, ho, ho," smiled Nicolas. The two men liked each other a lot. They had the same sense of humour and, more importantly, the same sense of values. While Nicolas loved Ballymore and the people there, he had his reservations about some of the men that he had met. He hadn't liked Richard Dalton at all on the one occasion that he met him. Nicolas knew that he probably had misgivings about the man before he even met him. He had seen the look of fear, or was it mistrust, in Saskia's eyes when she talked about him. She hadn't said anything, but Nicolas could sense it. Likewise Dave Parker seemed to be quite a hard nut. Sue seemed to be soft and timid around her husband. Why? Nicolas wondered. At least Dave was very attentive to his wife. Barney, on the other hand was a big softie. That was why Nicolas was convinced that he was the man for the job.

"Barney," Nicolas started, "I won't beat about the bush. I want to offer you a job."

"Nicolas, I'm flattered, but I have a job. I'm the vet to practically every farmer within thirty miles of here. My practice is growing all the time."

"I know that. That's why I'm going to make this offer as attractive as I possibly can. If you don't like it, we'll part friends. But perhaps we can work something out."

Barney was intrigued.

"As you know, I'm building an animal refuge centre here. The builders start on it now that the Manor is finished. Here are the plans and an artist's sketch."

Nicolas pulled some large sheets of architect's drawings from the coffee table.

"Barney," he announced, "this is The Rathdeen Refuge!"

The first showed a pretty sketch of a courtyard. On three sides were stables and on the fourth, a tack room, a feed room and various offices. Barney let out a low whistle.

"Wow, Nicolas. That is ambitious! It's fairly huge. How many horses do you plan on keeping?"

"Who knows, but I don't want space to be a problem. There are thirty stables here and the feed rooms are just next door for easy access. Here, this is the bit that I think will interest you."

Nicolas pointed to the room marked medical.

"This is the clinic, right next to the offices. Barney, it'll be a complete veterinary clinic. Now don't get me wrong, but I know you work *in situ*, in the homes of your patients. Wouldn't it be nice to have your own clinic?"

Barney stared at Nicolas in shock. "What exactly are you saying?"

"What I'm suggesting is that you become our resident vet. I don't think it would be a full-time job. The truth is I don't know how much time it would take up, but any time that you weren't with the animals of the refuge would be your own. You can use the clinic for your own clients. There's even an operating room."

Barney studied the prints. This must have cost a couple of hundred thousand pounds. More! There was nothing to compare to it in all of County Wicklow.

"I'll also pay you a full wage as the resident vet, and I assume you'll want a few assistants. Perhaps a stable hand and somebody for the kennels?" Nicolas pulled out the second artist's sketch. About one hundred yards away from the courtyard, a large brick building was to be built to house the kennels, hutches and other smaller domestic animals.

"Jesus, Nicolas, it's like an animal hospital! I've never seen anything so big. I would need a lot of help."

"Well, wouldn't two others be enough?"

"No, I would need at least three and maybe a part-timer."

"Christ, this is going to cost me!" Nicolas winced.

"Ah, relax, Nicolas. It will take us some time to work through your millions!" Barney laughed.

"Does that mean that you're interested?"

"I'd be mad not to," Barney smiled. As it was, Barney had to rent surgical facilities from a practice in Wicklow.

Nicolas heaved a sigh of relief. As soon as he met Barney, he had known that he was the man for the job. He just wasn't sure that he would be able to get him interested.

"This would be your office, next to the surgery," Nicolas pointed to the largest office in the complex.

"Well, I've got to hand it to you. It's spectacular."

"I'm relieved that you approve. Come on, let's go over to the site. I'll walk you through it. Then perhaps we can head over to The Hitching Post and see if we can agree on a fee for you that won't see me bankrupt!" Nicolas slapped Barney on the back and the two men headed back outside.

Later that evening, Lauren complained bitterly when her mother asked her to go over to Rathdeen Manor with a large casserole dish of Irish stew.

"Just because I've finished my homework first. It's not fair that I should be penalised."

"Honestly, Lauren, it's the work of five minutes and it's a lovely evening. I thought you'd be delighted to have a legitimate reason to go over there. I'll never understand you!" Saskia snapped at her daughter.

"I'm embarrassed about the bloody casserole, not meeting the Flattery parents!" Lauren knew that Nick Jnr was in the middle of his Christmas exams, so there was no way he would be over there.

"It's just a neighbourly thing to do," Saskia explained. The truth was that she would have loved to bring it over herself but she didn't know if she was brave enough to meet Jessica Bell. She still hadn't met the woman and listening to Nicolas talk about her, she seemed to be a real bitch. Saskia tried not to think about Nicolas Flattery in any way other than as a neighbour, but it was getting more and more difficult. The truth was that she had grown *very* fond of him. She had even begun to dream about him.

In Richard's absence she had seen a great deal of Nicolas, but the day they had spent in Wicklow together was the day she realised that they were getting too friendly. It had started out innocently enough. They had decided to go to Wicklow for a walk around the shops and they took baby Robin with them. For some reason, while they were laughing, Nicolas had put his arm around her shoulder. It was just a momentary gesture but a woman passing by had commented. She had actually stopped and smiled at them in the street!

"It's nice to see two people in love," she said and then she walked on after admiring their baby.

Both Saskia and Nicolas were too embarrassed to correct her but the mood had changed decidedly after that. They returned home to Ballymore almost instantly and they had barely seen each other since. Nothing had been said. They just both became terribly *busy*.

"Look, Lauren, are you going to do this one small thing for me or not?" Saskia asked, beginning to lose her patience.

Lauren could hear the tone in her mother's voice.

"OK, I suppose." She took the casserole dish and headed out the back of the house. It was much faster to go across the back fields and over the River More than to go along the road.

"Hi, long time no see!"

Lauren hadn't seen Connor Cantwell approach, she was so engrossed in conversation with Woody, who had decided to keep her company for the little walk.

"Hi, Connor. How are you?"

"Fine. We're nearly finished here, so I'll be out of your hair soon enough!"

"Look, Connor, I'm sorry that I was such a bitch the first time I met you. I was working my butt off that night and Dad was a complete embarrassment!"

"Forget it! What have you got there?"

"Oh this? This is an even bigger embarrassment. Mum has sent me over to the Manor with an Irish stew to welcome the Flatterys to Ballymore. Cringe."

"Here, let me carry it for you," Connor took it from her and began to walk alongside her. "Yea, they strike me more as the sushi kind than the stew kind!"

Lauren laughed at him. She liked his sense of humour. "Are you a full-time builder, then? Have you finished school?"

"No way, although I do think I'll go into the business. I'm in transition year and so I'm taking a lot of time off to get the training. A job like this one is a pretty cool experience. I'm working on the swimming-pool at the moment. It's not every day that Cantwell Construction builds one of those."

"They're going to have a pool! That's so cool. Rock on the summer!"

"Yea, I'm going to spend it in the States. Building, of course. But I can't wait for those American chicks who'll *dig* my soft Irish brogue."

"Oh, you're going away for the summer?" Lauren asked a little sadly.

"Yes, and I can't wait."

"Of course. I'm sure you'll have a great time."

They had reached the back of the Manor and so they parted company. Connor handed Lauren back the casserole dish and hovered for a minute.

"Well, bye," he said. "Good luck with your stew!"

"Thanks." As he turned to leave Lauren realised that he was a really nice guy. Why am I such a fool, she fumed. He used to fancy me and now he doesn't and he's so cute. She trundled around to the front of the Manor with her stew, feeling utterly miserable.

"Shit, shit, shit," she mumbled. "I'm going out with the wrong guy!"

CHAPTER 24

Sue Parker was up to ninety. She was surprised to hear from Saskia because they didn't have a lot in common. They had in fact drifted apart quite a bit over the last two years. Many women grow closer when they live in the same village and are having babies around the same time but not Saskia and Sue.

Sue spent most of her time on the golf course in Rathdeen and Saskia spent all of hers taxiing her elder girls to and fro. So the women didn't see much of each other. The last time they had dined together was at that dreaded dinner party two years ago. It felt like yesterday, Sue reflected. Now here she was, yet again, invited to Innishambles to dine. Her first impulse was to say no, but she couldn't do that without consulting her husband.

"Of course we'll go. Why didn't we ever have them

back here after that wild night in their house last Christmas?" Dave enthused.

"It was two Christmases ago," Sue replied despondently.

"No way, it couldn't be that long, could it?"

"It was before Guy –" she stopped herself.

"It was before we made Guy, you mean!" Dave wrapped his arms around his wife's waist. "Do you think you're ready to *make* a third Parker baby?"

Sue pulled away from him "God no, not yet, Dave."

He concentrated on the task of his bow tie. He studied his handiwork in the mirror of their bedroom and asked, "So who else is coming tonight?"

"I'm not altogether sure. I don't think it's a big affair. There's the two of us, the Daltons, the Flatterys and I think Barney has been dragged in, to make up the numbers because that lady Kim is coming too."

"Who is she anyway? Why is she living at the Manor?"

"I don't know. In the beginning, I thought that she was their interior designer, but she seems to be a good friend of Jessica's. They go everywhere together."

"Hey, maybe they're lovers!"

"David! Don't be obscene."

"What's obscene about that? Jessica Bell is a real Hollywood babe. You know they're all a very alternative bunch."

"Even so, Jessica Bell isn't. Surely that's why they've

moved to Ireland? Now they have a nice stable environment for their young son."

"I still say it's a bit odd, two grown women living with the one man." Dave put on his dinner jacket. He dusted himself down with a clothes brush, and was pleased with the result.

"Can I fix you a drink before we go?" he asked.

Sue was still doing her make-up. She sat at her dressing table; the only give-away that she was even going out tonight was the beautiful way her hair had been professionally clipped up. Usually dead straight, tonight it was a mass of soft curls tied up in a formal style, with wisps gently framing her fragile face and neck. She looked up at her husband and her face softened.

"You know, maybe it's a good idea. Can I have a glass of white wine, please?"

"That's my girl. Come on, it's Christmas. We should enjoy ourselves. The kids are happy with Jenny downstairs and she doesn't clock off until four pm tomorrow, so we can really let go and have a bloody good sleep in tomorrow morning." He left the room, having blown Sue a kiss, and bounded down the stairs to fix them both a glass of wine.

Dave knew whatever had been bothering his wife was only getting worse over the last few months. If anything, it seemed to be coming to a head. As he examined the contents of his humidor, he wondered what it could possibly be. Depression was the obvious answer but somehow that didn't quite fit with the symptoms. He took four large Romeo Y Julieta cigars from his humidor, and then he checked its humidity levels. They were perfect, indicating that at least his collection of cigars was in excellent condition. He closed the humidor again.

As he poured the wine, he thought about the night ahead. He had already met Nicolas Flattery once. Nice enough guy in an actor sort of way. Flattery seemed to be a bit of a dreamer, a little soft for Dave, but fairly inoffensive. His wife was a sex kitten, even if she was on the wrong side of forty. Dave genuinely didn't know what to make of the Kim one. Barney obviously was good old Barney. Then there were the Daltons. Sas was a sweetie, she was a great mom and she seemed to be keeping the whole house together pretty well, considering she had just had another sprog.

Dave didn't really like Richard Dalton, however. It was a gut-instinct thing; just a few comments Dalton had made over the last few years. It occurred to Dave that Richard *had* been a nice guy, but he seemed to be getting tougher or greedier over the last few years. He thought back to their recent business deal. God knows Richard hadn't done him any favours, not that he expected any. Dave had paid the market rate for his leasehold in Rock Tower, but he thought it was a good site. The profile he would get over the next few months, as the Tower and Rock FM were relaunched, would pay good dividends. There was also a very nice advertising rate for residents of the Tower on Rock FM. That was the clincher for Dave.

He planned to have their top store there with the

premier stock. He knew it made good business sense, even if Richard wasn't his favourite person.

Sue Parker walked into the kitchen and Dave had to put down his glass. She still took his breath away.

Her dark hair was swept up, her make-up classic and chic as always. She used natural colours, accentuating her natural beauty. It never looked false. Her eyes looked huge under large doe-like eyelashes and she had dark red lipstick on, covered in lip gloss. Dave wanted to take her straight back up to bed.

He continued to stare at her. The dress was dark navy, almost black. It plunged down, revealing her generous cleavage. This she had emphasised with a long gold necklace. The sleeves were fitted, highlighting how thin and long her arms were. As he looked down her body he saw that the dress was full length, gently resting on her hips and flat stomach. It fitted her like a silk glove. She was drop-dead gorgeous!

"Sue," he smiled, "I love you."

"I know," she looked at him, "and I love you too." She took the glass of wine that he offered her and downed it in one.

"Hey, you were thirsty," he laughed. "Do you want another, or shall we go."

"Let's have another and then go!"

"OK."

It was, as always, pandemonium in Innishambles. Saskia examined the dining-table one more time. It looked very festive. One of the biggest advantages of living in an old house was how well it looked at Christmas time. The huge fireplace was draped in a garland of holly and ivy. Saskia absolutely refused to bring any synthetic greenery into the house. "We have acres and acres of vegetation around this house. Christmas is one of the best times to utilise it," she explained to her mother-in-law who suggested that they get the plastic garlands that were all the rage.

Looking around the room now, she was pleased with the effect. The table happily sat eight. In fact, she had had to take out a few of the centre leaves of the table to make it this small. The tablecloth was white, but it was covered with gold sparkle at the girls' insistence. Evidently sparkle was essential this festive season. The silver cutlery sparkled too, she thought, as did the Tipperary crystal. Everybody had a Christmas cracker at his or her place mat, which gave it an instant Christmassy feel, but the most festive aspect was the flower arrangement in the centre. Saskia had mentioned to Cathy Taylor that she was having a few friends around just before Christmas and Cathy had promised one of her show-stopping flower arrangements as her Christmas present to the Dalton household. Cathy hadn't let her down. Fortunately, the colour theme she had used was white and gold and it fitted the table perfectly.

Richard stuck his head around the door.

"Sas, where's my bow tie?"

"I have no idea. When did you have it last?"

"Ah, Sas. I don't know." His tone made it clear to her that she should go and look for it.

"OK, I'll see what I can do," she sighed and left. Richard glanced around the dining-room. It looked great, and then he spotted the name cards. At each seat, just beside the dessert spoon was the name of the person Saskia had intended to sit there. He walked around the table to see who was to sit where.

"Ah, shit. I don't want that weirdo Kim beside me," he whined. He had begun to change the place settings to his satisfaction when Dudley and Dexter started barking.

"Mum, Dad," Tiffany yelled up the stairs. "Barney's here! Lauren and I are off. You'll see us later, that's if you're not blind drunk!"

"Charming chat out of my daughter," Richard laughed, as he walked into the hall. "No need to yell, honey, I'm right here. You don't have to shatter the windows! Hi Barney, Happy Christmas. What will you have to drink?"

"Hi, Richard. Happy Christmas to you too. A beer's good."

"Look, buddy, would you mind fixing it yourself? As you can see, I'm not quite ready." Richard stood in the hall with his trousers and dinner shirt on, but the shirt was unbuttoned and he was in his bare feet.

"Relax, I know where the fridge is in this house." Barney smiled. He turned to Tiffany, "Are you out on the town?"

"No, Lauren and I have been invited over to Rathdeen Manor to watch some movies on DVD with Nick Jnr. We thought we'd leave you fogies to it!"

"Thanks a lot, Tiff." Barney couldn't understand how casual she was around him. He still felt very awkward. Their past didn't seem to knock anything out of her. He wandered into the kitchen as Lauren and Tiffany headed out. Kelly was sitting on the sofa cooing to her little sister.

"You look like a natural, Kelly," Barney said.

"Oh, hi, Happy Christmas."

"Are you joining us for dinner?"

"Too much like hard work, Barney. Mum very kindly offered but I'd mess up the numbers. Anyway I have to study."

"On the twenty-third of December! Come on, surely not?"

"It's my Leaving this year. You of all people know what a big deal that is."

"Any thought on next year?"

"Not a clue, Barney. Strictly between you and me, I would have loved to study to be a vet but I'm too thick!"

"Kellser, you mean you're too beautiful!"

She looked at him shocked. Barney had never said anything like that to her before.

"Seriously," he continued, "when was the last time you saw a beautiful vet?"

She laughed at him. "You're the best, Barney. You

always cheer me up, even on the smelly nights when I have to study and everybody else is having a good time."

"How about this for an idea? Would you like to come and work for me after your leaving?"

"Doing what?"

"Well, I've decided to take the job that Nicolas Flattery has offered me. I'm going to be the resident veterinary surgeon at The Rathdeen Refuge. I'm going to have two or maybe three assistants. Would you like one of those jobs?"

"Barney, you're joking! Yes I'd *love* one of those jobs. Omigod, looking after little puppies and lost donkeys. It's probably the best job in the world." She threw her free arm around Barney's neck, still holding Robin in the other. He loved the feeling. There was now no denying it. He knew he had a major crush on this gorgeous girl. Kelly on the other hand seemed to be absolutely oblivious to it.

"Woa, slow down, girl. There'll be a lot of mucking out stables and washing mangy dogs. Have you thought about the amount of animals that we may have to put to sleep? Kelly, it's not going to be a picnic."

"Oh yes it will. Barney, you're the best!"

"Well, I'm not going to disagree with you there," he smiled at her, "But you'll have to discuss this with your folks and I do think that you should continue a correspondence course."

"What?"

"You know, one of those stable management courses by post."

"OK, yeah sure, but you're serious about the job offer, aren't you?"

"Absolutely! I've seen the way you can handle a horse. You're a natural. If it's what you want, you'd be mad not to pursue your career in it."

"Oh, it is. Thank you, thank you, thank you." She hugged him again.

"What has Barney done now?" Saskia walked into the kitchen.

"Mum, he's offered me a job."

"As long as that's all he's offered you!" Saskia exclaimed seeing her eighteen-year-old hug Barney. "Doing what, in heaven's name?"

There wasn't time to answer, however, because the dogs started up again as the doorbell rang and the Flatterys arrived at the same time as the Parkers.

All the men looked splendid in their black ties. Saskia had found Richard's spare bow tie in his chest of drawers after remembering that he last wore the formal stuff to a function in Dublin. Obviously he had left his tie somewhere in Rock Tower. Richard, however, remembered the truth. He had met up with Robin Maher after that function two weeks previously and suffice it to say, he wouldn't be using that bow tie again . . .

"Bellinis for everyone," Richard announced expansively.

Saskia explained, "He had this drink at a work do recently and he has become converted. I must admit they are rather delicious! I've just had one."

Everybody was willing to give it a go. Jessica followed him into the kitchen to help.

"What's in them?" she asked.

"That's the secret," Richard enthused. "They're liquid dynamite. They're so easy to drink but they are potent." He explained as he made them up. "Here, taste this." He gave her a glass. "It's Grand Marnier, champagne and liquidised strawberries. The trick is that the strawberries mask the strength of the drink."

Jessica took a champagne glass from him and sampled the Bellini.

"Oh, this is delicious! You're right about it being easy to drink. I could take any number of these, easily!"

"That's the general idea, Jessie!" he smiled conspiratorially.

By the time they had returned to the drawing-room, Saskia had found the Christmas compilation album and everybody was sitting comfortably listening to Mel and Kim *Rock around the Christmas Tree*. They each took a drink with festive cheer. It was obvious that this group had the makings of a good night.

Saskia had decided on a simple meal. The less complicated, the better, she thought. Nicolas Flattery had the effect of making her nervous and she didn't want to cook anything too ambitious. The starter was a fresh salmon mousse wrapped in a smoked salmon parcel on a bed of salad. The advantage was that it was prepared a few hours before. The main course was wild game goulash in a pastry case with potato dauphinoise and winter veg.

The noise level had already risen considerably by the time they moved into the dining-room. The Bellinis were working a treat and everybody seemed to be fairly relaxed, Richard thought. It was only when they actually went to sit down that Saskia saw what Richard had done to the place settings. She had been too nervous to sit beside Nicolas but Richard had changed the settings and now he was at her right-hand side. Dave Parker was at her left. To compound her nervousness, Nicolas had barely spoken to her so far all evening.

Richard had put Jessica to his right and Sue to his left. Saskia was furious but there was nothing she could do about it now. Kim was next to Jessica and Barney was next to Sue, in the middle of the table. In Richard's defence, everybody seemed to be happy with where they were sitting and dug into their starters with great relish.

The conversation moved freely from talk of Rock Tower and the now imminent publicity campaign to chat about The Rathdeen Refuge. Barney was very animated about the project and so Nicolas stayed relatively quiet and let him talk.

Jessica's accent got stronger as she drank and she enjoyed comparing LA to Ballymore.

"They don't really have a whole lot in common, Jessica," Richard remarked, as he finished his main course. He was beginning to slur his words slightly. "Except, of course, they're both full of beautiful women!" He put his hand on Sue Parker's knee under the table but she jumped and so he took it off again.

Dave had seen her – he tried to catch her eye across the table, but she dropped her eyes guiltily. Saskia also saw her husband. She squeezed Dave's hand on top of the table and asked him about his children.

Jessica, however, was commanding the attention of the table again.

"What I find amazing about Ireland is the price of the land here. Gawd, it's as expensive as back home." She took another mouthful of Bellini.

"That's because of the Celtic Tiger," Barney explained.

"The what?"

"We have had a booming economy here for over the last five years now," Dave Parker explained. "As you probably know, when an economy is on the up it's called a tiger economy. Well, this being Ireland it's obviously a Celtic thing, hence the expression Celtic Tiger."

"I prefer Celtic Pussy, myself," Richard growled flirtatiously at the women sitting next to him. This time he grabbed both Sue Parker's and Jessica Bell's legs. Both women jumped. Their knees banged the underside of the table causing the crystal to clink loudly.

"Only because you're such a bloody tomcat, Richard

Dalton," Sue snarled. "Excuse me, I have to visit the ladies'." She had lost all looks of serenity as she stood and half-walked, half-staggered to the little toilet beside the study.

Jessica Bell burst out laughing, however, and looked at Kim.

"I'd say I like Celtic pussy too," Kim smiled and purred.

"Richard, are you flirting with me?" Jessica asked in a whisper louder than most people would shout.

"Would that be so awful? What harm is there in a little innocent flirting?" He looked at his wife who was scowling down the table at him.

Jessica however was looking at Nicolas who had a look of horror on his face. "Don't," he mouthed at her. She shrugged and ignored Nicolas.

"There's no point," she said succinctly.

"There's always a point," Richard laughed, "at least there is when I'm involved."

"Not with me, Richard!" Jessica took Kim's hand and held it above the table. "You see, I'm gay."

"Jessica, you promised," Nicolas raised his voice.

"You're what?" Richard ignored Nicolas Flattery. "You and Kim here?"

"Yep. There's no point in trying to hide it from you guys. Damn it, you're our neighbours. But we would appreciate it if you kept it to yourselves."

"You don't look like a *talk-to-the-newspaper-set*," Kim commented simply.

Saskia saw the colour drain from Nicolas Flattery's face.

"Who's for pudding?" she asked in an artificially high-pitched voice. "It's Death by Chocolate." Everybody looked at her.

"OK, I'll go and get it." She stood to leave.

"I'll help you," Dave Parker added. He actually wanted to find his wife. Richard seemed to be the only one not remotely bothered by the turn of events.

"Don't fancy your chances of scoring tonight, Barney!" he laughed. "Well, I'll be damned," he added, "What about a *ménage à trois*?" he asked Kim and Jessica. "Would you be game?"

"I think I should help with the dessert," Barney stood and left the room, heading for the sanctuary of the study where he knew Kelly was reading.

"How's it going?" he asked her as he walked in.

"I'm reading up on stable management," she smiled.

"I thought you were meant to be studying, Kelly!"

"I was, but I'm too excited. How's dinner?"

"Don't ask. I've just discovered the woman your folks were setting me up with is a lesbian."

"You're kidding – Kim?"

"Kim and Jessica. They're a couple," he said with an American accent.

Kelly burst out laughing. "I don't believe it. Hey, it would explain a lot. Jessica and Nick don't sleep together. Lauren said that Nick explained that the family were a little alternative. Yeah, it makes sense. Wait till I tell the girls in school."

"You can't. Jessica has asked us to keep it quiet."

"You must be kidding!"

"I'm not, Kelly. Come on. That's not fair!"

"It's not fair to ask us to keep it a secret."

"OK, well, how about thinking of it this way. It's your boss's boss's secret. He mightn't be impressed if he heard that you were blabbing it all over the place."

"Ah, when you put it that way."

Saskia was worried about Dave Parker. He had seemed particularly subdued all night.

"Dave, are you all right?" she asked as he followed her out to the kitchen.

"Work has been hectic in the run-up to Christmas. Sorry, am I being a bore?"

"No, not at all. Look, I'm sorry about Richard. He's flirting far too much with Sue. I'll have a word with him as soon as I can. In the meantime, thanks for the help. Can you get the dessert? It's out here, in the scullery."

Dave followed her through the kitchen and out into the scullery. They heard Richard arrive in the kitchen. "OK," he shouted back to the dining-room, jovially. "Another batch of Bellinis coming up!"

Saskia was going to walk straight back into the kitchen to give him a piece of her mind and to tell him to calm down but Sue Parker beat her to it.

"You bastard," she snarled at him as loud as she

could, without being overheard by the guests in the dining-room. Sue had no idea that Dave and Saskia were in the scullery. They froze.

"What's wrong with you, pet?" Richard laughed.

"What's wrong? Have you no shame?"

"What the fuck's wrong?"

"How dare you lay a hand on me!"

"You didn't complain the last time," he laughed.

"That was two years ago and it was a terrible mistake."

"You didn't think so at the time."

"I was high as a kite!" she snapped.

"Yeah sorry, I have no snow this year. I have to keep my nose very clean. I've had a few problems lately, with the law."

"I don't want any coke. I didn't want any then either, in case you've forgotten."

"Ah, come on, Sue. It was all just a bit of fun."

"A bit of fun?" Sue sounded like she was going to snap. Dave held Saskia and wouldn't let her move a muscle in the scullery. "You fucked me when I was so high that I didn't know whether I was coming or going."

"Well, if I remember correctly, neither of us came. There wasn't enough time!" he laughed.

"What?" she asked nervously. "You didn't come, Richard?"

"No, I didn't. Why, does that make it better? It's like kissing somebody with your teeth shut. I didn't come so it doesn't count. Hey, if that makes you happy, no, I didn't come."

"How can you be so sure?"

"Well, if you must know, cocaine gives me a permanent hard-on. I'd be up all night. It's nothing personal, you understand."

"Quite the opposite. I'm delighted."

"Selfish bitch."

"No, it means Guy is Dave's son, not yours."

"You thought Guy was mine? I should be so lucky. My bloody wife never gave me a son. Sue, there's no way I'm Guy's dad because I was wearing a condom!"

"What?"

"You really don't remember, do you? You said something about perhaps getting pregnant and so I grabbed a rubber. I always have a few on stand-by – just in case I meet some frisky housewives."

"Fuck you," Sue stormed out of the kitchen.

"So I suppose a rematch is out of the question?" Richard called after her.

He followed her back to the dining-room a few minutes later, with a fresh jug of Bellinis. It was only when Richard and Sue had gone that Dave realised his fingers were digging into Saskia's shoulders. It must have been painful.

"Oh God, sorry, Sas."

"Oh no, it's me who's sorry, Dave. I'm so very very sorry. What kind of animal am I married to?"

He looked at her intently.

"Saskia, not a word of this to anybody. You must put it out of your head. Do you hear me? Not a word, not even to Richard. We'll talk in a few days, when we've had a chance to think this through. Do you hear what I'm saying?"

She nodded mutely.

CHAPTER 25

Dave was totally in control of his emotions. He smiled politely at all the other guests and apologised.

"I'm afraid we have to go. I think those Bellinis were a little too strong for Sue's constitution," he explained gallantly, every inch the understanding, loving husband.

Saskia watched Dave as he smiled at Richard and clapped him on the back, thanking him for a great night, agreeing to do it again very soon and leaving amid gentle slags of being a party pooper.

Saskia herself was still in a state of shock and so she offered no resistance. She just reflected on how stupid Richard was to make an enemy out of a man as powerful as Dave Parker.

Sue didn't even try to make sense of why her husband was gently guiding her out of Innishambles and into his large car. In a daze, she thanked Saskia for a lovely evening and left.

"Where are we going?" she asked, as they turned left for Wicklow and Dublin, as opposed to right for their house.

He looked at her lovingly. "It's a surprise, darling! Why don't you try and rest. I'll wake you when you we get there."

"Oh Dave," she looked at him nervously, "can't we just go home?"

"Hush, love, it's OK. I'm not going to try and seduce you. Trust me. You'll like it. Now go to sleep."

As soon as they hit the motorway for Dublin, the gentle purr of the engine put Sue to sleep. She had had a lot to drink and Dave knew that she had been through a serious trauma. He noticed that his own hands, which should have been gently holding the power-assisted steering wheel, were white-knuckled with rage. He was holding on as if his life depended on it.

I should kill him, he thought, as he played the scene between his wife and Richard over again and again in his mind. I'd probably be doing Saskia a favour into the bargain. What a low-down bastard! His fury grew as he drove towards Dublin. The roads were practically deserted on the eve of Christmas Eve and he was able to put the foot down.

Dave thought of Sun Tzu's *Art of War*. It was one of his favourite books. Know your enemy, he thought. Surprise your enemy, he remembered, and show no mercy; let destruction be absolute. He began to control his breathing and in due course, his temper. I must give myself time to sort out my head and my poor poor Sue. Dave glanced at her, asleep in the passenger seat.

So this was the demon that had been haunting her. He didn't blame her in the least. Everybody knew that Sue Parker couldn't hold her drink. A sniff of champagne was enough to get her twisted. Dave assumed that among friends she was free to let her hair down. He never thought that a neighbour would try to take advantage of her, let alone practically rape her. He tried to control his breathing again. It wasn't easy. He hadn't known that Sue had tried a line of coke that fateful night. God knows what effect that would have on her.

He turned his thoughts to tonight. Firstly he dialled Jenny. It was only midnight and so she was still up, watching TV.

"Hi, Jenny, it's Dave. Everything quiet at home?"

"Yes, thanks. India and Guy are both in bed and sound asleep."

"You're a star, Jenny. Look, I just wanted to let you know that we've had a slight change in plan. I'm taking Sue up to town to stay in a hotel tonight. You know, to get a real sleep-in tomorrow morning. No screaming kids outside our bedroom door!"

"Good idea," Jenny agreed. "Don't rush back. We'll see you when we see you." She smiled into the phone as she thought about the huge Christmas bonus she would inevitably get from the Parkers.

"Thanks, Jenny, you're great! You can always

contact me on the mobile for an emergency. Goodnight."

"Goodnight."

The next phone call Dave made was to the Hilton Hotel in Dublin city. He did a lot of business with the hotel and as such he had a *valued customer* membership card. The girl on the reception didn't know Mr Parker in person, but when she typed in his membership number and got a five-star rating, she contacted the night manager instantly.

Dave Parker was given the Bridal Suite.

Sue woke when the car engine stopped.

"Where are we?" she asked sleepily, unable to get her bearings in the underground car park of the Hilton.

"We're at the Hilton, my love. We're staying here tonight so I can take you into town tomorrow morning to buy you your Christmas present. Is that OK?"

Sue looked at him and smiled. "Dave, you're the nicest man on the planet and I love you. Yes, that's very OK."

Back at Innishambles, things had fallen apart rather spectacularly.

"Won't anybody have some Death by Chocolate?" Saskia tried. Richard was totally locked at this stage and insisted on talking American politics with Nicolas Flattery, who was not in the least interested. Saskia could see that he was still furious with his wife for letting their little secret out. Kim, as always, sat quietly watching the action.

"Look, Richard, it's been a very nice evening, but I think it's time we headed for home." Nicolas tried.

"Rubbish, you just got here. We haven't even had dessert. You can't go yet."

"Richard," Saskia tried to help her friend, "if Nicolas wants to go, I think we should let him. Perhaps they have an early start tomorrow."

"Yes, yes that's it. We have all the last-minute shopping to do tomorrow. You know how it is," Nicolas lied to Richard.

"Well, surely you don't have to take your lovely wife with you? Or should I say wives?" Richard dug Nicolas in the ribs with his elbow, in a laddish gesture that made the American pale with anger.

"Jessica? Do you *want* to come home?" he asked his wife.

Jessica Bell knew that she was in hot water with him.

"Perhaps we should go," she replied meekly. "Thank you for a lovely evening, Saskia and Richard, and I love those Bellinis!"

"Maybe we should call them truth serums in future," Richard slurred, utterly oblivious to the tension in the dining-room.

"Thank you, Saskia, for a lovely meal. You obviously went to a lot of trouble," Kim whispered to her hostess as she headed out of the room behind the Flatterys.

Suddenly the house was empty and quiet.

"Hey, where did everybody go?" Richard asked.

"Oh, Richard. Just go to bed and sleep it off. I'm going to have a look at what state the kitchen is in."

He grumbled something incoherent as he headed to bed with an extra large whiskey.

Saskia filled the sink with soapy water, to let the saucepans soak while she loaded the dishwasher. The conversation she and Dave had overheard was just too overwhelming for her to take in and so she put it aside, as if it had never happened. She continued to clean just as she would on any other night after a dinner party. After a while, Saskia went in search of Kelly.

"Barney, I didn't realise you were still here," she smiled at him.

"Hi Sas, to be honest I'm hiding. What a night! Have they all gone home?"

"Yes, poor Nicolas. He really looked dejected. Did you tell Kelly?"

"Er, yes. It was kinda difficult not to!"

"I understand." Saskia looked at her eldest daughter who had fallen asleep, snuggled up to Barney. Robin was asleep in Kelly's arms.

"You look like a perfect family there, the three of you," Saskia teased.

"Ah, Sas, she wouldn't have me."

Kelly stirred, but continued to sleep.

"Well, there is a bit of an age-gap there, Barney." As she said it, Saskia saw Barney tense up. Was it her imagination or did it look like Barney was developing feelings for her eldest daughter? Surely not. If it wasn't for the age gap, they would make a wonderful couple; then again up until a few weeks ago, she thought Nicolas Flattery and Jessica Bell were a match made in heaven. As for Dave and Sue Parker – perhaps Saskia wasn't the best judge of characters. She didn't dare think about her own husband. Dave Parker was right; wait a few days. Let the dust settle.

Saskia took the sleeping Robin from Kelly's arms and brought her up to her cot. The little girl was the most tranquil of her children. She always seemed to be serene and satisfied.

"Goodnight, angel," she whispered as she put the little pink bundle down in her cot. "Sweet dreams."

By the time Saskia was back downstairs, Kelly was bidding Barney goodnight.

"I'm off, Mrs D. My job as a pillow is over!"

"Goodnight, Barney, I hope you had a good night. Thanks for coming."

Kelly followed her mother into the kitchen.

"God, this place is a mess. Do you want some help, Mum?"

"I'd love some help, Kelly, thanks. Your Dad has gone to bed. The girls are still out in Rathdeen Manor and Edu is up in Dublin until tomorrow, for her annual Christmas shopping trip."

"Is she coming down with Grandma Dalton?"

"Bright and early, no doubt. That's why I want to get this mess cleared away tonight. I'm not having that old bat criticise the house as soon as she arrives."

Kelly giggled at her mother, "You know she will find something to complain about, no matter how hard you try. Hey, what do you make of tonight's events?"

Saskia froze, but Kelly continued.

"Lesbians? Would you believe it? Jessica Bell is so glamorous."

Relieved that Kelly was only talking about the Flatterys and not Sue and Richard, Saskia relaxed.

"Well, you never judge a book by the cover. I just feel sorry for Nicolas. They obviously had some agreement about keeping it quiet, probably for Nick Jnr's sake."

"Surely he knows?" Kelly asked aghast.

"How should I know?"

"Actually I think he does, Mum. Lauren was saying that he was saying that his family were a little *alternative*," she snorted.

"I don't think those two are good for each other," Saskia sighed, acutely aware of how little control she had over her girls' lives.

"Well, I think you can relax there," Kelly added as she closed up the loaded dishwasher. "I think they're beginning to agree with you."

"Oh, Kelly. That would be wonderful. Do you think they're breaking up?"

"Well, that's the good news."

"What's the bad news?"

"I think Tiffany has developed a bit of a crush on him."

"Oh heavens, I'm getting too old for this," Saskia

sighed as she finally wiped down the table. "Come on, pet. It's bedtime."

Wearily the two mounted the stairs together.

"What about you and Barney?" Saskia asked her daughter tentatively.

"What about us?"

"Well, he does seem to be a little keen on you, pet. Or do you think he's perhaps a little old for you?"

"Mum, you were barely older than I am now when you got married!" Kelly laughed. "Anyway, I think you're dreaming. He has said nothing to me and I couldn't go out with him. He's going to be my boss in a few months."

"Good," smiled Saskia, suddenly eager to get off the subject. She knew that the fastest way to get Kelly going out with Barney was to ask her not to.

"You promised. It's the one thing I asked of you, not for me, for our son and you blew it. What kind of selfish bitch are you?" Nicolas was yelling at his wife and he didn't care who heard. As far as he was concerned, once a secret was out it was out.

"I only told our neighbours. They probably knew already," Jessica tried to defend herself.

"They may have had their suspicions. Now, thanks to you, they are in no doubt!"

The Flatterys were in the front reception hall of their house but they were yelling so loudly Nick Jnr, Lauren, Tiffany and Connor Cantwell came up from the den to

345

see what all the commotion was about. Kim had sneaked off to bed to let them have the space they needed for this domestic.

"What the heck is going on, folks?" Nick Jnr interrupted his parents.

"You can tell him," Nicolas snarled.

Jessica looked at her only child and at his friends.

"I think it would be better if your friends went home first of all, Nick."

They didn't need to be asked twice.

"Bye Nick," they chorused as they headed out the door together.

Connor wasn't drinking because he had to drive to Dublin so he offered the girls a lift home.

"I wonder what the hell that's about," he commented as he started the car.

"It didn't look pretty," Tiffany agreed.

"Family fights, they happen in every house for God's sake," Lauren commented. She was still in foul form, having sat with the other three for the night watching videos and *doing* nothing. When Lauren heard that Nick had invited Connor Cantwell over for the evening, she hoped against hope that he might say something to her, but he didn't. To add insult to injury, Nick, who she was meant to be going out with didn't even make an effort to snog her. Life was so uneventful.

"Are you OK, Lauren? You suddenly seem a little upset," Connor asked.

"Ignore her, Connor," Tiffany snorted. "She's a moody little twerp!"

They had reached the front door of Innishambles. "I am not a moody little twerp. Happy Christmas, Connor. Thanks for the lift." Lauren flew out of the Cantwell Construction jeep and into the house.

"What's suddenly got into her?" he asked, confused.

"God knows. Happy Christmas, Connor, and thank you for dropping us home – it has got colder!"

"Hey, Tiff," Connor grinned. He pointed to the mistletoe that he had suspended from the rear-view mirror.

"Connor Cantwell, I'm shocked!" she teased. He reached over to kiss her on the cheek, but he turned at the last minute and kissed her on the lips, gently teasing hers apart. Tiffany hadn't planned it but she kissed him back and enjoyed the sensation.

"Happy Christmas," he smiled at her as she got out of the car. Tiffany didn't trust herself to speak and so she just grinned at him and waved as she ran inside.

There was a loud knock on the door.

"Room service," the voice said insistently.

Reluctantly, Dave Parker pulled himself out of his slumber. He shook himself awake, glancing at his watch as he headed for the door. It was already ten o'clock.

"Just a minute," he mumbled as he looked for his wallet for a tip.

"Christ, I don't remember the last time I slept this late," he smiled at the young girl who brought in two trays overflowing with food. She beamed back at him when she saw the twenty-pound note that he was handing her.

"Thank you, sir. Please call if you want anything else and Happy Christmas, sir."

"Happy Christmas to you too." He walked her to the door of the suite to see her out and then he went over to his wife, still asleep in bed.

"Good morning, Mrs Parker. How are you this Christmas Eve?"

She grinned in her sleep but made no effort to speak.

"Which would you prefer, a full Irish breakfast or the continental?" he asked. She raised an exquisitely sculpted eyebrow but still made no effort to speak.

"Do you want breakfast in bed or would you like to sit at the table?"

Sue suddenly realised that she wasn't at home. She sat up in bed and looked around.

"I forgot that we're in town!" she exclaimed. "This is wonderful. Dave, I've nothing to wear. These surprises are wonderful but –"

"Hush," he soothed her. "Sue, you worry too much. You are too precious to have to worry about anything. We'll sort everything out!"

He took her by the hand to guide her from the bed and offered her the Hilton dressing-gown he had found behind the en suite bathroom door.

"Thank you, Dave," she whispered as she put it on and tiptoed over to the table. "This is a feast. There's enough food here for four."

"You need it," he laughed. "You have to build up your energy. You always say shopping is exhausting and today we're going to buy the town out. So eat, woman!"

Sue dug into the fry with great gusto.

Dave hadn't given much thought to what he had to say but he knew he had to speak fast before he lost his nerve. He was terrified of only one thing in life and that was losing Sue Parker, his queen. When they had finished eating and she was obviously in a good mood, he decided to just jump in.

"Sue, we have to talk, darling."

She knew instantly that it was serious.

"I thought we were going shopping, Dave."

"Yes, we are and I'm going to buy you whatever you want but first we have to talk."

"What is it?"

"Sue, I heard your conversation with Richard Dalton last night." She covered her face with her hands, and began to shake.

"It's OK, Sue. I don't blame you. He's the bastard here. So help me, I'll kill him."

"No, please don't talk like that. Oh, Dave, what did you hear? What do you know?"

"I know that you did a line of coke with him two Christmases ago and that he – well he took advantage of you and, eh, up until last night you weren't sure who Guy's father really was."

Sue slid off the chair she was sitting on, as if too weak to even sit upright. She slumped on the floor. She began to sob like India, her three-year-old daughter.

"I'm so sorry. I'm so sorry. I'm such a silly silly woman. I've fucked up the only thing that really meant anything to me and that's my life with you, Dave. How big a fool can one woman be?"

It broke Dave's heart to see her. Sue was always so regal and composed. She practically never used bad language, this morning and last night being the big exceptions. Over the last two years, if anything she had become more composed and aloof. This was a side of her he had never seen. He realised that this was the first time he had ever seen his wife cry. He sat on the floor beside her and wrapped his arms around her, hugging her tightly.

"Sue, baby, it's OK, really. I know what you're like with one gin and tonic not to mention a line of coke. I don't blame you, really."

She looked at him incredulously. "You don't? How could you possibly forgive me for such a dreadful thing? Dave, don't you get it? Your next-door neighbour has been – he's been," she stuttered.

"Yeah, yeah, he's been there, done that. So what. You don't love him, do you?"

"Love him. God, if you knew how much I hate him!" Her venom shocked Dave, as she spat out the words.

"Well, that makes two of us. Sue, don't worry. Revenge is sweet."

But she had begun to cry again. He held her and held her while she let go of the guilt and the horrible secret that she had been bottling up inside her for the last two years almost to the day.

Slowly, as they talked, her sobs gave way to sighs and eventually Dave saw the first sign of a slight smile brighten her face.

"That's my girl," he encouraged her.

They sat on the floor for almost two hours talking about their love for each other and their life together. It was such a precious and vulnerable thing.

"There's one thing you must promise me from all of this, Sue."

"Anything."

"No more secrets. Do you promise?"

"I promise, no more secrets," she echoed.

"Do you think you can stand yet?" he asked tentatively.

"I think so."

They stood up together, still arm in arm.

"Would it be OK if I took a bath first, Dave?"

"Sure. You do that and I'll nip down to the hotel boutique. See if I can find us something more suitable for daywear. Mind you, what you were wearing last night to dinner was gorgeous."

"I think I would prefer if you stayed with me, if that's OK," she asked hesitantly.

351

"Whatever you want, queen," he whispered.

Sue hadn't let him near her in the bath in the last two years.

"Just sit near me, on the loo and keep talking to me, please."

Slowly as the bathroom filled with steam and Sue regained her strength, she wanted Dave nearer and nearer, until he was in the bath with her and they made the slowest and most intimate love of their lives.

CHAPTER 26

Christmas whizzed by in a flurry of tinsel and turkey. Richard was so preoccupied with the relaunch of Rock FM that he left for Dublin on St Stephen's Day, much to the chagrin of his own mother and his daughters, but to the delight of Robin Maher who eagerly awaited his return to her in Dublin.

"I swear Daddy has left this family!" Kelly fumed when she heard.

"He'll be home for the New Year, sweetheart, and anyway, that's not a very nice way to talk about him, especially after the Christmas present he has just given you!"

Saskia was shocked at Richard's generosity with his girls. Probably his guilty conscience, she thought, but for the most part she forced the memory of Richard and Sue Parker from her mind.

She couldn't think about it, wouldn't think about it

until she had time alone and perhaps she got the chance to talk to Dave Parker, just to make sure that it wasn't her imagination.

Richard had discussed a skiing holiday with her in November and she agreed that she couldn't leave Robin with Edu. Even though Edu seemed to have come through her lackadaisical phase, Saskia was not nearly confident enough to leave them alone in Innishambles for an entire week or ten days.

Richard subsequently suggested that he take the girls away by himself for a week in early January. He would be over the pressure of the relaunch by then and it would give him time to catch up with them, considering he had seen so little of "his angels" over the autumn. Saskia thought that this was a great idea. Richard said that he would organise it as *their* Christmas present to the girls. She kicked herself now for being so trusting. Richard never kept his familial obligations and naturally enough on Christmas morning, despite his promises to Saskia, he had nothing to give the girls except his words. She had been furious with him later in the day, when they were alone.

"Honestly Richard, would it have been too much to ask for you to get a brochure and a couple of plane tickets?"

"I've been up to my eyes, Sas," he complained.

"Fine, then why didn't you call me? I would have gladly gone into Wicklow Travel and booked something for you."

"Don't be daft. You know that I'll do it through the company!" he snapped.

"Will you? When?"

"Next bloody week. Don't hassle me."

When the girls discovered that there was nothing tangible under the tree from their parents, they were not happy. In an effort to bolster them, Richard got carried away and promised them a skiing holiday in the Rocky Mountains.

"Colorado, here we come!" he enthused.

"Where in Colorado?" Kelly asked suspiciously.

"Where do you want to go?" he asked.

"Vail," Lauren replied in a flash. Nick Jnr had been telling her where the coolest spots were and what to avoid.

"What's so good about Vail? You've just heard the name on TV shows. I'm sure there's plenty of other terrific places in Colorado," Richard laughed a little nervously, thinking that Vail must be one of the most expensive places in the world to ski.

"Well, Keystone is quite near Vail and it's meant to be quite a good family resort, but I hear Vail is way cooler," Lauren quoted Nick. She continued, "Aspen is for oldies – even older than you, Dad!"

"OK, let's go to Vail," Tiffany backed her sister up, aware that she was repeating what Nick had said. "Anyway, we'll be snowboarding this year. Nobody skis any more!"

"All right, I give in. Vail or Keystone it is, depending

on which one still has availability!" Richard said
expansively to his girls.

In view of the third of January being such a big event,
the Daltons agreed to have a quiet New Year's Eve.
Saskia watched the television with Edwina Dalton and
Edu, while Richard worked in the study. The girls
headed over to Rathdeen Manor where they met up
with Nick, Connor Cantwell, Barney and a few other
friends. Much to Lauren's dismay, Connor seemed to
be pursuing Tiffany and so she continued going out
with Nick, even if neither of them seemed that into
it.

On the evening of the third, Richard had organised
for a stretch limo to collect his three elder daughters
and his wife and drive them to Rock Tower. He left
Saskia to inform Edu that she was baby-sitting Robin
for the evening.

The au pair was furious with Richard. She knew
that she looked terrific at the moment and Richard had
barely acknowledged her over the holidays. It was
definitely true what they said about the glowing phase.
She still had no tummy to speak of, perhaps just a tiny
bump, but her hair shone like the girls' in the shampoo
commercials. So did her skin and her eyes were
terrifically bright. The sickness was over and she had
been planning how she would break the news to
Richard that he was going to be a father again.

It occurred to her that this evening would have been

a good time. Richard would be celebrating the new
listenership figures for Rock FM, making it Dublin's
most successful radio station. He would also be putting
his terrific Rock Tower on view for the first time. She
hadn't even seen the building yet. As the evening drew
to a close, she planned on taking him aside and giving
him the terrific news. Naturally he would be delighted
that his beautiful young lover was going to bear him a
love child and they could at last go public about their
wonderful love affair. Now her plan was shot to pieces.
She wasn't even going to the bloody party.

She sulked around the house, minding Robin while
the others dressed and giggled.

As the girls at Innishambles were in a tizzy getting
showered, made up and fighting over who was
wearing what, Richard was in Dublin city getting a
manicure. He had worked so hard over the last few
weeks, everything was ready. His speech was written
and the caterers were booked. Parkers, the chain store,
had moved into their new premises over the Christmas
and New Year, and they were going to open their doors
to Richard's guests tonight. It was going to be a huge
party.

It was all going to plan. Just as Robin Maher had
promised, the figures had been released that morning.
Rock FM had gained listeners in all the relative age
groups and even in some areas where they didn't
expect to. Rock FM's interest was the twenty to thirty-
five age group primarily and then the fifteen to twenty-

year-olds. Thirty-five pluses were a bonus. To Richard's delight, they were up in all these categories.

As soon as the figures were released that morning, he had a celebratory bottle of champagne with the management team down in the station. Then he had gone around and personally congratulated the DJs. After that, he took the advertising staff out for lunch. All in all it had been a very busy day. Robin had been at his right hand all day. In fact, if anything she had been a little too close, he thought. While Richard enjoyed her company, he felt like she was taking some of the credit for their current success, which was not really the case. Corporate Affairs had only been given the account a few months previously. This success was the culmination of years of hard grind.

This evening's manicure and facial had been her suggestion, however, and he had to admit it was thoroughly enjoyable. He had never had a facial before and he only came to the Berkeley Hotel because it was a 'men's only' salon. Up until now he had always thought of facials and manicures as being slightly poncey, but he was beginning to change his mind. At the end of the pampering, his hands looked really terrific and his eyebrows had been slightly reshaped. Even Richard had to admit he looked fantastic, and he felt great.

He arrived back to Rock Tower at seven o'clock, an hour before the doors were set to open to the public for the first time. He took the elevator from the car park up to his penthouse.

"Richard, is that you?" Robin called him

"Yes, it's me. Who the hell else would it be? Where are you?"

"I'm up here."

Richard looked up and there was Robin standing at the balcony of the upper level, wearing a tiny dressing-gown, and, it seemed, not much else.

"What the hell are you doing?" he asked.

"God, what kind of a hello is that? I'm waiting for you if you must know. I have a little surprise for you!"

"Robin, what the fuck are you messing at? Do you know what time it is? Damn it, my wife and kids are set to arrive any minute. What would have happened if I had them with me?"

"Richard, Richard, you worry too much. I'm a smart little girl. I was watching out for you on the security cameras. I would have seen, if you had company. As it happens, I saw you arrive alone and park your car in its usual place. Then I quickly got ready. Now do you want to play or not? I have everything ready."

"What do you mean 'everything ready'"? he asked, calming slightly and getting a little horny.

"Come and see," she giggled. "Or should that be 'see and come'?"

Richard bounded up the stairs to see what she was talking about.

"You're a naughty, naughty girl to take such risks," he growled as he squeezed her bare bum and took her into his bedroom.

The camcorder was set up next to the bed and she had placed an array of black leather whips and handcuffs on the bedside.

"While you were in the Berkeley, I paid a visit to the Ann Summers sex shop on O'Connell Street. You want to see the things they have there!"

Richard wasn't sure that he did. It was all very well when *he* decided what they did and how they did it. In fact that was the turn-on for him. If Robin was going to take the initiative, he felt more threatened than turned on.

"Look, Robin, I'm not sure that we have time for this," he stalled.

"Oh, baby, please," she put on her little girl voice.

He looked at her and then at the camcorder.

"OK, then but it had better be a quickie."

When the buzzer rang out twenty minutes later, Richard was in the shower and so Robin answered the door. She was fully dressed when she greeted the Dalton ladies.

"Welcome to Rock Tower," she smiled and stretched out her hand to Saskia. "I'm Robin Maher from Corporate Affairs. You must be Richard's wife."

"Yes, I'm Saskia and these are three of my daughters, Kelly, Tiffany and Lauren but it's funny, I have a baby called Robin. Isn't that a coincidence!"

"Why yes, it is. I think Richard is getting changed. I'm not sure," she laughed shyly like a true pro. "I wouldn't go up –"

The daughters laughed at her apparent embarrassment and ran up the stairs.

"Daddy, where are you?" Lauren yelled.

"I'm coming. Wait downstairs," he yelled as he saw the state his room was in. With the towel pulled around his waist, he quickly threw the camcorder and Ann Summers stuff into the cupboard. Just as he slammed the door on the evidence, Lauren pushed open his bedroom door.

"Hi, this place is so cool, Dad!" She jumped onto the bed where Richard had just shagged Robin.

"How big is this bed? It's massive."

Then there was a more tentative knock on the door.

"Dad, are you in here?" It was Tiff.

"Hi honey, come on in. You may as well. Your sister is already here. Does a man get no privacy these days?" he laughed companionably with them.

"Where's your mum?" Richard suddenly panicked. He had no idea where Robin was in the penthouse.

"It's OK. She's talking to your PR woman. She's a bit sexy, Dad."

"Is she?" he asked, sounding as uninterested as possible.

"What's the rest of the penthouse like? Hey, can we live here when we're at college?

Kelly walked in next as Tiffany began to open presses.

"OK, this is getting ridiculous. Can you ladies just leave me alone for five minutes so I can get changed

361

and then we'll head down to the others and have a drink or a Coke or something?"

Richard was getting nervous about any tell-tale signs that Robin might have left around the penthouse.

Reluctantly the girls headed back downstairs. They joined the women in the drawing-room. Robin had already fixed Saskia a drink and she was pouring Richard a whiskey.

"Would you girls like a drink?" she asked as the sisters entered the room. Robin could see quite clearly that the elder and younger daughter took after the father, while the middle one looked like the mother. They were all striking however and full of excitement. They looked at their mother when the drink was offered.

"Soft drinks only," she said sternly. "You are not going to get giddy at your father's press conference.

Begrudgingly they did what they were told and had a Diet Coke each.

"Now, how are my angels?" Richard swept into the room. He looked wonderful, fresh and energetic and brimming with confidence.

Robin looked at him in admiration and wondered if he would be staying in The Tower tonight or going home.

Saskia looked at him and began to worry if perhaps she had imagined the conversation between him and Sue Parker.

The girls rushed into his arms.

"Before we go any further," he announced. "I have a surprise for my little ladies." From his inside breast pocket, he pulled out three white envelopes and handed one to each of the girls. "It's OK. They're all exactly the same."

The girls ripped them apart, but Tiffany was first.

"Oh Daddy, it's an aeroplane ticket," she gushed, "and, and oh, my we're staying at the Hotel Marriott in Vail and all this money –"

"Five hundred dollars, to be precise and that's it. You're not wangling another penny, or in this case cent out of me over there. How you spend it is up to you! Happy Christmas, girls."

"Hey," Lauren chirped up. "This ticket is for the day after tomorrow, the fifth of January. Omigod, that doesn't give us much time to get ready."

The girls' cheers were explosive.

Saskia watched them each hug their father in gratification. She felt a pang of jealousy. Was this present not meant to be from the two of them? It certainly didn't feel that way.

After a few more hugs and kisses, things settled down again.

"How many are you expecting tonight?" Saskia asked Richard.

He looked at Robin, who had the list with her. She answered for him.

"About three hundred, Saskia. That breaks down into groups from the press – newspapers, magazines other radio stations and television stations. We're hoping they'll give the event a good deal of publicity. Then we have practically all the advertising agencies in the country coming. They're the ones who buy the airtime from us, so we'll be fawning over them. In effect, they pay our bills! There'll be a large corporate section, the head of Renault Ireland, Mercedes, and Fiat. We do a lot of car giveaways! We'll also have a fair amount of hoteliers, bankers and the like. And of course the celebs; DJs and their wives, a sprinkling of TV presenters and so on.

"Will you have celebs from other stations?" Lauren asked.

"Yes, honey, the whole market has opened up for broadcasters. They move around between radio stations now. Not like the old days when there was only RTE. In fact I'd say we'd have a good number of them here tonight, checking out the station's facilities."

"Where is the party actually happening?" Tiffany asked.

Richard answered, "It'll be downstairs, angel. You didn't even stop there, did you? If you came up directly from the basement, you'll have missed it. The reception area has been set up with a bar and buffet, so the guests can watch the DJ in action. There'll also be tours up to the offices of Rock FM and Parkers, which opens its doors for the first time tonight."

"Will anybody be coming up here?"

"No. This is strictly private."

"Are the Parkers coming?" Saskia risked asking.

"They said they were so I assume they are," Richard answered, then he asked, "What about the Flatterys? Did you ask them, Sas?"

"Mum asked me to," Lauren butted in. "They said yeah, sure. So is Barney Armstrong. It's going to be a great night!"

"Speaking of great nights, I think we'd better head down, ladies," Richard urged. "I don't want Mum to be alone down there."

There was a collective groan at the mention of Edwina Dalton's name.

"Robin, could I just have a word with you? I want to go over the list one more time, make sure I know everybody!" he smiled. "Sas, I'll see you downstairs in a few minutes with the girls, OK?"

"OK."

He walked his family to the lift and sent them down to the ground floor. Then he turned to Robin.

"Just what the hell do you think you're playing at, girl?" he thundered.

"What are you talking about?" she asked shocked at his outburst.

"You're swanning around this place like Lady of the Manor. Do you know that the girls nearly walked in on all that stuff you bought and left lying on the bed?"

"Oh shit. Richard, I am so sorry about that. I fully meant to hide the stuff but then they arrived and it went clean out of my mind. I'm sorry."

"Yeah, this is not good enough, Robin." His eyes were dark and his eyebrows furrowed. "Lay off a little, OK. And you don't come up here without me. Is that understood?"

"I was just trying to give you a little treat."

"You nearly got me a little caught, stupid bitch – think."

"Don't call me a bitch. Richard, this is not the time for this. You have a very big speech to deliver in a half an hour. I'm sorry I mucked up. We can talk about it later."

"You don't come up here without my prior permission. Is that understood?" he repeated.

"Yes, I understand."

"Now, where did you leave all your stuff?"

Robin pointed to an overnight bag, concealed behind the rubber plant next to the elevator door.

"Good, let's go," was Richard's reply.

She had never seen him this angry before. Robin couldn't believe how furious he could get. Richard looked like he might have even hit her. Instinctively, she knew not to antagonise him. Going down in the lift, she kept her eyes lowered, subserviently, but quietly steaming.

"Ground floor, reception area," the lift informed them.

"Now, shall we smile for the cameras?" Richard asked as if absolutely nothing was wrong. He gave her a broad friendly grin.

"Have a nice day," the lift advised.

"Absolutely," Robin beamed right back at him. Christ, she thought, I'm sleeping with Dr Jekyll and Mr Hyde.

"Have you invited Connor?" Lauren asked Tiffany.

"Eh, yeah, and I gather you've invited Nick."

"Yep," Lauren answered as she swiped a vodka and coke from the free bar, hoping to pass it off as regular Coke. The reception was filling up quickly.

"You and Connor seem to be getting on pretty well then," Lauren persevered as she took a drink.

"Well, it's OK. But to be honest I don't really think he's my type."

"Poor Tiff, what is your type if it's not Connor or Barney?"

Tiffany turned to her younger sister. "That's not fair. Barney was just too old and Connor, well, he's lovely. It's just we're a little too alike, too quiet I guess."

"That's ironic, because I think Nick is a little too wild for me. We bring out the worst in each other. There's nobody around to keep things calm."

Tiffany grabbed a glass of wine and took a deep slug, "Yeh know what, we should do a swop!"

Lauren burst out laughing. "Tiff, I'd love to!"

"You're kidding."

"No, seriously, I'd love to. Oh, were you just kidding?"

"Yes, no, I mean well I don't know." Tiffany thought about it. "You know what? I don't think I was kidding.

I just thought you were *madly* in love with Nick Flattery."

"Ah, that was before I knew him," Lauren explained.

"Oh, right yeah. Well, even if we did both want to swop, there is the small matter of the boys to consider. They would think that we had really lost it."

But Lauren was fired up. "Look, Tiffany, do you really want to give this a go?"

Tiffany thought about it for a minute, but in her heart she knew that she really had a crush on Nick and here was her sister, offering him to her on a silver platter.

"Yes."

"OK, well, they're both here tonight, so we'd better start racking our brains!"

"Well, if you want to think straight," Tiffany interrupted her, "put that down." She took the vodka from her younger sister and handed her a Coke.

As the room filled with beautiful people, Barney Armstrong walked in. He had got a lift from Jessica and Kim, but they were loitering outside.

Saskia was the first person he saw whom he recognised. She was baby-sitting her mother-in-law, as Richard worked the room with a rather gorgeous blonde at his side.

"Hi, Sas, how are you?"

"Hi, Barney, welcome to Rock Tower! You know Edwina."

"Yes, of course. This place is rather spectacular. It's like something out of America."

"It's all rock and marble as in Rock Tower and Rock FM, get it?"

He laughed, "Yes, I had twigged that much."

"Speaking of things American, did you see the Flatterys yet?" Saskia asked, hoping she didn't look too anxious. She hadn't seen Nicolas since their dinner party and she really wanted to talk to him. He hadn't returned her two phone calls. Tonight Saskia was determined to corner him and help him over his current domestic problems.

"They're outside, at least Jessica and Kim are. Nick Jnr is making his own way from Blackrock, I gather and Nicolas is in the States. Did you know he was going back there?"

Saskia's face fell. "No, I had no idea." She felt crushed. It was only when Barney told her that Nicolas wasn't even in the country did she realise how much she *really* wanted to see him. The pain she felt was actually physical, in the pit of her stomach. She couldn't ask Barney any more questions with her mother-in-law listening to every word, but she desperately wanted to know when he went, how long would he be away for. Would he be back?

"Sas, are you OK? You've gone really pale all of a sudden," Barney took her arm.

"I'm sorry. It's just getting a little smoky in here. Perhaps I need a little air."

Barney looked at Edwina for assistance.

"Oh, honestly, Saskia, it's not smoky in here. It must

be something else. Are you eating properly?" Edwina snapped at her daughter-in-law impatiently. Even Mrs Dalton had noticed how thin Saskia had become. "I'll take her out, Barney. You go on with the young folk."

He walked the women to the door of Rock Tower as Jessica and Kim were walking in. Nick Jnr and Connor Cantwell were just behind as were some very well-known faces from RTE TV. Barney didn't get the chance to ask Sas where Kelly might be and so he joined up with the other two young men.

CHAPTER 27

"Hi girls," Nick walked up to Lauren and Tiffany and gave them both a kiss on the cheek. Lauren had a gut instinct that his interest in her was waning as fast as hers in him. She just didn't know how to broach the subject.

"Have a drink," Lauren handed him a vodka and coke as Barney and Connor joined them.

"Hi, Tiff," Connor smiled shyly at her.

"Here, Connor, have a drink. You're going to need it." Lauren smiled.

"Why?"

"It's going to be a long night," she said by way of explanation.

Barney was just about to ask the girls if they knew where Kelly was when a voice boomed through the loudspeaker they were standing next to.

"Ladies and gentlemen, please put your hands together for your host, Mr Richard Dalton."

The girls cheered and stomped their feet. Nick let out a loud whistle.

"Who is she?" he asked, ogling the lady who had introduced Richard.

Lauren elbowed him in the ribcage. "Hump off. She's Robin Maher, Dad's PR girl."

"She is a bit cute," Connor conceded, glancing sideways at Tiffany to make sure that he hadn't offended her.

"Come on, boys. Drink up," Lauren encouraged them despite Tiffany's dirty looks. "It's a free bar!"

Richard Dalton came to the microphone.

The reception area was now packed to capacity.

"You're all very welcome to Dublin's newest and tallest building, Rock Tower, the home of Rock FM," he smiled expansively.

The audience cheered and he continued.

"By the way, if you feel like heckling, just be aware that everything we say here is going out live on Rock FM!"

There was more thunderous applause.

"Firstly, I'd like to thank all our listeners at home, who are tuned in right now – listening to us party." Another cheer. "I'd like to thank them for making Rock FM Dublin's number one radio station. We couldn't have done it without you. We have some listeners sprinkled among our VIP guests tonight, winners of some of the competitions that we have been running over the last few weeks here on Rock FM. To all our other guests I just want to say thank you for doing business with us. Together we make a great team – hell, the *best* team and let's just keep it that way. All that remains is for me to say dig in to the food and drink and Rock on with Rock FM!" Richard nodded at the DJ who was in the studio. He pushed up a fader and Tina Turner began to sing out, "The Best".

Richard stepped down to more rapturous applause and people immediately swamped him, as his wife and mother looked on from the back of the reception and the girls watched proudly from the bar.

Kelly was the only one in the family who hated these sorts of dos. As soon as she arrived into the reception hall, she spotted her old friend Denise. Denise had been a few years ahead of Kelly in Mount Eden and she was equally delighted to see her old smoking-buddy.

"Kelly, welcome to Rock Tower. Here, have a beer," Denise greeted her.

"Thanks, Denise. How are you getting on here? Is my dad an ogre?"

"No way, he's dead cool."

"Yeah, in his dreams. Look will you show me around the studios and the offices. Is Gerry Dempsey here? He's such a ride!"

"Yes, Kelly, and so is his wife and their three kids! Come on, I want to have a look at Parker's anyway. They've just opened."

The girls took off, clutching a bottle of beer each, to have a look around the building.

Their first stop was the first floor. Inevitably they met some of the young guns in the advertising department.

"Hi, Denise, who's your friend?" Dermot Ryan asked. He was probably one of the best-looking guys in the department, and damn good at his job. He always beat his sales targets, thanks to constantly hustling and not taking no for an answer.

"Hi, Dermot, this is Kelly Dalton and she's far too good for the likes of you."

"Nothing to Dick Dalton, are you?" he laughed.

"If you mean your boss, Dermot, Kelly is his daughter."

Dermot nearly fell off the table he was casually draped over. The other two reps he was chatting to also sat upright.

"Jesus, I didn't know he had daughters let alone such a beaut." Dermot was over by her side in a flash offering his hand and a cigarette.

"Can I escort you ladies around the building? I'll show you our supersoft sound rooms!"

"Don't you even think about it, Dermot," Denise defended the honour of her younger friend. Then she explained to her. "The sound booths are tiny rooms, barely bigger than a toilet cubicle, where the jocks sit when they're recording ads. There's nothing in the room except a microphone. Obviously the rooms are totally soundproof for recording purposes and the walls are covered in foam, so they're kinda kinky too if you know what I mean! Anyway, Dermot has brought more than one temp into them in his day."

"Denise, I don't know what you're talking about!" He feigned shock.

"And what about the recording of that poor girl you seduced last week?"

Kelly spoke for the first time to him. "You recorded bonking someone?"

"*I* didn't. I was otherwise engaged." He glanced at his two friends, still sitting at their desk, smoking and staring at the floor pretending that they weren't even there.

"I'm sure Dad would love to hear that story," Kelly smiled, "especially as you've only been in this building for a matter of weeks! Fast work."

Dermot lost his composure for an instant, as did his two cohorts until the girls burst out laughing. When they realised that Kelly was only joking they nervously joined in.

Elizabeth Wright, Richard's PA, stuck her head around the door. "Hey, you guys are going to miss the speeches if you don't get downstairs straight away."

"Well, what are you doing up here then?" Dermot snapped at her, hating her prudish efficiency.

Elizabeth got surprisingly uptight. "I, er I just had to do a message upstairs for – I was just doing something. Now do you want me to hold the lift or not?"

Denise, Kelly, and the boys joined her in the talking elevator. They hit the foyer just as Richard was starting and they fell out of the lift crying with laughter because Dermot Ryan could mimic the lift perfectly only he was saying much ruder things than the lift would ever say. Even Elizabeth Wright was laughing despite her best efforts not to. They calmed down and listened to Richard.

Barney had heard the commotion however and as Richard finished and Tina Turner started, he saw Kelly being guided to the buffet by a very good-looking young man in a suit. He had jet-black hair, which was gelled back from his face. Barney thought he looked like a rat, way too slick. Kelly however seemed comfortable when he put his arm around her waist gently, to guide her to the food. Barney desperately wanted to go over to break them apart but he was rooted to the spot.

Robin Maher was anything but rooted to the spot. She clung to Richard like a leech. As different photographers approached her she would gently put her hand on Richard's shoulder to get his attention.

"Richard, this is Noel from *VIP* magazine. He wants us to smile."

Richard turned and smiled as Robin slipped her arm around his waist and squeezed. Robin had been a little cross with him after his outburst earlier but when she saw him deliver his speech, all was forgiven. The man had such style and finesse. Richard Dalton was hers and that was that. To celebrate that fact, Robin had been drinking gin and tonics like water and now she felt no pain.

Richard turned away again to talk to a politician who had just arrived while Robin gave the correct spellings of their names to Noel.

"Yes," she smiled, "Richard Dalton and Robin Maher," she smiled.

"I know that bit, Robin," Noel laughed. "What's the connection though? What do you want me to put down as your title or relationship?" He held his pencil and notepad expectantly.

In a fit of recklessness, Robin giggled and decided. "*Friend*, Noel. Put down *friend*."

Richard's peripheral hearing was in perfect working order, however, and he swung around to the photographer, cutting the politician off mid-sentence.

"Noel, Ms Maher's title is Account Manager, Corporate Affairs. Got that?" Richard's smile was as warm as a deep freeze.

"Got it, loud and clear, Mr Dalton." Noel backed off to photograph some of the celebs.

"Try that again and you'll be in serious trouble," Richard whispered into Robin's ear. With so many people around however, the smile never left his face. He didn't want to create a scandal.

Robin saw the smile and ignored the sentiment and she laughed at Richard. She whispered back, "Will you spank me later?"

Richard turned and walked away, aware that he was getting nowhere. She was too pissed.

Queen boomed out 'We will rock you', and Lauren

got the notion that the boys would love the view from the penthouse.

"Would you like to see the view from the top?" she asked Nick.

"If you want to," he replied unenthusiastically.

"What about you, Tiff, Connor? Do you want to see the penthouse?"

"Yeah, that sounds like a great idea," Tiffany enthused. "Oh, Barney, do you want to come?" she asked as an afterthought.

"I think not. Five is a crowd," he laughed amiably, delighted to see Tiffany beginning to hang around guys her own age. He was also amazed how easy she was in *his* company after their brief encounter. Maybe it's just me, he thought, as he took another glass of wine and wandered off to find Saskia and Edwina.

"Penthouse," the lift told the young people as they arrived at the top.

"Wow, this is some building," Connor enthused, leaving Tiffany's side to admire the view from the window. "Look," he laughed, "there's fish in the table!"

"Who's for a drink?" Lauren asked.

"Lauren, we don't have to get pissed every time we're together, you know," Nick suggested.

"Well, what do you want to do?"

"We could just sit here." He flopped into the deep sofa and patted the spot beside him.

"You want to snog?"

"Snog means neck, doesn't it? Yeah, now there's an idea!"

"I've a better idea. Let's play another game."

"What did you have in mind?"

Lauren hesitated. "Have you ever heard of the game 'Swop'?"

Tiffany swung around when she heard her sister.

"Omigod, I think a drink is a good idea, Lauren. That's a pretty wild concept. Where does Dad keep his gargle here?"

"What is 'Swop'?" Connor asked, turning away from the spectacular view.

"Gin, vodka or beer?" Tiffany, asked having found the drinks cabinet.

"Vodka and coke, please," Nick asked. Giving up on the idea of getting Lauren onto the sofa, he joined Tiff at the booze.

"Well," Lauren started, "you boys could swop clothes for a start."

Everybody looked at her in surprise.

"This game could have merit," Nick conceded, looking at Connor to make sure that he wasn't that much smaller than him.

"What's the point of the exercise?" Connor asked, slightly less convinced.

"Well, it's a drinking game obviously," Lauren, laughed. "Whoever finishes last has to do a shot."

"Can we keep our own jocks?" Nick asked. Tiffany was dumbstruck.

"OK," Lauren replied, making up the rules as she went along.

Nick was peeling off his clothes at lightning speed. The girls laughed gleefully; even Tiffany who was very shy couldn't help but appreciate what an amazing body Nick had.

"Do you work out?" she asked him. Then she suddenly felt guilty about Connor.

"Come on. I'm ready. Connor, strip," Nick yelled, standing in only his jocks. "Ah man, this game is crap. How can I win if the other guy is going to be so slow?"

"Relax," Lauren tried to calm him. "Don't forget he still has to get your clothes on. You're in the lead."

Under the influence of the alcohol, this seemed acceptable to Nick.

By the time Connor had managed to get all his stuff off and Nick's gear back on, it was obvious that he had lost by about two minutes.

"Drink, drink, drink," the others chorused as he downed a large shot of something clear and strong. He didn't even know what it was.

"OK," Nick smirked. "Now it's the girls' turn!"

Tiffany looked at her little sister in horror. "You didn't really think this through, did you?" But Lauren was half-stripped already.

"Lauren, have you no shame?" Tiffany squealed as she tried to take her little dress off behind her sister so the boys couldn't see.

Fortunately, both girls had known that they were

meeting their boyfriends that evening and so both were wearing slip dresses and their newest, poshest underwear. Tiffany was wearing the teddy that Kelly had given her for Christmas and Lauren was wearing a very cute matching bra and knicker set that Tiff had given her. The job was easier than it first sounded. They kept their underwear on, despite the boys' protestations and so a simple exchange of dresses was all that was really involved.

Three minutes later it was Tiffany who was obliged to drink drink drink.

"What can we swop now?" Connor asked innocently, feeling surprisingly well after his shot.

"We could swop partners!" Lauren suggested, in a voice barely above a whisper. The other three heard her loud and clear, however.

"What?" Connor asked astounded. He had fancied Lauren for so long now, he couldn't believe what she was suggesting.

"You want to swing?" Nick asked laughing. "Usually it's the adults that do that."

"Oh, Lauren, where do you get your ideas?" Tiffany asked, absolutely mortified.

"Just one kiss," Lauren suggested, too shy to look at Connor or Nick.

"Surely, not in front of each other?" Tiffany asked shyly.

"God, no, sis!"

"OK, come on then." Nick's bravado took over, combined with his deep wish to get closer to Tiffany.

He stood up and took Tiffany by the hand. "Connor, just one kiss – you don't mind, do you?"

"Hey, if it's OK with Tiff, it's OK with me. What about Lauren? Is that OK with you?"

Nick looked at Lauren and smiled. "Lauren, behave! And no more booze, OK?"

"God, you sound like my father!"

Tiffany was amazed at how gently Nick took her hand. He put his other hand under her chin, gently bringing her face upwards and her eyes to meet his.

"OK," he spoke softly, "where can we get a little privacy?"

Noel from *VIP* tapped Kelly softly on the shoulder.

"If it's OK, I'd like to get a photo of you with your mum and dad."

"Yeah, sure," she smiled shyly. Noel knew she would make an incredible model.

Barney and Edwina looked on proudly as the threesome was photographed by a number of the paparazzi.

"Are you having a nice time?" Barney stepped in just as the flashes stopped. He could see rat-man already making a beeline for Kelly again.

"I certainly am. What about you?"

"I'm a little lost to be honest."

"Barney, why didn't you tell me? You should have come over to me. You know I would have minded you!" she teased.

"Will you show me around the building now?"

Rat-man descended, not willing to let go of his prey that easily. "Kelly, do you want another drink?" he asked.

"Oh, Dermot. This is Barney – Barney, this is Dermot Ryan. He works in the advertising department of Rock FM."

They shook hands, sizing each other up.

"What do you do, buddy?" Dermot asked with a slight edge to his voice.

"I'm a vet."

"Well, I'm afraid you won't find many heifers around here," Dermot sneered.

Kelly didn't like it. "Actually, Dermot, Barney is going to be my boss next year."

"Ah right – so you like animals, Kelly?"

"Yes, do you?"

"Me? Love them. I have a pet snake. Well, I *had*. It er, died."

"Do you know why?" Barney asked.

"Nah, it just died."

"Animals don't just die for no reason, Dermo. " Kelly looked at him.

"I'm going to take Barney around the building. We'll see you later."

Dermot knew that he was temporarily beaten. "Yeah sure. See you later."

As he returned to Denise and the gang, they teased him. "Did you get pipped at the post by the home boy, Dermo? That's not like you!"

"Yeah, remind me to buy a hamster," Dermot grumbled as he took another free beer.

"Come on. Let's check out Parker's first, Barney," Kelly suggested.

As they walked into the brand-new clothes store, she commented, "Hey, that's strange. I don't think the Parkers are here. Isn't that weird?"

Barney's mind was elsewhere however. He had nearly died tonight when he saw that sleaze trying to worm his way into Kelly's life. Barney knew that he just had to say something.

"Kelly?"

"Mm."

"Can I talk to you?"

"Sure. Oh, look at this!" she pulled out a long cashmere wool coat.

"It's only ninety-nine pounds. This is a great store," she was already rushing off in another direction.

"Seriously, Kelly. We have to talk."

She stopped abruptly and stared at her old friend.

"What is it, Barney?"

"Kelly Dalton. I am hopelessly in love with you. I know that this sounds crazy but I think it's always been there. The day you nearly fell off Polly was the day it came home to me. You are the most beautiful, kindest, sweetest creature that I have ever met and I love you!" He stopped and looked at her.

Kelly was lost for words. Her eyes had grown huge and confused.

"Barney, what are you saying? I don't understand. I thought. . ." She stopped because she no longer knew what she thought. "But the job?"

"Oh, that's genuine. Even if you told me to sod off now and pretend that this conversation never took place the job would still be there. It's for real but so is this. Kelly, I've never felt this way about anybody in my life. When I saw that animal trying to get friendly with you downstairs, well, let's just say that it was the moment of truth for me."

"Hang on a second. What about you and Jenny Quinn?"

"Nothing ever happened there."

"Barney, I'm not stupid. I know she stayed the night."

"I know, but that's it. Nothing actually ever happened. The one that I do need to mention to you is your own sister Tiffany. Now she and I *do* have a past, even if it was very brief but she seems genuinely cool about it."

"You don't have a *real* past with her, Barney."

"Yes, I do."

"No, you don't."

"What are you talking about, Kelly? Tiffany and I were as intimate as two people can get!"

"No, you weren't. Are you telling me that you think that you had sex with my little sister?" Kelly burst out laughing

He looked wounded. "Well, to be honest I was very very drunk, but I was pretty sure we did."

Kelly's heart melted for her dear friend. Maybe he really was the man she had been waiting for and he was right under her nose. God knows that they had enough in common!

"Barney, you can take it from me, you funny man," she moved into his arms and hugged him as she had done so many times in the past, only this time it was different. "You never had sex with my little sister." Then she kissed him on the lips. He kissed her back as softly as he could, terrified that the spell would break.

"God, I can't believe that this is really happening," he said when they eventually stopped. She rested her head on his shoulder as he stroked her long soft curls.

"I'll tell you something that'll really make you laugh. Not only did I think that Tiff and I had sex but I've also been having these wild dreams about Edu. She steals into my room at night and does the craziest things to me!"

Kelly pushed him away. "What?" She stood back. "What the hell are you saying, Barney?" She tried to make sense of it. "Is this some kind of joke? Ha ha, where's the hidden camera? You bring me up here. You tell me that you love me. OK, the Tiffany thing I understand. You were drunk, but then you tell me that you're having wet dreams about my au pair and you expect me to fall into your arms? What kind of sick bastard are you? You bloody men – you're no better than the rest of them!" Her eyes had glassed up like deep dark pools of pain.

"No, no. Kelly it's not like that. I really love you.

You're all that matters to me. Please, you've got to believe me. Forget about what I just said."

"Tell that to Edu!" Kelly yelled at him through her tears, as she stormed off, leaving him in the middle of the lingerie section alone.

It was well after midnight when Jessica Bell bumped into Saskia and Edwina Dalton who were sitting at a table to the side of what had become the dance floor.

"What a swell party, Sas. Aren't you dancing?"

"No, not just now. I was earlier with that lovely young man from the advertising department, Dermot something."

Jessica and Kim sat down beside them.

"Jessica Bell," she stuck her hand to shake Edwina's. The reason Saskia hadn't done any introductions was because she wasn't sure how to present Kim to her mother-in-law.

"How do you do?" Edwina replied taking her hand.

"And this is my partner, Kim," Jessica continued.

"Partner in what?" the senior Mrs Dalton asked over the music.

"Why, in life, of course! Oh, I love this one. Come on, Kim." Jessica jumped to her feet when she heard the words of 'Part-time Lover' start up.

Edwina simply shrugged and commented to Saskia,

"What a strange lady."

Robin Maher was well and truly pissed when she heard

'Part-time Lover' start up over the sound system. She was already fed up with Richard for snapping at her so much throughout the evening and she had noticed the politician's wife flirting outrageously with Richard. Robin sidled up to him.

"Listen, Richard, they're playing our song!" she whispered, trying to take his hands.

"Would you can it, Robin," he hissed back, still smiling.

"Come on, darling. Dance with me." She began to dance as he stood ramrod still.

"Robin, I think you've had rather too much to drink tonight." He tried to disentangle himself. "She's been working too hard," he explained to the couples standing around, now looking on, with interest. "I think you're a little tired, Robin."

Richard saw Dermot Ryan looking on in bemused surprise.

"Dermot, I could use your help." He was over in a flash, gently guiding Robin towards the lift.

"Shall we go upstairs, darling?" She looked up dreamily at Dermot and stopped short. "Wait a minute. You're not my darling. Richard, where are you?" She tried to look behind her as Dermot bundled her into the lift.

"Right behind you, Robin," he snapped as he joined her and Dermot Ryan. At this stage Dermot was half-restraining, half-balancing Robin in an upright position.

Richard stabbed the penthouse button. Then he turned to Robin.

"Just what the hell do you think you're playing at? Are you totally thick?"

"You've ignored me all night, you brute," she sulked.

"I've been bloody busy working the room, pumping hands and spouting inordinate amounts of bullshit. That's what tonight was all about. You organised it. Remember?"

"That was before you shouted at me earlier. I was only trying to give you a nice surprise, Richey."

"Penthouse," the lift interrupted them.

"Well, here's a little surprise for you," Richard stepped out of the lift and grabbed the weekend bag that she had left there earlier.

"You're fired!" He threw the bag into the lift.

"Have a nice day," the elevator carried on.

"You can't do that to me!"

"Oh, yeah? Well, I just did. You're fired and I don't want to set eyes on you again. You're a loose cannon, Robin, and far too dangerous to have around the place." Richard turned to Dermot. "There's a bonus in this for you, buddy. Take her straight down to the basement and get her the hell out of here. Don't let her go through the reception area. Do you understand, son?"

"Perfectly, sir."

Richard turned back to his now ex-lover.

"Goodbye, Robin." He bashed the basement button with far more force than was necessary.

"Going down," the lift responded courteously.

"Enjoy the ride," Richard snarled as the doors silently closed.

"He's a bastard, an utter bastard," Robin sobbed into Dermot's shirt.

"I know, honey. You're too good for him."

Robin looked up and noticed Dermot properly for the first time.

"Who are you? Where do you fit in?"

"My name is Dermot and I'm here to mind you," he answered silkily. "Where I *fit in* remains to be seen!"

She looked at the young man, easily ten years younger than her.

"Where are we going?" she asked.

"Down," he grinned wickedly as his hands began to snake their way around her waist.

In the comfort of his penthouse and away from the mayhem of downstairs, Richard collapsed into the nearest sofa and mumbled, "I'm too bloody old for this shit!" As he rubbed his temples he remembered the stuff that Robin had bought and he had shoved into his bedroom cupboard. He went straight to his room to retrieve everything and dump them before anybody could find them. Robin's lingerie would not be used again. Best to throw it all away. Everything that is, except the video! he thought wickedly. Richard had plans of making a large library over the next few years. Little mementos, he called them. As he threw everything into the black refuse bag, he realized that the video cassette was missing. "Shit, Robin must have put it somewhere safe," he said to himself. "Hell, I'll see to that later."

"Daddy, is that you?" Tiffany put her head around the bedroom door. "Are you talking to yourself?" she giggled.

Her hair was slightly dishevelled and she looked a little messed up.

"What the hell are you doing up here?" he asked shocked.

"Eh, hi, Mr Dalton," Nick stuck his head around the door too.

"Right, that's it. You two, downstairs right now. Have you been drinking?"

Richard shoved his black bag back into the cupboard and frog-marched the two back to the lift.

"Hi, Dad," Lauren arrived looking fresh-faced and untouched with Connor walking behind her, slightly more guiltily.

"Not you two as well! My God, where's your mother? Does she know what you've been up to? I thought I said that nobody was to come up here."

"We were just showing the boys the sights," Lauren replied as if butter wouldn't melt in her mouth.

"That's what I'm worried about," he sighed. He was exhausted.

"Come on. Let's find your mother and sister and get the hell out of here."

The following morning, when Victoria arrived into the special care room, she was not surprised to find Tom Anderson sitting with his daughter.

"Have you been here all night, Tom?"

"In God's name, how could I leave my little girl?"

She sat down beside him and put her arm around his shoulders.

"You can't go on like this for ever, Tom."

"I know, but switching off the machine. My God, I'm practically killing my own daughter."

"Now, Tom, don't talk like that. After all the chats you've had with the medical counsellor." Her voice was a little firmer.

"I know, I know," he sighed. "Who knows, she might even start to breathe herself."

"Now that's a possibility. She's a lot stronger than she was a few months ago, even if she is still in a coma."

"I think I'd rather let her go to Jilly than have her live her life like this, a vegetable."

"Be brave, Tom. I'll go and get Dr Walsh. Has Fr Kennedy been in?"

"He has. I'm tired of seeing that fella. He's in here every twenty minutes."

Later that morning Victoria held Tom in her arms as Fr Kennedy prayed over Katie's deathly still body and Dr Kennedy switched off the breathing apparatus. Tom looked on as if it were all a dream. The doctor could have been switching off a television set or a kettle. It was all so *normal*. They all waited for something or nothing to happen. The atmosphere in the room did not change. It took a moment for Tom to realise what that meant. His first inkling was when he saw Dr Kennedy's face. The doctor was smiling broadly.

"She's breathing by herself, Tom. Katie is breathing herself!"

It was then that he realised his old friend, the heart monitor, was still beeping away merrily.

"Thank you, Jilly," Tom whispered in a quiet prayer to his wife. "Thank you for letting me have her for a little longer."

CHAPTER 28

January was the coldest on record, the temperature dropped to well below freezing and the man on the radio was saying that it was, in fact, too cold to snow. Despite the snug warmth of the kitchen, Saskia shivered as she looked out the window. It seemed to reflect her mood. Little Robin had had an appalling night's sleep and so, after a six am feed, she promptly fell back to sleep in her mother's bed. Sas wondered if the baby could be teething already.

Richard and the girls had been gone for three days now and it felt like two weeks. The house seemed desolate. Innishambles was far too big for just Saskia, Edu and the baby to rattle around in. She wondered how she was going to fill her day. Without her girls to chauffeur around or clean up after, there was precious little to do.

The dogs could do with a good walk, she thought, and if pushed, she could saddle up either Polly or Mooner and give them a little run. They wouldn't thank her for it in this weather, she mused. Saskia thought about her phone call from the girls the night before.

She had been just getting into bed when the phone rang on her bedside table.

"Mum, is that you?" The line was surprisingly clear.

"Yes, Lauren. How are you? Where are you?" Saskia replied, delighted to hear from her daughter.

"Mum, you know where we are! We're in totally cool Vail. Oh, Mum, you should be here. It's amazing and everybody is so, so cool." Saskia warmed to hear the excitement in her daughter's voice.

"Have you been skiing yet? What's the snow like?"

"Yeah! I'm phoning you from the top of Vail Mountain. I'm in a place called Two Elk Lodge," she put on an American accent for the name of the restaurant. "It's just after lunch here. We're eating like pigs but skiing takes up a lot of energy."

"Is the skiing good?"

"Oh, yes, it's amazing – here, I have to go now. Tiffany is pulling the phone from me. Bye, Mum, I love you!"

"Bye, baby," Saskia wanted to talk to Lauren more but Tiffany was suddenly on the line.

"Mummy, we miss you!"

"I miss you too, angel, but I gather you're having a great time."

"Oh, it's amazing. The snow is like powder and the Americans are all so polite. There's loads of room on the slopes too. Mum, you'd love it."

"I'm sure I would, maybe next time. What slopes are you trying?"

"Well, we took it easy this morning, so we could get our ski-feet back. We just did green slopes. They're the easiest."

"I'm glad to hear it. Don't go doing anything too rash, Tiff. I want you back all in one piece!"

"Oh, Mum! We're off to try a bowl now."

"What's a bowl?"

"It's just like a giant basin, not a regular slope that you ski down. It's totally crazy because you can ski down any way you like."

"I see," Saskia lied.

"Yeah, well we'd better go now because the bowl lifts close at three thirty pm, so we have to go fast."

"What about Kelly and Dad?"

"Here's Kelly. Love you, Mum. Byeee."

Saskia heard the phone get handed to her eldest.

"Hi, Mummy!"

"Hello, darling. How are you enjoying yourself?"

"It's fantastic. Mum, you'd love Vail village. The shops are out of this world."

"Well, don't blow all your money on day one. How's the skiing going?"

"It's great. We did a green run called Overeasy and then into Gitalong Road. What Tiff and Lauren don't know is Gitalong started green, but then went into blue and they still went down it. No problems."

"Are the blue runs more difficult?"

"Yeah, but they're still fairly easy by European standards. It's much nicer skiing over here though. I just want to try a Black run now!"

"Please don't push it too hard, Kelly, and don't push the girls any harder than they want."

"Relax, Mum. We're having a ball."

"Whatever happened to the snowboarding plans?"

"Oh, yeah. Maybe tomorrow. Look, I have to go. The others are calling me."

"Where's your father?"

"He's already back into his skis, outside. I've got to go. Love you."

"Kelly, I have some very good news for your dad. Tell him I need to speak with him." Saskia listened as her daughter yelled at Richard.

"He says he can't come to the phone. He has his skis back on. You know how cumbersome they are, Mum."

"Oh, well, perhaps you could tell him then. Katie Anderson is off her life-support machine and breathing herself."

"Who?"

"Katie Anderson. The girl that Daddy– er, the girl that Daddy had the crash with."

"Oh yeah! Hey, that's terrific. I'll tell Dad. Now I really have to go. Love you Mum."

"I love you too, pet. Bye, love." Reluctantly Saskia put the phone back into its cradle.

It was a strange feeling that just as she was getting into bed, her girls were climbing into a snow-lift to spend the afternoon skiing down a bowl, whatever that was.

Now, thinking about the phone call this morning only served to make her feel more isolated because she knew that her girls and husband would be sound asleep at this stage. The time difference was something like eight hours. Nine am here meant one am there.

This morning, the ground outside Innishambles was covered in a thin film of white ice and Saskia felt depressed. A far cry from Vail, she reflected miserably. Christmas and New Year certainly hadn't been as happy for her as she had hoped but at least her girls seemed to be very content. Saskia thought about Richard.

She had done nothing about her husband and Sue Parker. The further it faded into the past the more difficult it seemed to be to tackle. Saskia was beginning to come to the conclusion that least said was soonest mended. Obviously Dave Parker had decided to let the matter drop. Perhaps she should do the same.

There were other matters upsetting Saskia too. Edu was proving to be more of a hindrance than help of late. Any time she brought the matter up with Richard, he just brushed it aside.

She also dearly missed Nicolas Flattery. Saskia could not figure out why he had dropped her like a hot potato. She was surprised that he had returned to the States without so much as a goodbye or a phone call. Obviously he was embarrassed by Jessica's revelations but Nicolas didn't strike her as the running away kind.

Dudley and Dexter barking frantically at the postman shook Saskia back to the present.

"Hi, Declan, Happy New Year," she greeted him at the door. "It's cold for you this morning."

"You have a lot of post today, Mrs Dalton. I hope it's all good news!"

"So do I, Declan. We don't want the Christmas bills just yet!"

She took the bundle and bade him good-bye. As she wandered back into the kitchen with the dogs, she saw that the top envelope was a padded one and it was addressed strangely: *Fao; Dalton*, it said.

"Maybe it's a late Christmas present, Woody!" she giggled, ignoring his excitement at the parcel.

She fixed herself a cup of coffee and settled down at the large pine table to sort out the bills from the personal stuff and her post from Richard's and the girls'.

The padded envelope was difficult to open and when she did, the grey fluff inside the padding managed to spill out. Inside, Saskia found a handwritten letter and Wilma's collar. In her horror and shock she let the collar slip through her fingers onto the floor while she tried to read the note.

Dear Sir/Madam,

I know this seems like a strange thing to receive in the post but my daughter found it in our garden recently. It looks like a precious item so I thought I would take the liberty

*of sending it back to you. I would have phoned you, but there
is no number on the dog collar, just your name and address.
I hope your little dog is happy with her returned collar.*

Regards

Mrs Judi Williams.

Saskia read the letter again and again, trying to make
sense of what it said. Woody was pining at her feet,
licking the collar when she picked it back up. Obviously
he could still pick up the scent of his sister from it.

"I don't understand either, Woody, but I'm bloody
well going to get to the bottom of this."

Saskia dialled the phone number at the top of the
letter. The phone was answered quickly.

"Hullo, Williams residence,"

"Hello, may I speak with Judi Williams please?"
Saskia asked.

"Speaking, can I help you?"

"Oh, yes. My name is Saskia Dalton. You posted me
my dog collar recently."

"Ah yes, you got it. I'm so glad. How's Wilma? Is
she happy to have it back?"

"What?" Saskia was utterly confused now.

"Wilma. I think that's the name that was on the collar."

"Oh, yes. That's right. Well, you see, that's the problem.
Wilma is missing and she has been since last September.
I was hoping you could shed some light on the subject."

"Oh my, I'm so sorry, Mrs Dalton. I had no idea.
I've seen no stray dogs around, although – last

September? That's a long time. To be honest the only reason I posted it to you was because it was such a lovely collar – the diamonds, you know."

"Oh, yes. Well, obviously they're fake but Wilma was a right little madam. Diamonds suited her. Where do you live, Mrs Williams?" Saskia continued, trying to make sense of the situation.

"In Foxrock. It's on the letter heading, isn't it?"

"Oh, yes, so it is. Thank you very much for sending the collar back to me. I do appreciate it."

"Not at all. Goodbye," Mrs Williams hung up.

Saskia's head was spinning. Foxrock was miles off her normal car journeys. The only time she had driven through it recently was coming home from St Helen's with Richard and Robin. Then it hit her like a bolt of lightning. Richard's accident. That was the only possible solution. Wilma must have been in the car.

"Oh, God, Woody. It was Wilma," she spoke to her little dog who was still very distressed by the arrival of the collar. "She must have jumped up on his shoulder, the way she used to with me. I don't believe it. He thought my little Wilma was a rat. Oh, poor little Wilma."

"Anybody here?" Barney knocked at the kitchen door and came straight in. When he saw the huge tears slipping down her cheeks he rushed straight over to Sas.

"What's wrong?"

"Oh, Barney. It was Wilma. That's why Richard crashed into that poor girl."

He hugged her as she told him the story and showed him the letter and the collar.

Barney gently suggested that, in all probability, Wilma had been thrown a good distance from the car in the accident. That would explain why nobody found her small body. To soothe Saskia, he insisted that she would most likely have died instantly. As gently as he could, he continued, "Being so tiny however, it would stand to reason that she would have been eaten by other animals, and now almost five months later, there would be nothing left of her to find." He spoke as softly as he could, but the horror still struck Saskia full force.

"You're talking about Foxrock," she howled, "not bloody National Geographic!"

"I know it sounds awful, Sas, but it's nature at work. You know, the circle of life."

"The only circle I want to see is the noose I'm going to hang Richard from when I get at him." Her tears turned to anger towards her husband.

Barney stayed with Saskia and soothed her while she came to terms with the developments. As she slowly calmed back down, he got up the nerve to mention his reason for visiting in the first place.

"When are the girls leaving for the States?" he asked as casually as he could.

"Oh, Barney, they went on Friday. They'll be back next Friday."

"Ah right." He couldn't hide the disappointment from his voice.

"Did you want to say goodbye?" she asked sympathetically.

"Well yes, but I guess they'll be home soon."

"They've only gone for a week. You'll last that long, won't you?"

Barney looked at Saskia. Could it be that she knew he was in love with Kelly?

"If I have to," he said with a shy grin. "Well, I'd best be on my way. Are you OK?"

"Oh, yes. It's just that this little collar brings back so many fond memories."

"You should put it away if those memories bring you so much pain."

"I will soon," she sighed.

"In that case I'm off. I need to check the plans over in The Rathdeen Refuge."

Saskia tried to contain her curiosity.

"How is it going over there? How's Nicolas?" she added as if it were an afterthought.

"I don't know to be honest. He's gone back to the States. I'm dealing with Kevin Cantrell on the refuge. The one thing I did hear is that Jessica is flying over to the States too. So maybe they're patching things up. Wouldn't that be great?"

Saskia clutched the table that she was standing beside for support. She actually felt like she had been dealt a physical blow.

"Back together?" she asked incredulously. "But how can that be? Jessica and Kim –"

"Who knows," Barney smiled. "I hope it works out for them anyway."

He left Saskia, unaware that his last throwaway comment had done more to hurt her than a thousand Wilma stories might. As she sank back into the nearest kitchen chair, Saskia had to admit to herself that she was miserable at the prospect of the Flatterys getting back together.

"How could I be in love with a man I barely know?" she asked Woody. Absentmindedly, she continued to open the post. She opened three more Christmas cards.

"There are some people in the world even more unorganised than me," she sighed out loud. Most of the rest of the post was for Richard or the girls until she came to a small parcel marked for her personal attention.

Casually she peeled away the brown paper and found a video inside.

"What's this?" she asked, even though there was nobody to ask and no note with it. There were no stickers on the video either. She wandered into the living-room and slipped it into the video player, switching on the television at the same time. Just as she flicked the remote control to zero, for the video channel, Robin began to cry again.

How does she do that? Saskia wondered. Just as you're about to sit down to eat or watch a video. She dragged herself upstairs, still exhausted from her sleepless night and got her little girl. Then she returned to the living-room, having changed Robin's nappy, and retrieved a bottle of milk from the kitchen.

Saskia was sitting comfortably feeding Robin her bottle before she realised what she was watching.

"Oh, that is disgusting. Don't look, baby," Saskia winced as she reached for the remote control, to switch it off. "Who would send us such a thing? If this is one of the girls messing again –" Saskia stopped in stunned silence as she saw the woman on her television screen turn around to face the camera.

"Christ, that's Robin Maher!" she eventually exclaimed. Frozen with shock, Saskia blinked as the man sat up on the bed beside Robin and slapped her on the bottom affectionately.

"Now go and get dressed. My wife and kids will be here any minute," he said as casually as if he were asking her for a cup of coffee. His voice was so familiar but the picture was unreal.

"This is some kind of joke," Saskia spluttered. The time and date were printed at the bottom of the home video, nineteen thirty-five on third of the first, it said. Saskia, who still couldn't use the twenty-four hour clock, did the sums in her spinning mind.

"Christ that was at seven thirty on the night of the re-launch. We arrived about ten minutes later," she screeched.

In a state of total shock, Saskia grabbed her car keys and still holding Robin in her arms, she ran out of the house. She left the doors wide open in her wake and ran out into the yard.

Ignoring the dogs' whines to come with her, she climbed into the Landrover.

"I have to get away," she kept saying. Oblivious to the fact that she was holding her daughter in a most dangerous manner, she started up the engine and tore down the driveway.

As she drove through the village of Ballymore, Saskia was about to turn right up to Rathdeen Manor when she remembered that Nicolas wasn't there.

"Who can I turn to?" she howled as Robin also screamed with displeasure, cradled in Saskia's right arm.

Instead of going right, up to Rathdeen, Saskia swung the car left and headed for Sue Parker's house. She accelerated up the driveway so fast Sue heard the engine of the Landrover outside her house and came to investigate.

"Saskia, it's nice to see you," Sue looked at her neighbour dismount from the jeep. When she saw the look on Sas's face, however, and Robin in her arms, she knew that something was seriously wrong. Sue rushed to Saskia's side just as the woman began to collapse. She took Robin from her and yelled for Jenny. The childminder rushed out and sizing up the situation instantly, half-carried, half-dragged Saskia inside.

Saskia was put lying on the deep sofa in Sue's living-room, while Jenny Quinn took little Robin away to play with India and Guy.

Sue Parker brought Saskia a large glass of brandy.

"Drink this first. Then we'll talk if you want. Do you want me to get a doctor, Sas?"

"No, please, no doctors," Saskia spoke in a whisper, as she looked into space, unsure even of where she was.

CHAPTER 29

It was after lunch by the time that Saskia was ready to talk. She had taken another two brandies and promptly fallen asleep on Sue's sofa. Sue was horrified by the state her neighbour was in. She called Rock Tower, despite her own issues with Richard Dalton, and was secretly relieved to hear that he was in the States with his daughters. The telephonist told her that he was uncontactable, except through his wife. At least she wouldn't have to deal with him. That meant that there was nobody up in Innishambles so she could mind Saskia and Robin all day. It was obvious that they needed a lot of minding.

At lunchtime, Sue peeped into the living-room to check on her patient. Saskia was awake.

"How are you feeling?" she asked gently.

"Numb."

"Can I get you some food?" Sue came over and sat on the side of the sofa.

Saskia looked into her neighbour's eyes for the first time that day. Sue thought Sas looked like she had suddenly aged by twenty years. Her eyes were deep in her head and they had a hollow look to them.

"He hurt you too. Didn't he?"

Sue Parker froze. "I don't know what you're talking about."

"I know about you and Richard. I'm so sorry, Sue. I'm so very very sorry. He's evil, you know. I had no idea how evil. He was screwing his PR agent, Robin Maher. I've just seen the whole thing in glorious Technicolor. It's just been released on video!" Saskia laughed but it was a kind of mad laugh, not a funny one.

"Oh, Saskia, what a thing to see. Oh my God, I'm so sorry."

"*You're* sorry, why? You've done nothing wrong. He's the bastard."

Slowly Saskia's colour began to return to normal and she started to act a little more like herself. They had a little food together and then a bottle of wine. Robin was happy in Jenny's care and Sue and Saskia sat and talked for the entire afternoon.

It was getting dark when Dave Parker's car pulled up outside his house. He had skipped his habitual pint in The Hitching Post under the circumstances and come straight home. Sue had phoned him earlier in the day to let him know what was going on. He felt sorry for Saskia.

"How's my favourite neighbour?" he asked playfully but gently as he entered the room. She looked up sheepishly.

"Oh Dave, I'm so sorry. I was talking to Sue about Richard."

"It's OK, Saskia," he sat beside her and hugged her. "That's all over. Sue and I are sorted. What's important now is how we mind you. Will you stay here tonight? We want to mind you."

Saskia nearly started crying again at Dave's kindness. He was the exact antithesis of her husband. His question however shook her back into reality.

"No, I must go home," Saskia explained. "The poor dogs will be starving." Then she remembered Edu. "God, I didn't even phone her. She'll be beside herself. I really must go."

Sue began to protest but she knew it was useless; Saskia had made up her mind.

"It's OK, really. Richard is away for the rest of the week. I have plenty of time to decide how I want to deal with this. You've both been so kind to me. I am deeply indebted, but there's just one more thing. Could I please impose upon you to keep this to yourselves just until I decide how to handle it? There are the children to consider, you understand."

"Of course," the Parkers chorused.

"At least let me drive you home," Dave offered.

"I'll follow you in the Landrover, so your car will be at home too," Sue added.

Saskia looked at the two Parkers. "You're the nicest neighbours anybody could have. Thank you." Her bottom lip began to quiver dangerously again as if she were about to burst into tears.

"I think I should really go now," she continued. She thanked Jenny Quinn profusely for minding Robin all day and then she climbed into the warmth and security of Dave's car. As promised, Sue Parker tailed them in Saskia's car to get it home. The last thing any of them expected to see up at Innishambles was the ambulance that greeted them.

"Saskia! Where the hell have you been?" Barney attacked her the minute she got out of Dave's car.

"Easy, Barney," Dave interrupted. "What's wrong?"

"Edu's what's wrong. I've just found her collapsed on the living-room floor."

"What?" Sas clutched Robin as they all watched the ambulance drive off with Edu inside.

Barney explained as they all walked into Innishambles to get out of the cold January evening.

"I was coming up to check on you – after this morning's little episode, you know – Wilma."

"Barney, what episode?" Sue asked, but Saskia explained quickly, anxious to find out more about Edu.

"It was nothing. Some do-gooder posted me Wilma's dog collar. They found it recently."

"Nothing?" Barney asked incredulously.

"Sorry, Barney, in view of what's happened since

411

then, it was nothing. Now tell me about Edu. What's wrong with her?"

"Well, I only got up here about an hour ago. I just walked in the back door and I found Edu collapsed in a pool of blood in the living-room. Judging by the fact that she had a bowl of pasta with her. I'd guess she was about to have her supper so at least she wasn't there that long."

Saskia was getting impatient. "Yes, but what's wrong with her?"

Barney looked very uncomfortable as his gaze moved from the blood to the Parkers to Saskia.

"Sas," he said softly, "it looks like it was a miscarriage."

The Parkers gasped as Saskia fell into the nearest seat. "How? Why? That's just not possible. She didn't even have a boyfriend. Even if she did – what would cause her to miscarry – I had no idea." She was rambling a little now and so Barney tried to assist.

"It's just nature's way, Saskia. There is rarely a reason for a miscarriage. Maybe if she was under a great deal of pressure or perhaps if she was malnourished or if she had a bad shock –"

He kept talking but something in Saskia's mind clicked. A shock, she thought, like me. My God – the same shock. "I must have left the video running."

"What video?" Barney asked, not understanding.

Saskia started to cry again as she walked over to the machine and ejected the tape.

"This stupid video. When the tape runs out it will rewind back to the beginning and start again."

Within ten minutes, Saskia was driving back out of Innishambles. She had gratefully taken the Parkers up on their offer to baby-sit Robin and she was heading for Wicklow County Hospital. How could Edu possibly have had a miscarriage? Saskia didn't even think that she had a boyfriend, not that she would have minded if she had.

Edu was in a private room sobbing quietly when Saskia walked in.

"Edu?"

"Go away."

"Edu. I've spoken to the doctors. I know about the miscarriage."

"Leave me alone," Edu cried.

"I can't do that, Edu. You're like family to me and this – well, this explains a lot. I didn't have any idea. If you had told me, I would have helped. I certainly wouldn't have made you work when you were sick. Oh, Edu, you're like a daughter to me."

Edu glared at her old boss. "You understand nozing!" she snarled.

Her rage shocked Sas. "Please help me understand, then. How can I help?"

"You want to help? Zen go away."

"Can I get somebody else for you, the father perhaps?" Saskia spoke tentatively.

Edu looked up at her in surprise and laughed. She actually laughed.

"You want to get the fazer? Really? OK, off you go – he's in Vail!"

"What?"

"You heard me. Ze fazer of my baby is in Vail with your daughters."

"No, this can't be true!"

"Oh, yes it can. Ricardo and I have been lovers for years. Do you want times and dates?" Edu's eyes were wild and she spoke with a kind of delirious laughter. "Your husband first took me in your familee bazroom –"

"Edu, you're making this up!"

"I whish I was, ze bastard. I saw ze video. I saw heem with zat other woman."

"You and Richard? That's not possible! He was like a father to you."

"Oh, Saskia. You are so naive. You don't deserve Ricardo. He was too good for you." Edu began to cry again.

Saskia had stopped listening, however. Why couldn't it be true? He seemed to be screwing everybody else in town. Having seen the video with her own eyes, she now realised that she had been walking around with eyes closed for who knew how long. She turned her attention back to Edu and ignored the tears. If what she was saying was true, how could she show the slightest bit of sympathy for the young girl? In fact Edu wasn't a young girl to be pitied. She was a dangerous, venomous, husband-stealing monster.

"The doctors say you can leave tomorrow. I'll be back to collect you then." She walked out of the room without waiting for Edu's reaction. As Saskia walked out of the hospital, she remembered Edwina's warning about Saturday's flitting making for short sitting.

I am not some pawn of destiny, she thought in fury. I can and will control my own destiny.

Innishambles was freezing by the time Saskia got home. It felt as if winter had crept in and curled its freezing claws around every stick of furniture and up every wall. Saskia went around all the rooms of the house and switched on all the lights as if trying to exorcise the chill. She found Barney's note on the kitchen table. She had left him in Innishambles when she took off for the hospital.

Hi Sas,

I hope everything is OK. I've fed the dogs and cleaned up. If you need me, just call.

Love Barney

She cranked up the heating and soon the house was beginning to feel like its old self again. Saskia realised that she hadn't really eaten all day but she wasn't the slightest bit hungry. She fixed herself a large whisky and walked into the study. She chose Richard's favourite old leather seat and curled up into it to think about her situation. She switched on the lamp beside the chair, casting a soft pyramid of light over it. The dogs joined her. Exhausted from the strange day they flopped at her feet.

"Oh boys," she sighed, "what's to become of us?" Slowly, the tears fell down her hollow cheeks as she relived the day's events and pondered on those of the last few months or, if she was totally honest with herself, the events of the last few years. How long had she been voluntarily blindfolding herself? Deep deep down, how long had she known about Richard's true nature? Had she always known? Now however, thanks to this bloody video and Edu . . . that was an even bigger shock. Saskia realised that she could no longer live in denial. Messing around outside was one thing but under her roof. Richard bonking the au pair. That was definitely the lowest of the low.

Slowly and painfully, Saskia listed Richard's biggest misdemeanours over the last six months. As far as she was concerned, he was responsible for that poor girl Katie Anderson who was still in a coma in hospital. He had also managed to kill her favourite pet in the whole world. Some people might think that not so bad but Saskia had been closer to Wilma than any other living soul on the planet. She told that little dog things that she wouldn't dare tell anyone else. Richard had raped Sue Parker; there was no other word for it. That was the bitter ugly truth. He had had an affair with his PR girl Robin Maher and now it appeared that he'd managed to get their au pair pregnant.

Saskia knew that she now had no choice, for her sake and that of her four daughters. Revenge was her only option. She would call Dave Parker in the morning and then she would get to work. Saskia had four days before Richard returned from the States. Four days in which to destroy him.

CHAPTER 30

When Saskia woke the following morning, her head was crystal clear. The whiskey, which had so successfully lulled her to sleep, seemed to have no after-effect on her. It felt like adrenalin was coursing through her veins as she jumped out of bed and threw on her jeans and denim shirt. The house was empty which gave her the silence and space she needed to think.

"Sorry, dogs, you'll have no walk today," she told them as she fixed herself a slice of toast and cup of coffee, and then she headed to the study.

"All right, Richard Dalton, if it's war you want, it's war you'll get!" she exclaimed to the room as she set her breakfast down and sat at the desk.

Saskia got out a pen and paper to help her think. Rock FM started to broadcast on the first of January 1996, so it had got the licence in January 1995. That meant that Richard was pitching for the licence in the spring of 1994, she reasoned. She remembered that summer vividly because she always had such misgivings about what he did.

"What happens if somebody finds out?" she had pleaded with him. It never occurred to her that she, Saskia, would be the one instrumental in the revelation of such sordid details. The application had gone to the licensing authority in the spring of 1994. Saskia remembered Richard at that time. He had been so excited.

"It's a really good pitch, Sas," he exclaimed. "We should get this licence. Imagine owning part of a radio station!" Looking back now, Richard seemed so different. He was young and enthusiastic, so full of hope. It was during the summer of that year that Richard began to get nervous. The Irish Radio Licensing Committee were taking longer than anticipated to reach a decision on which of the three contestants would get the Rock Radio licence for Dublin city. As the weeks dragged on, Richard got more and more restless. It was June or July of that summer, Saskia couldn't remember exactly, when Richard came to her.

"I have to do something more, Sas," he said. His expression was very sombre. She remembered the conversation vividly because she was so surprised.

"You've done all you can, Richard. There are five people on the selection committee. They will decide. Look, you already know that Patricia O'Reilly is on your side. That's one vote already," Saskia tried to ease his concerns.

"That's not enough," he snapped. "I need two other people on side to ensure that we have a majority."

"What are you saying?" She could tell by his tone that he was up to something untoward.

Richard became animated. "Sas, there's Joe Sweeny, Fintin Joyce, Martin Fitzpatrick and Michael Quinn. If I can *persuade* two of those four to vote for our application, we have the licence!"

"Richard?"

"Saskia, you'll have to trust me on this. Everybody does it. It's the only way."

"Does what?"

"I'll have to pay them off."

"Who?"

"Well, I've been thinking about it and I think Joe Sweeny and Fintin Joyce can be bought off."

"I can't believe you're saying this. How much are you thinking of?"

"To be sure it works, it'll take twenty grand each."

"That's a fortune. Who's going to pay for it?"

"Well, honey, I'm afraid it'll be me, but it will be in our interest in the long run."

"How the hell do you figure that?"

"Well, as you know, I want to buy out the other members of the syndicate who own Rock FM in a few years. That's if it's as successful as I think it's going to be. This will be my *persuader*, so to speak. Think of it as buying an option on the future earnings of the station!"

"Richard, this is insanity." Saskia tried to dissuade him but it was perfectly clear that he had already made up his mind.

"Trust me," he said.

Saskia shivered now, as she thought about him. Trust him? Look where that had landed her! She shook herself back into the present and went to look through Richard's and her bank statements.

"Thank you for keeping such a good filing system, Richard!" she laughed bitterly.

Lined up on one wall-shelf was a series of black folders, each one marked with a year. Saskia pulled out the folder marked 1994. She began to wade through their different accounts, paying particular attention to the June and July transactions. It was surprisingly easy. She was able to ignore their Visa and American Express accounts. These came first. Then she skipped over their current accounts. Saskia remembered Richard being so careful about "no paper train". She knew that he had paid out cash, not a cheque. Next she came to their savings account. On the fourth of July Richard had withdrawn twenty thousand pounds and then on the sixth on July, he withdrew a further twenty grand.

"Moron," she laughed. "Did you think that by withdrawing them a few days apart that you would draw less attention to yourself!"

Carefully she extracted the bank statement. Then, to her

amazement and utter delight, Saskia saw the most slanderous piece of evidence. Richard had actually penned in JS and FJ into the margin, next to the withdrawals.

"Oh, Richard. You really have given me enough rope to hang you. You pet!" Joe Sweeny and Fintin Joyce deserved what was coming to them, she decided.

The phone made her jump when it started to ring. She thought about not answering it, in case it was Richard. She wasn't ready to talk to him yet. Then to her relief, she remembered that he would be asleep because it was the middle of the night in the States.

"Hello," she answered it tentatively.

"Saskia, it's Dave Parker. I just wanted to check that you were OK. How's your au pair?"

"Oh, Dave, just the man. I really need to talk with you. Everything is absolutely fine but I do need to talk something over with you. Can we meet today."

Dave was amazed at how together Saskia seemed. "Yeah sure. I'm actually running late for the office. I'm in the car now. If you like I can swing by now or we can meet later?"

"Come by now. No time like the present."

After she hung up, Saskia quickly tidied away the files and her own notes. She slipped the one important bank statement into her handbag and then she sat down to eat her cold toast.

Within minutes, Dudley, Dexter and Woody were barking at the front door. Saskia opened it before Dave even got to ring the bell.

"Come in. You're welcome, Dave," she smiled at him.

"You seem remarkably chirpy this morning."

"I'm busy!"

"What are you up to?"

"Dave, I see no reason not to tell you because the whole thing is going to blow wide open over the next week anyway. In fact, I think it only fair to warn you."

"This sounds ominous," Dave looked concerned.

"It is. I'm going to hurt Richard, the same way he has hurt me."

"Saskia, you're still in shock. You need to think about this before you do anything too radical."

"Dave. My husband raped your wife. Do you really want to do nothing about it?"

Dave's face turned to ice. His hatred for Richard Dalton was so deep he didn't dare discuss it with Saskia.

"What do you have in mind?" he asked.

"I have information that may cause Richard's radio licence to be revoked. If this happens, your new shop will be in trouble. I doubt Richard will be able to keep up the repayments on Rock Tower if he loses his biggest tenant, the radio station."

"That would mean that my new store would be in a building that is being repossessed by the banks."

"Exactly."

"I guess the prudent thing to do would be to move out before the shit hits the fan." Dave understood completely. If he moved out suddenly, with no notice to Richard, it would be another nail in Mr Dalton's coffin. With two tenants not paying, the Tower would definitely be repossessed.

"It would be the smart move, Dave," Saskia smirked at him.

Dave was still worried about her. "What about you and your children, Sas? If you destroy Richard, how will you survive?"

"Dave, Dave, don't make the same error Richard has."

"What's that?"

"Don't underestimate the power of a woman."

Dave felt a freezing chill tingle down the back of his neck. Richard Dalton had made a terrible, terrible mistake. He was as good as dead.

When Dave left her that morning, they agreed that Friday would be D-Day. He would move his stock and staff out on Friday morning and if necessary make a press statement on Friday night. They promised to stay in close contact by phone and Saskia would notify him of any changes, not that she expected any.

It was already mid-morning. "Time flies when you're destroying tyrants," she mused as she phoned her mother-in-law.

"Dalton residence," Edwina answered the phone in her usual condescending manner.

"Edwina, it's Saskia."

"Oh hello, how are my son and my grandchildren? I hope you're minding –"

Saskia cut her off before she got onto a roll.

"They're fine, Edwina. Look, I need you to do me a favour. Can you please go to Wicklow General Hospital and collect Edu. I think she should stay in your house until things are sorted out."

"Oh my heavens," Edwina exclaimed. "What happened to the girl?"

"Well, Edwina, she's been screwing your son for the last few years. So I don't really want her here, under my roof, but I'm not quite ready to throw her out onto the street. I thought you could mind her for a while. By the way she's just had a miscarriage with Richard's baby, so be gentle. OK?"

Edwina was silent.

"So you'll collect her then, as soon as you can. Yes?" Saskia continued.

"OK," Edwina muttered, sounding totally shell-shocked.

"Fine. I'll call the hospital and tell them to tell Edu to expect you. I'm sure you and she will find a lot to talk about. Goodbye, Edwina."

"Wait. Where's Richard?" Edwina managed to say.

"Aha, I'm damned if I'm telling you, Edwina. He'll be home in a few days. You can talk to him then. In fact you can have him back then if you like, for all I care. Now I have to go. Goodbye." Saskia hung up without waiting for Edwina to respond. It felt remarkably good!

Next she put in a quick call to the hospital and then she sat down to study all of Richard's and her other bank accounts. My survival and that of my girls is the only thing more important than Richards's destruction, she thought. "But I reckon I can do both," she said aloud, "thanks to Richard!"

Saskia collected Robin from Sue Parker at lunchtime that day.

"Sue, you've been so kind to me. I can't thank you enough." She hugged her neighbour.

"Hey, we women have to look out for each other. I'm so sorry about your situation and my –"

"For goodness sake, you didn't mean to get involved with him. No, all blame lies firmly at Richard's feet and he will pay. Believe me."

"Well, if I can be of any other assistance, let me know," Sue offered.

"There is just one more thing. Could I borrow Jenny for a few hours this evening?"

"I'm sure that'll be fine. I'll take Robin anyway if Jenny can't baby-sit."

As she drove away, Saskia knew she had a real friend in Sue Parker, despite what Richard had done to her. It was good to know because she had a feeling that she was going to need all the friends she could get after the dust had settled on this saga.

That afternoon, Saskia made the phone call that would really start the ball rolling. The phone took ages to be answered.

"Hello, RTE."

"Hello, may I speak to Brian O'Malley please,"

Saskia asked nervously. The operator didn't even reply. She just clicked the phone through.

"Hello, newsroom," a bright and happy voice answered up the phone.

"Hello," Saskia persevered, "I want to speak with Brian O'Malley."

"He's not here. Can I help you?" The cub reporter smelt a story.

"No, it has to be him. When will he be in the office?"

"I don't know. Can I get him to phone you back?"

There was no way Saskia was going to leave her name and number with a stranger.

"I'll call him back," she put down the receiver, cutting the line.

Shaking with nerves, Saskia couldn't believe how uptight she was. Planning the revenge was one thing. Now that she was actually doing it, it was pretty scary. She took Robin out for a walk and let her mind further formulate her plans.

It was after tea that evening before Saskia mustered up the nerve to phone Brian again. This time he was at his desk.

"Brian O'Malley, is that really you?" she asked.

"In the flesh. To whom am I speaking?"

He sounded different to the way he did on the television but Saskia had no choice but to believe it was him.

"I can't tell you my name, at least not yet. I have some information I need to give you. It's really important."

Brian O'Malley had developed a name for himself as the man who blew open quite a few of the political scams in Ireland over the last few years. He had even developed a cult status with most of the schoolgirls around the country as a sex symbol. That said, he knew instinctively when he was being led up the garden path and when there was the possibility of a real story. Brian had been furious when the cub reporter manning his desk for him for the afternoon told him about the hang-up.

"Give them my mobile!" he had thundered at her. He was now pretty sure that he was talking to the woman who had hung up earlier.

"How can I help you?" he asked softly.

"Can we meet?"

"Absolutely. Can you give me an idea what we're meeting about?" he asked with a slight laugh. His manner was easy and comforting and Saskia felt his confidence warm her.

"It's about backhanders that were wrong," she managed.

"Lady, all backhanders are wrong," he said lightly. "OK, I'll meet you, when and where?"

"The story mustn't leak tomorrow. It has to be the next day – Thursday."

"Look, lady, you're getting a little ahead of yourself. I don't even know if you have a story yet. Let's meet and talk and take it from there."

Saskia forced herself to calm down and they

arranged to meet in the Belleview Hotel in Wicklow, at eight o'clock that night.

"Jenny, you're a dote," Saskia thanked her profusely as she left the Parker's baby-sitter in charge of Robin that evening in Innishambles.

Saskia had given herself plenty of time to get to the Belleview. As she was leaving the house, however, she decided to take Richard's car. Why not, she thought. It's considerably more comfortable.

The Belleview was a new, state-of-the-art hotel just north of Wicklow town. The car park was next to the hotel and security cameras monitored it. They winked at her as she drove the large black Merc in. She walked into the foyer and towards the reception desk. Saskia knew what Brian O'Malley looked like, from the television. She was only going to the reception desk to grab an *Irish Times*, so she could hide behind it while she waited for him.

"Mrs Dalton, you're very welcome again," the receptionist beamed at her.

"Again?" Saskia looked at her confused.

"Yes, you were here with your husband in October." Suddenly the receptionist looked a little worried.

Saskia quickly recovered however. "Yes, I know that but how do you know that?" she asked, improvising. Saskia knew that this was her first time in the hotel.

"It's our new security cameras," the receptionist enthused. "They're wonderful. They scan the registration number of your car as you drive in and then they give us a print-out of your history with the hotel. It's all aimed at improving the service," she concluded.

"Ingenious," Saskia replied half-heartedly. "Do you remember me personally?"

"No, I didn't even work here last October," the young girl laughed, "But I know that you came here twice for the night with your husband in October. Will you be staying tonight, Mrs Dalton?"

"No, not tonight," Saskia tried to keep her tone civil as she grabbed the newspaper and left the young girl.

She fell into an armchair in the reception area to wait for Brian and wondered which of Richard's women had been the Mrs Dalton to stay here, and what she herself had been doing those nights. Christ, had he no shame? she fumed. He definitely deserved what he had coming to him. When Saskia saw Brian O'Malley walk in, she was so fired up she practically yelled at him across the foyer.

"Brian," she waved, "over here."

He smiled at her like an old friend and quickly came to join her. He was obviously used to meeting strangers.

"Hi," he smiled at her and offered his hand to shake.

"Hello, thank you for meeting me," she said shyly. Then she began to talk. "My name is Saskia Dalton. I am Richard Dalton's wife. I want you to broadcast the truth about how he got the Rock Radio licence for Dublin city in 1994. He broke the law, Mr O'Malley, and that's not right."

"You mentioned backhanders on the phone, Mrs Dalton." Brian pulled out a mini-tape-recorder. "Do you mind if I use this?" he gestured at the recorder. "It's much easier than writing," he added a little sheepishly.

"Whatever," Saskia replied, more interested in getting her story off her chest, than how he kept a record of it.

The two sat down together and talked for over an hour. Saskia produced her bank statement and Brian listened, stopping her to ask questions when the need arose. As she spoke, he realised that he had a real story here, but he just needed more proof, a third party.

When she had finally finished, he looked at her and smiled. Richard Dalton must have hurt her pretty bad to drive her to this, he thought.

"Mrs Dalton, I want to thank you for calling me first with this information and you're absolutely right. What he allegedly did was against the law. All I have however is your word. Your husband could claim that he withdrew those two sums of money and blew then on the horses."

"Even though the dates coincide with the announcement of his getting the licence?" she asked incredulously.

"That does make it look more convincing but it's not proof."

"What about the fact that he wrote their initials in the margin of his bank statement?"

"Pretty stupid, yeah, but he could say that they're just doodles and mean absolutely nothing. In truth, all we have here is your word against his. What you need is a witness. Did anybody see him give the cash to Joe Sweeny or Fintin Joyce?"

Saskia racked her brains. "It was a long time ago. The only thing I can think of is Elizabeth."

"Who is she?"

"Well, she was Joe Sweeny's secretary, but she was so damn good Richard stole her. Naturally, under the circumstances, Joe didn't object."

"Do you have a contact number for Elizabeth?"

"Of course. Elizabeth Wright is Richard's PA. She's at Rock Tower all the time. You can phone her there in the morning, or I can if you like."

Brian looked at Saskia. "Now, Mrs Dalton, we have a story."

The following morning Saskia took Robin with her and they met Brian O'Malley in the reception of Rock Tower. She had already phoned Elizabeth to ensure that the girl was there. Elizabeth seemed agitated but she agreed to meet them. It didn't take long for Saskia to crack the PA.

"Richard has done something very bad, Elizabeth, and I'm pretty sure you know about it," she said gently.

"Oh Sas, I'm so sorry. I didn't know what to do. I couldn't just sit back and let him continue with it. He had to be stopped."

"What do you mean?" Saskia became aware that they were having different conversations but she was getting adept at conversing with only half the facts.

"Well, the video," Elizabeth faltered. "It was all so sordid and so dreadfully wrong of him and you've always been so nice to me. I just had to let you know."

Saskia's brain moved up a gear. So the video of Robin and Richard was a little gift from Elizabeth, she realised. Sas didn't know whether she wanted to thank her or hit her! Then she focused on the moment.

"Oh, yes, the video. I'm very grateful for that, but I want to go back further in time."

Slowly Saskia explained to her about the real relationship between Joe Sweeny, her old boss and Richard.

"How could I have been so thick?" Elizabeth exclaimed.

"Did you see the money or hear any of their conversations?" Brian asked, knowing that the story depended on it.

"See it? I lodged the bloody money for Joe! I saw the whole thing. I just assumed it was part of the licensing payment or something. Jesus, the account was a personal one of Joe's; at least it was in his name."

Brian beamed. "Bingo!"

CHAPTER 31

The following morning, Saskia was awake before dawn. Obviously there was no point in listening to Rock FM, she thought gleefully. They would hardly cover the story. She tuned in to Radio 1. She didn't have to wait long. Brian O'Malley was the top story.

His clear, crisp voice began:

Rock FM, Dublin's independent radio station, is shrouded in controversy this morning as news breaks that the Irish Radio Licensing Committee, who gave the licence to Mr Richard Dalton and his syndicate, had in fact received cash gifts to the value of forty thousand pounds. The alleged recipients of these cash donations were not available for comment last night but the Licensing Committee has said that it is looking into the matter urgently. It will give a statement as soon as possible.

And then it was over. Saskia couldn't believe how

fast it was. Was that it? Hardly enough to tear down the mighty Rock Tower empire. Saskia stewed for half an hour but eventually she could stand it no longer. She phoned Brian in a panic.

"Is that it?" she cried.

"Are you joking? This is so hot, Mrs Dalton. Every journalist in the city has been on to me. So has every newspaper. The other radio stations are going to go to town on this one. Just sit tight." He paused, "Mrs Dalton, have you thought about how this is going to affect your family? You might need to contact your solicitor. You're going to need a spokesperson."

Saskia had already explained that Richard was out of town and not likely to be contactable, unless he phoned home, but she hadn't thought about the press arriving at her door.

"I'll think of something," she said with a lot more conviction than she felt. "I'll stay in touch," and she hung up.

Saskia phoned Barry McCourt next.

"Sas, I was just about to phone you. What the hell is going on? I just heard the news."

"Were you listening to Radio 1?"

"No, it was 98FM. Why? Do they have it too? Shit, where's Richard?"

"Never mind Richard just now, Barry. I want to officially engage you as my solicitor in divorce proceedings against Richard Dalton."

"What?" Barry McCourt couldn't believe his ears.

He knew that Richard played a little dangerously professionally, he had often sought Barry's advice on slightly obscure deals, but he never thought that it would come to this. All things considered, Barry thought, if the shit was really going to hit the fan, and the Daltons were going to divorce, on balance he would rather be on Saskia's side of the battlefield.

Following her rather detailed conversation with Barry, Saskia turned her thoughts to where she could go with Robin, to hide from the press for the next twenty-four hours. The doorbell interrupted her thoughts. Oh God, they're here already, she panicked. Then a familiar voice shouted through the letterbox.

"Saskia, it's me. Jenny."

"Jenny. What are you doing here?"

"Sue sent me over. She heard the news this morning and thought that you might like my company."

"That woman is a saint! What about India and Guy?"

"She's going to mind them herself for the day."

As Saskia let Jenny in, the phone rang. Jenny got to it first.

"It's *The Star* newspaper. They're looking for Richard."

"Tell them he's out of the country and will be unavailable for comment for the next few days."

As soon as Jenny put the phone back down, it rang again.

"It's *The Irish Times*."

"Tell them all the same thing, Jenny: no comment."

Then the doorbell rang.

"Oh God, I don't know if I'm up to this," Saskia panicked. She opened the door.

"Nicolas!"

"Quick, we have to move fast. There's a *Today Fm* van hurtling up your driveway."

Jenny looked at them. "You go out the back and down through the valley, over to Rathdeen. I'll stall these guys. When the coast is clear, Robin and I will follow you. Go, go, go!"

Saskia and Nicolas ran out through the kitchen, freeing the dogs from the scullery as they did so. Dudley, Dexter and even little Woody came bounding out to the front door to ward off any possible intruders. They were highly excited by the amount of action in the house that morning.

As Saskia slammed the back door behind her, she heard the phone start to ring again.

"I hope Jenny can handle the mayhem."

"It'll be much easier for her than for you, because they won't expect her to give any sort of statement but they would hound you," Nicolas took her hand and pulled her into Polly's stable. He looked at her for a second, examining her face as if to check it for signs of damage. "God, I've missed you," he said and kissed her.

Saskia's heart was already beating as fast as possible. Her life was already a mass of contradictions – why not one more, she thought, as she let her arms wrap around his body and she kissed him back.

He broke away and grinned from ear to ear.

"I love you, Saskia. I have from the moment I first saw you."

"But you and Jessica, I thought you were getting back together."

"Back together," he laughed hollowly. "I was in the US finalising our divorce! We had an agreement that we would stay together for Nick's sake on the condition that she kept her relationship with Kim confidential. It was just so Nick could have a so-called normal upbringing. I guess it was just too much to expect from her. She couldn't keep it a secret. If she's going public on it, there's just no point in keeping up the façade."

As he spoke, he was saddling Polly up. Then he did the same with Mooner.

"Come on. Let's give them the ride of their lives."

Saskia mounted Polly and Nicolas mounted Mooner. The animals could sense the adrenalin and excitement and they took off at the speed of light across the fields. They tore through the woods and down the other side. Saskia had never ridden so fast in all her life as she galloped to keep up with Nicolas who strode ahead. He looked like some mythical hero from an ancient Irish legend. Nicolas hadn't had his hair cut since she first met him and it was beginning to grow slightly long. Now that he was galloping at full speed on Mooner's back, he looked divine, she thought. The man and animal moved as one. Before she realised it, she saw them take the River More in one wide leap. Nicolas glanced over his shoulder at Sas.

"Come on," he yelled. "You can do it!"

Saskia let go of the reins and grabbed Polly's mane. She closed her eyes as she felt the animal's huge hooves leave the riverbank and soar into the air. Saskia screamed.

"I'm flying," she screeched as Polly landed steadily and slowed from a gallop into a canter and then into a trot as she caught up with Nicolas and Mooner.

"You were wonderful," Nicolas looked at her proudly. "These are some animals. Such spirit!" He petted Mooner's steaming neck as they took a gentle canter up to the Manor.

Cathy Taylor and Barney Armstrong were waiting for them. Barney took the horses.

"They'll be the first animals to try out our brand new stables," he smiled as he took them away to give them a good brush down and a warm blanket each.

"Cathy has agreed to help me out here at the Manor," Nicolas explained when Saskia saw her. "She's a great woman – keeps the place running as smoothly as possible under the circumstances."

"Where are Jessica and Kim?" Saskia whispered.

"They've already gone. I got home last night and they left for the US straight away. She was just staying in the country for Nick's sake until I got back. To be honest, I'm not sure that she would have ever really settled here."

"How are you, *a grà*?" Cathy asked Saskia as she gave her a big Irish Mummy hug.

"Oh, Cathy, where will it all end?" The sympathy weakened Saskia's resolve. She could feel her eyes glass up at Cathy's soft touch.

"There, there, pet. You're among friends now. We'll mind you. Everything will be just fine."

As they settled into the Manor and Cathy busied herself making everybody tea, Nicolas switched on the radio.

"Listen to Radio 1, Brian O'Malley is the one with the story," Saskia said.

It was still the top story.

Following revelations on Radio 1 this morning, Joe Sweeny from the Radio Licensing Committee has resigned from his post. He denies any illicit dealings with Mr Richard Dalton but he feels under the circumstances he is left with no choice but to resign. The Taoiseach has expressed his concern that such a prominent committee could be involved in any underhand activities and he has agreed to expedite the investigation.

"Things are unfolding quickly," Saskia sighed. "Could I possibly phone somebody?" she asked Nicolas.

"Sure." Nicolas brought her from the kitchen into his den. "I meant what I said, Saskia. I love you," he offered again.

"Oh, Nicolas. You're going to have to give me a little space. My entire world is currently turning upside-down."

"OK," he said, looking slightly crushed as he

closed the den door, leaving her alone with the phone. Saskia phoned Brian O'Malley's mobile.

"Hi, it's Saskia Dalton. How are you?"

"Buzzing, Mrs Dalton. This thing is unravelling like a ball of string. Your husband – well, it's all going to be over before he even gets home at this rate!"

"I think it's time you called me Saskia, Brian! What's happening now?"

"Well, naturally Joe Sweeny is still denying everything but when I managed to get to talk with him this morning, I told him about Elizabeth Wright. Then he knew he was dead. Chances are Fintin Joyce will crumble too now. He's shit-scared, now the Taoiseach is freaking. We reckon Fintin will resign this morning too. If that's the case the Licensing Committee is as good as dead in the water. Saskia, there's a good chance they'll suspend Rock FM's licence until this matter is resolved."

"Good," Saskia exclaimed coldly. "Keep up the good work, Brian."

As she hung up, the phone began to ring and so she answered it herself.

"Saskia, it's Jenny. Do you know a very cute cop called Donal Walsh?"

"Yes, he's a friend of the family. Why has he phoned?"

"No, he's here. He just thought he should check up on you when he heard the story. He's in uniform, Sas, very cute! Anyway, he can get Robin and me out of here in the police car. Nobody would dare tail him.

Do you want us to join you or do you want me to keep fielding the phone calls?"

"Damn the phone calls, Jenny! They can swing for it, for all I care. No, just put some food out for the dogs and give them the run of the house and then come on over with Donal. That would be great."

She hung up and returned to the others.

"Saskia, could I have a word?" Barney asked tentatively.

"Sure, what's up?"

"Well, it's Edu? Where is she? Is she OK?"

"She's fine, Barney," Saskia heaved a heavy sigh. "It appears she was having an affair with Richard. I can't be with her just at the minute, so I sent her to Edwina's."

"Jesus, I had no idea."

"No, neither did I."

After Jenny's arrival with Donal Walsh and Robin, things settled down into a bizarre calm. No press knew that they were there and so they were not badgered. Barney went to O'Reilly's for the evening papers and they all gave Rock FM the front page. It was only as the evening drew to a close that Saskia permitted herself to think about all the staff of Rock FM.

"I feel so sorry for them," Saskia sighed.

"There's nothing you can do about that now," Nicolas tried to soothe her, fairly ineffectively.

"It's time I went home. The dogs will think I've deserted them!"

"I'll take you and Robin. Polly and Mooner can stay here."

"Thanks for everything, Nicolas."

"Well, you know I have an agenda."

"Oh Nicolas, I was so sad when you left without so much as a goodbye. I thought that there was something between us too but – well, I wouldn't have done anything about it back then, when I had a marriage," she trailed off.

"I know all about it." He went to embrace her.

"Wait a minute. How do you know?"

He looked at her lovingly. "Saskia, it was like you told me. This is a village. Everybody knows everybody's business!"

"I guess." She looked at Nicolas. "It's just that all of this has happened so fast. I don't know how it's going to finish."

"You mean you and Richard could get back together again?"

"Over my dead body! Not after all I've discovered over the last few days – no, that's definitely over. It's just the girls I have to think about and there's no way I'm going out of one relationship into another. I couldn't, Nicolas."

"I understand. Let's just mind each other. How's that?"

"That sounds absolutely wonderful." Saskia hugged him with a platonic hug but she knew that despite herself she wanted to kiss him.

"Where's Jenny?" Saskia asked.

"She's still talking to Donal Walsh, who managed to spend the entire day working here!" Nicolas laughed. "I think she'd be thrilled if you asked Donal to drive her home."

"Oh, is there love in the air?"

"Everywhere," Nicolas said. "Everywhere."

Saskia and Robin returned to a remarkably quiet house. The dogs were delighted to see them but other than that there was no evidence that the phone had been ringing all day or that a news crew had been camped outside.

Saskia put Robin to bed. The baby was exhausted after her energetic day as was Saskia. She ran herself a bath and fixed herself a glass of red wine and soaked to the sounds of Vivaldi's flute concerto.

The bath was a huge old Victorian one that had been re-enamelled. It carried a vast amount of water, which made for fantastic baths but massive water-heating bills. Just as Saskia began to feel a little soothed by the warm water, she remembered something Edu had said in the hospital a few days before.

"Your husband first took me in your familee bazroom —"

"Oh Jesus," Saskia jumped from the bath and got to the loo just in time, as she puked her red wine down the toilet.

She went to bed, sick and tired.

CHAPTER 32

With the exception of a bad taste in her mouth, Saskia once again woke full of fire. It was Friday. D-Day. Richard and the girls were coming home today.

Saskia's first call was to Barry McCourt.

"I've checked and double-checked those details, Saskia, and it would appear that you are in the clear. You're a very lucky woman!"

"Do you really think it's luck, Barry?" There was a sharp edge to her voice.

"Oh, I didn't mean any offence, Saskia."

"I'll be in touch. Keep those files to hand; I think Richard will be looking for them within the next few days. Thank you."

She cut the call short, ignoring all the little pleasantries that had been so typical of her in the past.

Saskia switched on the radio but there was no

mention of Richard Dalton or Rock FM on the news, so she phoned Brian for an update.

"No new developments overnight I'm afraid, Saskia, but this story isn't dead yet. I think we'll have something before tea tonight. I'll keep you posted."

Unsure how to fill her day, and fearful that some journalists might come snooping around the house again, Saskia took Robin for a walk over to Parkers'. Once she was away from the house, she knew she was safe from journalists,

"One of the advantages of keeping a low profile, while your Daddy was in the limelight," she explained to her baby. Robin beamed back up at her mother.

Sue was minding her own kids again too.

"Be careful or this may be habit-forming," Saskia teased.

"Well, actually, I'm really enjoying it. You know, the kids are a lot better behaved when I'm with them. I'm beginning to wonder if their bad behaviour was *because* I was away so much."

"You might have something there," Saskia said diplomatically. The two women sat down and Saskia began to slowly tell Sue her entire story. Her neighbour was dumbfounded.

"Jesus, I knew he was a bastard, but I had no idea that he was that bad!" she exclaimed. "Saskia, if there's anything I can do –"

You've been so much help already, Sue, I can't thank you enough." They talked for almost the entire day.

"Well, I'd better go home and face the music. They'll be home around tea-time," Saskia sighed unenthusiastically.

"Why don't I keep Robin?" Sue offered.

"She already thinks you're her mother!" Saskia laughed.

"To be honest, minding her these last few days has given me notions!" Sue smirked.

"Sue Parker! Are you thinking of making another baby? Go for it," Saskia smiled. She left Robin with her neighbour yet again and headed home alone.

Saskia sat in the study in silence and prepared herself. She knew this was going to be the hardest thing that she had ever done in her life, but it was probably the most important too.

"It's not just for me," she kept saying. "It's for the sake of my daughters too. I will not be a doormat!"

Brian O'Malley phoned her, to tell her that Fintin Joyce had just resigned. Rumour had it that he was pushed, but there was also talk that the entire Radio Licensing Committee was going to dissolve itself in view of the scandal. He told her to watch the six o'clock news.

Wearily Saskia went upstairs and got changed. Dressed for war, she thought, as she put on her new favourite jeans, the size eights. Then she did her hair and her make-up. War-paint, she thought, because this is war! When she was happy with her reflection, she returned downstairs. She thought about where she wanted the showdown.

"In the conservatory," she said out loud, to Woody. "That's my home ground. I'll be stronger there." She was gently pruning her fuchsia when the dogs went into a barking frenzy. The front door burst open. "Hi Woody, hi Dudley, Dexter. Mom?" Lauren yelled loud enough to wake the dead. "We're home!"

"So it would seem," Saskia smiled as she came out to the hall to welcome her girls. She was unsure how much or how little Richard would know as he walked in the front door of Innishambles. If he had turned on his mobile, doubtless there would be hundreds of frantic messages. If he had turned on the radio, he could know something. If he had even stopped to buy a paper, chances were he could have got wind of it. As he walked in behind his three sun-tanned and healthy-looking daughters, however, Saskia knew in that instant he knew nothing. She hugged her three daughters and kissed them but as Richard reached over to give her the perfunctory hug she pulled away.

"Girls, your father and I need to have a chat. Can you please bring your bags upstairs and start to unpack? I do not want to be disturbed for the next fifteen minutes. Do I make myself clear?"

"Where are Robin and Edu?" Tiffany asked.

"Out, now off you run. This won't take long." She turned to her husband. "Richard, could I have a word, please? This way." She walked back into the conservatory as he followed her and the girls dispersed, sensing nothing too untoward in their mother's manner. "Probably our bloody school reports," Kelly suggested as she dragged her huge bag upstairs.

"Everything OK?" Richard asked, feeling a little uneasy.

"No, Richard. Everything is certainly not OK." She looked at him straight in the eye. "Please close the door. I don't think the girls should hear this conversation."

He did as he was asked.

"To start with, I know about you and Robin Maher."

"What?"

"You heard me. I know about you and Robin. In fact I've even seen the video. Richard, I also know about you and Edu."

"Ah, Jesus."

"Jesus nothing. Edu is just out of hospital. She has just miscarried your child."

"That's impossible."

"Why?"

"Look, Sas, I was going to tell you this sooner but there hasn't been time. Well –" he stalled looking for another way of saying it, but there wasn't an indirect way and so he blurted, "I've had a vasectomy."

"There hasn't been time? How long does it take to say those four little words? When the hell did you have a bloody vasectomy?"

"After you told me you were pregnant again, with Robin."

"Well, that doesn't change anything. Didn't you know that you could still impregnate a woman after you've had one? Christ, this only makes you an even bigger bastard. I also know about Sue Parker."

"What the fuck is there to know there?" Richard was beginning to feel panic.

"You still don't get it, do you, Richard? You raped her. You could go to prison for that."

"Saskia, this is madness. OK, I admit, Sue Parker and I got a little frisky at the Christmas party here a few years ago but it certainly wasn't rape. We were high as kites and it was a wild once-off thing. It's certainly not worth all this craziness and it's all in the past now." He was thinking as fast as he could on his feet.

"And what about Edu and Robin?"

The blood began to drain from Richard's face.

"Look, I'm really sorry. You and I haven't been very close lately and the baby, Saskia –"

She cut him off before he got a chance to start soft-soaping her "Lately?" she snarled. "Lately? You and Edu have been at it for some time, it would appear, Richard."

"That's over now."

"Damn right it's over. So are we, Richard. We are so over, you wouldn't believe it! By the way, would you like to know where Wilma is? You managed to kill her. It was poor little Wilma who *attacked* you in your car the day you crashed, but you probably know that, you shit."

"Hell, I didn't know that!"

"Yeah? Well, now you do." Her venom was

palpable. "You were attacked by a dog that barely weighed a pound!"

"Look, Sas," Richard made one more stab to take control of his wife – she was usually so manageable. "I'm sorry you've heard some stuff while I was away. What you and I need is to get away for a while, just so we can have some time alone. How about that new hotel – The Belleview, for a weekend?" He gave her one of his best puppy-dog looks with a slight glint in his come-to-bed-eyes.

"The Belleview?" she screeched. "Why, do you get a group discount there now? Yes, I know about that too!"

Holy shit, he thought, deciding to change tack.

"We can't just throw away what we've had for the last twenty years."

"What *did* we have for the last twenty years, Richard?"

"It was love," he tried to sound convincing.

"No, Richard, I don't think so. I've spent a lot of time thinking about that over the last week. What we had was emotional blackmail. Twenty years of it. I thought getting pregnant with Kelly was the biggest mistake of my life, but it wasn't. Agreeing to marry you because I was pregnant was! You acted like the big saviour, getting me out of trouble, when in fact you were the one that got me into trouble."

"You were bloody grateful at the time if I remember correctly."

"Save it, asshole. We're over."

"Ah, for fuck sake, if you're not even going to meet me halfway –" he started, but she didn't give him the chance.

Saskia picked up her secateurs and began to turn her attention to a small bonsai tree that sat on its own display table.

"You know this tree is six years old?" Her voice had taken on a slightly menacing tone.

"What does that have to do with anything?"

"This little tree had begun life before you started dishing out back-handers, just so you could get your blessed radio licence."

"Ah Jesus, Sas, forget about those," he snapped.

"Why did that bloody licence mean so much to you, Richard? Was it the power thing? The ability to control a radio network, influence people's minds? Was that it? We were OK before that, weren't we?"

Then Saskia remembered Robin Maher.

"Or was it a licence to thrill? You fucker."

She mustered up every atom of strength and pride her body still held and regained composure.

"So, where were we? You're the lying, cheating, murdering husband. Oh, one bit of news that you'll be glad with. It looks like you've got away with nearly killing Katie Anderson."

"What are you talking about?"

"I had a long chat with Barry McCourt; well, actually, I've had quite a few chats with him recently. Your file has come back from the DPP. They're not going to throw you in jail for dangerous driving. I assume Kelly did tell you that Katie is now breathing for herself. She is however still in a coma, Richard, thanks to you."

"Ah, hell. That's just not fair. That was a complete accident. Jesus, I was even rushing to get to you!"

Saskia was in no mood to be rational however and so she ignored this comment.

"Talking of things legal," she continued, "I've engaged Barry as my solicitor in our separation and ultimately in the divorce."

"The what, Saskia?" Now he was shaking like a leaf and he had fallen into one of her large white wicker chairs.

"Here's the deal and it's non-negotiable. As you know Innishambles is in my name and has been ever since you had to put your own name down as a personal guarantor for the radio. The house is mine, Richard. All mine. As you also know, our monthly living expenses and the girls' educational bills are catered for by the trust fund in Guernsey. That continues. All of this stays the same. In fact, the only real thing that changes in our lives is that you move out on a permanent basis – oh, and Edu too, of course. If you two want to shack up together, that's up to you although I'm not sure what Robin Maher would say."

"That's over," Richard replied honestly, all anger gone.

"Now Richard, I think you'd better go."

"Where?"

"Well, there's a very good chance that your radio licence is about to be revoked." She looked at her watch. "It's five to six. You can catch the whole thing on the six o'clock news as you drive up to Dublin. But don't drive too fast. Remember another dangerous-driving charge would land you in prison."

Richard looked at her incredulously.

"What the fuck is going on, Saskia? What have you done?"

"I've simply redressed the balance, Richard. You hit me where it hurt most, within the family, and now I'm hitting you where it hurts you most – in the office!"

"Are you mad? You've destroyed both of us!"

"No, I haven't. Guernsey is secure. So is this house. I admit I have given you a fairly tough going over but I dare say you'll claw back," she clipped the bonsai, "slowly."

Richard stood up and clenched his fists. For one dreadful second, she thought he might thump her.

"You'd better hurry."

"You won't get away with this. I'll be back." He began to storm towards the conservatory doors.

"If you do come back, Richard," her tone was so threatening that he stopped and listened to her, "I will use the rest of the artillery that I have."

"What else do you have?"

"Well, there is that rather tasteful video."

"You wouldn't dare."

"I also have in my possession the bank statements from those *other accounts*. You know them. The ones the Rev Com never got to see. You do know that tax evasion is a criminal offence, Richard. You may have got away with dangerous driving but you won't get away with that!" She let the threat hang in the air.

"Where did you learn to be such a bitch?"

"I had a good teacher, Richard," she stared straight at him, leaving him in no doubt.

"You'll implicate yourself if you show those bank statements."

"Little old me? I'm just a helpless housewife. Obviously, I would hand over *all* bank statements to my lawyer for the separation agreement," she was using a bimbo voice. "If I implicate you in the process – oops!"

He looked at her with new disbelieving eyes. His whole world had been turned upside-down in just a few minutes. He stormed out of the conservatory to get his keys from the kitchen.

"You'll need petrol," she said calmly as he stormed back past her.

He looked at her and shook his head incredulously as he stomped out the conservatory doors. Richard slammed the stained-glass doors so hard that both peacocks came crashing out of their frames. They fell onto the terracotta tiles, smashing into a million little pieces. Richard didn't even turn around.

The girls came bounding down the stairs at the crash. "What happened?" they each chorused as they reached their mother. The freezing January air began to pour in through the gaping holes.

"Omigod, Mum, your peacocks!" Lauren gasped.

Saskia smiled. "You know something? I was getting tired of them anyway!"

The girls looked at her as if she were mad.

Saskia looked at Kelly, Tiffany and Lauren.

"You are all so beautiful and so wonderful. Give me a hug. Girls, we have to have a talk."

She gathered them into her embrace and, leaving the rapidly chilling conservatory behind them, they headed back into the warmth of the kitchen.

Richard was still in shock as he tore out of the Innishambles driveway. The six o'clock news was just beginning and Brian O'Malley had the lead story.

Following the exclusive we brought you yesterday about certain members of the Irish Radio Licensing Committee receiving cash gifts to the value of forty thousand pounds, we can now confirm that Mr Fintin Joyce has resigned from his post. This follows the resignation of Mr Joe Sweeny and we now go straight over to Mr Michael Quinn, president of the committee, for a brief statement.

Richard had to pull the car over to the side of the road, to listen. He didn't think he could listen and drive simultaneously. Michael Quinn came on the radio. His voice sounded tense and strained, like somebody who hadn't got much sleep lately.

Following recent information brought to the attention of

*this committee, we the undersigned have tendered our full
and complete resignation to the Taoiseach. The IRLC will be
dissolved as of one o'clock tomorrow morning. As a last act
of office, however, the licence awarded to Rock FM will be
rescinded. This rescission is a temporary measure and will
last for the duration of the investigation into alleged
payments to members of the committee. It will take effect
from midnight tonight. There will be a full and thorough
hearing into any wrongdoings between members of the
committee and the said radio station in the coming months.
Thank you.*

Brain O'Malley came back on the air. He began to
talk about other scandals involving backhanders over
the last couple of years in Ireland and Richard turned
off the radio.

I'm ruined, he though. She's bloody well ruined me.
He started the car again and headed for Rock Tower at
breakneck speed.

Back at Innishambles, things were surprisingly calm.

"I knew," Kelly sighed.

"So did I," admitted Tiffany.

"Well, I certainly had my doubts," Lauren added.

"What?" Saskia couldn't believe her ears. She had
planned to give the girls bite-size pieces of information.
They need never know the full extent of their father's
philandering. All she had said this evening was that
their father had behaved very badly, in fact he was a
little off-side and that they were going to live apart for

a while. She also said that there were problems with the radio licence.

"What did you know, Kelly?" she asked.

"Dad and Edu were having an affair. I got a lift home from school early one day. Do you remember, Mum, I was sick and Dad was meant to have the same bug. It was last year. Anyway you weren't here and I caught Edu coming out of your room, looking – well, looking very guilty."

Saskia felt a new wave of anger, turning to hatred for her husband. She knew that Kelly had *changed* over the last year. She seemed more distant and distrustful of men. Not until now did Sas suspect that her own husband, Kelly's father, might be the source of that mistrust. It also explained Kelly's hostility towards Edu. How could she have missed these signs?

"Jesus, I wasn't talking about Edu," Tiffany sounded shocked. "Sorry about this, Mum, but Nick and I heard a rip-roaring argument between Dad and Robin Maher on the night of the relaunch in Rock Tower. It sounded like he was firing her from more than her post in PR!"

Saskia didn't reply. She just hugged Tiff.

"Ah, well, what I saw was nothing as bad as that," Lauren smiled. "It's just, do you remember that Christmas party that you had two years ago, Mum? And the Parkers were here –"

Saskia couldn't bear to hear any more.

"What matters is that your dad and I really love you. We just don't have strong feelings for each other any more – that is to say we don't have a strong affection for each other any more," she corrected herself.

"Tell us something we don't know!" Kelly laughed.

"You knew?" Saskia was appalled. "I've only cottoned onto this myself recently!"

"Mum, Dad was a real plonker in Vail!" Lauren said. "He kept chatting up girls younger than Kelly."

"Thanks a lot," Kelly snapped.

"Oh, girls, I'm so sorry – I had no idea."

"It's hardly your fault if Dad is a bit of a prat, Mummy," Tiffany offered. "You know that Nicolas is thrilled his parents are splitting. He reckons it'll be a lot easier."

"Now there's a nice guy for you, Mum, Mr Flattery," Lauren suggested giggling.

Saskia blushed profusely, "Well, he was a real friend yesterday when I was trying to get away from the press. Kelly, we rode Polly and Mooner over to the Manor. I'm afraid you'll have to go over there if you want to see them tonight."

Kelly didn't answer. She couldn't stop thinking about Barney for her entire holiday but she couldn't forgive him for fantasising about Edu either. The last thing she wanted to do was to bump into him in Rathdeen Manor.

CHAPTER 33

The following morning Nicolas Flattery Snr and Jnr looked at each other from head to toe.

"You look good, Dad."

"So do you, son."

"OK, then let's go getem!"

En route to Innishambles, the Flatterys stopped at O'Reilly's for the morning papers.

"There's a load of papers today, it being the weekend!" Maureen announced. "I don't suppose you've seen the Daltons lately, have you?"

Both the men feigned surprise,

"No, no I haven't. Why?" Nicolas raised an eyebrow.

"Oh, no reason," Maureen replied, refusing to start the mud-slinging.

"She could barely keep it in," Nick Jnr burst out laughing as they climbed back into their own car, laden down with fresh bread and the day's papers.

The dogs heard the Flatterys' car before the girls did

and started barking wildly. This morning, nobody was in a particular hurry to answer the door in case it was another bloody member of the press, asking unpleasant questions. Eventually Saskia was obliged to.

"Oh, hi. You guys are welcome," she beamed.

"We weren't sure if you'd want the papers or not, so we brought them anyway." Nicolas was suddenly unsure of himself.

"You can dump them if you don't want to read them," Nick Jnr added.

"You know for the first time I can see how similar you two are!" Saskia laughed at their uncertainty. "Come on in. To be honest, we're all fine." She turned and yelled up the stairs, "Tiffany, Nick is here."

Tiffany came bounding down the stairs to greet him.

They brewed up fresh coffee and began to sort through the papers. Everyone had given it the front page. The tabloids were having a field day. This morning there were photographs of Richard on most of them as he arrived at Rock Tower late the evening before. *Richard Dalton on the Rocks*, one read, *Caught between a Rock and a hard place*, another read. *Dalton is shattered as Rock FM crumbles* was another headline.

"Are you sure that this isn't going to upset you?" Nicolas asked Saskia when they found themselves alone.

"He's getting what he deserves," she replied frostily.

"It's going to hurt for a long time, Sas," he tried to soothe her pain.

"Yeah, well. At least the farce is over."

Kelly walked in with *The Irish Times*.

"You know it says here that Parker's has pulled out of Rock Tower too and that means that the banks will probably foreclose on the building unless Mr Dalton pulls a rabbit out of the hat. What do they mean by that, Mum?"

"It means that your father will need a miracle to get out of this mess, Kelly, but I wouldn't put that past him."

"No, what I meant is how would the paper know that? Surely who owns the building would be confidential information."

"It must have been leaked to the press," Saskia said with a sly smirk.

The doorbell rang again. Saved by the bell, she thought.

"God, this place is like Heuston Station this morning," Saskia grinned.

"Do you want me to go?" Nicolas whispered.

She thought about her answer for a moment and then she looked at him.

"No, Nicolas. I'd like you to stay."

The smile spread throughout his face and into his eyes.

"Hello, the house," Dave Parker arrived into the kitchen looking wonderful and brimming with life. He was holding India, who was holding a bouquet of flowers as large as herself.

"These are for you." The little girl handed them as best as she could to Saskia.

461

Dave Parker gave Sas a kiss on the cheek. "Hello, we're just popping in to check that you're OK and to bring you your baby back! How are you?"

"Fine thanks, Dave. How about you?"

"Never better," he boomed. "I must admit, last night was a lot of fun. Poor Richard didn't know what the hell was going on when he saw us loading our stock up on trucks and moving out. It was very satisfying!"

"Will you have any problems with contracts or legal obligations?" Nicolas asked.

"Not at all. Richard Dalton was too egotistical for contracts. He reckoned that by having none with us, he had the power to kick us out if he got a better offer. I knew what he was up to, but as it happens, it suited my cause too."

"Did you get any hassle from the press?" Saskia asked.

"I only made one statement," Dave replied, "which I must say I rather enjoyed. I think it was to *The Irish Times*. I just said that Parker's the chain store was a professional and honourable organisation and we no longer felt comfortable in Rock Tower!" He laughed, "It was great fun."

Sue Parker walked in cradling little Robin in her arms and with Guy running around her feet.

"I don't want to give her back, Sas!"

"You know what you want, Sue," Saskia looked at her neighbour knowingly.

"Well, actually, Dave and I are planning a second

462

honeymoon so maybe I'll have some news after that!"
Sue whispered.

"Do you want me to mind your kids?"

"No, you're OK. Jenny and her new boyfriend are
going to play Mummies and Daddies!"

Kelly was nervous when she overheard about Jenny's
new boyfriend; perhaps she was back with Barney.

"Who is Jenny going out with?" she asked.

"It's funny you should ask, Kelly. I think he's an old
friend of yours," Dave laughed.

Kelly froze. Only now did she realise how much she
wanted Barney.

"Barney Armstrong?"

"No, a garda called Donal Walsh. She met him the
day she was minding Robin here," he explained.

Kelly suddenly knew what she had to do.

"Mum, can I borrow the Landrover?" she asked,
urgently.

"Where do you want to go?" Saskia asked.

"I need to talk to Barney, but I don't know whether
he's in Peartree Cottage or Rathdeen Manor."

"He's not at the refuge," Nicolas offered.

"Go on!" Saskia said to her daughter. In a flash,
Kelly was gone.

The next person to arrive at the door was Connor
Cantwell,

"Hi, Mrs Dalton," he said sheepishly. "Is Lauren here?"

He didn't need to ask twice. As Lauren heard his
voice she appeared from nowhere.

"Here I am. Let's go! Oh, Mum, er, can I go out for a while?"

"OK, but be back for tea!" She turned to Nicolas and the Parkers, "They're only back in the country for less than a day and they're gone out already. They obviously really missed their mother!"

"It's because they're so happy with you that they're comfortable coming and going so freely," Nicolas gently corrected her.

It was midday when Robin Maher awoke from her deep sleep. She had spent most of the previous night trying to keep up with the stamina of her new young lover.

"I had no idea that young men had so much energy," she teased Dermot Ryan, as he began to play with her for the fourth time.

Warm in the comfort of his double bed, she had dozed all morning, while he went out to get the day's papers. Like the rest of the Rock FM staff, Dermot had got royally pissed the night before. He was stunned that his boss had been so crooked and made a point of telling him, when Richard rolled up in his big black Merc the evening before.

When he got back to his apartment, with all the papers, he was delighted to read that Richard would most likely lose the infamous Rock Tower into the bargain.

"Go on, switch on your mobile. See if he has phoned you," Dermot encouraged Robin.

"Well, if he phones Corporate Affairs, they'll tell him that they let me go quick enough."

"I'd say he'd phone you directly."

"Can you believe that they fired me? The bastards!"

"Don't worry, Robin. You'll set up your own PR firm and it will be the best in town," Dermot tried to console her. He was secretly worried because they were now both unemployed. "Go on. Switch on your phone," he encouraged her.

Eventually she agreed. She switched it on and found three new messages from Richard, each one more desperate than the last, begging her to call him. Robin and Dermot giggled as they listened to them. Then they had sex again.

Within half an hour her phone rang, and she answered it.

"Robin, thank God I got you. Look, honey, I really need you. It's Richard here. Have you seen today's paper yet? I'm in a spot of hot water and I need a positive publicity blitz done fast. Can we meet?"

"Why would I want to meet you?" she asked with disgust.

"Ah, honey, look, I know we had a little domestic before I went away, but I need you. Baby, you're my PR wizard."

"No, Richard, I *was* your PR wizard. You fired me. Remember? Goodbye." She hung up as he began to protest and threw the phone on the bed.

"Let him feel what it's like to be out in the cold," she sneered. "Now where were we?"

It was mid-afternoon when the phone rang in Innishambles. All the girls were out and the Parkers had left. Nicolas and Saskia were alone in the kitchen with the baby. Nicolas offered to answer the phone.

"No, I may as well get used to handling the bloody press," Saskia sighed. "Besides you're doing such a great job there amusing Robin."

She went to the study to take it there.

"Sas? Is that you?" It was Jessica Bell.

"Yes, it's me. How are you? Oh, are you looking for Nicolas?"

"Well yeah, but it's kinda cool that I got you, honey. I just phoned the Manor but Cathy Taylor told me that he was in your place."

"Sure, will I get him for you?"

"Look, Saskia, Cathy told me about the events in your life over the last week. I'm real sorry that we weren't there for you."

"Thank you, we're starting to cope."

"I sure hope so. Look, it's probably good timing then that I'm phoning. Can you please tell Nicolas that I've just come from the attorney's office and I've signed all the forms? It's official. Nicolas and I are divorced!"

Saskia was stunned, she didn't know whether to congratulate or commiserate with Jessica.

"Oh, Jessica, isn't this something he would rather hear from you?"

"Are you kidding? Saskia, you're the woman he loves. It's funny how things work out. I think he would rather hear it from you than from any other person on the planet!"

"Jessica, I don't know what you're talking about –" Saskia tried to deny what she was hearing.

"Chillax, Sas. I think you're good for each other. Hey, maybe you two will get married. If you want to, you have my absolute blessing."

Saskia couldn't believe what she was hearing but Jessica continued.

"Kim and I are getting married. We'll send you two an invite when we've got our dates finalised! Well, I gotta go now. My fitness trainer is here. God, it's good to be home. I missed these simple pleasures when I lived over there! A big Hollywood Hi to everyone!" and she hung up.

Saskia returned to the kitchen in a slight daze and gave Nicolas an abbreviated version of the conversation. Before he could react, however, Barney barged in the back door.

"Saskia, close your eyes," he said enthusiastically.

"What is it, Barney?" she asked.

"Just do as I say!"

Obediently, Saskia closed her eyes while Barney rushed out and came back in carrying a very excited bundle.

"Now open them!" Barney was carrying a tiny dog that looked exactly like Wilma.

"Oh Barney, she's beautiful. She looks just like . . . " Saskia faltered. "It is! It couldn't be!" She rushed over and took the little dog from him.

"Yes, Sas, it is Wilma! I got to thinking after you got that letter and eventually I thought what harm if I just threw up a few notices and pictures around the Foxrock neighbourhood. Anyway, to cut a long story short, some kid found Wilma and liked her so much, she took off her collar and brought her home to her parents, pretending that she was a stray. The mother saw my notice up in a local shop and called me. No major harm done."

Wilma was furiously licking Saskia's salty tears of joy as they got re-acquainted.

"Now to matters more urgent," Barney continued. "Where's Kelly?"

"She went out to look for you hours ago," Saskia looked concerned.

"Don't worry. I'll find her. If you see her first, tell her I love her."

Saskia and Nicolas burst out laughing. "I think that would be better coming from you, Barney," Saskia suggested, but he was gone already.

"It appears that all the Dalton women are driving the men of Ballymore mad with love!" Nicolas said.

"Well, I don't know about that," Saskia replied shyly.

"Kelly has stolen Barney's heart, Tiffany has stolen

Nick's and Lauren and Connor Cantwell seem fairly inseparable! As for you –"

As Barney tore back down the gravelly driveway of Innishambles, he didn't even see Lauren and Connor walking back towards the entrance.

"He's in some hurry," Lauren observed.

"I'd say he's looking for your sister," Connor guessed.

"How would you know?"

"Well, I've seen him nearly every day for the last week up in Rathdeen Manor. He's been in and out to check up on the work of the refuge but all he really did was talk to me about Kelly."

"Poor you!"

"Yeah, well, it's not like I could exactly give him any inside information, but I tell you he has it bad!"

"Speaking of having it bad," Lauren gently pulled Connor closer.

"Well, to be honest, he's not the only one. Lauren, can we talk about this once and for all?"

"What do you want to discuss?" Lauren asked a little shyly which was very unusual for her.

"Look, I know you and Nick have a past. Then you and Tiff pull that stunt at the re-launch – well, what I really want to know is, is this just a little game for you or are you as crazy about me as I am about you?"

Lauren couldn't believe what she was hearing.

Connor was still crazy about her, that's what he had just said – "crazy". She beamed at him.

"Well," he asked nervously.

"Let's just take it one day at a time," she suggested. Connor's face fell and he pulled away. Kelly and Tiffany had always told her to play her cards close to her chest, "Never tell a guy you're crazy about them," they would say. "It's emotional suicide!" When she saw how dejected he looked, however, she couldn't help herself. Damn it, she always said what was on her mind. Why change the habit of a lifetime now?

"Connor?"

"Yeah," he looked at the ground.

"I think I'm probably as crazy about you as you are about me."

"What? I mean . . . that's not possible. I'm crazier!"

"No. I'm crazier!"

"No. I'm crazier!" He picked her up and swung her round.

"Put me down," she giggled.

"Only if you promise to go out with me for ages and ages and not to even look at another guy!"

"I promise –" but she couldn't finish her sentence as he smothered her mouth in eager kisses.

Outside The Hitching Post, despite the cold weather, Nick and Tiffany sat on one of Mick Molloy's pub benches. Barney whizzed by and headed up to the Manor.

"Have you decided when you're going back to the States yet?" Tiff asked tentatively.

"Eh, no. Mom has gone back with Kim,"

"I thought you'd be delighted that she was going to live back in LA again. Now you can go home."

"But it doesn't feel completely like home any more really."

"Why not?"

"Well, Dad is here and I know this sounds nuts, but I'm beginning to get settled in the American College and there is, of course –" he stopped.

"What?"

"Well, gee, Tiffany I don't know how to say this. I mean my family are a little weird but your family, well, you guys are spacers!"

"Thanks a lot," she snapped, hurt at his comment.

"Naw, hell, I'm no good at this. What I mean is well, I'd kinda like to hang around you. I think you need a lotta minding right now."

Tiffany looked at him wide-eyed.

"I really care about you, Tiff, and I know what you're going through. Most of my friends have been through it. You're gonna need a shoulder to cry on and I was kinda wondering if I could apply for the post."

She threw her arms around his neck. "Nick, you're the best friend a girl could have. I'd love it if you were the one I could turn to."

"Well, er, I was wondering if perhaps I could be a little more than a friend?" He put his hand under her chin

471

and raised her face up to meet his. Their eyes locked.

"Would you be my girl, Tiffany Dalton?"

"Yes," she whispered and he kissed her. They didn't even see Barney come hurtling back past them, through Ballymore. This time he was heading towards his own house.

Outside Peartree Cottage, Barney saw Saskia's old Landrover. He pulled up beside it and sure enough, looking cold and as lost as any stray he had ever taken in, there sat Kelly on his front doorstep. Nina and even Orinoco had come out through the dog flap to sit on the doorstep and keep her company.

"Kelly, honey. Why didn't you just go in through the back door? You know I always leave it unlocked."

"I didn't want to intrude," she looked at him uncertainly.

"My God, you're freezing." He felt her hands and face which were like ice.

They both began to talk at the same time.

"Look, Barney, I'm really sorry –"

"Look, Kelly, I've been doing a lot –"

"You first," she smiled at him.

"Well, it's a long story and please don't panic when I tell you I've spent the morning with Edu."

Kelly froze with terror but said nothing. Barney had put her in his favourite chair, the one with the dog prints and he sat on the little coffee table next to her, holding her hands.

472

"OK, here it is in a nutshell, Kelly."

She sat and listened as he explained about the miscarriage and how he began to think about the possibility of there being a connection. Eventually, he decided he had to go and confront her, especially as there was a good chance that she would not be coming back to Ballymore.

"Poor Edwina is in shell-shock," Barney sighed. "Richard got home really late last night. He's staying there at the moment. Anyway, Edu had been waiting up, to talk with him." Barney looked at Kelly, aware that he was talking about her father. "Let's just say that your dad and Edu had the mother of all battles in Edwina's house and he left her in no doubt that she was going back to Spain. Well, when I met her this morning, she had lost all her fire. It's as if she has finally copped on to what a, well er, what sort of man your father is. Anyway, Kelly, Edu crept into my bedroom and bonked me the night Tiffany and I had our 'brief encounter'." He continued as delicately as he could, explaining how everything now made sense.

Kelly looked at him in horror but slowly a small grin touched her lips. It spread to her cheeks and then to her eyes. Then Kelly gave Barney a broad, beaming, loving smile.

"My God, Barney. You got to be with Edu, after all the years you fancied her, and you don't even remember it!" she laughed.

"What makes you think that I fancied Edu?"

"Ah, Barney. Everybody in Ballymore knew. But that was a long long time ago. I'm so sorry. I don't mean to make light of the fact that you were, well, interfered with."

"Ah, that doesn't bother me that much although I am fairly fed up that I actually slept through it!"

"God, she's some bitch." Kelly's face began to cloud over.

"Don't go there, honey. There's no doubt that Edu was a nasty piece of work but she met her match in your father. Anyway she's going home to Spain soon and she was talking about heading off to LA after that. She's met some guy called Bush!"

"Oh, Barney, I'm so sorry. I wasn't much support to you over the last few weeks, while you were trying to sort out the confusion –"

"Kelly. Will you marry me?"

"What?"

"Will you marry me? I love you and I know you're the only woman for me."

"Oh, Barney. I'm only eighteen. I'm still at school!"

"Well, I'm thirty-three, that's a fifteen-year difference. But we wouldn't be the first couple in history with that much of a gap. Will you at least think about it?"

"Why don't you ask me again in a few years, time, boss!"

He pulled her to her feet and wrapped his arms around her, tightly.

"I love you, Kelly, and I'm never going to let you go.

Never. I'll protect you and mind you and love you forever."

She looked into his eyes, feeling warm and secure in his strong arms. "You know, I'd like that," she smiled.

Much later that evening, when all four Dalton girls were tucked up in bed in Innishambles, Nicolas Flattery and Saskia sat in front of a roaring fire.

When the phone rang again, Saskia seriously considered ignoring it but she couldn't do it. Instead she went into the study to talk.

"Hello," she answered it lightly.

The voice on the other end was weak and sounded unsure of himself.

"Is this Mrs Saskia Dalton?"

"It is. Who am I speaking to?"

"Mrs Dalton, my name is Tom Anderson. I'm Katie Anderson's father."

Saskia felt her stomach turn to lead. "Oh, Mr Anderson. How do you do? I'm so so sorry for the trouble my family, my husband, has caused you."

"Hush about that now." His voice was soft and warm. "I know all about your weekly phone calls into the hospital here. Victoria has regularly told me about your kind words and thank you very much for the flowers. They were lovely."

"Oh, they were the least I could do. Mr Anderson, I would have dearly loved to call in but I didn't want to impose upon your grief."

"Mrs Dalton, you're a very kind woman and that's why I wanted to talk to you personally."

Saskia's heart sank. "It's Katie, isn't it?"

"It is. She's going to be OK, Mrs Dalton. She came out of her coma this morning and she has been eating like a horse all day. My little girl is going to be fine."

Saskia felt the warm tears not just trickling down her face, but pouring down like little rivers.

"Oh, Mr Anderson, that's the best news I've heard all day! No, in fact it's the best news I've heard all week. Thank you so much for phoning me."

"Yes, eh, I was reading papers over the last few days. It would seem that you have a few issues going on in your own life at the moment. Anyway, I just wanted to let you know and thank you for your support."

"Thank you so much for calling," Saskia hung up and returned to Nicolas with wet cheeks, blotchy eyes and a huge smile.

She told him all about it and they got another drink.

"Well, how did your first day as a separated woman feel?" he asked.

"Surprisingly good! I think the truth is that the last few years have been a limbo. I'm really worried about the girls, however."

"With your unconditional love and understanding, they'll come through it, slowly. To be honest, they're very lucky. They'll stay in the same house, the same school, and they have a fantastic network of friends for support."

"You mean the boys?"

"Them and the girls from their school."

Saskia continued, "I'm not too worried about Lauren and Tiffany; they're teenagers in love. That will pass although I wouldn't dare say that to them now! Kelly though, now that's another matter . . ."

"Yes," Nicolas agreed, "I think the boys are a good source of support for them at the minute and who knows about Kelly and Barney. He is a good man."

"Don't get me wrong, I love Barney, but he is too old for Kelly. She needs to date young guys and live life a little. I don't want her to make the same mistakes I did. Barney is at the settling-down stage. I certainly don't think Kelly is ready for that. Not for at least another five or six years."

"Now who is panicking? Kelly has been through a lot this last week, Saskia. Let her enjoy Barney's company for a while. You can worry about them getting too close *if* that happens. Anyway, they'll probably have broken up long before it gets that serious!"

She sighed. "Yes, I suppose you're right."

Then he continued a little more softly, "I know he's been a bastard but their father does still love them. Needless to say, I think you had to part company from him, but he'll still be around for the girls. If the break had to come, however, it was better to do it sooner rather than later."

"Speaks the man who was married to a gay woman for how many years?"

477

"Well, she wasn't gay when we got married! To be honest, I found it easier not to rock the boat. That is until I met you."

"Ah, Nicolas," Saskia objected meekly.

"It's true, Saskia. I remember the first day I saw you. You were walking down the valley towards the river. You were surrounded by dogs and you looked wonderful. I thought that you were walking towards me, but you may remember that you hadn't even seen me."

Saskia just laughed.

"That day is scorched into my very soul," he continued. "It's the day my life turned around."

"Nicolas, I think you're getting a little carried away now."

He got up from his comfy armchair and moved over to her. He knelt at her feet.

"Don't make fun of me, Saskia."

"Oh, I didn't mean to. It's just that you're embarrassing me."

"Saskia, you're right. I've wasted the last fifteen years of my life. That was a terrible mistake. Let's not make the same mistake again. You know I love you. I know I love you. Please tell me that you love me too."

Saskia stared at the man she knew she felt so much for. Her eyes glassed up. "Oh Nicolas, I don't know what I feel. This has been the most unreal week of my life."

He took her in his arms as she began to cry again.

"I'm sorry, Saskia. I shouldn't be pushing you so hard. I just want to mind you. Look, here it is. I'm not a multi-millionaire but I do have a few million stashed away thanks to *Freedom*. It's enough to support us for a few years, until I publish my first novel!"

Saskia managed a weak laugh and so he continued.

"You know, this has actually been the most *real* week in your life as opposed to the most unreal, but I do understand that you need time. I'll wait."

She looked at his face. "Will you? Will you wait?"

"I've waited for the last fifteen years. What are another few?"

"Nicolas, there's bound to be a mountain of trouble over the next few months. I need to be here for my girls."

"And so you shall be," he soothed her.

"The media may try to drag me into this backhander mess," she continued.

"You know that won't last more than a few days and I actually don't believe that the businessmen get into too much trouble over those scandals. It's the recipients who have to answer the tough questions."

"What about the publicity of Rock FM? That's really going to hurt the girls."

"You're here for them," he continued to reassure her. "And I'm here for you."

Just then, a gust of wind crashed against the window.

"There's a storm brewing," Saskia said.

"This bloody country is so cold. I have an idea: can I take you on a holiday to LA in the summer? Just you and me?"

Saskia looked nervous again.

"We can go as friends if you like, not lovers!"

"Just good friends?" Saskia laughed.

"Very good friends."

"Nicolas, LA? I've never been there."

"No? Well, over the next thirty years I'll take you all over the world country by country. Hey, you can travel with me when I have my book launches! That way, I'll never have to be apart from you again."

That idea appealed to Saskia. She still remembered clearly how much she had missed him when he was back in the States.

"Will you take me to China?"

"Yep."

"Will you take me to Tasmania?"

"Yep."

"What about Africa?" Saskia was laughing now.

"Saskia, I'll take you anywhere and everywhere you want to go."

"That sounds like fun," she smiled at him over her glass of brandy.

"You know what they say, schweetheart," he put on his Humphrey Bogart accent. "Flattery gets you everywhere."

Saskia rewarded his appalling pun by gently thumping him with a cushion.

"Ouch," Nick laughed. "OK, it was bad. Let me fix you the other half of that nightcap by way of compensation." He left her alone in the drawing-room.

As the silence settled around her, the only noise to intrude on her thoughts was the merry crackling of the fire and the wind which was safely locked outside.

Saskia reflected on her life. I have four beautiful healthy daughters. I love this house. It's our home. I even have Wilma back! As if she could read her mind, Wilma, who hadn't left her mistress's side all day, promptly jumped up onto Saskia's lap. "And speaking of lap-dogs, Wilma," she stroked her little friend, nodded towards the kitchen and laughed, "it looks like we have another one! Seriously though. He is a lovely man and he does seem to be very sincere about his affections for me. I'm certainly very happy he's here. I'm not going to start relying on him the way I did on Richard, but I am glad he's around. I'm a lucky woman," she decided. "I believe in my girls and I believe in myself. I know I can do anything I put my mind to."

Wilma licked Saskia's hand in agreement.

"I have the power," she concluded, "the Power of a Woman."

THE END